DANGEROUS PLACES

"You are called Lee Rivers," said the bigger of the two Sikhs, the one with the gun massaging my temple. "You know what our purpose is here. Give it to us the Buddha Head and there will be no problem. Or else, we will gladly kill you."

He nodded his turban toward Tysee. If any man had eyes like a tiger, he did.

She looked at me, her eyes wide with panic. There was no use arguing. There was nothing to barter with.

"Well, Sikh and ye shall find. I think you'd better give it to them, Tysee."

She stood and reluctantly reached under her dress. After a brief fumble, the round relic appeared, still swaddled in its protective layers of cloth. Their eyes fixed on the bundle, fascination and excitement lighting their cold, professional stares. The larger of the two, standing beside Tysee, rattled something off in Sikharian.

The other Sikh used the point of the Bulgarian's knife to lift off the coverings, as if touching them with his bare hands would contaminate him.

There was little time. Once they had confirmed that it was indeed the Head, we'd lose ours. . . .

Jason Schoonover

Thai Gold

BANTAM BOOKS
NEW YORK · TORONTO · LONDON · SYDNEY · AUCKLAND

*This is a work of fiction. Any resemblance to a living person is
purely coincidental.*

*This edition contains the complete text
of the original hardcover edition.*
NOT ONE WORD HAS BEEN OMITTED.

THAI GOLD

A Bantam Book/November 1989

PRINTING HISTORY
Seal hardcover edition published October 1988, originally titled
THE BANGKOK COLLECTION

The author has attempted to stay true to historic, geographic, archaeological
and anthropological fact, with one notable exception: The fertility/good luck
talisman herein ascribed to the Shan of The Golden Triangle is borrowed from
the ex-headhunting Igorots of Luzon's Cordillera Mountains in the Philippines.
He thanks them very kindly for the use and returns it forthwith. Regarding
any other discrepancies, he appeals to license.

He also wishes to state that he has the greatest respect for Buddha and
Buddhism and deeply regrets any possible misinterpretation on the part of the
reader that might place Him in any other light but the brightest.

ISBN 0-553-27892-4

Published simultaneously in the United States and Canada

*Bantam Books are published by Bantam Books, a division of Bantam
Doubleday Dell Publishing Group, Inc. Its trademark, consisting of the words
"Bantam Books" and the portrayal of a rooster, is Registered in U.S. Patent
and Trademark Office and in other countries. Marca Registrada. Bantam
Books, 666 Fifth Avenue, New York, New York 10103*

PRINTED IN THE UNITED STATES OF AMERICA

O 0 9 8 7 6 5 4 3 2 1

This novel is dedicated particularly and deservedly to my friend and agent, Jack McClelland.

And generally to the collectors and correspondents, mercenaries and mountaineers, archaeological and anthropological explorers of jungles and their primitive tribes, photographers, pilots, bar keeps, writers, drug cops, spooks, smugglers, sailors, divers and all the other expatriate treasure hunters of the Far East. They form a nation unto themselves. Patpong is the capital. They are some of the real-life adventurers of our times.

Cupid and Bacchus my Saints are,
May drink and love still reign.
With wine I wash away my cares,
And then to cynte again.

UPON DRINKING FROM A BOWL, John Wilmot,
the 17th Century Earl of Rochester

If it burns, smoke it.
If it flows, drink it.
If it moves, fycke it.

Snake

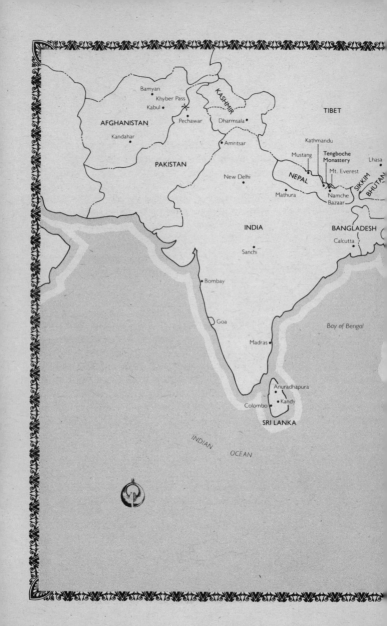

PROLOGUE

April 1959

 THE EXHAUSTED TIBETAN refugees, strung out thick and thin like a long strand of yak yarn, struggled down the 18,753-foot Nangpa *La*, or pass, and into the squalor of the Nepalese relief village of Thami.

Their ordeal was far from over. It was now a contest less with the Chinese Red Army, breaking in a huge, crimson wave over the rooftop of the world, than with the stark fear of an unknown future. And they had reason to be fearful.

Tragedy of typhoonic proportions was ravishing their land. Even their most powerful protective deities had abandoned them—including the glaring, fang-toothed Bhairab, the Almighty Defender of Buddhism, ubiquitously portrayed on *thankya* wall hangings with the skulls of his enemies strung around his neck like a garland. He had failed to halt the atheistic invasion in 1950, when Tibet was first overrun by the Red Devils. Now he had failed to support the revolt.

Even the Dalai Lama—the Living Buddha, the spiritual

and temporal leader of Tibet—had been forced to flee, on March 17, from Norbulingka, His summer palace in Lhasa. Disguised as a soldier, He had mixed in with some 30,000 of His loyal followers who had protectively surrounded His compound, not a few of them having been machine-gunned by the Red Hordes.

It was true Bhairab had seen the Dalai Lama and His retinue safely through the dangerous escape to India and exile, a success that quickly traveled the yak grapevine. But wasn't he to do more? Had the god-demon been guiled by the false promises of religious freedom? Or were the Tibetans being punished for some primal failing? If so, they knew they could expect little quarter from Bhairab's almost equally powerful colleagues.

After a day's rest the destitute Tibetans straggled on from Thami. They joined with another trail from the even higher Tesi Lapcha La and plodded along the high handle of the fork, toward the 12,000-foot Sherpa capital of Namche Bazaar, three hours away. This region presents the incomparable Himalaya at her most magnificent, with glistening white, knife-edged peaks soaring miles high into the bluest of skies, out of dark, plunging gorges. They hardly gave it a glance.

From Namche Bazaar, the long line threaded south, dropping 2,000 feet to the valley floor, then trudged down the huge Sola-Khumbu canyon until it opened out to the lush but still daunting foothills of central Nepal.

It was here at Namche that one man broke rank and leaned north, slowly and arduously climbing the steep walls of the natural amphitheater behind the scatter of stone huts, then past Kunde and Khumjong.

Despite wearing a balaclava, he had been frequently recognized by the Tibetans, and treated with the gravest deference and respect. Even among those who knew nothing about him, expressions of surprise lit up their dark, liquid eyes. He was a man not to be expected to be there.

Not only was his stature substantially greater than that of the diminutive Tibetans, but it was also obvious from his bearing—and his new broadcloak, which covered a much-too-tight Chinese army uniform—that he came from a markedly loftier station in life than did the average Tibetan. Among a people virtually bereft of possessions, he had fewer still, consisting solely of a rounded bundle about a foot in diameter slung securely by a cord over his shoulder. The material the bundle was wrapped in was of a rough Tibetan weave, which did not augur that the contents were of any greater value—except for the importance he seemed to ascribe to it, never for a moment releasing his grip.

His objective was a tiny huddle of buildings perched halfway up an enormous valley wall across from him, atop a great wooded spur jutting out from the lower lap of the 22,493-foot Ama Dablum, one of the most majestic mountains on earth. There was situated Tengboche, the most famous Buddhist monastery in the Himalaya, its setting unsurpassed for magnificence anywhere on the planet.

From the top of the spur, one's eyes sweep twelve miles up the stupendous Dudh Kosi canyon to the six-mile-long granite wall of Nupste at its head. If Ama Dablum is the Gatekeeper, then the sheer cliff of Nupste, never less than five miles high, is the Final Protector of the highest and mightiest of them all: Chomolongma, the Mother Goddess of the World, to the Tibetans; Sagarmatha, the Head of the Seas, to the Nepalese; and Everest to the rest of us. And over the great barrier of Nupste She demurely peaks.

It was late in the afternoon, when the great shadows cast by the colossal mountains were descending into the deep valley floors, before he reached the crest of the spur and shuffled to a stop just past Tengboche's entrance *gompa.* His chest heaving in the rarefied air, he removed his hand from the bundle—the first time he had done so—and wiped the grimy rivulets of sweat from around his eyes with the fingers of his mitted hand.

His narrowed eyes took in the open sweep of the quiet grounds, the pagoda-like monastery itself, and the stone buildings that tumbled down around it like a protective skirt. In the distance the magic light of the magic hour lit up the plume flying off Chomolongma's 29,029-foot-high crest like a bright, welcoming banner.

His breathing calmed, he slowly, stiffly struggled forward and up the rough stone steps to the monastery entrance. There he was greeted with a respectful *nameste*— "I recognize the divine in you"—from a tall, slim monk of about thirty-five years, who hastily set aside a twig broom he had been using to sweep the flagstones of the inner courtyard. While he did so, the visitor noticed that the monk was missing the small finger on his left hand. The stranger spoke a few formal words in Tibetan and then the two disappeared inside.

The next morning the emissary—lightened of his load— appeared at the monastery entrance, accompanied by the same monk and the elderly abbot. After a brief bow of his head, which was returned much more deeply by the two ocher-robed residents, he took his leave. The two solemn monks watched, motionless, until he dipped over the ridge on which the monastery sat, and out of sight.

Then, without a word, they turned and disappeared back into the monastery.

ONE

The Lion's Den

A HIROSHIMA-CLASS thunderclap directly over-head propelled me through the door of The Lion's Den and out of one of Bangkok's late-monsoon cloudbursts. The conditioned air inside immediately chilled my clinging clothes and made me shudder involuntarily. Water dripped off the brim of my hat. I yanked it off, shook it dry, and squinted through my hangover into the darkness of the small bar.

Through the jukebox hoedown of "The Rodeo Song," my eyes began to focus on the hundreds of pictures of the Lion's friends that covered the walls, the stickers from various international construction jobs, and the large banner proclaiming that this was a designated watering hole for members of China Post One of the American Legion Operating in Exile Out of Shanghai—the post of preference for soldiers of fortune, ex-*special* Special Forces, and others whose common link was a vile view toward anything colored red. The place was mostly deserted of regulars—the mercs, retired spooks, pilots, divers, and correspondents who hung their beer bellies out here—but then the floodwaters in Bangkok had transformed the city's infamous traffic jams into a solid, barely quivering jelly.

As my bloodshot eyes adjusted to the gloom, I made out the backs of only two hunchers at the bar, both familiar.

The dumpy one in epaulets, crumpled over a mug of beer, belonged to Hal Lawson, a Canuck foreign correspondent; we'd known each other since our Saigon days when we used to hang out at Mimi's on Tu Do Street. After the fall, he traded in his job there as the AP Bureau Chief, which involved jumping out of Hueys into hot LZs, for a freelance career in Bangkok and sitting in The Lion's Den, running up enormous tabs that caused the Lion's mane to thin and gray even more.

Looming on his right was Brock Stambuck, a monster with the shoulders of a water buffalo, who was still trim beef despite being the same age as Hal, about forty-three. Brock was with the drug boys, the DEA. It was he who just a couple of months before—when I had been getting the bends from diving into the mekhong and Coke a little too long and a little too deep—had talked me into providing a retirement home for his aging pistol, saying he needed something a bit bigger, a Magnum .357 that could kill two birds with one stone, so to speak. I didn't really want it, not being that familiar with the make, but in the end I had drunkenly accepted and paid him 500 baht—which was the deciding factor, it being only twenty dollars. It was a well-used Walther 7.65 with a clip that held seven rounds. I kept it back at the house.

Neither had seen me. I couldn't resist. I waited until Hal's mug of beer touched his lips before I cupped my hands to my mouth.

"Dead bug!" I shouted as loud as I could.

Instantly, the two men plunged off their high bar stools, slamming heavily to the floor on their backs, their arms and legs skyward. Whiskey and beer flew like fireworks. A moment later they were peering around warily, looking for the perpetrator.

"Well if it ain't Jungle Boy." Brock grunted cynically, crawling to his feet and readjusting his Magnum under his sports jacket.

"Son of a bitch. I've got beer all over me, eh?" the correspondent complained, pulling at his sticky shirt while he picked up his bar stool.

A couple of aging but giggling barmaids wiped up the spilled drinks. I couldn't talk. I was laughing too hard. Between my shout and my convulsions, my head felt like it was about to explode. Again.

"Well, you know the rules, asshole. You didn't hit the floor. Set 'em up! Old Crow for me. Hal here needs a new Singapore Tiger."

"Sounds like the entire sky is breaking open," Hal muttered, as an enormous crack of thunder overhead almost split my head with it. Bottles rattled behind the bar. "Can't even suck back a quiet beer without the sky or some jerk interrupting."

"It was worth it," I croaked through the tears, twirling my fingers in a circle when I caught the bartender's eye. *"Nam som* for me, though."

Orange juice. The other juice could come later. As I would as well, once I headed out raping and pillaging on Patpong Road that night, which I intended to do, come hell or another hangover. I'd been away a long time. Too long.

"Well, Jungle Boy," Brock semi-growled, taking his seat and eyeing my well-jungled safaris with mock disgust. "I must say you look like hell on a hot day. Where you been this time?"

I looked down at my soaked and soiled safaris. They and me needed a long, hot bath. A veeeery long, hot bath. My head felt like Krakatoa the morning after; my mouth like a herd of elephants had spent the night wallowing and fucking in it. Still, fond if foggy memories of the previous night with Lette at the Statue of Libertine Bar in Angeles City sashayed through my mind. How a tiny, four-foot-ten, seventeen-year-old go-go girl could rattle the knees of a grown, 170-pound man I could never know, but that little pussy of hers had something to do with it. It had the appetite of a Bengal tiger. It didn't purr—it roared like a lion. She was an a-go-go dancer there, though she was so petite I liked to kid her that she was really an a-goo-goo dancer. Angeles City is in the Philippines, of course. A whorehouse of 350 bars servicing Clark Air Base.

"I just got in from Manila," I replied, my laughter having faded to a ragged cough. "Nog picked me up at the airport and drove me straight here. I haven't even been home yet. I got this bloody wet just crossing the curb."

I didn't bother mentioning that Nog, my driver and houseboy, who was sitting in my car outside, had given me some tiny green pills of questionable content that he'd picked up in Chinatown for my thundering head; hopefully they would soon cut in. Nog's wife, Po, looks after my house, a converted Chinese temple on the Chao Phrya River near the Oriental Hotel. They both live in, along with their baby, Pac, named after Nog's electronic passion at the time of her birth. Nog had once been a champion-class Thai boxer, so was handy to have around; we kept in shape working out together, and besides, with the place stocked with collections and pieces I had picked up on expeditions all over the Far East, he was a good man to have around the house when I was away. Which was often. Too often.

One of the old crows brought Brock his Old Crow, Hal a beer, and me a juice. She stuck the bill in a plastic cup and set it in front of me. I grinned, glanced around the bar to see if I'd missed anyone, then slipped onto a bar stool beside them. Neither the Lion nor Wolfgang Krueger was in sight.

The latter was the reason I was here. The neatly typed note Nog had greeted me with when he had met me at Don Muang Airport an hour earlier was too urgent to ignore, despite my delicate condition:

Lee,

I must see you immediately about an extremely important matter. Please bring your packed suitcase and passport and meet me today at 1700 at The Lion's Den.

Wolfgang Krueger

Just lucky that I happened to be arriving today. I checked my dive watch. 4:50 p.m. I scratched my beard. It needed a good trimming, too.

Brock reached into a breast pocket, pulled out a huge

Cuban cigar, and examined it for a moment before lighting it, relieved that it wasn't broken. We raised our glasses.

"Loose shoes, tight pussy, and a warm place to shit," we said in unison.

"What held you up?" Hal Lawson asked, setting down his fresh frosty. "I thought you were supposed to be back a week or two ago, eh?" He was still pulling at his wet clothes. So was I.

"Oh, I had a hell of a time with their Cultural Properties people clearing a collection. Lemme tell you about it."

I'd been there putting together an ethnological collection of Ifugao artifacts, ex-headhunting gear from Luzon's Cordillera Mountains, for a Zurich museum. I had gathered up spears and shields, and ritual gear such as generations-old *boluls*, or rice gods, thick with a bloody patina from decades of having sacrificed chickens' blood poured over them at harvest *cañao* time; I had added bronze gongs with human jawbone handles, basketry, textiles, tools, musical instruments, bowls and other cooking ware, which Nelson Rockefeller had once taken an interest in and which were auctioned off at often 500 dollars a spoon after he croaked. Indeed I piled in all the hardware of their fascinating lifestyle—as long as it was smaller than one of their stilted lodgehouses—that I could carry out.

I had also stopped off in Sagada, where hanging coffins decorate the sides of cliffs, and limestone caves are always being found, stuffed full of 500-year-old skeletons resting in hand-hewn coffins piled in great jumbled heaps. One of these, dried-out tenant and all, I had added as an auxiliary collection, it always being my philosophy as a collector to give the museums the very best of what they'd contracted me to find—and then an extra. While not legal to export, of course, it had been managed, but that's what had caused the delay. Filipino officials, despite their American English and Catholic beliefs, are still Oriental. We just had to come to a meeting of minds and pocketbooks, if you know what I mean; I could have just slipped one hundred or two hundred pesos to the customs man at the airport and saved a lot of exasperation, but Zurich wanted those damned legal exit papers. In this business I've done more greasing than a pit mechanic.

Lette had gone with me into the jungle and the higher

pine forests acting as my translator since my Tagalog has
never progressed much past *gilling-gilling*— though the
little nympho made sure we did enough of that. Snow
White, the papa-san of the bar she danced a-goo-goo in,
was good enough to exempt me from having to pay the
daily bar fine to keep her out, thus saving me a considerable amount of money. Not that I really needed it—I didn't
—it was just a gesture among friends.

I had put together a 146-piece collection, which, once
given Cultural Properties Clearance Papers, I had shipped
Air Express from Manila to Zurich. Having already shot a
Kodachrome of each piece, I just needed a few days to
hammer out the documentation before sending it on from
Bangkok. Then I could sit back and wait for another fat
check, which I had every intention of investing in the
same shrewd manner I had invested so many others—in
the ladies and liquor of Patpong Road.

I collect anthropological collections, mainly primitive
art and antiquities, for museums and galleries around the
world, and the private market. The jungles and high rock
of the Far East are my fields. My name's Lee Rivers. My
friends call me Brook for short. That's their joke. They
don't really.

"You gotta have the looniest way I've ever heard to
make a living, you know that?" Brock said with a slight
smile of admiration, raising his glass. It looked like a thim-
ble in his hand.

"A guy has to make a living. It's a jungle out there," I
replied with my standard retort.

"Gonna be around awhile?" Brock asked. "What's your
next outing?"

"I'm meeting Snake down in Singapore in about three
weeks. He's got some leads from some fishermen where
there seems to be a pottery wreck. We're going to check it
out."

Snake is one of my best friends, a Tasmaniac and a treasure hunter. Mike Cheevers, his real name, owns a sixty-
foot, Bermuda-rigged Swan, the *Riquer.* With liquor you
can lick her, but the *Riquer*'s quicker, he always likes to
say. We've done a bit of diving together, old Chinese Ming
wrecks in particular being scattered fairly liberally around
the Far East. We've made a good few baht at it in the past.

"Where's the Lion, by the way?" I added, pausing until another explosion of thunder faded away. "I've never seen it so dead in here."

As I glanced around for him, my eyes scanned a plaque on the wall that succinctly summed up the Lion's philosophy: WHEN I DIE BURY ME FACE DOWN SO THE WHOLE WORLD CAN KISS MY ASS. An ex-iron worker with the face of an old football, he had drunk, fought, whored, and been thrown in slammers all over the world, until the day he woke up from a fifty-four-day drunk to find himself married and the owner of a Bangkok bar. That had been twenty years ago. His Thai wife was long gone but he still had the joint, a delightfully seedy place on Suriwong just a short stagger from the brighter lights of Patpong Road, the red-hot nightlife capital of the world. He had recently taken a new bride, a pretty Filipina in her late twenties named Marrissa. The Lion was holding up the bottom side of seventy, which doesn't mean that his roar had mellowed to a meow: the lion in winter still had teeth, even if they *had* been acquired from a dental lab.

It was obvious that some of his girls must have been there as long as he had. In the spiraling sexual galaxy that is Bangkok, The Lion's Den was in a twilight zone all of its own: *no* sexy, young, nude and seminude Thai girls jumped on your lap here. This was a bar where men came to drink and talk, free of being hassled by airheaded bimbos asking you to buy them one drink. Thus, the Ancients, as we kiddingly called his girls.

The Lion chose that moment to charge creakily out of his office lair in the back, clutching a handful of bills.

"Hey, Noi!" he roared at his cashier. "Where the fucken hell is . . . well, I'll be goddamned! If the Rivers didn't just flow in here! Welcome back to civilization!"

"Thanks. Where is it, by the way?" I said. I just couldn't get the fuzz out of my throat.

"It's always nice to see someone who fucken pays for their drinks when he gits 'em," he growled in his familiar Tennessee rasp. He shot a squinty glare out Hal's way.

Hal nobly ignored it, as he had so many others in the past. I noticed that Hal's chit box behind the bar, a shoebox with his name on it, was overflowing again.

"Hey, you gonna be around Friday night for the Hobo

Feed?" the Lion asked me. "The old Air America fly-boys
are in town for a reunion and they threatened to come
down and wreck the fucken joint. There's even a couple of
the old Flying Tigers and Ravens gonna make it. We're
servin' pork chops."

"Sounds terrific. Wouldn't miss it."

"By the way, there's been one of the boys askin' about
you. Where the hell did he go? Wolfgang was jist in here a
minute ago."

"He'll be right back," Brock interrupted. "Said he just
had to jump down to a drugstore for something . . . and
talking about drugs"—he checked his watch—"me and a
few of the boys have a meeting in a couple of hours, with
some Hong Kong gentlemen coming down from Chiang
Mai who don't know about it yet. I gotta go."

He chucked back his whiskey, stuffed his chit cup with
some baht, and headed for the door. So huge was he that
the Magnum made no bulge whatsoever under his jacket.

Hal Lawson also drained his new mug of Tiger.

"Look . . . sorry, Lee, Lion . . . I gotta head off too.
Working on a story about how the Libyans are using their
medical students in Peshawar to recruit Afghanis as terrorists, blowing up Pakistani government buildings. I have
it traced right to the Libyan ambassador himself. Lion, I'm
going to grab a *Soldier of Fortune* off the rack. Just add it to
these and stick them all on my tab, eh?"

He pushed a poker hand of chits in the old man's direction, and was gone before the Lion could warm up his
drawl to call him back. Shaking his head dejectedly, the old
man shoved them in the direction of the overflowing box
behind the bar.

"You'll have to excuse me, Lee," he said, his voice agitated. "I gotta get these goddamned bills straightened out.
Noi! Dig me out last month's ledger and git it into my
office, all right?"

Left alone to wait for the Wolf to enter The Lion's Den, I
pondered his note and felt a spark of adrenaline hit my
bloodstream, working with Nog's magic pills to clear my
fogged mind and damp discomfort. It wasn't the first time
he had sent a message to me, though never had one been
of such urgency. They had led over the years to some very
exciting and lucrative discoveries.

The first time had been a dozen years ago, about a year after I had moved to Bangkok, determined to make a go of it as a collector. It had come at a time when I had sold only a few collections—five or six—but enough for me to think there just might be a future in it. I'd made something of a risky career choice; to this day I still don't know of anyone else who's doing this full-time, at least in anthropology.

I had taken to hanging out at The Lion's Den soon after. Bangkok has a way of attracting the most fascinating people in the world and all of them seemed to pass through his bar. Of course it was Wolfgang Krueger's hangout. It didn't take me long to learn that not only was his knowledge of the Far East phenomenal, to say the least, but he also took a real and rich interest in primitive art and antiquities. He had been in the Orient longer than I had been alive. A friendship quickly struck up between us.

I had wanted to do some more collecting among the hill tribes of The Golden Triangle, but on the less accessible Burmese side. The trouble is that the area, like a goodly portion of Burma, is not controlled by the Burmese in Rangoon but rather by some twenty distinct tribes with names like Akha, Mao, and Lahu, most of them involved in the opium business, which is controlled by various drug warlords.

I had been interested in one of those tribes, the Shan—a short, light-skinned people of Chinese background and dialect. They are by far the largest tribe—indeed, they make up a state-within-a-state—and their own armed force of an estimated five thousand to ten thousand men, the Shan United Army, easily keeps both Thai and Burmese troops at bay. They were and are difficult and dangerous to visit. The Shan, who are engaged in the multimillion-dollar opium and heroin producing business, are led by Kun San, the most powerful warlord in the area, and greet strangers less with open arms than with arms full of arms.

While talking over my impossible desire with Wolfgang, he had taken me completely by surprise by offering to lead me in! He had contacts with Kun San, and obviously very good ones, from his old reporting days. At the crowded dump he called home on a narrow *soi* off Sukhumvit Road, he showed me an old magazine article he had written. I couldn't read it, it being in kraut, but he'd explained that the story was on the ethnic warfare in Burma and that he had pointed out that the Burmese were the legitimate rulers only by way of being the majority, and that the minorities were often treated as second-class citizens; this had automatically made him an ally of all the minorities. He was now planning to do an in-depth story on the Shan for *Der Spiegel*, and why didn't I join him as company?

And despite his age—he was in his mid-fifties at the time —we had hiked in, led by a Shan guide we had met in Chiang Mai. For almost a month we trekked the trails and villages of the Shan countryside with our own small company of provided bodyguards, he scribbling his articles, me collecting the ethnographic artifacts that make up their unique lifestyle.

For the most part we worked out of Kwan Mae, a town of three thousand or four thousand, set atop a high ridge, a well-equipped stronghold with a view of many other jungled ridges silhouetting off to the horizon. Kwan Mae was strongly defended by a perimeter of bunkers and concertina wire, 60mm, 81mm, and 82mm mortars, and 50-caliber machine-gun nests. It was no secret that this was Kun San's headquarters and several hundred of the Shan United Army were in evidence. Their uniforms were motley but they were well-equipped in terms of weapons, which were a jumble of aging M-1s, a few HK G3s, and numerous AKs, as well as the ubiquitous M-16s plus a few I couldn't identify that probably dated back to when the frogs were still trying to control the horror show—which Southeast Asia often is—before getting their warts burnt off at Dien Bien Phu and hopping back home with their spots between their legs.

Kun San even had his own air force, a tiny, four-seater, camouflage-colored Maule, small enough to take off and land on the short strip cut out of the jungle along the top of the ridge the town sat on.

Heroin production, of course, was the town's raison d'être. I knew from the English-language Bangkok *Post* that The Triangle produced about seven hundred tons of opium a year, which processed down to seventy of heroin, seventy percent of it controlled by Kun San.

Most of Kwan Mae's buildings were slapped together from teak clapboard; out toward the perimeter there were bamboo huts on high stilts threatening to fall down the steep hill. But on the crest itself was one very modern compound—even with a small swimming pool, I learned—that was camouflaged as best as could be done in a town that size. Kun San's home was strictly off-limits.

A satellite dish and a flurry of communications antennas on another building beside it raised my interest as well, particularly when I saw a large white man—the only other in the village besides Wolfgang and myself—frequenting it. Every time he spotted me he quickened his pace and disappeared inside; the one time I tried to introduce myself, I was hustled away by a pair of Shan with rifles.

I am never happier than when I am in some jungle or another on a collecting rampage—well, except for when I'm on a rampage down Patpong Road, of course—and it was made even more fun on that expedition by a delightful if somewhat ragged little urchiness of twelve or thirteen who attached herself to me. Although she was a skinny little thing, all elbows and knees, who it was readily apparent would never amount to much, she was exceedingly bright and high-spirited and—I had to admit—*did* own the cutest little dimples on a pretty little face. She took such a deep and genuine interest in all that I did and proved to be so helpful despite the language barrier that I let her tag along. For as long as I stayed in Kwan Mae, she eagerly joined me every day after school, helping me to identify the various pieces in my growing collection, and explaining through pantomime what they were. There wasn't a shy bone in her bony little body and some of those pantomimes set both of us laughing to tears.

By the time Wolfgang and I were preparing to take our leave, it was clear she had developed a fairly sizable crush on me. Seeing the listless look in her sad eyes, I offered her my hairbrush and mirror as a going-away present, she being at that age where girls begin to take an interest in such matters. But she gestured that she already had one. Then I saw that her eyes were set on something else—but on a something else I deemed somewhat inappropriate. I tried to discourage her but there was no doubt what she had her heart set on.

She coveted a button pinned to my shirt. The trouble was, it read FUCK COMMUNISM— the C a stylized hammer and sickle—so naturally I was hesitant. With only my rudimentary Shan, I wasn't able to explain why I wanted to refuse her such a small thing, but since she was so determined I finally shrugged and pinned it to the black tunic over her just-budding breasts.

I certainly had no expectation of receiving anything in return but she seemed to think otherwise, exchanging gifts being the Oriental way. Her present for me was a well-polished silver pendant. They're very common among the Shan; in fact they seem to be a cottage industry among the older women, who produce them from melted coins and market them in the province. It was very attractive, shaped like a flattened donut a half inch in diameter, but with a narrow gap leading from the outer edge to the hole in the middle. That made it at once a fertility talisman and a good luck charm. Before I could protest the inequality of our exchange, her gift being much more valuable, she had disappeared. I wore it around my neck for several years before eventually laying it aside.

Very unfortunately, although we had been in and out of Kwan Mae the entire time, Kun San's path hadn't crossed with mine. But, as Wolfgang had explained, he did have an empire to run, and it was the busy, dry season—opium-growing time.

The huge collection I'd acquired—some 168 pieces with all the appropriate slides and documentation—took twelve mules to cart out. I shipped it to my new contact of contacts in New York, François Giscard, whom I had recently met there at Christie's during the auctioning of a Tantric Buddhist collection of mine. I'd also come to New York that time to deliver a collection of Ban Chiang pottery to the American Museum of Natural History. The latter collection had also resulted from a lead from Wolfgang. I paid him twenty percent of the profits, which became quite a standard arrangement between us. I had very much been hoping to impress François, he being the dean of dealers and *very* impressive. He was delighted with my Shan collection and sold it to a well-known Chicago family in the hotel business that later, I learned, donated it to the Field Museum as a tax write-off—and for several times the sum they had paid for it.

I even made enough tickets from that collection to upgrade myself from the second- to the first-string dancers on Patpong Road, the sassiest and sexiest, flashiest and classiest street in the world. It hadn't taken me long to discover that the seraphic angels of this City of Angels could make you feel you'd died and gone to heaven.

Also, unbeknownst to me, my name was starting to be whispered around influential circles in New York. Soon the whispers had turned into a murmur. I was, of course, feeding other collections to museums at the same time.

The following year Wolfgang led me to an incredible windfall. I hadn't seen him for a month or two when he suddenly appeared in The Lion's Den. He was unusually excited—unusual because, like most wienerschnitzels, he normally displayed little emotion. He had a lead on a treasure trove of priceless gem-studded gold jewelry that in times past had belonged to Queen Supyalat of Mandalay. It turned out to be a magnificent collection of necklaces, bracelets, and rings that included a matching pair of fabulous broaches set with enormous, pigeon-blood-red rubies, their interiors richly decorated with the most uniquely beautiful feather and rose-garden inclusions imaginable. One doesn't live long in the Far East without learning something about gems, and these were stupendous.

The Queen's husband, King Thibaw, the Ivan the Terrible of Burma, once ordered some six hundred citizens buried alive as his cure for an epidemic raging through the city. This naturally caused a certain degree of panic and an exodus of citizens to parts unknown. Fortunately his bizarre cure wasn't given a chance to prove its effectiveness for at just that moment the limeys invaded northern Burma to seize control before the loathsome frogs could leap in before them, the poms having subdued Rangoon and the south some years before. The year was 1886 and in the ensuing conquest and confusion, part of the queen's collection of jewelry, clearly marked and sealed, found its way out of the palace and into hiding. Dr. Kildare, with his queen, was shortly thereafter exiled to Calcutta, where, presumably, he was able to continue his peculiar medical experiments on genuine insects.

The jewelry had been rediscovered by a Burmese farmer widening his rice paddy. The enterprising farmer sold it to the rebel Karen tribe, which controls the movement of black-market goods from Thailand to consumer-goods-starved Burma. Wolfgang had been duly notified by the rebels. He brought the find to my attention, we split the investment outlay, and I smuggled the jewelry from Pattaya beach resort in Thailand to New York aboard the *QEII.* Customs control on luxury liners is often slack, to say the least. In Manhattan, an ecstatic François disposed of them in a matter of a phone call.

We all made a handsome profit. That one flip-over paid for an abandoned Chinese temple I'd bought, and its renovation, and still left me bundles of baht to throw at the pussy of Patpong.

The whispers and murmurs now turned into a roar among the champagne-and-caviar crowd of Manhattan—a group I was introduced to at the first of many parties of François's that I would attend.

But the best part was getting in solid with François. Now that I had been accepted as one of his primary sources, there was nothing I couldn't move. He would cash pieces practically as fast as I could collect them, particularly those items a museum wouldn't touch, like Queen Supyalat's jewelry. For the museums I concentrated on the major ethnographic collections—but even some of those, such as the Shan collection, I flogged to François.

Typhoons of money began to swirl down around my bearded, curly-haired head. Besides a splendid market with François, I had an equally splendid source for leads in Wolfgang, with me lucratively in the middle. Naturally, to hold that comfortable position, I did my best to be sure neither found out about the other. That way there was no worry that the most important link of the three—mine—might be eliminated.

Like most huns over the age of thirty, Wolfgang Krueger had that pale, boiled-potato look, though his heavy face had been baked somewhat by the tropical sun. Slightly rumpled, gravy-colored safari suits were his standard dress, and although they couldn't disguise his lumpy figure, neither could they hide the fact that he had been an athlete in his youth, his handicap undoubtedly being partly responsible for his decline. A semicircle of Ben-Gurionesque, flaring white hair topped his strong features like tufts of sour cream.

Wolfgang's most obvious feature was his left arm, or rather his lack of it. The rumor was he'd lost it in World War II. But he was extremely nimble with his remaining hand, able to load and light his meerschaum effortlessly.

Despite his appearance, it was clear that he was of some breeding; unlike most boche, whose accents sound like a rusted vw krautcan going through an auto crusher, Wolfgang's articulate English issued forth with a relative lightness and ease, as if some warm olive oil had been added to the metallic mixture.

Yet any questions you had about his distant past, no matter how subtly phrased, were always diplomatically turned aside. he was the most intelligent man I'd ever met; he could pick the pockets of your mind, check the contents, and slip them back without your being aware.

What *was* known about him was that following the war he had migrated to the Far East, eventually settling at its hub, Bangkok. There, as a freelance journalist for a series of German-language newspapers and magazines, he had covered the various coups, national births, wars and insurrections, which were and are as numerous in this jungled corner of the world as kernels are in the homemade rice wine of the Orient.

He liked to be where the action was, although he was now into his sixties and had slowed down considerably. He was at an age where time is no longer money, but a far more important currency.

"Ah! Herr Rivers! I'm so glad you could come!"

I swung around on my stool to see Wolfgang's tall frame sliding into his favorite booth. I hadn't heard him enter. Scooping up my glass and chit cup, I slipped in across from him, setting my soggy hat on the table.

"That's just what a girlfriend of mine said in the Philippines last night . . . *Christ!*" I gasped when I looked up and saw his face clearly.

His right eye was blackened and almost swollen shut, his left cheek was bruised, and there was a lick of tape on his chin. He managed to smile through a cracked lip while he patted rain off his bald pate with a handkerchief.

"Let it just be said that occasionally parts of Bangkok, normally one of the safest cities in the world despite its dubious reputation, can be dangerous at night, Herr Rivers," he said cynically in his low, resonant, but commanding voice.

I had known Wolfgang long enough to know when not to probe.

"Well? How are *you* and what have you been up to?" he asked. "You look a little beaten up yourself." He stuffed the hanky in a damp pocket and pulled his mushroom-shaped pipe out of another.

"I'm okay. And doing the same old thing. You know, looking for old things all day and young things all night."

My voice was still a little raspy, but my head was rapidly clearing. What was in those green pills Nog had given me? Wolfgang smiled slightly and deftly loaded his pipe. An elderly barmaid of at least twenty-eight hobbled over, took his order for schnapps, and mine for another *nam som.*

"Since you brought up Herr Christ's name a moment ago," he said, "we will talk about religion for a moment."

He stoked up his large meerschaum. He was being unusually serious. The thunder was rolling off into the distance.

"You know much about Buddhism, I'm sure?" he asked, sipping from his tiny glass, then taking up his pipe again. "You even wear an ancient, and I believe golden, Buddhist amulet."

He paused. I noticed he was keeping the stem of his pipe away from the swollen part of his lip. Hell of a beating just over a mugging.

"I'm not a Buddhist," I said, "but I have a great respect for it. It's responsible for the great serenity of the Orient, I would say."

"Someone once said, I think it wass Voltaire, that if there wassn't a God, man would create him. The Buddha never claimed to be a god or a son of god but Hiss followers have made Him such. You could say that they made a legend out of Him, could you not?"

I nodded, trying to figure out what he was getting at. I didn't have to wait long.

"And one of those legends concerns the existence of the Buddha Head. The Rumor, ass we call it."

A squeeze of adrenaline squirted into my veins. I sat back and tried to probe his eyes. The light in those windows was bright, but the shadows it cast were too dark.

"What do you think?" he added, looking at me squarely. "Possible?"

"I don't say it's *im*possible," I ventured carefully.

It was a low-level rumor that had been raising its golden, gem-encrusted head in the Orient for years. Not infrequently, the subject would come up at the antiquity shops of North America and Europe, where it was taken surprisingly seriously—even down to the latest corollary, which stated that it had surfaced, then quickly disappeared underground again, in the last quarter-century or so.

Wolfgang's eyes burned into mine with a fierce intensity.

"Do you know something I don't . . . ?" I added, our eyes locked.

He flashed the corner of a smile, then turned, trading his pipe for the schnapps.

"Just speculating. But if places ass large ass Angkor Wat can be lost for centuries, why not something ass small ass a head? And what about that five-and-a-half-ton solid-gold statue of Buddha at Wat Trimat that wass only discovered back in '53 when it fell off a truck and broke the plaster encasing?"

"I can't deny the logic," I told him. "There's often reality in rumors, fact to fiction, leads in legends. It was by reading Homer that Heinrich Schliemann tracked down Troy."

"*Ja!* Let's speculate a little. Suppose it exists and it fell into your hands. What would you do with it?" He asked the question casually, though I could see he was watching me carefully.

I hesitated only a moment. It was a calculated decision.

"Well, being that I'm a professional collector, I would sell it to the highest bidder, of course."

Whether I actually would or not, I couldn't say for sure, but I had done enough black-market business with Wolfgang to know what his interests were. Instinctively I had very strong and immediate doubts whether it would be right to sell it. But I knew why he was interviewing me: he wanted to determine if I was the right person to handle such a piece. I didn't want to deal myself out of the game before I saw the pot.

He chuckled and leaned into the table, a little too far, for he suddenly looked pained and pulled back, his hand drifting to his side.

"Are you all right—?"

"But that sounds so . . . so cynical," he said, cutting me off, suppressing the strain in his voice. "You would have no compunction about not taking it to some appropriate Buddhist institution? A discovery that would directly affect the lives of untold millions? Particularly after what you have said about your very positive feelings about Buddhism?"

I thought for a moment, wondering if I should qualify myself, but then decided to press ahead with the angle of debate I had committed myself to. I fought down my excitement. I was sure he was on to something very special. My mind grew as clear as the ring of a tuning fork.

"It wouldn't . . . necessarily . . . be either cynical or immoral. Wouldn't it really be nothing more, from my anthropological point of view, than just another ritual object?" I worded my answer to give myself a back door.

"It sounds like an elaborate rationalization to me," Wolfgang probed. He was teasing me and I knew that he saw that back door ajar.

He tapped his pipe. It had already gone out. He reached for his matches.

"You once told me that a major pleasure you got out of collecting wass placing these collections of yours in museums, because then they are saved for posterity. Doesn't this conflict somewhat with something ass obviously important ass the Buddha Head?" He was still probing. He knew I was walking a tightrope.

"Well, that's normally very true. But for one thing, no museum in the world would touch it. It's unsalable on any open market because of its religious value. For another, I like to put my collections where they are most appreciated, and one criterion for judging appreciation is who is willing to make the greatest sacrifice of a most precious commodity—money? Buddhist pieces, bronzes and so on, are the most expensive antiquities in the entire Far East. Such an objet d'art as you describe would be of the ultimate rarity and would command an indescribably high price. Like anyone, I have to make a living as well. Anyone involved in a back-door, private sale would be set for life. Besides, it's not the first time I've flogged prize pieces. Remember those jewels of Queen Supyalat's you put me on to, for one thing?"

I twirled my drink, then took a sip.

"That iss true," he said, concentrating. "So, again—if it fell into your hands, what would you do with it?"

"To the highest bidder."

"Spoken like a true collector!" Wolfgang exclaimed, raising his schnapps to salute me.

There was now a broad smile on his face. His eyes were bright and alive, even the blackened one. I relaxed. I knew then that I hadn't fallen off the high wire. I also knew I was full of shit. Money considerations can only go so far. But at least I would be able to learn more about it before I took a different back door.

"Well, I *am* a true collector. But it's just a rumor anyway . . . or do you know something I don't, Herr Krueger . . . ?"

I gripped his eyes squarely with mine. It was my turn to ask a few questions. He read my gaze, nodded, and slowly set his glass down. His hand rose to caress the stem of his pipe.

"I . . . do not . . . really *know,* but I wanted to see how you would react, in case it *wass* true. I only suspect, myself, and only in the most general way."

I sat back, trying to hide my disappointment. It was just idle speculation.

"It wass something that wass said in a telephone call I received two days ago from New York," Wolfgang continued. "It wass from a Herr François Giscard—"

"François!" I exclaimed, suddenly sitting forward again.

"So you do know him? You keep rather good company, I see. I have heard of him, of course, and I gather he hass heard something of me ass well, which iss flattering. Apparently he had phoned all over Bangkok trying to locate you and when he couldn't, he looked around for someone who might be able to track you down. That turned out to be me."

"How did he get in touch with you?" I was stunned.

"Through Lion. I wass here yesterday when he called. He asked for me."

"What did he say?"

"Well, it actually wassn't all that clear. He said he couldn't talk over the phone, and even indicated he wass calling from a pay phone. He sounded terribly agitated and distinctly paranoid. Iss he always like this?"

"No, no . . . quite to the contrary," I replied, bewildered.

"Well, he said he might want my help for some time— and named quite a significant amount, I might say. But not knowing what it entailed, I said that I could hardly know if I wass interested or not. I'm afraid I am too old for mystery assignments. That iss when he hinted that it had something to do with, as he put it, 'the Rumor, the one that hass been floating around Asia for a very long time.' Well, the only rumor I know about that vaguely fits the description iss *the* Rumor, though I could be absolutely wrong. He promises that you'll be able to tell me all about it when you get back."

"Get back? Where am I going?"

I hoped it wasn't far. All I really wanted to do after weeks in the jungle was laze around on the back veranda with a couple of naked girls, and throw empty beer cans at the rice barges floating past on the Chao Phrya, without ever straying far from a hot tub. But he reached into the breast pocket of his safari shirt and pulled out with a ticket folder, which he set before me. I flipped it open.

"Cathay Pacific to London! Then Concorde to New York! But it's the start of winter there! There might be *snow* on the ground!" I shuddered. I'll do *anything* to avoid snow, along with *wind* and *cold,* all four-letter words of the most obscene kind in my vocabulary.

"That wass his request. The first thing he wanted me to do wass track you down and get you to New York ass quickly ass possible. He said he didn't dare phone you at your number in Bangkok for some reason. I found Nog and from what he told me, I learned you were at the Statue of Libertine Bar in Angeles City. This Snow White fellow there said you were flying back to Bangkok sometime today. There are flights in from Manila to Don Muang all day, too many to wait around for, so I just left a note with Nog for him to pass on. Check what time you leave on the ticket."

"Eight o'clock tonight!"

"Ja. And because of the floods I would suggest you leave immediately."

"Damn," I swore, grabbing my soggy hat and slipping out of the booth. I reached into my pocket, but a slight raising of Wolfgang's hand indicated firmly that the bills were on him.

"But I've only got a bag of dirty clothes! And I'm still dressed for the jungle!"

"Well then, you should be perfectly attired for New York." He chuckled, then he stopped suddenly as another stab of pain jabbed his side.

The rain had stopped when I stepped back out into the comforting blast of raw heat and humidity on Suriwong, into the rabid burp of three-wheeled tuk-tuks slowly plowing through the flooded streets. Despite the disappointment, I could feel sparks of excitement. Whatever François so urgently wanted to see me about—even if it probably wasn't the Buddha Head—it sounded like it would be exciting, and I thrived on excitement.

I looked longingly down the street to where the bright, flashing lights of Patpong Road, a few steps away, beckoned the horny men of the world. Even from here I could see beautifully dressed, sexy women sashaying around. Unfortunately, I wouldn't be getting abreast of things tonight.

"Damn," I swore under my breath as I tiptoed along a plank catwalk above the flooded street and crawled into the back of my Nissan. The thought that snow might lay immediately ahead sent shivers of horror through me worse than the Lion's air-conditioning.

Nog set his comic book aside and grinned at me from under a Foster's Beer ball cap Snake had given him. He adored the huge Hobartian, who always sent his too-big castaways in Nog's grateful direction.

"Don Muang," I said, "and hurry."

TWO

New York

THE YELLOW CAB swept down 5th Avenue, sending eddies of autumn leaves swirling for cover. Central Park was ablaze with color, the mountains of Manhattan rising steeply up from her margins like Himalayan cliffs while a full autumn breeze drifted languidly down the canyons. My relief was immense—it was still horribly, even deathly cold but it could have been much worse. The only earmuffs I like wearing are Oriental earmuffs—two silky smooth thighs.

François's penthouse in the building he owned on Central Park East overlooked the Met—so he could look down on the Michael Rockefeller Collection, he liked to joke, though it wasn't that far off the yen because his own collections were stupendous, to say the least.

His family had been premier in the antiquities business for three generations and his position at the top was accepted almost as a divine right. Nearby Madison Avenue is the Ming-plated heart of the antiquities and primitive-art business in the world. He didn't have a street-level shop;

he was so exclusive he *chose* his clients, inviting them up to his huge, lavish quarters, which had been constructed by joining four existing penthouses into one grand design, with galleries to hold his treasures. His power was such that he unquestionably had the finest, rarest, and most expensive pieces in New York.

His lifestyle and background were totally different from mine; I was a small-town kid from the frozen wastelands of North Dakota in the Deep North. What we did share was a common fascination with the Far East. How his developed, I don't know. I can only speak for myself.

I think I was always destined to be an anthropologist. One of my most vivid childhood memories is accidentally discovering an Indian hammerhead while taking a short-cut across a field to the ol' swimming hole gravel pit. That fired the fascination. My summers were often spent with my dad, crisscrossing freshly plowed fields, searching for projectile points. Only the amateurs called them arrowheads. Spring was the best time, right after cultivating, and after a good wind had balded the tops of the sandy hillocks. I diligently documented my finds as to period, place, people, and type of stone, having no idea at the time that it was superb practice for what I would eventually make a good living at.

Anyone brought up in a small town knows just how confining they are, and I escaped by joining Huey, Duey and Louis on their many adventures to exotic countries— again, without realizing that someday I would be roughly imitating their lifestyle. Of course, like every other peach-fuzzing boy with a rising interest in boobs, I graduated to *National Geographic;* unlike most, I had read every copy ever issued, cover-to-cover, by the time I completed high school. They were the only thing that made that thoroughly boring experience bearable.

After getting an honors degree in anthropology from North Dakota State, I was drafted. Being a baby-boomer, that meant Vietnam, but by the time I arrived the war was starting to wind down. Fortunately, I had a fairly easy tour, serving in Intelligence for the most part, out of the air base at Tan Son Hnut.

My love affair with Southeast Asia began immediately and was total. I was enraptured by Oriental culture—by the food, the rich world of smells, and all the other indelible sensory experiences, by the ornate art and arcane spiritual beliefs, by the calm people and the exquisite manners they used even while blatantly ripping you blind. For the first time, the word *exotic* took on real meaning for me.

And the women and nightlife were incredible; if the bars on Plantation Road near the base were good, they were even better on Tu Do. I knew that I had found the part of the world where I wanted to sink my roots. And sinking roots I did a lot of.

Field duty was fine with me too, when I had to do it. The incredible adrenaline rush when our chopper leaned back into a landing flare over some jungle clearing, the *tick* of enemy rounds clipping through the thin aluminum, the firefights with all the screaming and yelling, confusion and stark passions, but most of all, that incredible feeling afterward, when we were lifted out, of being more alive than we had ever felt in our lives—all of it had a fascination that burned into me. It was addictive and I was soon hooked. An adrenaline junkie. It was anything but boring.

And the best part was, it was always summer. There was none of that forty-below-zero bullshit. I'm still convinced I have some permafrost lingering in the marrow of my bones. I've always said that my favorite winter sport is scuba diving in the tropics.

Returning stateside after we had shuffled out of Vietnam was a hell of a comedown but for a couple of years I endured it. I kicked—and being a vet, *was* kicked—around California, through a variety of dumb jobs. There wasn't much of a market for anthropologists. Once again I was getting bored to the marrow.

In the middle of that I had a disastrous love affair, one that particularly chilled me because I had given it my all, while she had taken every bit of it but given nothing in return. It had been with a girl with the body of a gazelle but the mind of a lizard, though for too long her sleek, graceful lines had masked her flickering tongue. The last I heard she was trying to become a dog doctor, which I thought was thoroughly appropriate.

But it had been the last straw. I began to recall more longingly than ever the soft, subtle, responsive women of Asia, where females are feminine and not feminists. If I only had one life to live, I was determined to live it in paradise.

I had a vague dream about what I wanted to do. It was a wild throw, but I had always believed in following my dreams. I could never understand people who didn't. I didn't understand most people, in other words.

After selling what little I owned I took the long way around, through the museums of Europe and over the rough but well-worn groove that was the Asian Overland Trail across Turkey, Iran and Afghanistan, this a few years before that area went all to hell. By the time I had threaded the Khyber Pass and skidded down into and across that incredible irritation that, to me, is India, I was thoroughly exhausted. And, incredibly, still bored.

I stumbled on to the resplendent isle of Sri Lanka and serendipitied onto the Devil Dance Cult, the most terrible and terrific in the Orient. The Sinhalese along the southwest coast believe that illnesses are caused by demon possession, and that to be cured, the afflicted must undergo a complex all-night exorcism, complete with insanely screaming, leaping dancers who wear grotesque masks and wilder costumes and throw handfuls of flash powder onto torches. To my surprise I found myself more than welcome to attend, and was even given a place of honor before the Inner Circle. The entire village was in attendance, enraptured as much as I was by the brilliant drama of the ritual.

My exhaustion immediately sloughed off. I had found just what I had been looking for.

I spent two months rummaging around the jungle, piecing together a 111-piece collection: well-patinated masks of the six major demons, including Maha-Kola-Sanni, who comes in eighteen apparitions, each of which causes a particular disease; costumes, drums, whistles, bells, and jangles; all the other ritual paraphernalia; and literature and sound recordings. By shooting each piece and the exorcisms themselves, I had prepared complete documentation. It was a collection package-designed so that any museum could set up an all-enveloping, multi-media experience. I knew it couldn't go wrong.

After spending most of two frustrating weeks becoming initiated in the horrors of Asiatic red tape while trying to get a Cultural Properties Clearance Permit, I finally threw my hands in the air and simply crated everything up and shipped it Sea Mail out of the country, marking it as books, clothes and handicrafts, which wasn't really a lie. Right from the start I was in the primitive-art smuggling business, with all the risks and paranoia that entails.

Once back in San Francisco, I circulated the slides and documentation to museums around the world. It wasn't long before I received a positive response from the British. My investment had multiplied twentyfold.

Shortly after that, a phone call came from the Smithsonian. Did I still have the collection? No, I'm sorry, I had replied—thinking quickly—but if there's anyone in the world who can go out in the field after another one. . . . Soon a contract almost as thick as a stack of *Anthropology Todays* had arrived and I had tossed my toothbrush and malaria pills back in my knapsack. I was on my way.

My interests expanded—to the Tantric Buddhism of the Himalaya, the Kayans and Ibans of Sarawak, the Bataks of Sumatra and Palawan, the Penan of Borneo, the hill tribes of Southeast Asia and the Philippines, and the mask cultures of the entire region. I eventually became known as the man to contact in the Far East. I was steadily offering collections to the some 300 ethnographic museums in the world, and frequently taking contract orders from them. I was also working on the private markets, through the shops of London, Paris, Zurich and, most importantly, New York.

By then I had long since discovered Bangkok and Patpong Road; both were revelations, and were even better than my sweet little imagination. Paradise. I had found it. My boredom had disappeared that first night in the Sri Lankan jungle and had never returned.

Everything had worked out beautifully, and I owed no small part of that to François Giscard. He knew more about Oriental antiquities and cults than anyone else I had met. Needless to say, we hit it off right from the start.

I always looked forward to seeing him and did now as the cab jerked to a stop before his tower. After paying the cabbie I shivered out onto the sidewalk with my knapsack of dirty laundry, trying to straighten my soiled safaris. I just hoped the airline cologne I had liberally doused myself

with would camouflage some of the damage. That I hadn't
been able to resist the nonstop free champagne on the
flight from Singapore hadn't helped my overall condition
either. That herd of elephants had been at it in my mouth
again.

I passed lobby security and entered François's large, luxurious private elevator and rode it to the top. Within moments the ornate doors opened and I stood before my
beaming host.

"Entrez! Entrez! Monsieur Rivière!" he exclaimed, slipping naturally into French and his pet name for me. He
could slide around more languages than a Parisian prostitute. Gripping my hand, he drew me inside, taking my
beat-up old hat and dirty knapsack. Before the impeccably
dressed François, my attempts at neatness were in vain,
something an unconscious wiggle of his prominent nose
confirmed. His eyes danced quizzically. François was tall
and slender, his hand movements rapid but graceful.
Though in his early to middle fifties, he looked a dozen
years younger.

"Alors! It appears you *did* drop everything to come as
soon as possible. . . . My apologies," he added, in a concerned tone when he noted my embarrassment.

"Someone said New York's a jungle . . . ," I mumbled.

"It's been a long trip," he said diplomatically, exuding
that warmly dignified sophistication that one finds bred
only in the higher altitudes of New York, or in the finer
homes of Europe where he had spent his youth. He
mounted my hat and bag on a clotheshorse. "I'm sure you
would appreciate a shower and clean change of clothes."

I immediately relaxed, though I did detect a faint nervousness about him.

"Love to, but I'm afraid I'm wearing my best right now.
Half the dirt on Luzon is mixed in with the clothes in that
knapsack."

"Hmmm . . . we'll have to do something about that,"
he said thoughtfully, then led me down a broad, stark-
white hallway lined with masks from all over the Far East:
a complete collection of *kolam,* or playacting masks, from
Sri Lanka; clay *durgas* from Nepal; the delicately carved
Indonesian masks that relate the story of the *Ramayana,*
the ancient but still-living epic of Asia; the *barong* of Bali,

which teach of the universal struggle—and triumph—of good over evil. Most of them had been acquired by me, I noted with satisfaction.

The rooms we passed were a blur of cultures, both ancient and modern, from Himalayan objects d'art to meso-American terra-cottas, from Eskimo soapstones to Benin castings, from Viking jewelry to a vast collection of Oriental art, from carved ivories to wall hangings, from great jade sculptures to the huge, hideous, mud-and-woven-straw figures of the Sepic River valley. Spotlights breathed life into tapestries, gods and statues, from the tiny to the huge—the latter the reason for the large elevator. In one room I caught sight of an Egyptian mummy, undoubtedly the rattiest one I had ever seen in my life. I always wondered why he kept the disgusting thing, and the great mounted slab from King Tut's tomb bearing hieroglyphics, which were two of the rarer pieces, and not for sale. Everything in the complex had been arranged in such a manner that François and his young wife, Breenda, could live with and enjoy the pieces before they were sold, to be replaced by other treasures.

"Can you do me a favor, François?" I said, still shivering. "Could you turn the heat up just a tiny bit, please? I've never been here in the dead of winter before. I can practically see my breath."

"Dead of winter!" he said surprised. "It's a gorgeous autumn day! The leaves are just changing! But certainly. Where would you like it? It's room temperature now."

Yeah, and a meat locker is a room too, I thought.

"Ninety-five would be just about bearable . . . well, make it ninety."

His eyebrows danced involuntarily for a moment, but then he nodded.

He ushered me into his study. The room was warm and open, furnished with rich woods tastefully juxtaposed with the simple, modern lines of chrome and glass. It was a corner room; two entire walls were plate-glass windows that overlooked Central Park. One wall featured various yachting trophies, plaques and numerous photographs, many of familiar public and entertainment figures. Out from the other wall stood a heavy oak desk, on which rested a 1,500-year-old bronze ascetic period Buddha from the dead city of Anurad-hapura in Sri Lanka, which I had sold to François some years before and which he now kept as part of his personal collection. Beside the desk was a low bookcase stacked with rare books. Soft classical music drifted softly from somewhere.

"Please make yourself comfortable. I'll just run out and have the maid take care of your laundry and fetch Christopher from the nanny. We'll draw your bath when your clothes are ready."

He left to arrange that. To ward off hypothermia, I beat myself with my arms and stamped up and down a few times. Keep moving to survive: I hopped over to two large portraits positioned prominently behind his ornate desk. I'd seen them before, of course, but had never really studied them closely. They were of two of François's illustrious ancestors—his father and grandfather—and were executed in similar styles, with both gentlemen standing regally in front of drapes, the left hand of each resting on a small pedestal table. I noticed for the first time that there was a single object on both of the little tables.

Mildly curious, I stopped stamping and leaned forward. I recognized a German war medal, an Iron Cross. Glancing up, I could tell by the style of clothing and pencil-thin mustache that this portrait was of François's deceased old man.

I glanced over at the grandfather's muttonchop whiskers. Interestingly, one of his fingers rested on an object as well. It was an *ankh*, an ancient Egyptian symbol of life.

François swirled back into the room with his young son. Christopher immediately ran to play with a group of centuries-old bronzes and golds that lay on the floor, arranging them into competing armies.

"The heat's been adjusted, *mon ami,* and your clothes are being laundered. Have a seat. Would you care for a drink?"

Why not? I couldn't feel much worse. I sank into a thick sofa with a view of the park.

"That would be nice. Mekhong and Coke. But no ice. Please."

From a small bar François swirled together my drink, a Chivas for himself, and a milk for Christopher. He sat on another sofa across a glass coffee table from me, setting his glass down too hard, so that part of his drink spilled. It drew my attention to his nervousness again. He caught my eye and nodded. After swabbing up the spill with a handkerchief, he launched straight into business.

"There's no escaping it. This situation has caught me a little, ah, off guard," he said. "I must formally ask you to agree that the contents of this conversation will never under any circumstances be taken past these doors." He spoke very clearly, looking me straight in the eye.

"Of course." I shivered, hugging myself with my arms in the frigid room. "Scout's honor."

He paused and glanced out over the smoky lungs of New York, as if wondering how he should phrase something. He took the time to shakily light a Gauloise. I heard a throat clear impatiently. It was mine.

"You have heard of the possible existence of the Buddha Head," he stated rather than asked.

My heart leapt. Maybe Wolfgang was on the right track after all.

"The Rumor and all that. Yes, of course."

He took a nervous drag, blew out the smoke, and tapped non-existent ash into the ashtray. The smoke hung in the air like a shroud.

"I have reason to believe that it may exist," he said, in a quiet, still voice.

I chilled even more. I had half-expected to hear him say just that, yet it still came as a jolt. He saw the look of comprehending incomprehension in my face, and went on.

"Not only does it possibly exist, but I know where it is. Or rather, where it recently was. That's why I asked you here so abruptly."

"I don't know what to say—" I exclaimed when I found my voice.

He shook his head seriously.

"I was as surprised as you are. It's always been an intriguing rumor. Then I received an overseas phone call a few days ago. It was from my old friend Abbot Tengid at Tengboche Monastery in Nepal. You'll remember that I gave you a hello note to pass to him a year or two ago when you were going up that way after some Sherpa material."

"Of course. The old guy with the missing finger."

I knew François had been a friend of the abbot's for years, that he'd attended the annual September Mani Rimdu ceremonies there several times. The ceremonies are powerful lessons in the tenets of the Tantric Buddhist faith, often masked and always danced. In one of the dances Bhairab slays the enemies of Buddha; in another dancers don a skull mask, a not-so-subtle reminder of everyone's eventual end. Attending was always a major effort on François's part, because he had a phobia about flying, and each visit required that he travel by slow—if luxury—liner, then overland. But such was his interest in matters Tantric that he went to those lengths.

"He flew into Kathmandu and phoned me just four days ago," François continued. "The line was terrible and my Tibetan is only fair, which is unfortunate, because what he told me was almost unbelievable. He was very upset, almost hysterical. Something terrible had happened. He said that the monastery had been robbed the day before and that one of the things stolen was the Buddha Head! No one was supposed to know it was there, he told me. The thieves probably found it by accident when they were ransacking the place—probably for antiquities," François added, amazement in his voice.

"How did they rob it? The place is full of monks!"

"I don't really know. I made out something about a meal and that it happened at night." I noticed a new tension enter his voice. "There was a hitch, though—one of the monks had caught the thieves in the act, which perhaps explains why they got so little—only this Head, a couple masks and a *thankya.* And I shouldn't even say 'they,' because it could have been one. I just couldn't make out a lot of what the abbot was saying. He wasn't entirely coherent and my Tibetan is not terribly good. Unfortunately, the monk who interrupted the thief or thieves was wounded—though not terribly seriously, or so I gathered. They didn't carry him over to Hillary's hospital at Kunde, so it can't be too bad."

He took another nervous drag on his cigarette.

"This sounds incredible—how could anyone escape? You don't exactly jump into a getaway car and get lost in traffic a hundred miles from the nearest vehicle! It's all trekking trails up there!"

"I don't know. It could have been the airport above Namche Bazaar. I know so little."

I leaned back and thought deeply for a moment.

"François," I said finally, my excitement dissipating rapidly, "I'm not sure if you're not getting all worked up over nothing. That line seems to have been pretty bad. Don't you think it quite possible that you heard wrong?"

"I know what you're saying. But about the Head, I know that was clear. He had to say it twice because I wasn't sure I heard right the first time. It does all seem so incredible!"

He threw his hands in the air in his animated, Gallic manner.

"What would it be doing at Tengboche Monastery in the first place?" I argued. "Tengboche isn't even that old— built this century, in fact. The Buddha croak . . . I mean, died over 2,500 years ago." I corrected myself at the last moment. I always tried to speak a little more genteelly around François than I did with the lustful lads at the Lion's.

"That might explain the part in the Rumor about it reappearing in the last quarter- or half-century or so," François said.

"A robbery at Tengboche must be big news in Kathmandu."

"In the *Rising Nepal* I had one of the servants fetch from the international newsstand in Times Square, it's been headlined only as an aborted robbery. There's no mention of any head—just the masks and a *thankya* wall hanging. Oh, and a small Reclining Buddha, the kind that displays the Buddha when he was passing into Nirvana."

"Hmmmn. Why did the abbot call *you,* of all people?"

"Well, I was surprised at that myself at first, but then I saw why: we're very good friends. He knows I'm, well, a leading dealer. You know the tremendous amount that is stolen from Nepal each year and finds its way to the West; he is quite aware of it as well. He suspects the Head will appear on the market. The thieves probably don't even know what they really have, except that it's covered in gold. He turned to me because I know the business well. My friend is clutching at straws, obviously. He wants me to try to trace and recover it."

"You're kidding. . . .*You?*" I was incredulous. I thought of all the black-market business we had done together.

"*Non,* Monsieur Rivière, I am not 'kidding.' He wants it all very hush-hush. He hasn't told the police about it. He just wants to get it back, poor man; he really is distraught. He was extremely reluctant to even mention it on the phone but he had to. He wanted me to fly out immediately to investigate, but I can't fly—you know that. That's why I asked you to come here in such a rush." He paused before adding softly, "You must go for me."

I blinked uncomprehendingly.

"I know, since you're a collector, what your automatic reaction might be. I know I may be asking you to do something that is possibly against your grain: help find it, and then return it despite its obvious value. I wish to hire your services on this project. Although it won't in any way come to even a small percentage of what it could possibly fetch on the market, it's still generous. I'm prepared to offer you 25,000 dollars."

My eyebrows rose. It was finally starting to warm up in the room, enough that I stopped shivering. François loosened his collar and continued.

"I know you might think this runs against my grain as well, but it doesn't. Nothing you and I have ever channeled into quiet hands was ever out-and-out stolen, and certainly nothing we've handled is of this importance. Lee, you know my admiration for all things Buddhist. Abbot Tengid is a close personal friend whom I want to help in every way I can. One doesn't get a chance too often in this life to do something of benefit to mankind. This is it for me"—he threw his hands in the air again—"if this is the real Buddha Head, it's quite beyond commercial interest as far as I'm concerned. *Oui,* it could be sold on the black market but that's *exactly* what it would be, the very *blackest* of markets. I ask you to be my proxy. I feel so helpless and useless, being able to do nothing myself. *You* must scour the Far East for me."

I didn't say anything for a long time. This took some thinking. I had known François long enough that I didn't doubt his sincerity. But if I took up his offer I would be effectively cutting myself out of any profit on the greatest antiquity in the Far East. And yet, if I found it, could I really bring myself to sell it? I had had a tough time wrestling with precisely that question on the plane over, just in case Wolfgang's speculation was true.

"Why me?"

"You're undoubtedly the best man. The abbot is acquainted with you. He knows through me that you're very conversant with the business. Actually, in terms of smuggling antiquities, you probably know more about it than anyone."

"Do you have some sort of overall plan?"

"Oui," he said quickly, encouraged by my question. "In North America and Europe I'm in the process of putting out the word to the shops and galleries that if *anything* particularly rare and expensive in the Buddhist line is made available to them—even if it's a *little* warm, if you know what I mean—to give me a call. I don't think we have to worry about the museums; they wouldn't touch something like this. As for watching the markets of the Far East, I thought you'd be too busy to do that, so I took one other man somewhat into my confidence, this Monsieur Wolfgang Krueger. With you acting as a beater and Monsieur Krueger and I watching the markets of the world, there's a slight chance it could land in our net. Should you track it down, all the better. I understand you have known this German, Krueger, for some time. Do you think he can be trusted?"

"Wolfgang? Well, he's always been completely honest with me."

That wasn't really the truth, but I couldn't betray one friend to another. I had serious doubts about Wolfgang's reliability in this venture. If the point was to have the Head returned, I would have to watch him. Anxiety tore at my solar plexus as I forced myself to accept that two men I had always conspicuously kept separate, now knew each other. Before François could ask me what I knew about Wolfgang, I reversed the question:

"Do *you* think he can be trusted?"

"It is said that few people know Asia as well as he," François replied. "He seems clearly solid and reliable and I'm glad you agree. If you didn't, I would drop him. I have been aware of his reputation for some years. He occasionally used to sell pieces to the dealers down on Madison, though it appears he's somewhat retired and hasn't been around for several years."

"*Really!*"

That was a revelation. I'd never known Wolfgang to be a dealer. If he knew the markets, why bother going through me?

"*Oui.* When I couldn't find you, he seemed like the obvious man to contact. The publisher of the *New York Times*, a friend of mine, told me that some bar in Bangkok called The Lion's Den is the hangout for correspondents. Since this Krueger apparently was once a journalist, I suspected I would find him there. I was lucky."

"Why didn't you just phone my house?" I asked, not bothering to add that the Lion's was my hangout as well.

He nervously tapped the long ash from his dead cigarette, then butted the beast.

"Well, that's another thing," he said, drawing closer and speaking sotto voce, his nervousness increasing. "It was the very next day, and I was about to when I received a visit from a friend of mine quite high up in the Central Intelligence Agency. Their Kathmandu people had intercepted a coded message from the Russian embassy to Moscow. It mentioned my name! 'Tengboche' wasn't even in code. Apparently the Russians monitor telephone calls in and out of Kathmandu. He wanted to know what it was all about. I was flabbergasted, and admitted that the abbot had called me about the robbery and wanted me to watch out for the stolen *thankyas* and so on. I didn't tell him about the Head because the abbot had insisted that it be kept as quiet as possible. I don't think my friend entirely believed me, but he let it drop. And that's why I didn't dare call your place—I had also told the abbot over the phone that I would probably send *you!* I couldn't trust your phone—or even mine anymore. I had to speak to you personally."

No wonder François was nervous.

"It has all been a dreadful worry," he continued. "I even called Monsieur *Krueger* from a pay phone. Who knows? Maybe *this* place is under surveillance? I don't know how interested the Russians are, or why. Just the same, I didn't want to take any chances." He began to fidget. "And we have to be very quick—so much time has gone by already."

"I think you're being unduly paranoid. But tell me more about what exactly you have in mind me doing."

"I'd like you to start with Tengboche. Wolfgang Krueger will be supplied with expense funds for both of you. It would be best if you pass any messages for me through him so that there is a buffer between us—in case my friend at the CIA is correct, that there might be a cause for concern. These Soviet people may know about you and me but not about Krueger, and it's best we keep it that way. And I would ask you to give Monsieur Krueger this letter, which explains the matter in fuller detail, though it stops short of divulging everything. If he *is* interested in helping, I have asked him to phone me from a Bangkok pay phone to a pay phone near here at a certain time. Then I will fill him in completely. This package also contains a cash incentive. You can try to convince him to help as well. He was somewhat reluctant on the phone, but I couldn't tell him much then."

He drew a thick envelope out of his jacket pocket and set it on the table before me. From another pocket he pulled out another fat envelope. He set this down beside the first.

"This one is for you," he said quietly, his hands trembling.

I stared at them but made no move to pick them up.

"François . . . how is it even possible that the Head exists? I know you're better versed on it all than I am, but for one thing the Buddha was *cremated.*" I nodded toward what had to be a foot-high, solid-gold Standing Buddha on a pedestal near the window.

My skepticism, unleashed in part by lack of sleep and jet lag, was gaining strength. I could have used more of Nog's green pills. I hadn't had a decent sleep since leaving Lette's warm arms and hot thighs.

"That's correct," he said. "I've thought a great deal about that too, in the last few days, and have done a little research to freshen my memory." He swept a hand toward the low bookshelf near his desk. "And I learned many, many interesting things. It's all circumstantial evidence, but it's, well, *interesting.* . . . It *is* possible the Rumor is true, that the Head exists!"

"Convince me."

"Let me start at the beginning. His name was Siddhartha Gautama. There's considerable debate as to when He was actually born, with approximately a century separating the two schools. Generally in the South Asian countries, 623 B.C. is taken for His birth with Him dying eighty years later in about 543 B.C. But in the North Asian Buddhist countries the favored date for His birth is 563 B.C. — which is the date favored by non-Buddhist scholars, incidentally. He was born to a princely family in what is now southern Nepal. He married but, at the age of twenty-nine, left His wife and family in their palace to wander around India and Sri Lanka for six years as an ascetic in search of enlightenment, fasting and meditating. He finally achieved His goal at Bodh Gaya, under a bo tree, a slip of which grew into the sacred bo tree at Anuradhapura in Sri Lanka."

"And the oldest recorded historical tree in the world," I added with a twisted smile.

François flushed slightly, and continued.

"Thereafter he was known as the Buddha, or the Enlightened One. He spent the rest of His life teaching and died at the age of about eighty."

I rolled my eyes.

"Pardon. I know you know things like this. But please let me describe it in some detail to be sure we thoroughly share our knowledge. There should be no gaps. We're starting with little enough knowledge as it is."

I shrugged. François took a moment to light another Gauloise. He took a drag and set it in the ashtray, never to pick it up again.

"His disciple, Ananda, was in charge of the funeral," he went on. "The Buddha had given him explicit instructions on how it was to be handled. Details vary to a degree, but they match on the important points. The Buddha did not want any of His material body to remain, and here His followers certainly broke with His wishes. They lay Him in state seven days in Kushinagar in northern India. Then, keeping in mind His instructions to have a funeral of a King of Kings, they wrapped Him in 500 layers of cotton and cremated Him with fragrant wood in an iron case full of oil. The fire was later put out with milk. Sometime during the cremation the sky rained flowers—which is all part of the myth-building process. The Christians did much the same thing, conjuring storms during the crucifixion of Christ," François explained, raising an aquiline finger as he pressed to his point. "Whoever did the wrapping of the cotton had a full week to substitute heads. Think about it—500 layers of cotton would make a corpse, particularly a wizened, eighty-year-old corpse, look as recognizable as that Egyptian mummy out in the living room."

"But who would have done it? And why?"

"I've thought about it considerably and there are twelve suspects. First off, there's some reason to point a finger at the Buddha's wife or son. Or both."

"Really?" I said, noting sweat breaking out on his forehead.

"Yes. Remember, when the Buddha was still the pampered Prince Siddhartha, He had married. His wife's name was Yasodhara. She could very well have been alive at the time of the Buddha's death, certainly the son. The wife, being abandoned, might have carried a grudge. And the son, perhaps feeling rejected as a boy when his father deserted the family, possibly didn't feel he was subject to his papa's instructions—you know how children are who carry a parental grudge. At the same time, he no doubt respected what his papa had achieved and wanted some remembrance of Him. But as He was now a total nonmaterialist, He owned nothing that could be passed down. The head, of course, is the highest spiritual center for a Buddhist. It was the most valuable thing the Buddha had."

"It all sounds a little macabre . . . though I do recall an Indonesian tribe I once collected among who, on important matters, consulted with their dried-up ancestors they kept crammed in clay jars. . . ."

"*Oui.* Those were different times. My guess is that Yasodhara, the wife, perhaps with her son, bribed the corpse-preparer into switching heads. There's no evidence the corpse-preparers were Buddhists, since very few people were then. Like now, the corpse-preparers were Untouchable and very poor. Buddhism was still at the level of an influential cult. Like today, they came from the lowest strata of society. They were bribable."

"It could have been done. Undeniably. Though it still sounds awfully unlikely to me that Mom and the kid would have headed off with it."

"I agree, but let's examine each and all in turn. They could have kept it in the family, passing it down as an heirloom of sorts, until it surfaced again. And I believe there's evidence—strong circumstantial evidence—that this happened only 150 years later. But there are far more likely suspects I want to offer you first, that I think you'll find much easier to accept."

"Shoot."

"Look what was done with the rest of His remains! How His followers fought over them! They had definite *value.* To avoid an out-and-out war, His relics were divided between the eight ruling Mallas in the region, who were demanding them. As you can see, it is clear that He wasn't cremated very well, and probably wasn't meant to be. Don't you agree that *any* of the eight would have had the motive and could have easily forced the corpse-preparer to arrange the switch?"

I nodded thoughtfully, wishing my own head was clearer.

"They built eight *stupas* over these relics," François continued, in a carefully modulated voice. "Look at the Temple of the Tooth at Kandy in Sri Lanka; there they have built a huge complex over a supposed tooth of the Buddha's; it makes one wonder whose canine actually *is* in there, doesn't it?"

"Interesting indeed," I said, slowly stroking my beard.

"Oui. That's ten possibilities. But now we reach the executive level. There are two other considerations. One is Ananda."

"His disciple? His *faithful,* unquestioning sidekick? Not as much chance, I don't think."

"Not only Ananda—I think he and the Buddha Himself may, just may, have had a pact."

"How do you see that . . . ?"

"Think of it. First of all, as we have seen, the Buddha wasn't above a little self-aggrandizement for His final act—"

"The Mafia funeral," I interjected. Then I winced as I saw a single, large snowflake drift down outside the window.

"If you wish to call it that but I wish you wouldn't. Perhaps, being human, He harbored a few thoughts of leaving a legacy behind. He Himself once said He didn't expect His teachings to last more than 450 years. No doubt He wanted to do all He could to create as big an influence as possible. He probably foresaw that there would be a fight over His remains, and arranged for Ananda to get the best portion so he could build a suitable shrine for it."

"Yes." I nodded. "Possible indeed."

"And Ananda could have done it himself for the identical reason, on his own—which is my last choice. Being in charge, he naturally had access. He did fail to completely cremate the body—that is also certain. The point is that *any* of the twelve suspects had means and motivation."

"Okay . . . someone made off with the Head. What then?"

"All roads appear to lead to Sanchi. Some time after the death, an inconspicuous monastery was built at this site in north-central India. It was the seed monastery of them all and probably was used to house some of the over one thousand monks the Buddha had ordained. True, there's no real mention of it historically for some century-and-a-half, but those monks had to stay someplace. I suspect very, very strongly that the Head was placed there—but in secret. The monks at Sanchi had a double motive in keeping it thus: first of all the Buddha had publicized that His remains were to be obliterated, and the monks would have looked bad if they had been seen ignoring the Buddha's deathbed wish; secondly, it was kept quiet to protect it from the other, stronger cult groups around them, who could have overpowered them and held the Head for ransom, or destroyed it, or whatever."

I nodded thoughtfully. It was undeniable. I was getting caught up in François's story.

"Tell me more about this monastery?" I asked, taking a sip of the mekhong. "I know of it certainly, but not the background."

"*Oui,* but it's hardly mysterious. It came to be called the Great Stupa at Sanchi, and it still exists. It first crops up in the books when Alexander the Great invaded through the Khyber Pass from Afghanistan in 325 B.C. or so—which has an impact on this story that I'll get back to. When Alexander left India to return to Greece, he left a general in charge, one Seleucus Nicator. Then a certain Chandragupta Maurya led a native uprising and threw him out, becoming the first true Indian emperor, the founder of the First Dynasty, that of the Maurya. *His* grandson was the famous Ashoka, who lived from 273 to 232 B.C. Ashoka took Buddhism, this new and growing cult, to his heart, and spread the belief all over the subcontinent and even down into Sri Lanka, which he conquered. It was Ashoka who built the Great Stupa on the site of the previously insignificant monastery at Sanchi. He also took the relics from the original eight *stupas* the Mallas had built and divided them further, building some 84,000 others. But neither those nor the original eight remain in any identifiable form today."

"You suspect he discovered the Head at the monastery and was moved to these extremes?"

François nodded. It occurred to me that his nervousness was disappearing as he warmed to his theory.

"And under him, the cult graduated to a religion, if one presumes the only difference between the two is the number of converts."

I gazed out the window. Above Central Park feathery autumn clouds tickled the sky's broad, blue belly, turning golden as the sun retired.

"Interesting. . . ."

"The Great Stupa was sixty feet in diameter and twenty-five feet high," François explained. "Like all religious buildings, even the pyramids and the Gothic churches of Europe, it was shaped like a mountain, for that is where the gods traditionally live, whether it's Olympus or Sinai. The Great Stupa at Sanchi represents Mount Meru, the mythological central mountain of the universe. Like all its successors, it was probably white, symbolizing snow. You can guess what was in it," he added, pausing significantly before continuing. "Then, years later, in the middle of the second century B.C., during the Sungas Dynasty that succeeded the Mauryas, the shrine was *doubled* in size. Why?

What else!" he exclaimed with such enthusiasm I almost spilled my drink.

Christopher looked up from his play, then returned to bashing centuries-old sculptures together. I could only nod in increasingly deeper thought. What else could have been in there? They all contain some relic or another and it *was* the big one. . . .

"Go on," I said.

"It was the first *stupa* ever built with a three-tiered umbrella on top symbolizing the Buddha, His law and the community of monks—the idea of the Trinity, which is also used by Christians. The 112-year reign of the Sungas was a period of almost constant warfare and they eventually gave way to the Andhras from the south of India, while at the same time the Kushans took over the north. The border between the two empires passed near Sanchi, and though it fell into the Andhra sphere of influence, it appears the two empires shared the site. The new owners apparently learned the secret of this most sacred temple in India and built it even bigger! It was now the greatest stone monument in India, and was copied everywhere Buddhism was exported. It and its tiered umbrella directly influenced the design of the stacked *chortens* in Nepal and Tibet; and from there the multitiered pagodas of first, China, then Korea and Japan; the pointed, bell-shaped pagodas of Burma; and even the mammoth World Mountain of Borobudur in Indonesia, the largest of them all. Sanchi's was the most important temple in the Buddhist world. The splitting of India was a prominent factor in the spread of Buddhism. Do you think all that could have been stimulated by a . . . a *toenail?*"

I nodded for him to continue. He lowered his voice and did just that.

"It was at this time, the end of the first century B.C. when the Andhras were taking over the south and the Kushans the north, that the new religion was at a growth stage and in need of an icon to focus on. Roman trade, which Alexander had been instrumental in opening up, was at its peak. Roman ships traded with India, and the Great Silk Route from Cathay to Roma traversed half the globe. There's an Andhra mirror handle of an attractively built lady—to say the least—that was found at Pompeii and is at the museum there. Artisans also traveled the Silk Road. At the heart of this trade route was the Kushan Empire, which encompassed Afghanistan, Kashmir and as far south as Sanchi. Their king, Kanishka, who lived from about A.D. 78 to 144, was known as 'the Second Ashoka' for his work in spreading Buddhism. He was the first to put the Buddha on a coin, which during those illiterate times was an important way of broadcasting information about military conquests, a new ruler or, in the Buddha's case, a new religious idea. Before that, a deer, a footprint, a wheel or the bo tree was used to symbolize His figure, since the Buddha didn't want His image reproduced. The king thought otherwise. Here. Look at this."

He flipped open a coffee-table book to a marked color plate. It showed a blown-up gold coin embossed with the unmistakable image of the Buddha, His thumb and forefinger forming a circle. That was the teaching sign, or *vitarka mudra*— the scuba diving A-OK sign—that had been used by both the Buddha and Jesus Christ. It was ironic, because both were known for having some trouble getting under the surface of water. The Buddha coin also showed a solar disc behind His entire body. His Jewish colleague had often been portrayed in the same way, the iconographies of both having been influenced by the broad-based sun-worshipping cults in the western half of Asia. The coin even had the Buddha's name recognizably stamped on it— BODDO— which hinted strongly at the "Indo" portion of the Indo-European roots of the West's alphabet. The Buddha's cranial protuberance, or *ushnisha*, representing superspiritual knowledge, was clearly evident, as were His elongated ears, caused by the heavy-jeweled ornaments He had worn while still a prince.

"I'm impressed," I said, closely examining the picture. "This Kanishka was sending a clear message."

"Yes. The first images of the Buddha began to appear on *stupas* after that, about A.D. 150 to 200. It was really Kanishka who oversaw an explosion in the visual representations of Him."

"The robe looks more Roman, though," I said, glancing at the picture of the coin one more time, and at the page opposite, before laying the book aside. "And those pictures of the Buddha's wife look a lot like Athena."

"It's not surprising. The artisans who traveled the Silk Route eastward in search of work brought Roman styles of sculpture home with them. Most settled on India's northwest border, at Gandhara, part of Kanishka's Kushan empire. It was the Kushans who built the huge stone Buddha in Gandharian style at Bamyan in Afghanistan. Hellenism met Buddhism at Gandhara. In Alexandria, sculptors used to store statues in inventories, all of them based on standing portraits of the Roman emperor, while awaiting orders to attach appropriate heads. The same happened in the East: the artisans attached what they imagined was a Buddhist head, adjusted the gesticulations into the various *mudras,* and sent them out. During Kanishka's reign *tons* of statues were produced and these were again copied elsewhere. The Kushan period lasted from 100 B.C. to A.D. 300. His impact was tremendous."

"And then the 300-year-long *gupta*— the Golden Age— took over, as I recall. And many of these early Buddhist heads looked a lot like the Greek god Apollo, the bodies like a Roman emperor."

"Oui. But what's *most* interesting to us are the features of the Buddha Head! Although the early sculptures *do* look like Greek gods, the caricature *itself* had to be based on the original. By this, I mean the protuberance, the hair and the elongated ears. It *had* to be available for this to happen! Which is further evidence to me that it existed. How else do you explain the tightly curled hair that is always depicted, among a people with wavy hair at the most? And the protuberance—word of mouth? Possible but not likely. And it's unlikely the sculptors were working from drawings since there's no evidence their artistic tradition had developed that far."

I was impressed by François's research.

"You're saying that Kanishka called his head sculptors together and gave them a peek at it?"

"Oui— or advised them personally after studying the actual Head himself," he said, missing another of my unintentional puns.

Sweat was pouring off his forehead. He removed his black blazer and began to undo his cuff links. Christopher was tugging at his pants; his shirt already lay crumpled on the floor. I was finally feeling comfortable.

"I suspect it was either Kanishka or Ashoka who decorated it with the gold and jewels and so on it's supposed to have," François told me.

"I wonder what the protuberance really is? A growth? His hair style?"

"Well, the Gandharian School seems to represent it as his hair tied in a knot, but who knows? Tell me when you find out."

"I seem to recall there was supposed to be a Buddha skull at a place called Hadda in Afghanistan," I said, ignoring his insinuation and slowly stirring up the long-settled silt that had buried my deepest memories.

"I think that's it. I theorize it was taken there for a short time, but that the emperor realized it was far safer and of better use where it belonged, and that was at the Great Stupa of Sanchi. But *that's* the historical basis to the Rumor, no doubt. It definitely, historically existed! How could something like that disappear forever?"

"Well, it could have been a piece of whoever's skull was cremated at Kushinagar," I said. A light snow began to fall over the darkening park. I hastily turned away and shakily gulped a drink of mekhong. "How did the schism dividing Buddhism into two schools come about? How does that fit in?"

"Between Theravada or Hinayana, 'the Lesser Vehicle,' and Mahayana, 'the Greater Vehicle'? Probably the more fundamentalist Theravada didn't go along with the radical sculpture movement, the blasphemy of portraying His image, though they certainly accepted it later. The Mahayana—the reformist group—broke off to incorporate other gods and animistic beliefs, as was done in Nepal and Tibet, and then moved across China to Vietnam and Japan, along the pagoda route. The more traditional Theravada settled in Sri Lanka, Burma and Thailand, though they didn't remain fundamentalist in a Christian sense; they incorporated a few animistic beliefs themselves and, of course, like the Mahayana, made the Buddha a god and created a spate of heavens to attain to. I believe the Head stayed at Sanchi until perhaps the twelfth century, certainly not much longer. By the seventh, Buddhism was waning in India. By the twelfth, Islam had invaded and spread all over the subcontinent, but its one god offered the Indians little more. Eventually Hinduism with its vast confusion of deities and demons—its extravagance was surely much better suited to the powerful spiritual needs of the people—began to grow out of the soil of India. It eventually pushed Islam almost completely aside as well but by this time the Head had been smuggled out of India."

"The Head would have been moved? Why?"

"Because of the Islamic invasion, of course! The Moslems spread their faith by the sword, remember. They had little patience with competing religions."

"Makes damned good sense."

"*Oui.* Logic says it would have gone north, following the line of least resistance and greatest support. Nepal, or Tibet. There it was safe for centuries, and under the wing of its natural inheritors—the Dalai Lamas. Then relatively recent events, at least in Tibet—"

"The Chinese takeover!" The pieces were beginning to fit as tightly as a Thai pussy. "And he sent it down to Tengboche for safekeeping, so it would still stay in Buddhist territory!"

"*Exactement.* That makes very good sense, to say the least. Perhaps you can find out from the abbot. He may even have a very different story than my own. Well, what do *you* think of my theory?" he asked, tugging at his tie. "But *mon Dieu,* it's hot in here!"

"I can't deny the logic at all," I said "There's not only circumstantial evidence, but damned *real* evidence too! You're making a believer out of me." I suddenly laughed. "And this might just all be hogwash, the result of a lousy telephone connection."

François joined in laughter and leaned back. There followed a long pause, by the end of which I knew what he was going to say next. There was an earnestness in his voice as he leaned forward.

"I repeat: Will you go and help return the Head? Or perhaps you see too much of the commercial value in it—"

I shook my head slowly, but it wasn't to say no. It was at the incredibility of it all. All the same, François blanched.

"What are your reservations?" he asked quickly, tensing again.

"The money."

"I am . . . prepared to pay you more. How does 30,000 dollars sound?"

I shook my head again.

"Mon Dieu! I can't go higher than 35,000!"

He was looking frantic. He patted the sweat off his face with a handkerchief.

"Why are you offering so much?"

He looked down, embarrassed.

"I want the financial inducement to be such that people assisting in the return won't be tempted to, ah . . ."

"To get something else into their *own* heads about it, right? Well, don't worry," I told him. "That's not it. What I mean is that if this is going to be a charity case on your part, I want it to be the same thing on mine. You know I feel about Buddhism the same way as you. I'm certainly not as well off as you but I'm still far from broke. I've lived in Asia too long not to have been affected by Buddhism. I could never look any of my Oriental friends in the eye if they knew I had made money returning the Head—or worse. I have to say I like the idea of doing something for the good of mankind and all that, too," I added, fingering my amulet. "You're quite right about this being far above commercial interests."

François's eyes opened briefly in shock. Then relief swept over them. I pushed the envelope meant for me firmly toward him.

"Très bon, Monsieur Rivière! That's generous of you, very generous! But you're not saying something you might later regret?"

I crossed my arms. Any doubts I might have had before were gone with the monsoon. He studied me carefully.

"Will you accept expense money? This might cost considerably more than you realize."

"If it's that much, I'll send you a bill."

"Lee, I appreciate very much your offer. You're a true friend and I knew I could count on your integrity in this matter. But, please, I *insist* that you take the expense money. It's not much—a few thousand dollars. Please remember that, as you say, I have considerably more money than you."

Steel had entered his voice. He took up the envelope

and slapped it on my lap. Before I could argue further, he raised his hand.

"Now, you know where your usual room is. Your tickets to Bangkok and then Kathmandu are in the packet."

Christopher roared by, naked except for one sock, pretending a Vishnu was some kind of jet. He flew out the door.

"You leave first thing in the morning, shuttling to Toronto. I have you booked back to Bangkok on Canadian Airlines International."

I shivered at the thought of flying over Canada, a six-letter word spelled w-i-n-t-e-r. But then there's got to be something good to say about a country that puts a beaver on their nickel.

"You have a day in Bangkok to get your things together before flying up to Kathmandu. In any case, remember to contact me through Monsieur Krueger as soon as possible with whatever information you have. If you have to phone me yourself, please be sure to talk in the most roundabout manner. Don't even identify yourself. I'll recognize your voice."

He stood to walk behind his desk, where he opened a drawer. Long shadows from the towers across the park bowed down to us, almost touching our feet.

"Now, to the Jacuzzi with you. Your clothes should be done shortly. Tonight I've booked a table for all of us at Elaine's for . . ."

A loud crash and a high-pitched cry out in the hall interrupted him.

"Here, help yourself, *s'il vous plaît,*" he said hurriedly, quickly placing in front of me a heavy hand-mirror that I knew had once belonged to Josephine, and a highly ornate snuff box with a large N monogrammed on the lid. I smiled. Invariably, both were table ornaments at François's parties. He excused himself and disappeared out the door. A moment later a litany of angry French issued from the hallway.

I flipped back the top, scooped out a small mountain of white powder with a tiny gold spoon, deposited it on the mirror, and rolled up a 500-baht note. A moment later I was lying back and sniffing. Raising my glass of mekhong, I saluted the two well-oiled gentlemen nailed to the wall behind François's desk. The adrenaline was flowing. I sensed I was soon going to have my hands on the finest piece of my life.

THREE

Patpong Road

THE LION'S DEN was packed with middle-aged pilots when I pressed through the door, their ample beer bellies stretching identical burgundy shirts with the Air America wings on the breast. All wore the heavy gold bracelets that are the trademark of their fraternity. "Everybody Is An Asshole" was raging out of the juke box and the noise level was at a happy din.

I stroked my freshly trimmed beard and peered around the smoky confines. Most of the regulars were out for the free weekly feed, including Hal Lawson in spirited conversation with a couple of cigar-chomping pilots with bottles of Kloster in their thick paws. Glancing around through the smoke, I made out the salt-streaked, smiling head of the retired spook who had been agency chief of the then top-secret air base at Long Tieng during the CIA's "secret" war in Laos in the sixties, his stocky football physique gone mostly to pasture, that pasture being Patpong's where he could always be found grazing or lapping from his favorite troughs. Nearby, one of his equally heavy-set colleagues,

now retired to Udorn in northern Thailand, raised the two
fingers remaining on one hand since he messed with a
booby trap; one of the decrepids dutifully served him up
four drinks; it was a standing joke. Both were chatting and
cracking dirty jokes with what had been their employees a
quarter of a century before. A former Raven—that breed
that flew forward air advance mostly, in tiny bird dogs—I
knew who was now a senior captain for United Airlines
and who dropped into The Lion's Den whenever he had a
layover was sharing a good-natured joke with another regular, a Belgian merc, a compact chunk of muscle with
bright, alert eyes whose career dated back to the Congo
and through Allende and who now handled special operations for the Thais out of the same city of Udorn.

Safari-suited correspondents, construction stiffs in from
Saudi and a few others—none of us ever knew what they
did, or if we did we didn't talk about it—were shoveling
into the free chow. The mood was light and bright, the
camaraderie warm, firm and real. The fly-boys were back
in town.

But Wolfgang Krueger was nowhere to be seen. His cus-
tomary booth was occupied by three men wearing reunion
shirts and listening attentively to the Lion raconteuring
one of his woolly tales from his wild and wobbly past.

Disappointed, I slipped over to the bar, greeting and
being greeted, and ordered a mekhong and Coke. Double-
checking around and still not seeing the Wolf, I pushed
through to where the Lion sat with his prey and waited
until the punch line to a story I had heard a thousand times
before came and passed before interrupting. The Lion
introduced me and we shared a few pleasantries before I
had a chance to put my question to him.

"Wolfgang? Hell no, I ain't seen him since you was in a
couple days ago. I was wonderin' where the fucken hell he
was myself."

The Lion was drawling into another reminiscence, this
one about some whorehouse in Calcutta right after the
war, so I drifted through to the phone at the end of the bar.
It rang for a full three minutes before I reluctantly returned the receiver to its cradle.

While I was deciding what to do next, an immense shout
startled me. It came from the direction of the door.

"Heil Hitler!" a Teutonic voice screamed.

The bar suddenly went cold as one of Jupiter's moons. Everyone turned to the door. It was Kurt the Kraut, or the Brussels Kraut as we sometimes called him, because he'd lived there for a time before moving to Bangkok thirty years before, eventually opening a bar of his own—Panties, on Patpong. It was one of the oldest on the strip though it was a complete mystery to many of us how he kept it going, Kurt clearly not operating with a fully loaded Luger. He was the most incompetent publican in Bangkok, it being a well-known fact that his girls, the cashier, mama-san and the bartenders had been ripping him blind for years. He claimed to be an ex-Waffen SS man and looked the part, being tall and—at one time anyway—well-built, though he had gone to spud long ago. He was standing stiffly at attention with his arm shot out rigidly at a forty-five-degree angle. The eyes in his equally rigid face burned with a fanatic's disjointed passion. Part of his shirttail hung out over his bulging belly. One of his shoelaces was undone. It wouldn't be the first time the Lion had kicked him out.

"Ve are *proud* to have the pilots of—" was all the Brussels Kraut managed to spit out before the Lion was on his feet, his teeth bared. The experienced old pilots read the situation quickly, relaxed, and looked on with amusement as the Lion ejected the protesting Prussian, then returned, his face still flushed with anger.

The bell above the bar clanged loud and long. Hal Lawson's hand was on the clapper cord.

"A show like that calls for one for the house, eh!" the Canuck shouted above the loud and general cheers.

While the bartenders went into a frenzy setting them up and the Ancients hobbled around distributing them, the Lion, his mane now up, stalked through to Noi, who was just to my right and behind the bar. He demanded the stuffed shoebox with Hal Lawson's name on it.

"Lion, can you do me a small favor?" I asked. "I've got something I need to get to the Wolf. Could I leave it with you to pass on?" I knew I should wait till he was in a better mood, but I had things to do. People to meat. I hadn't been laid for a few days and I was getting a little antsy. Out of my breast pocket I pulled the envelope François had given me for Wolfgang.

"Jist scrawl his fucken name on it and leave it with Noi here in the cash box," he growled, breaking away from the impossible task of adding up Lawson's chits.

Then his eyes fixed on the latest bill, the one Hal had stood for the house. The Lion's growl suddenly grew to a roar.

"Hey Lawson!" he bellowed. "Git yer fucken shrapnel-embedded goddamned arsehole over here fer a goddamned minute!"

A number of heads turned quizzically for a moment before auto-rotating back to their old conversations. I quickly scribbled Wolfgang's name on the envelope and added: GONE TREKKING. I knew it would be safe with the Lion.

Hal looked like he would sooner have been back covering the Tet Offensive as he walked by me, white-faced. I wiggled through the crowd to escape any debris from the explosion and was halfway to the door when a large hand reached out of the crowd, gripped my arm, and pulled me over.

"Well, it's Jungle Boy again," a deep voice said. "Haven't seen you here for a couple of days." Brock Stambuck eased his bulk onto a miraculously free bar stool, oblivious to its wobble. "I'm surprised."

"Been taking care of some business," I replied, thinking it best to avoid the subject of my quest completely. "It always takes a couple of days after an expedition."

He eyed my freshly laundered jeans and Hawaiian shirt.

"My God, even a haircut! I must say, you look a hell of a lot better than the last time I saw you. I was wondering if you'd like to drop over to the embassy range and get some practice with that pistol I sold you. You've still got it, of course?"

"Never fear, it's safe at home. But I'm afraid I'll be busy as hell for the next while. Things are a little crazy. But once I get everything squared away, you're definitely on."

The Lion was waving his hands angrily at Hal. The journalist tried to protest but the Lion shook a huge roll of chits in his face.

"What're you up to that's so important?" Brock asked,

taking a nip of the Old Crow that a decrepit old hag of at least twenty-six had brought him. He reached for a Cuban.

I glanced over at the corner again. Hal was handing the Lion a check. A moment later Hal trudged past us to his bar stool, a shaken look on his face. The thorn now out of his paw, the grimace that passed for a smile returned to the Lion's leathery mug. He hitched up his pants and resumed his favorite role of host to the unexpected and unusual.

"What am I up to?" I said. "Oh, just some piece I have a lead on that I'm trying to track down. I can't really talk about it. You haven't seen Wolfgang, by any chance?"

Brock shrugged his heavy shoulders, to my disappointment. Where could the old kraut be? He must have known I'd be back and that this was supposed to be important. I had to catch that plane to Kathmandu early in the morning.

"And talking about pieces," I said, checking my watch and draining my glass, "I've got an important appointment."

It was almost 7:00 p.m. If I didn't get over to the Cherry Blossom Massage Parlor damned quick, the best would be cleaned out, and that would include my favorite, Su, number 143. Also, I could hear the sirens calling from Patpong and was feeling the first stages of what I sensed was a powerful hunting trance coming on. Somewhere out there was a beautiful girl with whom, I just knew, I was going to have a serious meaningless relationship tonight.

"And leave all this?" Brock asked incredulously, before sending his nearly full glass of Old Crow flying past his tonsils.

"They'll be around awhile," I said, plugging my bill cup with some baht and leaning toward the exit. "I'll catch them later. *Ciao.*"

I paused at the door and looked back. The party was reaching altitude. I couldn't resist. I waited until Hal's mug of beer shakily touched his lips before I cupped my hands to my mouth.

"Dead bug!" I shouted, as loudly as I could.

Before the explosion of flying beer, crashing bar stools and the curses of injured men could reach me, I was out the door and down the street. Five minutes later I was standing in the pseudoluxurious surroundings of my favor-

ite massage parlor, sipping a mekhong and Coke in the
subdued Muzak and dimmed lighting, and admiring the
girls sitting on well-lit bleachers behind a wall-size picture
window. They were all dressed in the same outfit, and each
had a red button with a number on it attached to her
blouse. It always reminded me of those restaurants where
you pick a lobster out of the tank.

"Her, 143 please," I said to a discreet host in a suit,
relieved to see the girl with the magic hands was still
there.

"You no want 51 also? Same-same before?" he whispered, never forgetting a customer's predilections.

"No Siamese twins tonight. I just want a good bath and
rubdown this time. No trimmings. I'm saving it for somebody special."

Who that someone special was I didn't know, because I
hadn't met her yet. But I knew I would. I did every time I
headed out for one night in Bangkok. She was always beautiful, and had a different name each time, when I remembered to ask what it was.

He nodded and whispered into a microphone by the
window. A moment later a soft hand was leading me
gently to the elevator.

———— • ————

Ah. Patpong. Home. Finally.

And it was the evening of Loy Krathong, the most magical festival in Thailand, held on the twelfth full moon of the
year. Many of the bars had set up elaborate ponds before
their establishments and smiling Thai girls were strolling
around them, holding the pretty floats they would later
launch in propitiation to the Goddess of Water.

Powdered, pampered and perfumed, I was already floating on a soft cumulus on which winged nymphs sang seraphic tunes, as I drifted down the neoned strip, past the
deaf vendors flogging their watercolors and wares, past
touts flashing cards advertising "pussy Smoke Ckga Lett
show" and "pussy pingy-pong show" and "Resbien show
with dildow," past sexy, bikini-clad girls trying to lure me
into the throbbing hearts of bars with names like the Pussy
A-Go-Go, Erotica, Flashtastic. I ignored them all—there
was only one bar I was interested in tonight. My favorite

bar on my favorite street in my favorite city in my favorite country in the world.

Crazy Horse.

I skipped up the steps and bounced in, breathing deeply of the scented air that felt crisp and cool as a mountain morning, while the beat of the best of *Billboard* boomed out of the speakers. I surveyed the bright neon interior: the glistening white rectangular island bar, the high-tech room which center it dominated, the showcased a-go-go stage raised to high-heeled ankles at eye level. Above the bikinied dancing girls admiring themselves in the mirrored walls orbited a Star Wars satellite system of flashing, twirling lights. The place was doing wall-to-wall business as usual, and sexy, semiclad Thai girls were resting on the arms and laps of *farangs*— foreigners—all over the sparkling room. The energy level was high, hot and horny.

There was still a single stool open on one of the wide sides of the big bar. I slipped onto it and ordered the usual, mekhong and Coke. Looking up into the wall mirror, I caught the happy smile and sparkling eyes of someone familiar, obviously having a good time, and realized with a soft jolt that it was me. I gave the image a wink and a thumbs up. I had died again and was among the angels in Patpong Heaven.

"Hello, my friend . . . I don't know . . . but you *are* a lucky fellow," a tall, blond *farang* said, interrupting my reverie. From some Scandinavian country, by his accent. "What is it that you have that we do not?"

"Huh?"

"The lady on this stage. She is much too beautiful to call her a girl. I and many others have been wanting to take her home for the last couple of weeks but she will have nothing to do with any of us. But she has been looking at you since you came in. Are you the boyfriend of her?"

I hadn't had a chance to look at the girls yet. I noticed that all the men around the bar were as one in silently staring at the same point on the go-go stage. Their faces were tense, desirous, admiring.

Puzzled, I looked up and scanned the dancers. Then I blinked twice, and bit my bottom lip so my jaw wouldn't drop into my mekhong.

I'd seen a lot of incredibly beautiful women on Patpong,

and here you see *all* of them, so I quickly swept my wits together. I turned my head away deliberately and took a sip of my drink, waiting at least five seconds before casually looking up again.

It was true. She *was* incredible.

And she was beaming happily at me as she danced with fast and graceful energy to the beat of Michael Jackson. I looked down and pretended to stir my drink, trying to figure out what the hell was going on. I was vaguely aware that some of the men were glancing in my direction.

Nonchalantly I looked up again. I had my wits back in my pocket. She *had* to be flawed—they all were, particularly the beautiful ones, who the world over are sadly but invariably airheads, never having had to develop their brains since they were able to rely so easily on their boobs. But if this lady had a physical flaw, I certainly couldn't see it at a glance. Quite the opposite—she was magnificent.

She was sleek and lean and beautiful beyond belief, her string bikini a shimmering black satin that was a flimsy, teasing second skin to the Chinese white that was her color. Her legs flowed out of black high heels, their ankles strong but delicate, their calves curvaceous and full, their thighs lithe and firm, those sinuous and sexy limbs finally ending at a pert, black-satin triangle that barely covered her own. The strings of her bikini bottom disappeared between two fantastic firm cheeks that waved and wiggled in a language all their own. She had a tight little belly button on a tight little belly on a long, slender waist, and higher, barely concealed by her top, swelled two proud and protruding breasts. Long, long, jet-black hair flowed to her bouncing bottom, surrounding her face like a halo, framing two gleaming eyes and a beautiful white smile braced by two tiny dimples.

And there was no doubt. She was dancing for me.

Our eyes locked and immediately I knew I was lost. I tried to turn away but the joy and happiness I saw reflected in the flash of her smile took me captive. I held her easy eyes as she lowered her chin and danced down the stage to be in front of me. She shook herself around, high-kicked, and spun on her toes, her hands high above her head, her elegant fingers now tracing delicate Thai arabesques in the air.

While awed murmurs for her safety rose from the *farangs* she leapt high up onto a chrome pole, flipped upside down, and twirled around and around and around, always on the music's very beat and always, again and again those eyes and that smile flashing back at me. She sizzled, she souffléed, she stirred herself around. Her shining black hair flew. Her lithe body glowed with the exuberance of her dance.

I was mesmerized, suddenly being spun into a new kind of cocoon she was weaving around me, by the way this incredible female communicated with me. While she danced, we may as well have been alone in my bedroom, so oblivious were we to everyone else in the room. I could feel an uncontrollable sexual arousal starting to rumble— Ol' Thunder shifting, shuffling and snorting, seeking freedom from his cramped confines. She read my face, smiled even wider and a gleefully happy laugh rose with and above the music. She shot her hip at me on the beat. Boom. Boom. Boom. I flushed and looked down. When I looked up again, I could see in a glance that she was upset for embarrassing me.

The rocker segued to a slow ball-boiler. She smoothly transformed herself into a long and sinuous snake, the music melting and flowing through her, her hair covering her face teasingly, only a cat's eye glinting through. Her hands caressed her thighs and breasts unselfconsciously and I could see and feel her arousal. She was alone with me, feeling beautiful, looking beautiful, feeling sexy, looking sexy. She was aroused and raising her arousal to its highest level, and the air in the room crackled with her sexuality.

The song came to an end, the spell broken. The girls hurried off the stage to make room for the next line. She followed, reluctant but joyous, but not without a warm glance of longing that left my head and heart reeling. My eyes caressed her naked backside until it disappeared backstage.

My hand trembled as I raised my glass to my lips. The mekhong tasted dry. I set the glass down, and became aware that many eyes were on me.

"My God, you are a lucky man," my neighbor said incredulously.

I felt embarrassed again and mumbled something, my lips like rubber. My heart was beating too loudly. I tried to concentrate on the new line of dancers, but it was only with the gravest difficulty.

Five minutes that seemed like five hours later, she reemerged, refreshed.

"Oh, my God. Here she is coming," the Viking said. "I can not stand to be that close to her. You can have my seat, friend." He quickly slipped off his bar stool.

She floated up, looking much tinier than she had on-stage, a trace of shyness hinting at an inner vulnerability. I slowly spun around on my stool and she stopped before me. I was entranced by her eyes; they glistened like two unfathomable gems, the intelligence behind them unmistakable. Her nose was uplifted and pert, her skin fine as silk and glowing with health and vitality, her cheekbones high, her face, like the rest of her, voluptuous, perfectly proportioned. She had to be twenty, twenty-two at the most.

Her thigh accidentally, electrically brushed mine. It was a long moment before either of us spoke, and when we did she was the one who led.

"May I sit down?" she asked, embarrassment in her voice.

"Of . . . of course," I sputtered, feeling my face redden.

"Cup coon ca," she whispered, as she slipped easily onto the vacated stool. She gracefully crossed her long legs and shook her hair into place. The flow of it reminded me of music. Or poetry. I was only partially aware of the stares around us.

"Could I buy you a drink?" I asked, finding my voice. It came out with a soft richness that surprised me.

"It not necessary. If you want to buy me drink you can."

My eyebrows rose—something about how she spoke. Her accent was crisp and clean, even if she still fractured the syntax, falling back on Thai's much simpler structure. And yet it wasn't quite a Thai accent either. I signaled the bartender, then turned back to her.

"Do I detect a hint of an *English* accent?"

Her smile suddenly glowed like the sun breaking through clouds.

"Yes. My family send me boarding school in London and

study dance. But only speak English six month so no so good. I no like English food and weather much so I come back."

I raised my eyebrows again.

"Dance! Well, I'm not surprised," I said, although I certainly was. The families of virtually every other girl on Patpong were lucky to own more than a scrawny water buffalo to hoe their paddy fields. To send a daughter to London? To study dance? What the hell was she doing *here?* I asked her just that. Her face inexplicably darkened for just a moment, before returning to its beautiful inscrutability.

"I just work here for just few months. I accepted at Chulalongkorn University."

"University! I've never known a girl on Patpong to have more than grade six!"

"I know. I no same-same Patpong girl."

"I'll say. What are you going to study?"

"Anthropology."

"Anthropology! How did you ever get interested in that?"

"Because I live it," she said simply, offering no more. I was too puzzled to probe.

"I'm an anthropologist!"

"I know."

"What? How do you know?" I exclaimed, a little too baffled to think of anything else to say. I had to get myself together.

"There other reason I work here too," she added, ignoring me. Disappointment seemed to descend over her face. Somehow from her look I felt I should know why. "I come here work to surprise certain man. But he no seem to recognize me."

My heart fell. "Oh," I said, my turn to be disappointed. "Who?"

"You. . . ."

If I had been taking a drink I would have choked on it. *"Me?"*

"You mean you no recognize me?" she asked, her face now fallen.

"Am I supposed to?" I asked incredulously.

I had never seen her before in my life. I'd certainly

never forget a face like hers. I searched it for clues, crinkling my forehead as the wispy hint of the most distant of recognitions, like a sweet and drifting childhood memory, tickled the outer edge of my mind. But in a moment it was gone and I was left no further ahead. I swept my mind past the thousand-and-one bar girls I had banged in Thailand. Could she have been one of them that I was too drunk to remember? Not likely. Had I perhaps seen her in London a year before while I was delivering that collection of Mah-Meri woodcarvings from Carey Island to the Museum of Mankind? No.

Then I realized that she had to be taking me for a fool. I shook my head. A shadow of disappointment rose from her features and then dissipated, as if my response hadn't been entirely unexpected.

"If I knew you from before, you must have changed something about yourself. I'd remember hair like this for sure," I said, feeling its silky texture slip through my hand. I was a sucker for long hair. A glance down to her tight tummy further convinced me I didn't know her. I would *never* forget a waist like that.

"You go remember," she said, pouting and hiding in her hair.

Her drink arrived. I thought I should introduce myself.

"My name is Lee—"

"Rivers," she said softly, cutting me short.

I almost spat out an ice cube. I stared at her for a moment.

"La chew coon?" I asked. And your name?

She hesitated for a moment before telling me. I could see she was debating whether she should or not. The ayes won.

"My name Tysee. Do that 'ring bell'?" She held her neatly manicured fingers up as if she were tinkling a tiny bell. When she saw it didn't, she went on anyway, a glint of hurt now furrowing her brow, confusing and embarrassing me even more. "I should no be surprise. It be a long time. But I *no* go tell you more!" she stated defiantly. "You no even remember my name!"

A deep disappointment seemed to descend over her beauty, but a moment later her intelligent eyes flashed as she recovered. "I be here wait for you over one month. I know you come here. But you go Philippine. Now you come but you no remember me." She pouted while she spoke and I wasn't sure if she was serious or not.

"*How* did you know I come here? That I was in the Phil—"

Her soft, warm finger touched my lips, silencing me as her mood suddenly changed. She held it there longer than necessary, its touch communicating a wonderful surge of warmth. Slowly she took it away and picked up her tiny glass. Her hands were soft and elegant, their nails carefully manicured. Eminently holdable.

"*Chok dee!*" she toasted in a soft whisper. I wondered what she was thinking about.

"And good luck to *you,*" I returned just as softly.

Our glasses tinkled and I took a small sip. I was lost for anything to say. She wasn't.

"No one ever bar-fine me out," she said in almost a whisper, setting her glass down and looking away.

I couldn't see her face for her long hair.

"I can't understand why—"

"Because I no go with another man. I wait for you. Will you bar-fine me out of Crazy Horse Bar, Lee Rivers?"

Her voice was suddenly hot and wet.

"Jesus . . . I don't believe this," I mumbled as I reached into my pocket for the 300 baht. What the hell was going on . . . ?

———— • ————

"It Loy Krathong," she said easily as we dismounted The Crazy Horse a few minutes later, my eyes adjusting to the new vision beside me, one of grace and beauty in a diaphanous mauve dress that caressed her equally smooth form.

"Why don't we go to Lumpini Park?" I suggested, pointing toward Bangkok's beautiful central park named after Buddha's birthplace. "It's just a short walk away."

"I like that. I never hold hands with man in public before. It no so good but I see everyone changing. And with you it different," she added, smiling up at me, her smooth hand slipping into mine and giving it a squeeze. I could feel her whole being, her awareness, her lightness of spirit, in that delicate grip. Somehow I would have to remember where I knew her from. I had obviously made a good impression for some inexplicable reason.

We turned onto Silom Road and wended our way through the long, bright gauntlet of craft and food stalls that lined the broad sidewalk every evening to feed and entertain Bangkok's enormous night culture. We strolled past card tables selling twenty-five-dollar Taiwanese Rolexes and perfect Thai-made Gucci bags, past noodle stalls and fruit stands.

"Hey, let have look in here!" she cried, turning into a shop.

It was Simon Leather, the exotic-leather shop. We browsed among the crocodile handbags, eel cases and ostrich shoes. After ten minutes of good-natured bartering we left with Tysee happily holding a bag containing a cobra-skin bikini. A gift.

I pulled her over to a small food stall. In a giant *wok* was a round, red heap of huge, freshly cooked grasshoppers.

"You like?" I asked hungrily, turning to her.

"Pom chop!" she replied eagerly. I like.

We finished our stroll down the street, munching on the nutty-flavored delicacies, breaking off the legs, drumsticks and head, chewing up everything else. I shook my head slightly in amazement. She looked perfectly, guilelessly graceful nibbling the little beasts. Tysee. The girl with the pretty name.

I ventured to tell her about my experiences on the Rejang River, where I'd been abandoned by my Iban guide and porters and had had to survive on insects. She listened very attentively, moving closer as she did.

"That be dangerous!" she exclaimed with concern in her voice when I had finished.

"Not half as dangerous as my cooking."

Her laughter at my half-assed joke sounded genuine. It stopped as we approached the insanity of Rama IV Road with its broad lanes choked with snorting, rearing traffic. We somehow managed to survive the crossing and were soon mingling with the thick, well-dressed crowds gathered around the black statue of King Mongkut, who would later give Yul Brynner a career, and Rama IV its name.

So as not to lose touch in the press of people, we tightened our grips on each other's hands, hers every so often offering gentle squeezes I could feel in my heart like a caress. We flowed with the squish of people through the iron gates of Bangkok's beautiful central park, and soon were strolling at a relaxed pace in the ever-widening delta of humanity into a wonderland of fireworks, balloons, music, love and laughter. The air was warm and soft, the atmosphere light and happy.

"I only do this few time. Loy Krathong," she said merrily.

I expressed surprise. She was Thai and it was the most important celebration of the year. At least I presumed she was Thai. Thai-Chinese. She saw my look of disbelief.

"You remember. You try remember," she scolded teasingly, now treating my failure of memory with the same happiness of spirit that was in the air.

It puzzled me but I was also enjoying the new game. We gravitated to a hive of stalls selling the small, dinner-plate-size Styrofoam rafts used in the ceremony, each reflecting the artistic ability of the sellers.

"What you favorite color?"

"Green. Like summer leaves."

"Good. That my favorite color too," she said, tugging me over to a small stall, behind which perched a wizened old hag. "This woman, she favorite color red," Tysee laughed.

"How do you know her favorite color is red?" I asked, seeing no evidence in either her clothing or the boats. Then the old woman smiled revealing gums stained red from years of betel-nut chewing. Tysee giggled and hugged my arm.

"You rascal you." I grinned. "You even have a perverse sense of humor!"

She pointed at a marvelous round boat, one with banana leaves in-curling around the perimeter to create a flower-shaped design. The leaves forming the petals were dyed bright green. Besides a stick of incense and a candle, it even flew a tiny paper flag of Thailand.

I nodded. Tysee did the bargaining, with much good-natured bantering. I noticed again that unusual accent, but knew it was no use probing—that it was just part of the mystery. It'll out in time, I thought. Everything does.

"I think we get good price—twenty baht," she whispered to me conspiratorially as we left the stall, raft in hand. "I'm sure it should really be twenty-five. We lucky. That good sign."

She held the raft gently and we made our way in a leisurely stroll to the lake, a clean, strong attraction between us. Past the single musicians with their homemade instruments made out of tin cans, sticks and a few wires, past lovers holding hands and running, laughing children.

A large crowd was gathered on the soft grass that gently curled down into the large pond. The waters were already aflame with thousands of floating offerings, the candles winking in the reflection of the gleaming full moon and equally bright stars. We wound our way through the people and knelt by the water's edge.

"You make wish too?" she asked.

"I make a wish," I said.

She set the offering on the shoreline before us and placed her hands together in a prayer-like *wai*, then closed her eyes and, like many of the other singles and couples, slipped into meditation. I watched, breathing softly and easily, absorbing the gentle atmosphere.

Then I too formed a *wai* and closed my eyes. I thanked Mae Khonka, the female-water spirit, for another year of life-giving water, and made a wish.

Her wish is my wish, I thought.

Whatever Tysee's wish, it was a long one. Finally she opened her eyes and delicately placed the boat on the lightly lapping water. In a moment a small boy had swum over like an otter. After I quickly slipped a baht coin between two leaves of the boat where he could easily retrieve it, he pushed the raft out into the galaxy of others. For a long time we watched ours, Tysee slipping her hand again into mine, then drawing me closer until I could feel her warmth, her breathing, and catch brief wafts of the fragrant scent she was wearing.

Slowly we made our way back through the crowd, both of us feeling like all the sins of yesterday had been forgiven, that the new year would be better, brighter, that our hearts would be cleansed and more pure. She said nothing, and shyly avoided my gaze, but walked closer to me, now holding my arm with both of her hands.

———— • ————

"What's the matter?" I asked as Nog fidgeted with something in the front seat of the car. We were parked, idling, in the narrow *soi* in front of the solid doors of my compound. Tysee was sitting quietly beside me, interested in everything going on around her.

"Automatic door no work again, Mr. River. I have to get spare key."

"Damn," I mumbled under my breath. Again. . . .The last time it had taken a month to find people qualified to fix it.

Nog jumped out and scurried over to the *phi,* or spirit house, a dollhouse structure on a six-foot pedestal. Virtually every building in Thailand has one. They are most often shaped like a Buddhist *wat,* or temple, and are used to house the spirits that lived on the land before the trees and grass were cut down for construction. It was phallic-shaped, the same as Wat Arun, the Temple of the Dawn, the largest in Thailand—the original just across and down the Chao Phrya from us. Po kept ours well-stocked with little elephants, classical dancing statues and daily offerings of rice, fruit and flowers. In the tiny door of the spirit house is also where we left the spare key in the care of the occupants. Nog made a *wai* before it reverently, then reached inside with his fingers. In moments we were inside the high-walled courtyard and stepping out of the car.

"This real nice place, but no look like house," she said, her eyes scanning the twin-roofed affair with arching dragons at the corners.

I told her about its Chinese Buddhist past, how it had been abandoned and how I had discovered it, bought it and fixed it up. I led her to the cages of tropical birds Snake had given me, and the aquariums of tropical fish I had brought up on various dives. She seemed impressed with the small garden with its shrubs, bonsai, flowers and rattan.

A retiring Nog must have released Raffles, my mastiff, because he ran up, his huge muscular rump wagging back and forth, his tongue drooling happily out of the side of his goofy face. I introduced Tysee to him. Raffles took a couple of quick sniffs, liked what he smelled, and turned his attention more to her than me. Some pet. She crouched down and scratched him behind the ears, her face an inch from his. Raffles gave her a massive lick. She laughed. I patted

him a couple of times and ordered him to stay outside,
then we mounted the wide granite steps that led up to the
porch with its large red pillars.

Her eyes broadened with delight when the great door
opened to reveal the expansive living room with its sofas,
wool rugs, and carved furniture from all over the Far East.
Hanging tapestries, porcelain from a variety of dynasties,
and *thankyas,* as well as stone, terra cotta, jade and
wooden sculptures, decorated the open-vaulted room. The
atmosphere was relaxed and calm. Which made it at juxtaposed opposites to much else in my life.

"You have very beautiful home," she exclaimed as we
kicked off our shoes. "I like *mahk-mahk!*"

"Cup coon cup. Thank you. I've had the other large
room renovated into bedrooms, office, quarters for the
servants and so on. Look around if you wish."

She slipped gracefully around the living room, slowly
fingering the stone surface of a Vishnu stele, taking in the
low teak furniture, feeling the rich Kashmiri underfoot,
touching this and that. I flicked on the subdued lighting
that accented pieces around the room, lit some incense
and put on a tape of light, melodic, Burmese gong music.

"This picture of you parents?" she asked, lifting a framed
portrait off a mantel.

"Yes." I was feeling bad that I hadn't had time to give
them a call from New York.

"They good-looking. I think you have your mother's
eyes. What he do for living?"

"They just retired to Arizona. Dad used to be a small-
town pharmacist. I always tease him about being a drug
pusher."

Tysee quickly replaced the picture and moved on, looking decidedly upset. I wondered what I had said wrong.

"Tell me about your folks," I said. "What does your dad
do for a living?"

Tysee turned her back to me, ostensibly to inspect a
display of antique, erotic figures carved out of ivory—but
not before I got another glimpse of her face. She appeared
so uncomfortable it shocked me.

"My papa . . . he run farm," she answered awkwardly,
offering nothing else.

I quickly decided to drop the subject. Quietly, she

drifted on, a tentative smile returning to her face when she fingered some silver hill-tribe jewelry I had put together during various forays into The Golden Triangle. She beamed as something caught her eye. It was in a glass case I used for keeping some smaller objets d'art. I moved over to assist, but before I got there she deliberately, it seemed to me, moved on, turning her attention to my Buddhist shrine. Like all Thais, she was uplifted by the sight; she smiled cheerfully, and put her hands together reflexively.

"You have Buddha! Good! You also wear Buddha amulet. You are Buddhist?"

"I'm a little of everything. He is very good."

The answer seemed to warm her, for she drifted to my side, her soft hand slipping effortlessly into mine. Her hand felt so natural, her spirit so light. There was that something else about her too—an awareness, a sense of joy, of trust, of beauty beyond the merely physical. A presence.

I squeezed her hand.

She slipped into my arms. She felt light and slender and smelled like the freshest and most delicate of spring flowers. We stood there hugging in the misty light and soft music and tendrils of joss smoke while I lightly stroked her hair. It felt good. Very good. Too good.

She slowly pulled away and looked up at me, her warm eyes on mine, her open lips close. I kissed them tenderly, feeling their rose-petal-soft edges. They parted slightly and our wet tongue tips touched ever so delicately before our mouths slowly closed on each other. It ignited a blaze between my legs that took me by surprise. She sensed it and pressed her sinuous body to mine. The blaze turned into a roar, and my hands slipped down over her tight buttocks, pulling her in. I could feel her heat.

Then she pulled away from the kiss, panting slightly.

She made a slight move and her dress slipped down her long legs, leaving only a skimpy pair of black silk panties that accented the ivory whiteness of her skin. Her delicate fingers searched out my belt buckle . . .

In a moment we stood naked, our lips barely touching, both of us gasping slightly as Ol' Thunder brushed against her firm but soft-skinned tummy. I lifted her into my arms. She felt as light as a feather and was trembling. I carried her to my room and gently lay her down on the large bed.

Soft fans of light glowed out from beneath it. The delicate aroma of joss drifted in the air. A ceiling fan whispered as it turned.

Nothing had to be said. Words would only have been clumsy. I lay beside her and gently drew her to me. Our lips met as delicately as before, our tongues touching, caressing. My fingertips slipped down her long slender waist, caressed her hips, her strong thighs, her back, her full, firm breasts. Her sensitive fingers slid lovingly down between my legs, her touch making me draw in my breath. She lightly held me, squeezing imperceptibly, communicating, sending waves of pleasure coursing through me. We were both trembling.

My hand lingered on a firm breast. Its nipple was small, erect. I slowly pulled myself away from her lips and bent down. She lay back, her body open to me. My tongue's tip found a nipple, and touched, caressed its small, spiky protuberance, probing the base around and around to where it met the firm curve of her breast. It responded by changing, firming. I nibbled it. Her breathing deepened and soft, almost desperate sighs issued from her lips. Her hand became tangled in the hair on the back of my head as she pressed me to her. I sucked her nipple into my mouth. She breathed deeply, her soft sighs growing stronger, her grip on me strengthening slightly as she began to slowly stroke me. I sucked more and more of her breast inside, my hand molding it to feed me more until we were both trying to get the whole of it in. She guided me to the other. Then back again.

My fingertips slipped down her long, firm waist again, to her downy little patch, her skin, her body responding at each step. Her legs parted to greet my hand as it passed slowly over her firm, silky mound. She arched her hips as my fingers gently found their way down into her nest.

She nipped hotly at my neck as my middle finger traced the line of her vagina. On the second stroke it was greeted with a hot wetness. With each caress, it found more freedom, slipping into the slick little valleys on either side of her hard little *him* on her firm little *jum-jim*, until all was open and wet and eager. My fingertip found that little point of hardness, which I lightly caressed. She gasped and stiffened, holding me ever tighter. I gently probed the dwelling of her gods, my finger sliding slowly into her tightness, her firm around it, and wondered how I would ever fit when the moment came. She pressed her hot little pussy against my palm, forcing my finger inside her to the hilt, first tightening herself around it, then relaxing her grip, then squeezing again, rocking in rhythm and I knew it could be done and I could barely wait. She stroked me faster and faster as her own temperature rose into the red zone.

I slowly slid down her smooth body, my fingers and lips tracing its smooth, flawless beauty, down her tummy and along her strong hips, lightly tickling my nose in her silky down, sliding lower still, tracing and kissing the firmness of her thighs. Her breathing heightened in anticipation and her thighs quivered slightly as they parted to receive me, and I moved between them, now kissing the soft smoothness of their inner sanctum, now moving up closer and closer, kissing lightly, lovingly, sometimes more firmly and strongly, smelling the sweetness of her wetness.

She gasped in rich pleasure as the tip of my tongue made the ever-so-slightest contact with the tip of her little magic C. I caressed its tiny, firm wetness, feeling her entire body respond. I delicately traced the magic line with my tongue a couple of times, then began to stroke slightly deeper, moving with each slow, loving, enjoyable stroke to take laps to one side, then the other, probing deeper and ever deeper, shifting to trace the smooth, wider valley near the top, then skimming back down and probing into the mystery of her primordial cave, feeling the firmness, awareness and sensitivity even around my tongue. I nibbled the magic little button, teasing it, leaving it, and then, with a new-found determination, probing deeper on the sides, to the valley bottoms themselves, first on one side, then the other, as she grew hotter and hotter.

As her fires raged, I found the magic spot at the base of the hard little rosebud just where it meets the stem. Exhilarating gasps and labored breathing greeted my tongue; I began to press and roll her button lightly between my lips, then to munch it, sucking more and more and more of it into my mouth while her body went increasingly rigid, Ol' Thunder standing tall and rubbing against her smooth, tight calf, as her hands on my head pressed me into her—I was all but oblivious to her moans and sighs of ecstasy. Then all of her vagina was around my mouth, sucking and my head moved around in a loving rage.

I could feel the buildup, the increasing tension in her, and see, even in the dim lights, the flush spread over the beautiful landscape of her body, while I grazed and gazed adoringly up along her tummy to her upraised breasts and thrown-back head.

Suddenly she gasped once, then again and stiffened, her whole body rocking in rigid, spasmodic waves back and forth down on me, her voice crying and sighing and singing all at the same time.

Still hungry, she began to pull me up onto her, my chest and belly running along her prominent, upright little pussy. She covered me with kisses, then broke away, looking up at me with wide-open eyes, so imploring in their intensity, as she guided my pulsating *co-ay* toward her steaming *lek maew*, her little cat.

She held me, stroking me up and down in her wetness, finding the mark, wetting the head, our eyes locked all the while.

Spontaneously she rocked her hips gently up to meet me. Deeper and deeper into the sweetest, smoothest, tightest of quicks I slipped until we were locked tightly together, vibrating in each other's arms.

Never had I felt such a body as this, such a naturalness as this, such a communication as this. Such a pussy as this. The most beautiful of the beautiful, the most unique of the unique, like a snowflake with silky hair around it. It was a perfect fit. I felt completely inside. I held myself up on my elbows, partly not to crush her, partly to angle in to the maximum, partly to be able to look down on her ineffable beauty, her firm breasts, her cheek on the pillow, her closed eyes, her parted lips, while she sighed helplessly with each long, deep stroke.

For two hours or more we made love, lying on our sides, helicoptering, woofer style, her topside, sitting up together, alternately pounding the juiceburger into hamburger, then being gentle, sometimes stopping just to rest and caress, finally with her on her back with her legs together, an almost impossible position. Faster and faster we moved, long-covered in love sweat, now, our bodies joined as a single entity, one in mind, body and spirit.

Two more times her grasp tightened, her breath coming in shallow draughts. The third time I could take it no longer—she pivoted her vagina up to me higher and higher, until she was six inches off the bed. Her lips were by my ear, and her sighing reached a crescendo just as her grip on me suddenly stiffened and she spasmodically began to shake again, an orgasmic cry again torn from her.

I exploded like Mount Baker at the same time. The moment felt eternal, the ecstasy agony, as my white-hot semen burst into her. Then, after a long time, eons, the pulsations slowed, gentled, and she took them up herself, milking me completely dry with her beautiful little pussy.

When I came out of my reverie she was covering me with kisses and there were tears in her eyes. We lay together like that without saying anything, or having to, both of us slippery with sweat, licking it off each other's shoulders, lips, cheeks.

When we eventually disengaged I lay back, incredulous. Exhausted. Stunned. I'd thought it was all over, gone, done, that I'd grown out of that childlike, insecure need, that plague of the emotions. I'd thought I was safe, that it wouldn't happen again, *couldn't* happen again, that like too much of any good thing, you get enough of it. I'd slept with so many women—short women, tall women, beautiful women, even fat women, deaf women, crippled women, white, black and Oriental women, tight women, sloppy women, saints, semi-whores and whores—that even despite the novelty of a new tumble, it had become, if certainly not dull, then not like it had been in the car back in high school.

So this was totally unexpected. It burst through the clouds like a miraculous sunbeam, like in those El Grecos you see in the Prado.

"You're *incredible* in bed," I finally said. The words came out hoarsely, with a touch of astonishment in them. My own astonishment astonished me.

"*Cup coon ca.* You say nicest things," she cooed, snuggling in closer, now kissing my shoulder.

Out of the corner of my eye, I could see her smile and her eyes flash with delight.

"No. I take that back. You're not good in bed."

She pinched my thigh.

"You're *spectacular* in bed . . . *yet dee mahk-mahk.*"

"Well, you no go too high. Good maybe, I no know. That word, I no so sure. I no do it that much. You make me good if I good."

"In fact, you're the most *amazing* lover in the Far East!"

"You should know," Tysee said with mock jealousy, giving Ol' Thunder a loving squeeze. "You probably sleep with them all, you big butterfly."

"In *fact,* you're the most incredible, spectacular, amazing woman I've ever been with!"

"I bet you say that to all girl," she said, that wonderful lilting laugh giggling out from her. "You same-same in bed. For long time I want to find out and I happy now that I know."

There was no hint of insecurity in her. Her finger was on my lips. I kissed it.

Long-inert emotions, covered and dusted over for what seemed like centuries, were threatening to shake loose, the way a long-dormant volcano rumbles and rolls before exploding.

It scared me. I was looking that monster, love, in the jaws again. If it was lust at first sight, it was love at first fuck.

"Will you tell me who you are now?" I asked as I drifted off.

She didn't answer for a long moment.

"My name Tysee," she finally whispered, still teasing. "Now you go remember who I am."

The words drifted into my dream like a dream. I am in a garden. The sun is beaming down. Red roses the size of sunflowers are everywhere, sprouting, growing, blossoming all around me. Drawn by their fragrance and beauty, I lean forward to pluck one of the beautiful flowers. But I feel a sharp pain on my hand. Shocked, I quickly pull away. A growing spot of blood is on my palm. I look up. The thorns along the stem of the rose are the size of bayonets.

FOUR

Nepal

THE OLD TOYOTA taxi bounced and rolled over the great cobblestones of Durbar Square, turning right at the home of the Living Goddess, the sanctuary of the cloistered, flawless virgin Kumari, who annually dots the forehead of the king of Nepal with a *tica*, granting him the divine right to rule another year. To our left were high, sagging, ancient pagodas with their wonderfully dirty wood carvings; opposite rose the old palace, a mixture of British imperialist Greco-Roman columns and the traditional, finely carved filigree of the Newari artists who had built this enchanting dollhouse of a city in its present, medieval form during the sixteenth century. Everywhere were ramshackle pedal-rickshaws, fake fakirs, tourists, a few beggars, vendors of instant antiques, touts, snake charmers, fortune-tellers and the other magic people of this magic city. Everywhere also was the still, tranquil calm of this tumbledown capital of 300,000 that looks like it fell out of a painting by Brueghel.

I was still under the spell of another living goddess, in

another magic city. I knew Kathmandu's was eternal, but
the other . . . ? Time would tell. For now the emotional
virus felt nice and I wanted to indulge in it, make it linger a
little while longer. For surely it couldn't last. It never did. I
wasn't so sure I wanted it to. I knew its habits, its nefarious
ways, how it slipped into your life by stealth like a mist
under the door, as soft as lips, hiding its bared, blood-
dripping fangs behind veils of an all-enveloping heavenly
fog.

I tenderly fingered a new 500-baht bill she had given
me. She'd insisted on paying me.

"You got good buns," she had said with a laugh only
hours earlier. "Maybe I take you out again when you come
back Bangkok."

I had joined in the joking and taken one last probe.
"Won't you tell me now where I met you before?"

She had shaken an elegant finger at me, teasing.

"Maybe I tell you next time. If you good in bed again."

Then she had given me a moist and lingering kiss, and
was gone.

Now I looked at the bill, shook my head slowly in disbelief, kissed it and carefully placed it in a special slot in my
billfold.

"To the embassy quarter."

Richard Haimes-Sandwich's was my destination. Richard is one of about a dozen collectors who live here,
perched like praying mantises, waiting for pieces, usually
bronzes, to surface from the fertile Nepali culture, or sift
across the border from Tibet. When this happens, they
leap on them and whisk them off to New York where
80,000 dollars is not an uncommon price for a good piece.
Only half that figure is profits these days compared to a
multiple of about ten only a decade ago. Such are the ever
changing numbers in the Great Game. Richard does very
well at it. In fact, he's the best. Well, at least in Kathmandu. . . .

Richard had been here since the very early seventies
when, while in the midst of a round-the-world trip as a
young man barely out of boarding school, he had discovered Nepal. Like everyone, he had fallen in love with it;
unlike most, he'd wanted to stay. He found the means by
delving into the rich antiquities scene.

I had a like-irritation relationship with Richard. We both recognized that we were at the pinnacle of the business, although his area of specialization was antiquities and centered on the Himalaya while mine leaned toward ethnology and included the entire Far East. We overlapped when I drifted into his sphere of influence, and those times had no doubt created some of that undercurrent of brittleness and distrust he showed toward me. But the esoteric nature of our careers didn't allow us to ignore each other. We often dealt with the same shops on Madison. His name would pop up in the catalogues at Christie's and Sotheby's as often as mine. And there were certain kinds of information that could be had *only* from one or the other of us. Our meetings invariably were a tight game of give-little-and-take-all-you-can, though he played it far more seriously than I did, my attitude being one of bait and boff. I could enjoy the sport—I didn't feel threatened. Today, though, I *did* need hard information, though I'd have to garner it in a soft way.

It was a bit of a risk sparring with him on this occasion but very, véry little in the antiquities field went on in Nepal without his knowing about it. The robbery had been reported in the *Rising Nepal.* He, more than anyone, would be alert to the possibility of some greater significance to the break-in, and would have done some investigating. And there was also the possibility he'd had something to do with it. He was a seasoned antiquities smuggler too, after all. I had to learn what he knew.

Richard Haimes-Sandwich was a limey, of course, originally from Bray, outside Windsor on the Thames, and claimed to be descended from Lord Sandwich of Hawaiian Islands and soup-and-salad fame. The assertion seemed reasonable enough, although I had learned, on one of my trips to London in talking with the Director of Asian Antiquities at Sotheby's, who happened to have gone to public school with him, that Richard's branch hadn't fared so well over the centuries, and was barely able to keep up appearances. Appearances were very important to him, and in that, he fit in very well with Oriental culture, where one is often judged by the value of one's wristwatch. If his family was on the skids, you certainly would not have known from observing him; Richard always assiduously kept his pretensions up at nose level. At the same time, his success was a strong point in his favor. If he had any legacy, it was the haughty arrogance of his character, and the maddening downward-scaling cadences of his accent, which he shared with his social class, and which had hardly been softened by his years in the mellowing Himalaya.

He had the kind of infuriating self-centeredness that required one to always address him formally, as Richard, which he pronounced in an exalted manner as "Richawd." Not Rich or Rick, and certainly not Dick, and absolutely *not* Dickie. Richard. He was equally pretentious about the hyphen in his surname, as most people with broken names are, for some goofy reason. To keep him in his place, I would occasionally bait him with a Ham-Sandwich, which, the Sotheby's chap in London once slipped, had been his deeply loathed nickname back in boarding school.

"It's *hawdly* original," he had snapped when I first tried it on for size. Suppressing his fury, he had pushed back his thick glasses in his characteristic way, with an irritated sweep of his pudgy hand. It fit perfectly.

I knew that much of his social myopia was caused by his size. Unlike his name, Richard Haimes-Sandwich was a short man, with the hyphen between 5 feet and 6 inches. He had all the complexes of his kind, and was tense, brittle, overly ambitious, hyperactive, and the owner of, at best, a sardonic sense of humor. He overcompensated for his inherent feelings of inadequacy by strutting his supposedly superior breeding and his own—one had to admit—substantial achievements. He occasionally even tried to imitate the heavy, rolling gait of a heavyweight, which made him look decidedly ridiculous because he was somewhat on the plump side. Whenever he got especially intolerable, I would hum a few bars of Randy Newman's song "Short People." It wasn't necessarily cruel; he was equally prone to go for the psychological jugular. Yet in the final analysis he was self-made and that was a feature I always respected.

Richard was waddling stiffly around his airy yard when my cab clunked to a halt inside the tawny walls of his compound. He was directing the squat workmen who were adding a fountain to his English-style garden. Behind

him stood his boxy, brick, three-story house, plain and
utilitarian in the Nepali manner.

"Well, I do say," he called over carefully as I shoved
some rupees toward the driver. "This . . . is . . . a bit of
a surprise . . . isn't it . . . ?"

I could tell by the elongated hints of curiosity in his voice
that it wasn't entirely.

"Richard, how are ya?" I said as he limped up and I
looked down. He was the only person I knew who could
still strut with a limp—one he hadn't had before, I noted.

"Very well, thank you," he said as I shook his dishrag
hand and he probed my eyes. "To what do I owe the
unexpected pleasure of your visit?"

"I just wanted to get away. Girl problems, me boy. I
thought a little mountain air might cool things down a bit.
Thought I might check out some of the trails along the
border with Sikkim, but I'm pretty open."

He was the only person in the world I could do that to—
lie through my teeth and smile at the same time. He was
equally adept at it.

"Uh huh . . . fine . . . well, do come in," he said, thoroughly unconvinced, as he led me into the garden and
indicated a lawn chair. The air felt still and light, the images the light created clean and clear.

"And how long is Kathmandu to enjoy your company,
Master Rivers?"

"Not long, I'm afraid," I explained, taking the seat. "I
just want to grab a trekking permit and some gear in
Thamel and I'll be off."

Thamel is the tourist area of Kathmandu, freckled with
numerous shops inexpensively renting every kind of
mountaineering gear imaginable, most dumped cheaply
by the numerous expeditions that pass through here. I
didn't tell him that I'd also be looking for an expensive
kata— a white silk scarf. That would have been a dead
giveaway.

"You wouldn't be planning to stop in the Sola-Khumbu
region on the way, would you?" he asked bluntly, probing
my eyes as he pulled on a pair of leather gloves.

Tengboche is in the Sola-Khumbu region. Ham-Sandwich wasn't wasting any time getting to the point—if there
was one to get to. He noted my discomfort and surprise as

he took up a gardening tool with barbs like devil's claws. On a table beside us he had been potting a number of rosebushes. I glanced again at the barbs. They looked small, reasonably harmless.

"Well, as a matter of fact I was giving it some consideration," I replied, improvising rapidly and forcing myself to appear relaxed. "I also thought of heading onto Mustang for a bit—there's a girl at the Red House in Kagbeni named Mya I'm rather fond of. I'm also considering doing a little digging in those deserted hermits' caves in the Muktinath Valley. I'm pretty open."

He eyed me skeptically, lifted one side of his thin mouth into a half-sneer, then turned and airily ordered two tubs of *tumba* from an obsequious servant.

"Escaping one girl just to get tangled up with another? Hardly feasible, Lee. Cut the crap for once." Richard was being *unusually* blunt. "You're *really* going to Tengboche, aren't you?" he said pointedly, trying to keep me off guard.

"As I say, trekking in the area *is* a possibility."

"Come off it, Lee. I wasn't born yesterday," he said, shoving his glasses up his nose. They were as thick as the bulletproof windows at Tiffany's. "It has to do with the phone call, doesn't it?" he added with a dash of sarcasm, speedily poking the hand-tool into a potted rosebush.

"What phone call?" I asked, feigning innocence, sitting back and pulling my hat half over my eyes.

He turned from the pot he was puttering in and eyed me carefully before replying.

"The one the abbot from Tengboche made after flying down to Kathmandu from the monastery there. This is a pretty small town, you know. The telephone system is as barbaric as any you'll find. Bloody party lines practically."

"Well then, you should know more about it than me. I can hardly listen in from Bangkok."

The *tumba* arrived, two quart-size wooden tumblers heaped with fermented millet seeds. The servant poured boiling-hot water over each. While it steeped, I poked at mine with a wooden straw.

Ham-Sandwich's brow furrowed. He authoritatively slapped down his gloves and tool and sat down on the wooden lawn chair in front of me, and fixed his magnified eyes on me.

"I'll be completely open with you," he said more cautiously than I had ever heard him speak. "I'll be open because I believe you about as far as I can throw Mount Machapuchare. There's rumors coming from the telephone people. *Strong* rumors. I know he talked to François Giscard in New York."

"Really?" I said, genuinely taken aback. Then I bit my tongue. I had let out something. He hadn't missed my reaction.

"Yes. You didn't know that I knew François, did you? I also know you do a great deal of business with him, enough that you're quite possibly here at his behest. How do I know that you know François? You haven't known it but I've been dealing with him for years as well. He's my guest here every time he comes for the Mani Rimdu. I've been to his place in New York on a number of occasions. Once I asked him about an Anuradhapura Buddha he has on his desk. Modestly interesting piece."

"You're being too generous," I said, quickly recovering.

I shouldn't have been surprised that Richard dealt with François. That he was divulging it meant that he was playing his queen. Too soon.

"The word is that the call had something to do with. . . ."

He paused to study my expression.

I looked relaxed and happy to be in Kathmandu again with a trek ahead of me. Underneath I was sweating.

". . . with a somewhat rare ritual object that was stolen from Tengboche Monastery," he went on. "There's some mention of a . . . head of some kind, a head with some . . . *rumors* attached. What do you make of that?"

I shrugged innocently, trying not to react to the news that the word was slipping out. I was surprised—this hadn't stayed a secret long.

"It does seem like a highly unusual break-in," Richard continued. "Who the bloody hell would finger a bloody monastery out in the middle of bloody nowhere? It's not really worth it, is it? You can't get out of there easily. *Tremendous* risk. And now *you*, of all people—Mr. Collector himself—appears unannounced. Too much coincidence for me. Particularly since another name was mentioned in that telephone call, which wasn't caught by the operators listening in. It was the name of someone François did business with and was going to recommend, to go up there to investigate. But I think we both know who, don't we?"

"A robbery? Really? Tell me more about it?" I said, feigning surprise, though I knew I couldn't hide the tension I felt. I hoped he wouldn't be able to see it in the shadow cast by the brim of my hat.

He still had me on the defensive. His eyes turned to pillboxes. Big pillboxes.

"It was in the *Rising Nepal,*" he said didactically, knowing full well he was telling me things I already knew, but going along with the charade. "Everyone was drugged quite senseless. But before they finished whatever it was they were doing, it appears they were interrupted. Details are sketchy. The king has put a clamp on publicity; the newspapers are muzzled now. It's all rumors, but you know how rumors are in Kathmandu—they're usually accurate. Apparently the monk who came on them is badly injured. You're really going up *there* aren't you? It was something bloody important and they want you to try to track it down."

"Well, if all of *that* is going on, it does tip the scales in favor of my going that way. A bit of excitement!" But it upset me to hear the monk was more seriously injured than François believed. It was no use being overly coy about my destination; he could find out easily enough by checking my trekking permit at the Immigration Office.

"Come on, Lee," he said, eyeing me skeptically. "Tell the bloody truth for a change. Why are you going up there? Maybe I can help."

He fixed me with his gaze. With his thick glasses, it looked like a very small codfish with very large eyes was staring at me. Sometimes you can't lie to eyes like that. So I didn't.

"I'm going up because I like the Himalayan air," I said, covering my little smile by drawing a soothing sip of yeasty *tumba* through the straw.

"Humph. Being cute again. That old game of yours."

"Well, Richard, you know it's really *our* game," I said. "Give and take."

"Yes. And what have you given me?"

"The pleasure of my company!" I said, throwing my arms wide and taking on the innocence of a choirboy. "I really can't understand why you think otherwise. And, Richard, if you're so curious about this robbery, why haven't you gone up for a look?"

By way of an answer, he hiked his right pant leg up. Bandages covered an ankle.

"A fractured ankle. I just got the cast off yesterday, as a matter of fact. And now it's infected. Otherwise I'd be up there. But then I don't know what I could learn anyway. This is all being kept very hush-hush."

I clucked my tongue. "Too bad about your ankle. But that's what comes from self-abuse. Affects the balance. You fall down."

"Well?" he said pointedly, ignoring me.

"Well what?"

"Is it true about the Rumor? You may as well confirm it. There seems to be little doubt."

"No, Richard. It's about getting some air. And even if I *was* onto something I couldn't very well tell you anyway, could I?"

"Rubbish," he said, his eyes twinkling somewhat. "You owe me one, you bloody bastard."

But he knew it wasn't true. He had gotten something from me: that I was on the trail. He had guessed my intentions with a perspicacity that I hadn't expected. That was enough, in his mind, to substantiate the validity of the rumors concerning the robbery—rumors that were wider than I had expected.

But I had also gotten what *I* wanted: I'd learned that more than a hint of what had happened was out—much, much more. And more importantly, that it was likely he hadn't been directly involved in the robbery either—if the ankle wasn't just a con.

———— • ————

When flying over Nepal, it's easy to soar in your imagination and pretend you're tiny—the size of a butterfly—and drifting above one of those three-dimensional topographical maps architects use, the circling contour lines replaced by the terraced rice paddies that surround each high ridge.

Nepal is a small country and from the portholes of a STOL

Twin Otter floating eastward at 12,000 feet—about 5,000 above the average ridges—one can see clearly the brilliant white mirage of the high Himalaya thirty miles off the port window, the peaks like glistening white molars that chew mountaineers and Nepalis alike, inspiring admiration and respect like no other mountain range in the world.

Out the starboard porthole, the view is of three or four high terraced ridges giving sudden way to the plains of India beyond. As I watched, the smoke from a hundred million hearths was already drifting up from the subcontinent, woody-smelling smoke that would later, during the summer monsoon, mix with the humidity to shroud the Himalaya from view.

There were few roads visible below, most transportation in Nepal being by foot along the ancient trails that connect and bind the country together. There is also a network of dirt airstrips, which was fortunate for me, as I had no time for the two-and-a-half-week trek to the monastery. I was on a flight to Tengboche Airport, one of the world's highest at 12,435 feet and only a half-day trek from the temple of the same name.

The plane banked to port and floated toward the mighty Khumbu valley. Ahead were the very gables of the roof of the world, a jagged, brilliant-white mass scratching at space itself: Lhotse, Nuptse, and that mightiest of the mighty, Mount Everest, all of them prominent, plumes of ice crystals flying from their crests like comets.

The plane clawed for height as we entered the huge canyon that slashed toward the heart of this ultimate domain of the gods. Massive mountains rose from the deep gorge below and soared higher and higher on either side. Scattered here and there on the high mountain slopes, often nearly inaccessible to man but always where the mighty Himalayan mountain, sky, river and valley gods could see them, were tall *tarchins,* or flagpoles, their frayed prayer banners fluttering in the breeze, beseeching favor and protection.

On reaching the head of the canyon we banked slightly to starboard. Below us, out the port window, in a half-bowl on the edge of a cliff, clung Namche Bazaar. The country grew even more enormous: canyons sliced even deeper, mountains leapt even higher into the startlingly blue sky.

On the back of a high alpine plateau above Namche I saw what looked like a fingernail scratch leading to the edge of a sheer mile-high cliff. From my seat behind him, I watched the pilot adjust the trim controls and let out the flaps as he guided the mosquito-sized craft toward this tiny scar. Everyone's knuckles whitened as he concentrated on bringing the buffeted craft down onto the short, angled runway. So primitive was it that there were no buildings whatsoever.

He hit the brakes and feathered the props the instant we touched gravel. I don't know how much comfort and faith he placed in the knowledge that the plane—like all the aircraft of Royal Nepalese Airlines—has a goat sacrificed in front of it annually to the god of transportation, but he was beaming just as much as the rest of us when we deplaned.

I was also relieved that there was no snow yet at this altitude, and it was all still at arm's length, so to speak, on the mountain peaks. There, I couldn't deny, it looked magnificent. And a good place for it too—out of reach except for the crazies who climb to it.

I breathed in the clear, thin Himalayan air. I certainly hadn't lied to Richard, I thought, as I sucked it in. This was very rare air indeed. Delicious.

A polite Sherpa—his tribe's name means *Men from the East*, as they are ethnic Tibetans who migrated to this most sacred of regions four hundred to five hundred years ago— offered his services as a porter. I just as politely declined, and he touched the patterned, orange-and-yellow pillbox *topis* on his head and moved through the group of trekkers until he found a patron.

I swung my pack onto my shoulders, adjusted my hat to dampen the glare, and struck out in the direction of Tengboche. Moving fast at this altitude is impossible, and I immediately fell into the familiar baby steps of the Himalaya.

On reaching the crest of the hill above the airport, I was greeted by the magnificent view of Ama Dablum. She sat like the most regal of potentates on a great sofa of granite that is the planet itself, her white-draped head regally held high, one frosty arm raised in benediction, the other resting magnanimously on its natural armrest. Her broad legs draped down into the greenery of the deep valley before me to cool their toes in the raging Dudh Kosi. From bottom to top the panorama had an upward swing of over two miles. On a spur sweeping out from her flanks nestled a tiny huddle of buildings. I took another deep breath and set out.

I descended for two hours along a trail through a pine forest, past jingling yak caravans, past Sherpa porters straining under enormous loads of firewood and aluminum ladders for some climbing expedition or another, past *gompas* and *chortens* and piles of *mani* stones displaying the eternal mantra of the Himalaya—*Om Mani Padme Hum;* Hail to the Jewel in the Lotus

ཨོཾ་མ་ཎི་པ་དྨེ་ཧཱུྃ

—till I came, at the bottom, to a raging gorge. At my feet, smooth, emerald boulders the size of houses impeded the furious flow of the equally emerald glacial runoff. I crossed the river by a precarious swinging bridge covered with prayer flags, then had to slow even more for the long, two-hour climb on a winding switchback trail to Tengboche.

By the time I had trudged through the ancient gate at the top, with its Tantric pictures and mantras designed to halt any evil spirits that might be hitchhiking with a traveler, I was dead tired. I dropped my pack down heavily on a slate-lined resting ledge and crumpled beside it like an old, arthritic man.

The reward was the unprecedented view ahead.

It was like looking up the grand aisle of some enormous medieval cathedral to the most magnificent of altars. In attendance and paying tribute along either side, and accompanied by their gods, were giants, the greatest mountains on the planet—Kwangde, Tawachee, Lhotse, Kantega, Thamserku—not one rising less than four miles to the sky and many soaring over five. Behind the altar of Nuptse itself, the crest of Everest rose to preside over the congregation. Everything was awesome and huge, the valley, the sky—the silence. It was a sight to snatch away what little breath I had left at this rarefied altitude.

To my right, over the open ground, grazed a few huge, tame yaks, the monastery's mascots, black hair hanging like some kind of long, shaggy moss on their broad flanks. An ancient Sherpa shuffled across, slowly twirling his prayer wheel, his withered lips in silent motion. Two Gurkhas stood near the well in their World War II puttees and khaki wool sweaters, both leaning against their old Lee Enfield 303s, and I noted there hadn't been soldiers posted at Tengboche the last time I was here. They strolled over, politely and without haste checked my trekking permit, and wrote the details into a rat-eared logbook.

To the left stood the monastery itself—a low, pagoda-style structure, surrounded by a squat huddle of modest stone dwellings that housed the many monks, whom I could see strolling here and there in their blood-colored robes. Above the flat roof of every building a prayer banner flapped on a tall *tarchin*. Everything felt like a beautiful dreamworld.

Then I remembered I had a mission to carry out. Reluctantly, I heaved my pack over my shoulder and limped over to the modest stone cottage provided for trekkers. After sending a message to Abbot Tengid that I had arrived, I slung my pack onto a crude dormitory bed and washed up in a pan of shockingly cold water while a smiling old Sherpa woman boiled me some potatoes.

————— • —————

"You will please come. Abbot Tengid see you now," a polite monk said to me.

"Thank you," I replied, setting aside my wooden cup of steaming yak-butter tea.

I followed the short, plump messenger up the stone steps to the monastery entrance. On reaching the top, we stepped into the outer courtyard, used for part of the Mani Rimdu ceremonies François took such an interest in. It was of modest size, its cobblestones covered with yak droppings and with a flimsy gallery all around. A monk was taking advantage of the stark Himalayan light to copy a *thankya*. We crossed to the great entrance to the monastery itself. The heavy doors were ajar. My rotund guide politely beckoned me inside.

I climbed the handful of steep, stone steps, removed my Rockports and set them aside, being careful that the soles weren't accidentally left facing upwards—a grave insult—and then stepped over the high threshold, through the heavy wooden door and into the deep, gloomy confines of the inner monastery itself. As my eyes adjusted I made out stacks of scriptures in pigeonholes that lined each side of the room. Two low, bench-like tables ran the short length of the interior, parallel to each other and almost the same distance out from the walls as they were from each other. Cushions were placed so that monks could face each other across the two long tables. Musical instruments—cymbals, a large hanging drum with an intricately carved and brightly painted rim, a couple of ten-foot-long brass horns, and lesser-sized drums and horns—lay in position here and there.

At the head of the room was the altar, a relatively modest creation resembling an ornately carved and painted dresser. From its back rose ledges on which were set incense holders and tiny brass bowls filled with water. on the flat portion of the altar itself were a number of what appeared to be little trees, the stems and circular leaves made from yak butter. The altar was fitted against the wall. The incense wasn't burning now, but so rich was its patina in the room that it imbued the still air with a thick fragrance and darkened the old glass on the two small windows that allowed a little faded light to filter into the room.

A slight movement in one corner caught my eye and I realized I wasn't going to be led to a private office but that the meeting would be held here. As I reached the old abbot, I placed my hands together and bowed slightly. Then I sat cross-legged on the cushion that had been placed at a level below him and removed the *kata* I had purchased in Kathmandu. I let the white, silk scarf fall loose from one corner and offered it to him with my right hand. He received it with his left and with his right, mournfully gestured a *mudra* in the air. He chanted a brief thanks and blessing. I noted he was missing the little finger on his left hand. I had almost forgotten that.

He fingered the scarf's texture for a moment, savoring it

as a person would an object of sentimental value, then carefully, almost reluctantly, set it aside. He seemed pleased with the traditional present and his face showed a trace of the cheerful glow of older times. But when he turned to me again, his face had blended back into the sepulchral surroundings. It was a much older face than I remembered; though always thin, he had clearly lost weight, and its lines were like trenches in some Flanders no-man's-land.

The pudgy monk quietly sat in attendance beside the abbot. One short and fat, the other tall and skinny; Abbot and Costello flashed through my mind, but I immediately suppressed the thought.

Lama Tengid turned his head slowly toward his assistant and muttered a few words in Nepali. The chubby monk nodded and turned to me.

"My name Tarchin, like prayer-flag pole," he said, introducing himself. "I head monk. I will do interpret. Abbot Tengid bid you welcome. He remember when you here last. He ask that you have *chang*."

He poured me a small, greasy bowl of the rough, milk-white rice beer from a black, wooden container. I took a sip and nodded my approval.

"Please give him my thanks," I said, "and tell him that I'm very sorry to hear about the difficulties that have befallen the monastery, and that I will do everything I can to find and return the stolen objects." There was a pause, then the abbot turned his head slightly and murmured at length, his quiet tones resonant in the spirit-laden room. Even across the language barrier, it was impossible not to discern that the voice was low and heavy with depression. The monk listened attentively, collected his thoughts, and turned to me.

"He know you are friend of Mr. Giz-ard in New Yorks and he trust you like brother. But what is said must not touch other ear. He say this is much, much important. He know you are come to help, and he will tell you all he know. He think it be treasure hunters who do robbery and he know you and Mr. Giz-ard in that business that thieves sell to. He want that you make question to him and he will answer."

Sensing it wouldn't be appropriate to cut immediately to

the point I was most interested in, I began with the obvious. "Tell me about the break-in first, please."

The abbot spoke through the interpreter.

"It was six day ago. We all sit down together for meal. After evening ablution many monk get much tired but think it no problem. It bedtime. Everyone go sleep, but sleep much, much deep. There something put in evening meal, we sure later. Many monk no wake up to afternoon next day and much sleepy and heavy in head. But one monk, Sonot, he not eat because he on special fast in room in monastery. He hear something at night and wake up. He go inside monastery and find two men there. No monks the men. He ask what they do. They make stab with knife on him," the interpreter explained, his quiet voice belying the violence of the action. "We find him next day, much, much bad."

I furrowed my brows. François's information was indeed incorrect.

"He *is* still alive?"

"Very thankful yes, but he much too bad to carry to hospital at Kunde so doctor he come here, but he can no stay long. We no have much money for expensive helicopter from Kathmandu. Much thousands of rupees. Doctor leave medicine and nurse. Many monk pray right now."

"Good. The food. How were they able to drug the food?"

"We talk to cook. He say day before man come with big bag rice he donate to monastery."

"The rice," I asked, "is there any of it left? Can I see it?" My heart leapt to my throat. A lead.

"We will ask cook. But I think police take much."

"Could the cook describe the men?"

"Cook remember little," Tarchin explained. "He get food bring to him every day from pilgrim—that how we eat. Hard to remember all. He say man no speak Nepali but make sign language. Cook no know where he from, but he say no have face like us"—he pointed to his high cheekbones—"man have light skin, but no like you—he have slant eyes. Kind of like Chinaman or Japanman but not that. Later we learn that two man like that here. Both pretend be Buddhist pilgrim but they no Buddhist, that for sure."

My adrenaline flow quickened as I approached the big question.

"What did they steal?"

Abbot Tengid looked like a knife had suddenly jabbed him and his face drifted downward. When he finally replied, Tarchin had to lean over and strain to hear the words.

"I not supposed to talk about this to anyone, but must. I must get stolen thing back or my life nothing and I probably die and reincarnate as crow."

"I understand perfectly and will take this to the grave with me."

The abbot now spoke in a hoarse whisper. Tarchin's words mirrored no less the grave meaning of the message.

"They stole most precious thing there ever is and secret that could ever be in Buddhism, the most important Sacred Relic. It is very heart and soul of Buddhism. They stole . . . the Sacred Buddha Head."

The ominous silence that followed pressed in, and for a moment I found it difficult to breathe.

"Do you mean a stone head?" I probed, trying not to be convinced. My heart was beating wildly. "Or a bronze head of the Buddha?"

"No! It *real* Buddha Head. Revered skull of Enlightened One Himself. It covered in gold and precious gem."

I silently begged for time to gather this together while taking another sip of the *chang*. My hand trembled slightly as I raised the bowl to my lips and drained it. Tarchin obediently refilled it, then he and the head lama sat motionless and silent, eyes on me, patiently waiting.

"Please tell me everything you know about the Buddha Head," I said, trying to mask my excitement. "How did it come to be here?"

"It come in 1959 when Dalai Lama flee Lhasa. He afraid Chinese troop might catch Him so He send trusted man with most precious of treasures over Nangpa La here to Tengboche."

"Have you contacted Him about the loss?"

"*No.* No can do. When man come in 1959 with it he give order from Dalai Lama to old Abbot Lobsang—I just head monk then—that it to be kept here until He be able to return to Tibet. Only then He ask it back. Abbot Lobsang no supposed to contact Him about any matter to do with Buddha Head, not even if there be trouble with it. It all on letter from Dalai Lama."

"Really? Why not?"

"Letter say it be much hard for Him to explain that He have it. It might up . . . up . . . upturn? Make no feel good. How you say English . . . ?"

"Upset?"

"Thanks you. It might upset Buddhists much. Buddhists in Himalaya believe Dalai Lama very pure, like Buddha because He reincarnation of Enlightened One. But He not be pure if He have Head, because that be going against wish of Him when He in earliest incarnation, when He tell followers to cremate Him. People not understand. Human nature not same as God nature. Could hurt Buddhism. It upset me at beginning too. Letter even say that He would say He no never heard of Head if it get in news."

François was right on the money, I thought appreciatively.

"After He was safely in India, why didn't He have the Head brought to Him there?"

"India no safe place either for Buddhist. Hindu always fight with Moslem, and Sikh fight everyone. Head not safe outside Buddhist country. Nepal, at least this part, Buddhist and have closest big monastery to Tibet. Safest place but even here no safe. No much monks, and Chinese or India could take over country. Must be kept much, much secret."

While I thought for a moment, I took another sip of *chang*, half-finishing the small bowl.

"After man of Dalai Lama go, old Abbot Lobsang very different man, more secret, more saintly. It very much honor to hold Buddha Head, of course. I think monastery become so famous after because of holy energy it give."

"That's the area we have to explore," I told Abbot Tengid. "How many people knew about it? I see your interpreter here, Tarchin, knows."

"Always two supposed to know story—abbot and head monk," Tarchin translated. "I know from beginning when man bring Head. I see letter. When Abbot Lobsang die eleven year ago, I become head lama. I tell Tarchin. He my head monk."

I nodded understandingly, but glanced at the chubby monk. Could he be involved? It didn't *seem* likely, not after eleven years.

"The letter from the Dalai Lama. May I see it?"

"No possible. To keep Big Secret big secret, Dalai Lama man who come over *la* burn it in front of Abbot Lobsang. But there no doubt that it real, from Dalai Lama. It have His sacred seal on it and holy signature. Old Abbot Lobsang know both—he inspect it very carefully. After man leave sacred Head in great trust with Tengboche, he join with other refugees."

"Okay, where did you keep the Head?" I asked, finishing off my second tiny bowl. I needed it. Tarchin poured the final tumbler, then set the *chang* container aside. There would be no more. Himalayan hospitality decrees three glasses as proper etiquette.

"We keep it where holy letter instruct us to," he replied, gesturing toward the cabinet-like structure. "In special hidden place by altar."

I placed my hands together and bowed slightly, then stood. My legs were stiff as a dead dog's. I limped to the altar a few feet away but could see nothing amiss, or any obvious place where the Head might have been hidden. Seeing my confusion, Tarchin rose and lifted one end of the altar, then shuttled it clumsily away from the wall. Behind, the clapboard showed evidence of having been freshly renailed shut.

This was no accidental find, I realized with a shock. Someone had *known* it was there.

"We fix. Police take away curve metal stick with sharp ends the thieves use to get out boards."

A crowbar! There was *no* doubt at all.

"It seems . . . possible that this was an inside job, for them to know about this," I said carefully, watching for Tarchin's reaction.

There was none. But I couldn't rule out the possibility that a Buddhist monk had done it; they *are* human. Abbot Tengid looked very upset when Tarchin translated my comment to him after we had returned to our seats.

"That is no much possible. Tarchin and I only mans who know where it is. We both sure no one else in monastery know."

I thought for a moment, draining my third glass of *chang* while I did. The interpreter removed the tumbler and set it aside.

"Then it must be someone around the Dalai Lama who knew."

There was no answer. He clearly didn't feel comfortable entertaining the thought.

"There were other things stolen. What were they?" I wanted to check against the reports in the *Rising Nepal*. They weren't far off.

"They take mask from cupboards upstairs. Two mask. Bhairab and skull mask. Also old bronze statue Reclining Buddha, much revered. Come from Tibet when monastery built. And old *thankya.*"

"Do you have any pictures of them? Do they have any special markings so they can be recognized?"

"Can recognize if found."

That wasn't much help but I didn't say so.

"The Gurkhas. Why couldn't they do anything?"

"They new. Only here three day now."

"I presume they got away just by taking advantage of their head start," I said mainly to myself. "They just trekked down the Khumbu canyon ahead of the news."

"No. Maybe no," Tarchin said, sensing that he should take over for a while.

Abbot Tengid sat with his head bowed, the interview clearly tiring him.

" 'Maybe no?' What do you mean?"

"We learn that airplane land at Tengboche Airport at seven in morning," Tarchin explained. "No one there because usually plane come at nine. Some people see. It sound different. Very small. And color crazy—all green and brown in patches."

Camouflage?

"Did anyone see them get on it?"

"No. Just guess that plane. We learn that they no ask permission to land, they just do it. They trek in and fly out."

"The thieves," I said, changing the direction of inquiry, and hoping I wouldn't have to trace them back along whichever route they walked in on, if that was even possible. "Did they leave anything behind besides some rice? Clothes? Pack? Anything?"

"Yes."

My heart skipped a beat.

"Well what is it? *Please.*"

"Don't know. Sonot, monk who find thieves, must have tear it off mans who he fight with. It small metal thing hang around neck."

"A pendant?"

"If that what you call it."

"Do you have it? May I see it?"

"You may see, but we no have. It with Sonot. We not realize he have it till after police from Kathmandu leave. They take everything else. Sonot much injured but refuse to let it go."

"Well, may I see Sonot then?"

Tarchin translated this to Abbot Tengid. The latter slowly picked up the conversation.

"Yes, we see him. But he very ill. Not be able to talk much maybe."

"Fine. May we go?" I asked, as I began to stand. I wasn't sure if it was the *chang,* the altitude or my stiff legs, but I weaved slightly as I wobbled to my feet. I hated to face it, but I also felt the onset of a headache and nausea, both symptoms of altitude sickness.

Abbot Tengid rose slowly, and I realized then just how broken a man he had become. The change was shocking. The tall, bent figure shuffled dispiritedly through a side door and down a gloomy hallway, with Tarchin at his elbow and me following. The head monk knocked lightly at a door, then we quietly entered a small room.

Sonot lay on a hard bench softened by a Tibetan carpet, covered by oily blankets, their edges shiny from wear. A small candle flickered in a corner. Tending him was a Nepali nurse, worry lines at the corners of her drawn mouth. Against a wall sat a monk fingering *mani* beads and chanting quietly and rhythmically, following something in a palm-leaf book that wasn't the familiar "Om Mani Padmi Hum," the builder of good karma. Another monk also following was chanting in synchronization with the first, a scripture, directly into the ear of the prone, chalk-faced monk. Sonot, an initiate, couldn't have been over twenty years old.

"Monks chant from Tibetan Book of the Dead," Tarchin explained in a soft whisper. "We help monk Sonot on transition to next life."

I stared with compassion at the near-motionless figure. He clearly wasn't far from that next reincarnation. The only way I knew he was still alive was by his breathing, a bubbly gurgle intermittently broken by weak, wet, choking coughs. I could see there wouldn't be too many answers from him. Even the incense couldn't mask the smell of death.

"He stabbed in lung and stomach," Tarchin whispered.

The abbot took a rough stool beside the bed and waited for a break in the monk's chant, then leaned toward Sonot's spare ear. The cadence of whatever he said blended with the uninterrupted chants of the monk in the corner. Then the old man sat back.

Nothing happened for a long moment, but then a flicker of life revealed itself in the bedridden monk. His eyes slowly opened a crack and focused in my direction, the black pupils glimmering in the candlelight. They held me for a long moment, then their ashen lids fell shut as if he lacked the strength to keep them open. For another moment there was no other movement, and no sound except that of his tortured breathing. I was about to suggest we leave when his tightly clasped fist began to twitch. In an effort that seemed to drain his remaining strength, the fingers slowly trembled apart until his hand lay open like a dead, upturned crab. In its palm lay an object that glowed a soft yellow in the subdued light.

I reached over and picked it out of his palm. My hand brushed against his. It was cold and pallid.

"What . . . !" I exclaimed, before catching myself.

It was something I had seen many times, high in the jungled hills of The Golden Triangle many years before. It was a fertility talisman and good luck charm, only it wasn't silver—it was solid gold.

What was a Shan *doing here?*

"Is . . . is it possible to ask him if he saw if they had tattoos on their bodies?" Among the Shan, who are animists, tattooing is widely practiced as a way to ward off evil spirits, particularly among the men.

Tarchin translated. Abbot Tengid nodded and leaned over the monk's ear for a moment, then sat back waiting. A mouse scurried along the edge of the floor. Sonot's lips quivered for a moment, then fell still. An eye ticked. It was too much effort for him.

I looked at him sadly and shook my head.

"We may as well leave," I whispered, carefully pocketing the talisman. Abbot Tengid saw and nodded a quiet approval.

The chants diminished behind us as we slipped out and closed the creaking door.

"Could I speak to the cook?" I said in a low voice. "Perhaps he can give us more information. Hopefully there's some of that rice left."

The abbot nodded. We turned and I slowly followed the two men back through the chilly monastery and out into the courtyard, where we slipped on our footwear. We shuffled down the steps to one of the nearby huddle of stone buildings that had smoke issuing from a hole in its roof, and entered the warm confines of the black, sooty cookhouse. Great, hand-beaten brass pots slowly boiled over wood fires. Mounds of small Sherpa potatoes lay piled up in corners.

Tarchin translated my questions for the ancient monk, his face like an old crumpled paper bag, who functioned as the cook.

"He say only thing he can say more is that rice very hard and thick, take longer cooking," Tarchin translated. "But he say he can get you little. Police not take all back. There be much left."

Leaving the steaming pots to an assistant, the old monk slowly led us to a clearing in the nearby pine forest, where he dug down into the soft sand with a wooden shovel he had brought.

"He no burn it," Tarchin explained. "Smoke of poisoned rice would offend gods, so he bury here, where no bird, animal or even insect live, so it not hurt anything."

I took a sample, filling a pocket in my down jacket. "Who else had contact with the two men?" I asked as we left the old cook behind to carefully re-cover the drugged rice. "I would like to speak with them. How about the keeper of the trekkers' hut?"

"They no stay there," Tarchin explained. "They camp far on edge of campground, away from other people. They leave their tent and sleeping bag but police inspectors take back to Kathmandu."

I nodded. Of course they wouldn't have stayed in the lodge; they would have been observed getting up in the middle of the night, and run the risk of some of their burglary equipment being noticed. Unfortunately, approaching the police with a request to examine their gear was out of the question; they would want to know why a white collector of antiquities was making such inquiries. I doubted I would even gain much by learning the names on the thieves' trekking permits, although surrendering one's passport is necessary in order to obtain one. If they were as well-organized as they seemed to be, they would have covered that trail well, by using false passports. That had better be the case, I thought, because there's no easy way to get access to the permits either. In any case, the police would be following up that angle.

"We can show you place they camp, if you wish?"

But there was nothing to see except a magnificent view up the valley to Nuptse, and Everest beyond.

The three of us stood on the bare rise slightly above the monastery, surrounded by the crisp, silent air, the only sound that of our breathing. I could think of nothing else that could be done. Abbot Tengid rasped something to Tarchin, his hand gripping the younger man's forearm, his voice earnest. The head monk turned to me.

"He say you, please, do whatever you have to do to restore Sacred Head to Buddhism and not only he but Buddhists everywhere, even if they not know it missing, will be thankful deep in their souls. But you must be very quiet and not let anyone know."

The eyes in the older man's wrinkled face burned out at me, full of hope and expectation, of desperation and anxiety—confusing emotions that had been totally foreign to him until only very recently.

I nodded deeply, feeling the iceberg tip of the full significance of his loss chill me to the bone.

"I will do my best," I said, hoping I sounded strong.

The afternoon wind was beginning to low through the pines as we inched back down to the monastery.

The relative satisfaction of having gotten this far comforted me a little that night as I crawled, shivering and with a lightly pounding head and upset stomach, into my sleeping bag, haunted by that last imploring look on Abbot Tengid's face when I had taken my leave.

Asleep that night, I dreamt there was a beautiful, smiling young woman beckoning to me who only seconds before I had recognized as Tysee; she was wearing a brilliantly vermilion diaphanous gown that fluttered and flowed in the windless breeze of my sunny illusion. Then an uneven and faintly disturbing hum began to murmur in the background, quietly intruding, refusing to retreat. The next moment she was dissolving in a soft and misty light as, disappointed, I drifted and rose from the wonderful comfort of that midnight oblivion into the dawn of wakefulness.

In a fourth moment there was only the awareness of filtered, early-morning light on the other side of my eyelids, and the memory of where I was. And the intruding, resonant murmur itself. For a few heartbeats I wondered what it was.

Then I guessed. And my eyelids snapped open.

I scrambled out of the warm womb that was my sleeping bag and swung my legs over the side of the cot. Instantly I was shivering in the crispness that is a Himalayan morning. In a few minutes I was roughly dressed and pulling my hikers on. A trekker across from me grumbled in irritation and rolled over in his bunk.

"Sorry," I whispered hoarsely as I headed for the door. Already the Sherpa woman was up, finishing her morning ablutions by tossing aromatic herbs onto the freshly lit hearth to please the gods. For once she wasn't smiling, and hardly acknowledged me as I unlatched the door and stepped out into the crystal-clear morning light. The dazzling white of the nearby peaks made me squint in pain.

Those sounds, now more distinct, were emanating from the monastery. I hurried around the corner of the trekking hut and up the uneven stone steps to the courtyard entrance. No monks were about; normally some would already be sweeping, others collecting firewood. I strode across the enclosure. A raven cackled and lifted off from a *tarchin* as I hurried by.

The sounds were loudest at the door. Some of the different tones could be separated. I pulled off my shoes and, with apprehension, quietly unhooked the latch to the heavy doors and stepped over the high threshold into the shadowy interior.

As I had feared, the monks were all in their places at the instruments, unaware of me as I faded into a dark corner. The low, ponderous braying of the ancient brass horns blended in a strange, syncopated rhythm, with the low, heavy thump of the drums. Now and then, at further uneven intervals, a small clear-sounding bell was gently and briefly rung. The only sounds that kept time came from three monks chanting, in sonorous tones, the ancient mantra of the mountains:.Om Mani Padme Hum.

The room was full with the sound, the vibrations, quiet yet full, leaking out over the yard to the universe beyond, thicker than the broad tendrils of incense that curled slowly through the still, heavy air—air laden with an immutable mysticism as deep as the ages, that plumbed the depths of existence and attuned itself to that sadness and sorrow shared equally by man and God alike as a common bond. It was an indelible sound, one never to be forgotten.

I didn't have to look into Abbot Tengid's heartsick eyes in his waxen features to know that Sonot, the monk, was dead.

FIVE

Bangkok

"I KNEW IT! We must be living right, Herr Rivers!"
Wolfgang Krueger exclaimed as he slipped into
the booth across from me at The Lion's Den.

I'd found him three days earlier, right after flying back
from Kathmandu, and this time it had been easy. He had
been back in his usual spot at the Lion's. The reason he
hadn't been there when I returned from New York was
that he'd had to go to the hospital for emergency treatment on his ribs.

"There are several hundred varieties of rice in the Far
East," he began to explain, "grown in an equal number of
small areas by different groups, often tribes off in the jungle. But Professor Charupong at the agriculture department at Chulalongkorn University did not take long to
identify it."

He paused and began nimbly loading his meerschaum
with his one hand, still imbued with the enthusiasm the
Shan talisman and the hot scent had raised. And apparently François's letter had assuaged his hesitations as well.

I hadn't seen anyone so old so excited since the Lion married his beautiful young Filipina.

His renewed energy picked up my slightly dampened spirits—Tysee was nowhere to be found. She seemed to have disappeared into thin air; the mama-san at The Crazy Horse didn't know where she was or even if she would be back. The lousy part about letting a woman seep into your blood was already starting. Usually absence made the hard-on wander; this time it had made it grow fonder.

"And . . . ?"

"I did not even have time to tell the professor that we suspected it wass from The Triangle. He only had to take one look at the shape of the grains and he knew where they were from. He pointed out some of the peculiarities of the variety to me. Did you notice that they were quite thick but slightly hourglass-shaped? *Nein?* Well, they are. Apparently they have some particularly attractive features —size and hardness primarily. He had once experimented with crossing it with some other breeds to eradicate that indentation. He hadn't been successful but he is still watching for a suitable mate."

"Wolfgang—" I started, raising my eyes impatiently heavenward. A gecko on the ceiling snapped at an insect.

"*Ja.* Well, after slipping some under the microscope to look for some kind of hereditary line running from tip to tip, he came up with the central village from where the variety iss found." He tapped his forefinger on the table top for emphasis, and then fumbled for a match. I impatiently beat him to it, holding it while he stoked his large pipe into a blaze. As I did, I studied his scars from the mugging. They were still healing. He seemed in much better shape, though he was still tender around the ribs.

"Come on, Wolfgang," I said, exasperated. "I've been waiting three days for this."

And all I'd had to do in that time was wonder where the hell that juiceburger of juiceburgers had disappeared to. It wasn't like me to get irritated with him, particularly since he was surely the key to any success we might have in nabbing the Head once its suspected location was confirmed.

"We've dined on this species of rice before ourselves, although it wasn't spiced so interestingly, so to speak. The drug it was soaked in couldn't be completely analyzed, although a friend in the chemistry department tried—a Professor Somjet. He said it appears, judging from the impurities, to be from some natural source, though it has properties also found in many common sleeping pills."

The manner in which the monks had been drugged jived with a too-common method of robbery practiced all over eastern Asia—*farangs* in particular being duped into swallowing cooked Cokes and candies, then being robbed by "friendly" locals, often on trains and buses.

Wolfgang paused to look around for one of the arthritic barmaids. I was getting more and more impatient.

"Wolfgang, for Christ's sake! Is it from Kwan Mae or not?"

"*Ja.* It can wait for a minute," he said, leaning back toward me across the table, nodding his heavy, sunburnt head. "Our guess was correct. Kwan Mae. Kun San's headquarters."

"Good," I said, feeling the excitement returning, pushing thoughts of Tysee out of my mind. "That's all I wanted to hear. It confirms my suspicions as well. The plane used *had* to be Kun San's camouflaged little Maule, though the pilot practically must have filled the cockpit with helium to get it that high. And the description of the robbers fits as well—the Shan are light-skinned."

The Lion wandered over in a stroll as slow as his drawl, saw we were deep in a personal conversation, replaced my empty mekhong with a fresh one, and growled at one of the biddies to snap another schnapps to Wolfgang.

"Let me see that amulet again, if I may."

I pulled the gold pendant out of my breast pocket and passed it to him. It had rarely been out of my hands since I took it from the now-reincarnated Sonot. We were now looking for a way to steal the Head not from mere thieves, but from murderers—and these were killers who had been practicing their trade for many generations. Still, I thought there was a way of nabbing the Head in a way that held minimal dangers. It was only the residual ones that bothered me, like, what if Kun San wanted to exact revenge? He certainly would lose a lot of face on this one. I wasn't sure if life in Thailand would be safe for me afterward. And life without Patpong would be no life at all.

"*Ja*, there is no doubt," the Wolf said gleefully. His normally imperturbable demeanor had dissolved. "It must belong to one of Kun San's two top lieutenants. Either Chung Si Fu or Kayao. They both have talismans such as this! I have never seen any others in gold before but theirs! I am sure of it!"

"What can you tell me about this Chung Sea Food and Kayao?"

"Chung *Si Fu*. Early thirties. He hass eyes like a snake's."

"Say no more."

"*Ja*, there iss no doubt," he said with a trace of sarcasm. "My old friend Kun San iss behind it."

"I have a simple but pointed question for you, Wolfgang," I said, preparing to broach the key to the plan I had tentatively formulated while the Wolf was away having the analysis done. Everything depended on his reaction to my question.

"Please?"

"How would you feel about having to rip your old friend Kun San off for the Head?"

"That iss no problem," he replied without hesitating.

My eyebrows danced in surprise at his automatic reply.

"Well, with your contacts with him, we should be able to get in easily, ostensibly on another collecting mission like the one we went on before. Once we're there, I'm pretty sure we can find a way to draw around to the subject and make an offer to Kun San to market it for him. He must surely know we can do that better than anyone. We can make off with it that way or, at least, set him up for a sting later. Neat and simple. What do you think of it?"

He listened attentively. In the end he looked down, smoke trailing out of his wide nostrils, and shook his head. He carefully set the amulet down on the table.

"What do you mean?" I asked, taken by surprise again. It had seemed the ideal cover. Absolutely ideal. The obvious.

"It iss a very good plan, Lee. Very good. There iss only one problem. I am afraid I am unable to just walk up to Kun San and ask him. Our relationship iss not what it used to be. In fact, it iss non-existent now. That iss why I would have no qualms about stealing the Head from him."

I looked at him blank-faced. I had pinned all my hopes

on this. I felt an ominous sinking feeling in the pit of my stomach, mingled with an enticing sense of relief.

"It wass something I wrote for a magazine just six or seven months ago," he said unapologetically. "The first I've written in years and it had to do this. I wrote that he would be doing hiss people and the world more of a service if he turned to legitimate crops. It iss one thing to criticize a politician and then to sip cocktails together in a perfectly friendly manner, ass if it didn't happen. Kun San iss a politician of sorts, but he does not tolerate anything less than total subscription to hiss views. He hass let me know I am quite unwelcome back in Kwan Mae, I am very sorry to say."

"It's been a bit of time," I argued. "Couldn't you try an opening? Maybe he got over it." I was scrambling for a way to hold my perfect plan together. Of course that was the trouble with it, and with all obvious plans—it was too good to be true. Situation normal: All yeted up. . . .

He shook his head sadly and slowly.

"I tried just a couple of months ago. He did not even answer my message."

"Damn it," I said again, twirling my glass in irritation.

I could feel the Buddha Head being pulled away from me; up till then it had seemed just possible that my reach might meet my grasp. But there was still a way. I didn't like the backup plan I had formulated as much, but it could possibly work just as well.

"Well, I may have to go in alone, if it can be arranged. He may remember my previous visit."

Wolfgang shook his head heavily.

"It iss out of the question. He hass never met you and would think you're with the DEA."

I frowned. Hiring some of the local mercs would be out of the question. For one thing, it would take at least a fortnight before they were fully operational. For another, they'd have a hell of a time taking on an army of up to 10,000 seasoned fighters in their home arena. Besides, it had to be kept completely quiet.

"Damn it," I said, feeling a mixture of relief and anxiety rising in my stomach.

Still, it was an out. If I wanted out. And I was being torn, no doubt. I took up the talisman he had set down and rubbed it firmly between my fingers, as if trying to squeeze answers from it.

"Well, Wolf," I said, "it seems the only thing we can do is to watch for it to come onto the market, which is going to be a tough one. I doubt like hell it'll turn up here in Bangkok. We'd better notify our contacts in Hong Kong but I suspect that if he's willing to take a risk like flying his damned little airplane all the way to Nepal and risking one of his top men on such a wild job, he must surely know the value of the piece. With his contacts and smuggling lines it'll probably go to Europe or New York directly and we'll miss it." I was wavering between disappointment and abandon, not sure which would win out in the end.

"It iss true," the Wolf said, sipping his drink. "It could possibly be on its way out already. Though I would be interested in *their* contacts in that regard. It iss not just anyone who can market such a stolen piece—you know that. Contacts are everything."

"Well, I'm not so sure he *doesn't* have them. I'm sure he somehow knew the Head was there. I suspect the other little pieces that were stolen—the masks, *thankyas* and the little bronze—were just to throw people off the trail, to make it *look* like a standard burglary."

I thought of asking Wolfgang about his past collecting career but let it slide. I just wanted to get out on the street and look for that lovely, lively lady with the luscious legs.

Wolfgang nodded knowingly.

"Best contact François and tell him to keep a firm eye on the markets he's covering. Did you mention to him that you and Kun San had a falling out?"

Wolfgang had called him in New York shortly after I returned, to give him the details of my trip to Tengboche.

"No. I don't think he knew of my contact there. But I will."

"Well, I guess that's that then, isn't it?" I said, hoisting my glass and throwing back a swig.

Where *is* that delectable, comfortable, sexy creature? Where do I look? Why didn't I get her home address? I guess because I rarely haul the same one home twice.

Wolfgang didn't return my toast. Instead he remained looking down. I could see he was trying to find the correct words to open up some new line of thought.

"I don't necessarily think it iss over," he said quietly, now looking directly at me and pulling softly on his pipe. "There are other ways to skin a tiger, you know."

"You have a plan?" I asked, not sure if it was welcome or not.

"*Nein.* But I am an eternal optimist. In life I have learned that there iss *always* a way. You must remember that we have made considerable headway: we are virtually sure of where the Head went after Tengboche Monastery. *That* iss a very healthy and happy beginning."

I listened. Wolfgang's creative, daring perseverance had snared more than one other difficult piece.

"There iss a bigger problem and that hass to do with the eventual destination of the piece. I will speak frankly, for we have known each other many years: we just cannot let something like this go. You know the *value* of the piece? It iss surely worth a fortune! I would guess in the *millions!* If sold at Christie's or Sotheby's—out of the question, of course—it would smash all records—and I mean *all.* This iss not just a statue of the man! Or some mere Van Gogh!"

"I know. We already discussed the value," I said, eyeing him warily. A picture of the dying monk, Sonot, and Abbot Tengid's agonized eyes, flashed before me. I suddenly didn't feel comfortable with Wolfgang. I didn't want to tell him that I couldn't rip it off, that I never really could all along. He sucked on his pipe for a long moment, and took a sip from his tiny glass of schnapps, before replying. I could see he was trying to evaluate me.

"Are you willing to risk your life for an ideal, like this François Giscard wants you to do? Getting the Head back so it can be returned to the monastery, probably just to be stolen again? It iss not in the least secure there, particularly now. You have told me about your friend Richard Haimes-Sandwich, so word iss already leaking out. Every collector and crook in the world will be after it. We would be *fools* to give it away like that."

"Maybe it's time it went back to the Dalai Lama," I said, signaling my real attitude. "It could be secretly returned to him. No one would dare rob him."

His eyes narrowed for a moment. But he took up the line of thought.

"You think not? Where do you think it iss most likely

word leaked from, about its location at Tengboche? And what about the Indians? Hindus? They have a certain amount of tolerance, but would they be pleased with a ground swell of Buddhism on their land? Which could very well happen if the word got out, ass it assuredly would. Ass it *iss!* I'm afraid this hass gone past the point of no return."

"What exactly are you saying?"

"I just want you to recall a conversation we had not too long ago in this very bar. At this very table. When I asked you what you would do if something ass precious ass the Buddha Head fell into your possession. Remember?"

"We were talking hypothetically then, Wolfgang. Beer-table talk. Mekhong dreams."

"Were you? Think about it again then. We could sell it and retire to supreme luxury for the rest of our lives. We know that François Giscard iss already there—that iss why he finds it so easy to be altruistic in helping out hiss old friend at the monastery. The Great Philanthropist," he added sarcastically. "It iss no great risk to him, and he will probably end up with a paragraph in the history books that he was instrumental in retrieving it. *He* can afford to buy the glory, and that iss what he iss doing, Lee, plain and simple. I am being paid quite well, no doubt. Certainly, 15,000 dollars iss a handy sum of money, but it iss still little compared to the Head's value. You have been to my house? Don't you think one becomes tired of living like that? You are more well-off than me but you are not really rich either. Even you could use the money, but you have turned it down for reasons you did not really think about. *Ja*, Herr Giscard told me on the phone. . . .'This iss the big one. The biggest we will see in our lifetime!' And you say you want to throw it away!"

I had left François's message to him in this bar, where he had eventually found it. I shifted uneasily. Fortunately, Wolfgang couldn't see my discomfort, for he had closed his eyes for a moment, as if to slowly wring his hands together in his mind. I had never seen him like this. A man less obsessed with money, I had rarely met.

"Wolfgang, how do you justify this to your conscience? You've taken on a job, and now you're talking about double-crossing François. I must remind you, he's one of *my* best friends!"

Wolfgang sat back straight and formal. His voice was strong.

"Lee, your Herr Giscard iss using us at least in part for his own ends—his need to be glorified as a great humanitarian. We would simply be doing the same to him—using him. No more. No less."

"Well, I don't know if you can question his insincerity to that degree. And in any case, it's all moot. How the hell could I—or anyone—ever get in there anyway? As you say, if there ever was a sure way of committing suicide, it's crossing that frontier into Shan territory without clearance and a guide. We're just going to have to hope it turns up on the market somewhere in the Far East—slight chance as it is. Or do you have something up your sleeve?"

I immediately regretted the question.

"*Nein.* But I have a feeling that something will turn up. It *always* does. Ass I say, I am an eternal optimist. Why don't you go down to The Crazy Horse and loosen up? Who knows?" he added with a slight smile. "Some good ideas might pop into your mind there. Time for my physiotherapist."

He drained his glass and began to excuse himself.

"You'll phone François with the latest information?" I asked. "And tell him to heat up his spies?"

"Don't worry, Herr Rivers. I will punch the clock," he told me with Germanic disdain. "I do not want to jeopardize my 'salary.'"

I signaled the drinks were mine this time and remained staring into my mekhong. So near and yet so far. . . . I didn't know which find was more disappointing in not being within my grasp—the Buddha Head, or Tysee.

Fortunately, one of them found me.

———— • ————

"*Poo mah hah, ca,*" Po, my housekeeper, announced quietly.

"Huh?" I asked, looking up from my desk.

I had been plodding together the Ifugao documentation for a Swiss museum, hampered by the goddamned glitches in my word processor and the fact that the useless fucking machine worked at the speed of a retarded turtle. Already that collecting trip felt so long ago it was difficult getting back into it, and besides, the frustration of the Head and Tysee's disappearance and my bloody reaction to both was so great. Memories of Lette at The Statue of Libertine were already just that, memories—on the scrap heap of my mind with the broken, naked bodies of a thousand other casual and semicasual flings.

Po repeated herself. A visitor.

"Uh, *Cup. Pom awk mah.*"

I hit the keys to do a SAVE. The disk drive spit around a few times, then ratcheted. BDOS ERROR. I hit the ESCAPE key. Nothing. Hammered RESET. The screen went gibbly and a haphazard arrangement of alphabetic letters appeared—another composed page lost. I was about ready to ram my foot through the screen, but swore and switched the machine off instead.

"Rotten to the fucking core," I cursed.

I stomped out of my study and across the broad living room to the wide-open door, then stepped over the threshold onto the veranda.

"Tysee!"

She was wearing a silk outfit with vermilion patterns, and carried a matching handbag. I skipped down the stone steps and took her hands. Her face lit up and she laughed. The sound danced from her and flew with the birds. Suddenly the world was bright and alive again.

"I have gift for you."

In one hand was a single red rose.

"Well, thank you! That's very nice. My first gift from you."

I took it. Smelled its fragrance. Beautiful.

"No. It second."

"Huh?"

"You remember yet where you know me from before?" she asked as she slipped off her shoes. I led her in and offered her a seat on the sofa.

I placed the rose in a Shang vase on a mantel, then sat down beside her and ordered two glasses of orange juice with Perrier from Po, and some water for the rose.

"I'm afraid not," I said, scratching my head. "But don't think I haven't tried."

She looked at me, her eyes twinkling, a tiny smile on her lips.

"You want me give you small hint?"

"How about a *big* hint?"

She rose and glided over to the cabinet where I kept various knick-knacks. I recalled she had paused at the same one the last time she was over.

"May I open?" she asked, her hand on the latch.

I showed her my palm.

Carefully, she lifted the lid, reached in and picked up something. She rejoined me on the sofa and turned to me, smiling, her fist clenched around her secret. I watched her, feeling the anticipation of discovery brightening everything. Slowly she opened her hand.

In it lay the silver Shan talisman—identical but for the metal to the gold one I had taken from Sonot—which had been given to me so many years before. She looked up at me, waiting, smiling, but saying nothing.

"Well?" she finally asked, probing my eyes.

I shook my head in frustration and threw up my hands helplessly.

"You'll have to give me a bigger hint I'm afraid. *Farang* he no have good brain. Too much mekhong." I forced a chuckle.

"Who give you this, crazy man?"

I looked at her and thought for a moment.

Then I blinked. My stare froze on those dimples, then bulged with surprise. My finger jabbed toward her.

"It *can't* be!" I exclaimed, rising half-up on the sofa. I had forgotten her name completely, if I'd ever known it! The gawky little girl in Kwan Mae with the enormous crush on me! I immediately felt embarrassed that I hadn't remembered her.

She was laughing though, and while I half-stood half-sat speechless, she reached into her handbag and came out with something small and yellowing. Her hand hid it while she pinned it onto the lapel of her silk blouse. A moment later she was looking smugly at me, and I was staring at the button I had given to a little Shan girl high in The Triangle —was it a decade ago? *Fuck Communism* the button read, the C a hammer and sickle. I must have blushed.

"Now I know why you no want to give me button," she said, laughing gaily. "After you go, when Russia *farang* who visitor at Kwan Mae read it he get very angry and want to take away, but I cry and my papa no let him."

Russian *farang?* That white man I saw occasionally, furtively moving between buildings, was a Russian? Questions popped to mind, then just as quickly burst in the champagne euphoria of her visit.

"I keep for long time until I learn what English letters mean. When I find out I laugh and laugh and laugh. I think it very funny."

She was laughing then. So was I. All the tension had instantly dissolved between us. She was very good company, her manner completely and instantly disarming. Tysee slipped the talisman into my breast pocket.

"But why you no remember me?" she suddenly pouted, though I could see she was partially putting it on.

"Well, there's two good reasons right there," I said, pointing at the firm, nippled roundness lightly pressing against the silk of her dress.

She looked down.

"That no reason. There still nothing there," she said, waving a hand dismissively.

"Do you remember what you looked like?" I said laughing, while an idea sprang into my mind.

I stood and strode over to a black-lacquered Chinese cabinet and pulled out a photo album from the days when I still kept them. Flipping through a few pages, I quickly found my pictures of Kwan Mae. In another moment I was grinning nefariously and extracting a photo of the little girl Tysee. It showed a skinny-legged little urchin, one in a group of other scraggly kids, smiling uncontrollably at the camera. In the background, pigs were rooting around the supports of bamboo huts. I cackled with evil glee.

She was beside me in a second. She took one glance and tried to snatch it from my hands. I held it high above my head. She stood on her tiptoes and pressed herself against my chest as she tried to pull my arms down. Feeling her warmth and breath, smelling her scent, I couldn't stop them from descending by themselves. She snatched it from me and glanced at it, then blushed and pirouetted away, the dancer in her revealed.

"Now, how the hell could I remember you?" I roared in mock anger.

"I no change *that* much," she said, her voice for a moment growing serious.

She looked at the photo again, averted her eyes and flushed noticeably, then snuck another glance. Finally she tossed it facedown on the coffee table and hurried to me, slipping her arms around my waist, pressing her cheek to my chest.

"I dream about you many times," she said simply. "I meet other men my age and they too boring. I often lonely because no one I can really talk to and have same-same interest as me. I remember happiest times when I girl when I be with you, help you with collecting. You so interested in it. You so much fun to be with. And you no look you age."

I'm not sure if I act it either, I thought, but I said nothing. I held her and we began to rock back and forth. The caged cockatoos were cooing, and the glass wind chimes were tinkling in the trade winds, shooing away evil spirits and casting a magic spell that drifted in from the garden. She may have been young, I realized, but her aura was that of one much more mature.

I gently drew Tysee back down to the sofa.

"Where have you been?" I asked. "I've been looking for you since I got back from Nepal four days ago. I've been at The Crazy Horse and just about every other bar in town, looking for you."

Her face sobered and she drew away slightly.

"What's the matter?" I asked, wondering if I had said something wrong.

"You no like me anymore if I tell you," she said flatly.

Her hands were now folded primly in her lap. She was fidgeting with her silver bracelets.

"Tysee! There is *nothing* that could make me stop liking you. Though that might not be a bad idea. I think I may like you too much already. . . ."

She gave me a worried glance, then averted her eyes down.

"Tysee. You're perfectly safe with me. You know you can trust me."

She hesitated a long time, stealing tentative glances at my eyes. Then her face suddenly screwed up and she was crying, huge sobs welling and billowing from her. She reached her arms around my neck, her head falling against my shoulder. Bewildered, I held her a long time, gently rocking her, saying nothing, not knowing what to say. Finally, the storm began to blow itself away.

"That's what you say *now*. You no going to want me after I tell you. Maybe you know. Maybe you not know. But if you no know, you no going to want me be you friend after I tell you."

"Well, it couldn't be that big a deal. *Tell* me—"

I cut myself short as a smiling Po appeared at the entrance to the kitchen. She politely set our drinks on the coffee table before us. Looking up, she quickly read the situation, flushed, and quickly exited, though not before pouring some Perrier for the rose.

"Come on, dry your tears. Have a drink. And tell me."

She looked up into my face as I dabbed teardrops from her cheeks with a tissue. Her moist skin glowed and she looked as fragile as the Shang vase I'd placed her rose in. Her eyes were still brimming, threatening to overflow. Her lips quivered slightly. Our faces were inches apart.

"I go visit my parents."

"So? It's good to visit your parents," I said. "I wish I had more time to visit mine."

"I go to jungle outside Chiang Mai."

"I know. Kwan Mae. I was there, remember? It's beautiful country."

"Papa no beautiful though. Papa no good man. Papa name . . . Kun San. . . ."

I gripped her to me—I had forgotten all about the Head! I couldn't believe it.

"*See!* You *upset!*" Tysee exclaimed, when she saw my face. Her mouth began to twist in agony.

"No, I'm *not* upset. I'm excited, that's all!" And I was—staring at her like I had just discovered the Hope Diamond.

"Why?" she asked. "You no know who Kun San is?" Her voice quivered with insecurity as she revealed herself.

"*Of course* I do, everyone does! It doesn't matter a *bit.*"

The clouds burst forth once more. Only now she held me tight with gratitude. Her tears gradually abated until she announced the end of the flood with a nip to my shoulder.

"You good man," she said. "I know you good man when I

little kid and know you. But I so afraid to tell people who my papa is. When they know, they act different."

She tried to laugh and dry her tears at the same time. I passed her a glass of orange juice and she took a sip. Wet, embarrassed laughter welled from her.

"How *was* your visit home?" I quietly asked.

"It no good," she said, when her tears had again stopped flowing. "I happy to see Mama. She quiet woman and good. But Papa? *My dee.* No good. He very angry with me for dance in bar. He hardly speak to me except yell. And I yell back. Mama say I should no do that but I more modern girl after be in London."

"How does he shame you?"

She looked at me with a trace of scorn, and began to explain it as if I was a little limp in the lilacs.

"I think he big important man when I little girl. Everyone talk quiet around Papa and kowtow to him. Then he send me to Bangkok home we own off Sukhumvit, *soi* 71, to stay with uncle to go good school, and I learn what he do for living, that he big drug man and that drug no good thing. I feel big shame then. Papa no Buddhist. He think Buddhist crazy, monks no work, go around get food from people free. He call them beggars."

"So that's why you dance on Patpong? To get back at your father?"

"*Chi.* He shame me—I shame him. I chose Crazy Horse because Mr. Krueger he tell me you go there. I want to see you again too. I tell Mr. Krueger to no tell you because I want to surprise you."

"Well you sure did!"

"Papa let me go England six month ago to go school and learn English. He agree because he want me be like lady. I like dance since I little girl. I study dance there at finish school. But I get *mahk-mahk* homesick. I no like London. Many crazy people in Soho where I go take dance night-class. Then I see that many crazy people they on heroin and I know where that heroin come from. I feel bad. Then I go Amsterdam vacation with girlfriend and see too many junkie there near railway station. It ruin such beautiful city. Maybe same-same heroin in crazy people in London and Amsterdam come from Kwan Mae. Maybe same-same heroin from Papa. I hurt *mahk-mahk.* One time I watch telly and there show on Golden Triangle. They talk about papa of mine! I with other people and have same-same name! They joke about this but no know truth, and I no tell them but I feel *big* shame. I no can stay any longer. I come back and work in bar. I no go home with man like other Patpong girl but he no know. I know he hear I work at bar though. He have many spy in Bangkok. I make him feel shame like I feel. I no tell him I accepted into anthropology school so he think I will stay Patpong girl long time."

"So what happened on your visit home?" I asked, interrupting her so I could absorb all this.

"Oh, he much angry! He slap me! Call me *gly*— chicken. Same-same prostitute! I no *gly* but he heroin man, and I tell him that. He slap me. Mama stop fight. I think he going to kill me. But then he leave very angry. It good I no see much of him. He much busy. Something happening with business."

"The opium business? Or something else?"

"Oh, they all much excited about something. He and Chung Si Fu and Kayao, he two top men, talk much. Office in home and I hear through walls. They talk about airplane of Papa be on big trip somewheres. They have something important in office they keep and go look at many time. I think it heroin. They call it 'head.' I not sure but think that mean top quality, like Number Four. I get ashamed again. mama want me stay longer but I go."

"Could they be meaning 'head' as in *this* kind of head?" I asked, tapping my temple.

My heart was beating in faster. She shrugged.

"*Chi.* I suppose it could be same-same. Why you say?"

"First, just one more question: Did any of your papa's men wear a pendant like this one you gave me? Only made of gold?"

She thought for a moment, wiping her eye with a tissue at the same time.

"*Chi.* But only two lieutenants—Kayao and Chung Si Fu. They only people in town who afford that except Papa. I hear Kayao he say to Papa that he upset because his left behind somewhere. He say it be *mahk-mahk* bad luck. Papa tell him he buy Kayao another one, but Kayao still upset."

"I hope he's right about the bad luck," I said, digging into the pockets of my slacks. "Could this be it?"

Tysee's bright eyes broadened. Instinctively she reached for it, turning it over, inspecting it.

"*Chi!* This is it! He have for many year! How you get?"

There were to be no secrets. She trusted me, and now it was my turn to trust her. I told her the whole story, leaving out nothing except for my initial mixed feelings about the returning of the Head. As I went on, her eyes grew wider and wider until it was obvious that she was going to break down and cry again. She surprised me though—she *did* cry, but her tears were of anger, a raging, spitting fury. I'd never seen Orientals lose their cool before. Thais even forced a smile to their faces when standing before firing squads. A matter of face. But perhaps she got this from her father.

The suggestion was hers.

"Papa bring so much dishonor on family I have to take the Head back. No brother or sister. He must *no* get away with steal sacred Head of Enlightened One. I get it back. I go Kwan Mae and take it back to abbot in Himalaya."

I was taken aback by her forthrightness.

"Tysee, I wasn't thinking of getting you involved. I was just hoping you could help me with some information."

"Are you Buddhist?" she asked directly.

"Well, no, not really."

"Well, *I* Buddhist. So I involved more than you."

"Tysee, you can't," I said, a troubling thought nipping at me. "For one thing you'll never be able to see your father again if you were to do this to him. Even if he *is* wrong, you might regret this very much, later."

"Maybe before, I think I want to make up with him someday. Not now. Not if he do this to the Buddha. The Buddha more important than anyone. If I not do something, the Buddha be angry with me. Papa have to see I right afterward."

None of this sat well with me. I was never one to believe in burning bridges, and it looked to me like she wanted to raze the forest those beams had come from. Her youth was showing.

"You *mahk-mahk* good man. You help me?"

"Tysee—"

"Are you help me or no?" she demanded. "You no help me, I go alone."

I shrugged helplessly.

"Help you? Of *course* I'll help you if I have to! It's my *job!*"

I hoped that tomorrow, after a cooling-off period, she would think differently. She relaxed a little now, but I could see she was still troubled. Her soft hands found mine on my lap. I thought I noticed a change beginning to come over her. As if something else had entered her mind.

"Well, maybe I should go my home now," she said with a sudden shyness in her voice, "so get ready for tomorrow when we fly Chiang Mai."

She didn't look me in the eye, the way she normally did when addressing me. I grinned. She was so delightfully obvious.

"Why don't you stay here? It's more convenient."

"*Cup coon ca.* Maybe we go bed . . . now?" she asked in a small, sensitive voice, a twinkle deep in her black pupils as she looked up at me. "That way we get good rest and early start, *chi?*"

"*Chi,*" I agreed in mock seriousness, although it was barely dark. "It really is quite late."

A delicate hand touched the back of my hair, as her soft, moist lips found mine. Then the world dissolved into chemical magic.

SIX

The Golden Triangle

"OKAY. THIS WHERE we get off. We walk in jungle now."

The battered World War II vintage jeep bucked and growled through a final pothole that could have been a tiger pit before wheezing to a stop in the middle of the deeply rutted trail. It was little more than an elephant walk, and indeed, large, brown cannonballs that either they or some monstrous rabbits had left behind littered the way. The thick jungle margin on either side had been well chewed up by pachyderms. We were in the densely jungled hills near the village of Mae Hong Song, northwest of Chiang Mai, and as close as we could get by vehicle to the border point we wished to cross.

"Thank God," I groaned, extracting myself from the dusty machine. "I don't know how much more of that I could have taken." There wasn't an argument in the world that would have stopped her. I'd found myself being towed along almost against my will.

I hoisted our knapsacks out of the back and slapped their

sides. Yellow clouds rose from them. Tysee brushed off her black, Shan-style jumpsuit, then removed a small bag of provisions from the back of the jeep. The driver, of a vintage approximately the same as his jeep's, nodded without expression and ground the vehicle into reverse. Tysee had contacted him at a jade shop her father owned next to the police station in Chiang Mai, Thailand's second city and the gateway to The Golden Triangle. Slowly the jeep whined around a bend and out of sight. My ears rang as the relative silence of the jungle crashed down around us.

Tysee began rearranging my knapsack to find room to put the lunch, pulling out a forty-ounce bottle of vodka I had brought along as a gift for Kun San. Her face took on the expression of a question mark as her hand grasped something hard that wasn't me. She pulled it out. It was the Walther 7.65. When I had phoned an elated Wolfgang before catching the plane north—jokingly giving him hell for not telling me about Tysee—he had strongly advised me to take some firepower along, if I had any. I had plugged the seven-shot clip and thrown it, along with a box of shells, into the bottom of my bag.

She handled it deftly.

"It very small—lady gun," she said squarely. "Toy compared to what Papa have. Man of Papa already radio ahead and they expect us but we have to be careful. I think I should carry toy. Shan might look in you bag, no in mine. They know daughter of Kun San and no dare touch."

She repacked our bags, sticking the gun deeply into her own, a troubled expression clouding her face. We hoisted them onto our backs, secured them, and were about to set out when she gripped my arm tightly.

"You do what you have to," she said, looking me directly in the eye. "But you no do anything to my papa, okay?"

"Don't worry," I replied, putting my arm around her shoulders. "He's your papa." It was evident she had a few things to work out in that relationship.

Distant voices interrupted us and I spied the head of a work elephant swaying over the top of the trail behind us. I shoved on my battered old hat, grabbed my pack and we quickly dissolved into the jungle before the *mahout*— the elephant handler—could spot us.

We found the footpath with little difficulty and struck

out. Like Nepal, the entire Golden Triangle is crisscrossed by footpaths linking village to fields to village. We were to hike to the first of these settlements where some of Kun San's men would be waiting to meet us. We followed the trail through magnificent, double-canopied, Tarzanesque jungle, around huge fig trees and banyans with tangled roots, vines and dangling lianas everywhere. Bright sun-beams slashed through the top canopies and jabbed pillars of light down into the gloom, splashing onto huge orchids, huger pitcher plants and the giant fronds of spreading ferns. Iridescent birds flashed by and sang in the cathedral-like silence while monkeys hooted and scrambled through the upper foliage. It was always good be back in the jungle, the rich, moist aroma of the decaying forest bed filling my nostrils with its fresh, pungent scent.

It seemed we were always climbing—often for a half-hour at a time, to the crest of one jungled ridge from which we could see for miles, the view of other jungled ridges retreating in silhouette—then descending for an equally long time along narrow, twisting trails, before heading up the next laborious hill.

I was fading with the jungle light before Tysee finally deemed it time for dinner. Nocturnal sounds were awak-ening as we huddled in the wide, undulating roots of a giant banyan and snacked on our dinner while the curtain of darkness descended completely.

"How do we know when we're into Shan territory?" I asked, wiping my forehead with the back of my hand. Hours had gone by since we had left the jeep. During the trek I had heated up, and pulled off my sweater; now I thankfully crawled back into it. Jungle or no jungle, it got damned chilly at night in the hills.

"What time it is?"

I told her.

"We be in Shan territory about two hour now."

My eyebrows rose. She passed me a banana. I had been doing a lot of thinking on the trail.

"What are you going to tell your papa about me? You were just there and had a fight with him, and now you come back with me."

"I tell him I sorry I run away," she answered, obviously having done some thinking herself. "And that I bring you back because you my boyfriend. I also tell him I quit work bar and I go university. That make him happy."

"Good idea," I agreed. "Now here's what I suggest we do."

I explained to her my plan: interest her father in having me flog the piece for him. We just had to find some way to broach the subject.

"We find a way," she whispered, breaking off a piece of cake for me.

"One way might be to bring this up," I said, pulling out the gold pendant I had brought from Tengboche.

She stared at it and stiffened.

"I don't know if you should bring that. It might be no easy to explain."

"It's a chance. Whoever owns it would like it back, I'm sure. I'll only bring it out if the situation warrants it." I fixed it into the sweatband of my hat. "In any case I have this one."

I fingered the silver talisman Tysee had given me years ago. I had restrung it and added it to the Buddhist amulet that hung around my neck. She smiled happily. We ate in silence for a while before I brought up other considerations.

"But what if that doesn't work—if he doesn't want us to sell it for him? Where will we find it? And how do we get away?"

I thought of the gauntlet that would have to be run— from Shan State, through border patrols and back into Thailand. This area would be swarming like a kicked ant-hill. It was highly doubtful that we could get away with an outright snatch. With any luck, it wouldn't come to that— to Operation Snatch.

"You ask too many question. I think I know where Head is—in safe of Papa in office. How we get away? We think of way. I know trails."

It's a good thing I thought, because I'm completely lost.

"Okay, we better go," she said, pulling out flashlights for both of us. "Still have many hour walk to village. Not safe to be in jungle after dark. Many hungry animal."

I didn't need any persuading. We glided along the single trail, her in front, me admiring the panther-like ease with which she moved, her jet-black hair swinging back and forth, her tight little backside swaying.

We hadn't stumbled more than a hundred feet before the dark jungle suddenly shook on all sides and powerful flashlights exploded in our faces. A phalanx of guns converged on us. My heart went to my throat. Singsong orders in the Chinese Shan dialect rang harshly out of the dark.

Tysee spoke rapidly in a strong voice; a moment later the blinding flashlights dropped from our faces and the guns pointing at Tysee swung over to me. After a pat-down and a cursory search of my bag, the muzzles were lowered and we struck off in a long line, the lights cut back to one thin beam held by the point man. With our new bodyguard, we made good time along the well-used trails. We passed through a couple of hamlets and after four hours of steady tramping, reached the top of a high, broad plateau on which, I knew, sat Kwan Mae.

Although it was only 10:00 p.m., the town was silent and asleep except for the sentries. Our welcoming committee left us at the edge of town and faded back into the jungle. We shuffled through the ville. Occasionally a dog straggled to its feet and yawned a lazy bark before flopping back down, its duty done. Here and there the light of flickering oil-wick lamps seeped through the bamboo slats of stilted huts, the sweet, flowery aroma of opium drifting out with it.

We trekked straight up the hill to the big house, past the guards and through the compound gate. Other guards at the door recognized her but gave me a burning visual inspection. To my surprise, no one was up to greet us.

"Papa maybe not here," Tysee said. "Maybe with minor wife other house." Then she added in a softer, almost conspiratorial voice, "My mama sleep very deep always."

After lighting an oil lamp and pulling off our shoes, we tiptoed in. After all these years I was actually entering the home of Kun San. It was now almost as modern as any compound home in Bangkok—and out here in the jungle. . . .

Tysee led me into what I guessed was her room.

"We sleep here together. It okay. As long as man is good, and boyfriend, Papa and Mama no get upset. I have futon here I bring back from London. No like hard floor anymore. Soft bed much difficult to get use to but now no can sleep on anything else. With you sleeping bag on top of us we be much warm."

"You've slept with other men here, have you?" I teased, in a subtly probing whisper.

She didn't answer but disappeared out the door, returning a moment later with another pillow. She'd apparently adopted that habit as well.

We slipped out of our clothes and curled up together on the soft futon, the sleeping bag over us. Her back was to me, and she was holding my hand to her breast. I was exhausted and drifting rapidly down into sleep when the descent eased to a stop. Her hand had drifted behind her, slipping down between my legs. She squeezed me twice gently.

"Jeez . . . Tysee," I whispered, not having to try to sound groggy. "I'm dead tired."

She wiggled around to face me, her hand quickly finding its way back to Ol' Thunder.

"This help you sleep," she whispered back, her breath hot. She was panting slightly.

I felt uncomfortable. "But your mother might hear us," I argued, trying not to lose my downward drift. Christ, we had banged our brains out again only the night before.

"Mama sleep like rock, I tell you already," she replied, insistent. "One time there be earthquake and she no wake up."

She was trying to perk Ol' Thunder up. To my disappointment, she was succeeding. But I still wasn't sure if I could make the earth move tonight.

"I've got a bit of headache . . ." I said weakly.

I wasn't kidding; after last night's bout the head *was* aching. I was so sore that the friction of khakis against crotch had been irritating as hell on the long trek. Just the same, I realized I was losing the battle.

"I play flute and music help you sleep," she giggled.

"Ah, that sounds like a great idea," I whispered, relieved. I could drift off back to slumberland with my Asia girl serenading me.

That comforting thought dissolved in a puff of smoke when she gently pushed me over on my back and wiggled my legs apart. My closed lids popped instantly open when she slid down my chest, her mouth slipping delicately over my battered, uh, flute. I had *rarely* known an Oriental who would do that, except for some Filipinas—which did make visits to the archipelago a special treat.

Tysee gently stroked me with her hand while her head slowly bobbed up and down like a Halloweener after apples, her tempo increasing as Ol' Thunder almost instantly rose up like a trombone. A barely discernible laugh issued from the orchestra pit while she tongued the bottom of my stiffening instrument, then began to nibble around the horn. Returning to blowing the reed, she carefully stroked down with her mouth until she reached the point where, if she had sneezed, I would have been transformed into a kazoo. The sensitive allegretto of Beethoven's Seventh gradually built up into the crescendo of the allegro con brio as I approached the climax of her movement.

"T . . . T . . . Tysee," I said in a shrill whisper. "I'm . . . I'm . . . slow . . . slow . . . down . . . or I'll blow . . . blow the orchestra apart. . . ."

She pulled away just in time, then laughed hungrily and began to slide up my body, straddling my instrument. Her eyes gleamed in the near-darkness. She delicately spread her tiny lips with her fingers and slowly leaned back, soft sighs issuing from her open lips. She had only rubbed herself against me four or five times, just long enough for my wet mouth to find a stiffened nipple, before she began to shudder, trying her best to stifle her passionate moans. I let myself climax at the same moment.

Tysee collapsed on my chest. We held each other for a long, tender moment before she rolled off and curled up with her back to me. I drifted back to reality and rolled over on my side, gently placing my arm around her. Her hand slipped back between us, to gently hold my crumpled flute. It was a comforting feeling and I lay still awhile, enjoying the feeling of softness and peace.

"Tysee," I quietly whispered, a well of emotion filling me. I wanted to tell her something—*needed* to tell her. It was stupid. It was too fast. I didn't want to tell her yet that I loved her, even if I felt I did. I *did* want to tell her I cared about her.

When she didn't reply, I repeated her name. The only sound was a gecko chirping on the wall. Carefully raising myself on an elbow, I leaned over and looked down at her face.

Moonlight seeped through the shutters, softening her relaxed features. She was breathing in deep, relaxed droughts, already fast asleep.

———— • ————

A cold mist was rising from the body of the jungle in wide, slow-moving tendrils. The crows of roosters mixed with the intermittent pop of the homemade flintlocks Shan hunters use to bring down birds and monkeys for meals later in the day. From nearby came the sifting sound of a woman winnowing rice in a woven tray, farther off shuffled a backstrap loom that someone had just taken up. But it was the receding drone in the background that had really awoken me. It was a plane—probably Kun San's. I wondered with interest where it was off to.

To my disappointment, Tysee was already up and gone. I crawled out from under the warm sleeping bag and shivered in the chill, moist air. To loosen up, I slipped out for a morning stroll through the town. Breathing deeply of the fresh, clean air and stretching, I walked down the haphazard, still-familiar dirt streets, watching black pigs root and grunt while dogs lazed about, sniffing at me and each other.

The town had grown little since my last visit; it was still a humble-jumble of clapboard dwellings on a narrow, central plateau, with a tumble of bamboo huts on stilts at the edge where the land fell away to the jungle. From a flag-pole on a parade square, surrounded on three sides by military barracks, flew the Shan State flag, a red M-16 crossed with a fountain pen of the same color against an open book, the background a rich royal blue.

Kwan Mae wasn't poor, at least by hill-tribe standards, and was certainly better off than it had been during my last visit. A ghetto-blaster was quietly playing Burmese gong music somewhere, and Singer treddle sewing machines were whirring. Canned goods that had been smuggled across the porous border, and even jeans and printed T-shirts, were sold in hole-in-the-wall shops. The Shan were clean and courteous; they smiled at me and hid their curiosity as much as possible.

I returned and was happy to find Tysee, though it was clear that father and daughter had had their first argument. To my chagrin, I learned that it was over me. Tysee's face was set but sad as she drew me aside.

"Papa learn you here and very upset but you no worry. He no want you in house. He say there guest hut to stay in, but I say you *my* guest and that you stay in *my* home. He much angry and demand to see you."

"Oh God. When?"

"Right away."

"Great. May I wash up first?" I was not only still covered in dust from the day before, but sticky dry in certain places.

Tysee nodded and guided me to the washing area. I stripped down, dipped cold water out of a huge crock with a dipper, and splashed the frigid water over me, then raked a comb through my hair and quickly trimmed the few wild hairs out of my beard.

"Okay. I'm as ready as I'll ever be," I said, straightening the pockets on my safari shirt. "Lead on, MacSan."

"He having breakfast in office. You have breakfast with him."

Squaring my shoulders, I knocked on the door. An order, which I presumed meant "enter," greeted me. I turned the knob and stepped over the threshold into a smoky room filled with the pleasant aroma of Burmese cheroots.

Kun San wasn't alone. Two sturdy lieutenants in military greens were with him. Both were in their early thirties and had patterned protective tattoos on their chests, visible between the open flaps of their shirts. They sat on either side of their leader like protective hawks. On the wall directly behind them I saw a *thankya* and two masks, one depicting a large Bhairab, the other a smaller skull mask. I suspected they had deliberately placed them there to test my reaction, and did my best to concentrate on the men before me. Their eyes were burning into me, appraising me.

Kun San was in his mid-fifties, a not unhandsome man, short and stocky and still athletic. His face was open and mobile, his eyes bright, narrow as pillbox slits, and shrewd —the kind that can see through other men at a glance. He was clearly a man of intelligence and charisma, a man at ease with command. He was dressed casually but neatly in military-green fatigues. If he was still angry, it didn't show.

Kun San matter-of-factly pointed to a wooden chair at the round table, while one of the two lieutenants put aside the cigar-sized cheroot he was smoking and poured me a small cup of tea. An ornate Reclining Buddha sat in the middle of the desk. I ignored it and glanced at the aide who was serving me.

He was lean but strong with a clean-cut, handsomely chiseled face that betrayed no emotion. His narrow eyes revealed an obvious, though hard, intelligence. I glanced at his chest as I took my seat. A Shan gold amulet hung there.

The other lieutenant was short and stocky, developing that lumpy look that comes from too much rice wine and too little taking care of oneself. After a brief study of me he returned to what he had been doing when I entered—preparing his morning betel nut. He made a roll by folding a heart-shaped *bai plu* leaf around an areca nut, tobacco and lime, then pressed it into the side of his cheek and began chewing open-mouthed, revealing black teeth and red-stained gums. Almost immediately the bitter, astringent mixture went to work and he began to spit red jets into a discolored clay crock beside him. A hint of pleasure tinged his brutal features, otherwise devoid of emotion—and, I sensed, of just about anything else.

I tried not to notice that his chest was bare of gold.

From the vibrations in the room, I instantly knew that any move I made to return the missing amulet would cause more problems than it solved; suddenly I wished I'd left it at home. I could feel the gold amulet burning a hole in my sweatband; fortunately I'd left my hat in Tysee's room.

Once seated, Kun San checked his Rolex and pulled on a cord that hung down from the wall beside him; from a distant part of the house echoed the vague sound of a ringing bell.

"Food come. We have breakfast together," the lean lieutenant with the cheroot said evenly, revealing gold-capped teeth.

There was a chilling strain of malice in his voice, directed toward me, which didn't bode well.

"This Kun San."

He spoke the name forcefully, with visible pride, like he was announcing Kublai Khan. At the mention of his name, Kun San nodded nobly in my direction, reserved but not unfriendly.

"There Kayao," the thin one added. "My name Chung Si Fu. I speak little English and speak for Kun San."

The stocky one called Kayao remained impassive, mostly absorbed in his chew, waiting for orders to toast or roast—either would be carried out, no doubt, with equanimity.

"My name is Lee Rivers," I said. "It's good to meet all of you."

I offered my hand, trying to break the ice. They took it awkwardly, not used to the Western custom.

"Kun San know you here as guest of daughter Tysee. And he welcome you," Sea Food said, his voice cooling further.

There was a soft knock at the door, then a servant, dressed in a brightly colored Akha hill-tribe costume, entered carrying a large tray. On it were dishes, chopsticks, a large bowl of steaming rice, more tea and some side dishes of small bits of meat and rough green vegetables.

While it was being served I stole a glance around the room. There was also a rattan-backed plantation chair, but little else in the way of furniture—just a number of cabinets out of which protruded rough paperwork, the crude ledgers I guessed he used in his business. And, in a corner, a very old safe of a size that made me wonder how men or mules had ever shouldered it there. I also wondered how I'd ever get inside it.

Kayao loudly and reluctantly spat out the remainder of his hastily chewed alkaloids while the other two butted their cheroots. Kun San indicated to me to dive in. Nodding, I did so, not realizing until then just how hungry I was.

Once the food had been served, they didn't waste any time getting to the point.

"Kun San want to know if any other reason for you be here," Sea Food said with a full mouth.

It couldn't have been a better opening.

"Not really. I was a guest here several years ago doing

some collecting among your people: clothes, baskets, tools, that sort of thing. I enjoyed myself and always wanted to come back."

Kun San froze, his chopsticks in midair, as soon as he heard the translation. Then he placed the bowl of rice, which he had been holding to his lips, back on the table and studied me closely, scanning the hard disks of his mind. It was apparent that Tysee hadn't told him.

"You here before? Kun San want to know how you come here."

"I came with a *farang* man," I replied, carefully choosing my words, and wondering if I was making a mistake alluding to Wolfgang. I had no other option now, except to mention his name as innocently as I could. "Wolfgang Krueger. I traveled around Shan territory for almost a month. I was working out of Kwan Mae for most of it."

It was clear to me that I may very well have taken the wrong tack. Kun San pushed his rice bowl aside, his hunger evidently forgotten.

"Where you see German man last time?" the translator demanded, imitating his master's voice.

"Just a few days ago," I shrugged, taking a studiously nonchalant sip of tea. "I ran into him in Bangkok."

They absorbed this. I kept up my front of innocence, trying not to telegraph that I was aware of their acute interest.

"How he be?"

"Well, not so good actually. He's had a bit of trouble—he was beaten and robbed. Apparently he was in a part of Bangkok he shouldn't have been in one night, so he said."

"He say he *robbed* . . . ?"

"Yes. He had a few bruises and a black eye. Spent a bit of time in the hospital."

All three stared at me for a long moment before exchanging glances among themselves. Aware of their eyes burning into me, I picked out a piece of meat from one of the common condiment bowls with my chopsticks, and shoveled it into my mouth along with some rice.

"Kun San happy to hear old friend Wolfgang not hurt bad. He want to know what you speak about."

"Jeez, not a great deal. We had a beer. He told me about his accident. Actually," I ventured, "he mentioned you."

Kun San's face had gone immobile, a slight movement of his head to one side the only indication that he had absorbed this new bit of information. He was still off his feed.

"He said that he had written something in a magazine that you didn't like," I went on, "and he thinks that you're angry with him. He's very sorry about it, he told me."

Kun San pondered this for a moment.

"That true. Wolfgang old friend—not so much present friend, but we wish him good. What else you talk about?"

"My collecting, more than anything." I shrugged, seeing an opportune opening again. "That's all I remember."

"What you collecting?"

"Well, I often do antiquities," I said, "old statues and that sort of thing. Frequently black-market. Like this one"—I took up the Reclining Buddha—"this is a good piece, Tantric, Nepalese, Pala Dynasty I would say, about tenth- or eleventh-century. Let's pretend that it's stolen and you wanted to sell it. Well, I'm sure I could find the best market in the world for you. I take a very, very strong interest in Buddhist pieces."

I set the statue down. Their interest was visible. I let it sink in, and I picked up my chopsticks again.

"Kun San want to know if you do any collecting here this time," Sea Food said, a little more warmly.

"This time? Well, if something interesting turns up, certainly. I'm always keeping my eyes open. But I'm really just here on a vacation . . . and to meet Tysee's parents."

The translator's face tightened again at my words. Kun San also looked a little troubled when the translation came through, and glanced toward Sea Food.

"He ask how you meet daughter," Sea Food told me, his voice, tinged with bitterness.

"In Bangkok. She recognized me," I answered, avoiding mention of Patpong. "Of course, I didn't recognize who she was at first—it had been so long and she had changed so much. She's a very fine young woman. By the way, I brought you a present. I took these of her many years ago."

I dug out the pictures of Tysee as a girl and passed them to Kun San. He deftly opened the package. His eyes couldn't hide their pleasure as he studied the images, savoring them one by one as a treasure from the past. Having finished, he carefully set them down, then leaned back in deep thought.

"Where you get Shan talisman you wear?" Sea Food now translated.

That question wasn't from Kun San, but from the aide without a talisman, Kayao, whose hand subconsciously moved to his chest, his thick hand clenching air.

I described how Tysee had given it to me so many years before as a gift. There was no expression on Sea Food's face now, as he camouflaged his emotions more carefully but I sensed his inexplicable attitude toward me had hardened and set.

Fortunately, I could see my answer had affected Kun San in a significantly different way. There was a long pause, then my host's reserve dissolved and his face softened. He took up his bowl again and passed me a dish of sweetmeats, insisting that I help myself to more, then dug back in himself. Kayao followed suit, his chopsticks shoveling back rice like they were a large soup spoon. Sea Food was the only one to hesitate; he could barely conceal his mysterious bitterness toward me.

"He thank you very much for present," Sea Food explained, neither his eyes nor his tone expressing hospitality. "He like very much. You welcome to stay as guest of daughter. Only he ask that you no mind to stay in guest hut. He have business here that private."

"Of course. And thank you," I replied. "I don't mean to disrupt any business."

"Food good?" Kun San asked suddenly, in awkward English.

It was evident he knew a little.

"Very good," I said, my mouth a raging inferno from a chili I had missed.

Nothing more was said as they silently dug into breakfast. I was pleased with myself. My foot was in the door and not in my mouth.

I stole another glance at the safe before turning back to the food.

———— • ————

Tysee and I were returning from a late-morning stroll in the poppy fields directly adjoining the village. The Shan

workers were busy; some of the young fragrant heads of
the *Papaver somniferum* were already blooming out, with
large, beautiful red-and-white flowers. In a few weeks, after their leaves fell but before they were pulled from the
ground, vertical razor slices would be made in the large,
green heads, allowing the opium resin to ooze to the surface for collection the next day.

We were talking about another head, and reformulating
our plans on how to acquire it. I felt it best to take a little
time, and had to dampen Tysee's desire for more direct
confrontation. Still, she was at least as satisfied as I was with
our progress thus far. Operation Snatch—the grab-and-run
option—was pushed farther into the background, which
was perfectly fine with me, since there were men with
guns everywhere. Every able-bodied male in the area was
a soldier, whether he was in the fields or not.

I suggested the next step should be for her to talk to Kun
San in the manner daughters in love are wont to do, which
is, building up their boyfriends' imagined prowess in the
business or whatever world. Or in our case, filling Papa in
on the extent of my knowledge of the underground antiquities market. That I had once handled the Queen of
Mandalay's jewelry would have to impress him. It was a
strong plan and she quickly agreed to it. We just needed a
little time, probably just a day or two. Unfortunately, we
weren't going to have even that.

The first hint of an obstruction came in the form of a
dog's happy bark. As we approached the edge of town we
observed a couple of Shan men separating a black dog
from a frolicking pack. It was young, strong, healthy, male
and considerably better-fed than the rest. As the men
struck off toward a jungle trail, it tagged behind, its tail
swinging back and forth like a State-of-Washington windshield wiper. One of the men was carrying a club, another
a machete.

"What's the occasion?" I asked Tysee. "Is someone being
married?"

Black dogs are saved for special feasts because of their
reputation for having a superior flavor.

"No," she answered. "Mama say there feast tonight because important man come. Plane go secret airport near
Chiang Rai pick him up." She had named the major mar-

ket town north of Chiang Mai, in the heart of the Thai portion of The Triangle.

"Jesus, thanks for keeping me tuned to events," I said, perturbed, tightening inside at the news.

"You no ask me," Tysee snapped back, her eyes clouding.

"I shouldn't *have* to ask," I muttered, an edge to my voice. "It's probably just a big heroin deal. . . ."

"I not know. Papa never tell Mama about business," she said sulkily. "And you no get angry with me."

I looked at her slantways. I wasn't used to Oriental women talking back; they're usually more subtle—and more effective. But then, as I had already quickly learned, she was no typical Oriental woman. She could read my thoughts with a perspicacity that surprised me.

"In London, I see things different there. Woman no have to kowtow to man all time. Men no have second wife there either."

"Okay, I'm sorry, for Christ's sake. I just wish you'd keep me informed about everything going on. It's hard to plan if we don't share all the information we have. If your mother says anything else, please tell me."

I had met Tysee's mother earlier—a warm, quiet woman who felt most at home in the kitchen despite her cooks and hill-tribe servants. After shyly but graciously accepting my gift of several yards of vari-colored silk, she had disappeared back into her room. In that short meeting, I saw where Tysee had gotten most of her looks; although of the jungle all her life, mama-san had an erect, natural grace and soft beauty.

"Well, I think we can find out now anyway," I said, pricking an ear to the distant drone of the plane, the second hint that our plans were about to be pole-axed. The flight to Chiang Rai, only an hour distant the way a hornbill flies, actually takes much longer; the way Tysee explained it, the jungle pilot has to navigate around the corner into Laos—to outflank the Thai border stations—then shoot down between hills to one of four dirt strips near Chiang Rai, the choice of strip depending on the season and monsoon. She also said that it was very rare, because of the inherent dangers, that they flew into Thailand—or for that matter anywhere—which explained why even Kun San's daughter had to hoof in. It was, simply, safer. I wondered who it was that was so important and yet so disabled that he or she had to be lifted in.

"Let go see," she said.

We climbed to the top ridge, where the airport was situated close by Kun San's compound. It didn't take long for the drone to grow louder. In a moment the tiny plane had appeared around a jungled hill and was sweeping low up the valley toward us. The pilot waved around in the almost nonexistent wind, then bounced the plane roughly down on the runway, kicking up a great cloud of dust. It was the same plane that had been here on my last visit—a four-seater Maule, a STOL tail-dragger with fixed front wheels. Only a plane that small could handle the short jungle strip that opened out over the valley below—which meant it could also handle the short airstrips of Nepal. The pilot would be at home with a sloped Himalayan airfield: this strip was carved at a steep angle and had a cliff at the end that dropped off into the jungle below.

The plane was still camouflaged in greens and browns. It taxied to its rest position. With the propeller still sputtering down, one of the two Shan maintenance men picked up the tail of the craft and began to walk it around to face downhill. Two other men, soldiers of the Shan United Army armed with AK-47s, pistols and mobile rocket-launchers, sat in an open-ended shed on the margin of the runway only fifty feet from the plane.

Sea Food stood on the far side of the narrow runway, waiting to greet the arrivals. But his attention wasn't on the small craft—it was on Tysee. I didn't like the look on his face, even from that distance, and made a note to query her about him at a better time. It didn't take an Einstein to see that something had obviously gone on between them.

"I think I see an emergency way out," I said quietly, "if we have a way in, if you know what I mean. . . ."

"Tell me."

"We fly."

"You pilot? You no *tell* me that?" she asked, still a little testy.

"Sweetheart, I've been a bush pilot for years," I replied with a slight smile, patting her behind, trying to cheer her up. "Unfortunately it didn't have anything to do with flying airplanes, but we'll manage."

She smiled slightly and the twinkle returned to her eyes again.

"The tougher question is this: Just in case we decide on Operation Snatch, how do we get into the safe? If that's even where it is."

"Oh, that be no problem."

"Huh?"

"When I small girl and learn to count I play in Papa office and find piece of paper on floor. I ask Papa what it is. He tell me it for safe and show how it work to help me learn number. I never forget."

The other maintenance man was putting the chocks to the wheels. The pilot was fighting with his door.

"Tysee! Jesus, that's *just* what I mean! Why didn't you tell me this before?"

"You mad again?" she shot back, her fuse evidently as short as mine.

"Just a little pissed. That could change everything."

The pout deepened.

"Well, you no tell *me* everything. You no tell me you fly plane."

"Well, actually I don't. I took a few lessons from an uncle of mine when I was a kid but I've been around enough to know that there's no big mystery about them. They practically take off by themselves. It's landing that's a little sticky."

She gave me a highly dubious look.

"Look," I said, trying to lighten the situation. "If there's going to be any chewing out around here, it'll be *me* chewing out *you*."

She caught my meaning and jabbed me in the ribs.

"And that goes for poking, too."

She couldn't hold back a laugh. Her fingers touched my arm. Then she caught sight of Sea Food still staring at her and dropped her hand.

I ignored him. My spirits had lifted. The Shan Air Force, I chuckled to myself as we walked up to the plane to see who had arrived.

My private joke ended abruptly when I saw a familiar figure step down from a strut to the ground, then limp out from under the wing. Those huge fish-eyes fixed on me at the same time mine fixed on him. It was clear that Richard

Haimes-Sandwich was just as surprised to see me here as I was to see him.

I was the first to half-recover.

"Well, here I was just starting to miss Western food, and what arrives delivered by air but a Ham-Sandwich! Fancy meeting you here."

"Fancy meeting *me* here! What about you?" he replied, stiffening at hearing his sacred name used in vain. "I suppose you're here because you like the air as well?" he added, sarcasm dripping off his voice like slime. His hand was limper than usual. He had a briefcase in the other.

"Well, as a matter of fact, it is somewhat, ah—"

"*Heady*, would you say?" he interrupted, finishing my sentence.

There was little use in being coy any longer, except that Sea Food had walked up and taken an interest, having recognized that we knew each other.

"Yes," I said, squelching my disappointment, "as a matter of fact, there *is* something about that to the place."

Richard was the *last* person I wanted to see up here. But his presence certainly confirmed the Head hadn't left yet.

"I wasn't told you were going to be here. If I had been, I'd wonder why they'd need two of us to handle this piece."

"You weren't told because I'm an unexpected guest. I'm here on a different matter than you—whatever yours is," I added, regretting I couldn't lead the Ham-Sandwich on, and milk him for some information with Sea Food hovering on the edge of our little crowd.

Richard's face betrayed that he regretted his last revealing sentence.

"I'm here more on a social matter," I continued, softening the description for the sake of the intense Shan. "You see, Kun San's daughter is a special friend of mine. Tysee—this is a collector 'friend' of mine from Kathmandu. There's few people who know more about marketing Tantric Buddhist items than him. This is Richard Haimes-Sandwich."

"What kind sandwich?" she asked innocently, though I could tell by an almost imperceptible movement of her eyes that she hadn't missed my barb.

"Ham—though he really looks more like Spam," I added, patting his ample belly.

Richard's eyes turned flinty and he drew himself up to his full five-feet-six. But he bit his tongue. The significance of the introduction was not lost on him. This was the first notice he had taken of her, and his eyebrows rose considerably. He rapidly shoved his glasses up on his nose and took her hand with more feeling than he'd shown when taking mine.

"How long you be guest, Spam-Sandwich?" she asked solicitously, but I knew she was really interrogating him.

"Uh, it's actually *Haimes*- Sandwich."

"Oh, I sorry. How long you stay Mr. Hams-Sandwich?"

I almost choked, I had to laugh so bad. Richard's forehead furrowed but he gave up trying to correct the misnomenclature.

"Uh, not long actually. Just till tomorrow morning. Then we leave. I'd love to stay longer. I had no idea Kun San's daughter was so, uh, lovely. . . ."

"I hope you have happy stay. Now please excuse me, Lee and Mr. Hams-Sandwich. Chung, I promise Mama I help her with cooking big meal."

Richard's eyes were the size of a grouper's as he watched her glide to the edge of the field and disappear around a corner.

"Not only is she bloody incredible to look at," he said, startled, "but incredibly enough, I swear I caught a Kensington accent mixed up in that catastrophic syntax. . . ."

"You did," I said without explaining.

Seeing that others were waiting to take him to meet Kun San, he pulled me aside and spoke in low tones.

"Look, Lee, let's drop the bullshit. I suspect you're here for the same reason as I am, and I'm not going to bother saying what it is, just in case you're legit, but I'm damned sure you're not. That would also explain why you didn't drop in after you returned from Tengboche. You didn't want me interrogating you. I'm damned glad you didn't, actually, because a couple of days after you left I received a message from Kun San regarding the . . . item. Now it seems I'm holding the cards. And as such I'd advise you, as an old friend, to give me a wide berth."

"I have no choice with your wide girth."

He reacted by showing me his palm in a half-clench.

"You see this hand? These are your balls in it." He fluffed his fingers and enunciated very clearly: "They feel pretty tender. Keep in mind where they are."

"Fag."

"I think if Kun San learned you were recently up at Tengboche he wouldn't be too pleased," he continued. "Oh yes, I checked your trekking permit at the Immigration Office. I think you know that when you do business with Kun San, you bloody well do it his way or you don't do it—or anything else—ever again. I think you know what I mean. Now excuse me," he finished, "I can't keep the 'head' of this enterprise waiting." He couldn't keep himself from the jab, or from the little smile that went with it.

As Sea Food led him away, he couldn't resist another shot, and and called over his shoulder: "And the name is *Haimes-Sandwich.* I would suggest you remember that, me boy. Or you'll be a Rivers up the creek sans paddle."

He fluffed his fingers again.

He limped along with Sea Food, around the same corner as Tysee. My brow knit with worry. The Shan knew their business well, to bring in the best to unload the piece. Well, second-best. Ham-Sandwich would be whisking it away to New York, Europe or wherever. Anxiety flooded over me. We were being forced to punch up Operation Snatch. Somehow. And fast.

I turned away, leaned back against one of the plane's struts, pulled my hat brim low over my eyes, and crossed my arms, one hand worriedly stroking my beard.

The two maintenance men were refueling the plane. The cockpit door was open. I turned my head and glanced inside. Sunlight glinted off the key in the ignition.

———— • ————

"Come!" Kun San ordered good-naturedly, calling us from the small pool to an eating area set up on mats nearby on the grass. "The lamps are lit and we hungry. We start with good-luck drink!"

The interpreter had supplied the words, our host, by his voice, the hospitality in them. Actually, the interpreter's attitude toward me was little better than disguised hostility, which I did my best not to encourage.

The melodious, dancing tones of an eight-piece percussion band—including a large, horseshoe-shaped *kong wong* with its many different-size gongs—had been entertaining us for some time, which gave everyone time to sip a mekhong, or some of the volcanic, locally distilled rice brew, to puff on cheroots and to chew betel.

It was exclusively a male feast—a business feast—and I suspected it had nothing to do with the Head, that operation being a secret among Kun San's top staff, and his pilot. Most of his men were Buddhists. Also attending, besides myself, were some dozen or fifteen of what I presumed were the heads of the various village operations, many of them brightly costumed Meo tribesmen. There were also three ancient Chinese, who I guessed were old KMT generals. They were the reason for our starting so late, but I could see Kun San hadn't been overly upset—he more than anyone understood the importance of their role in his enterprise. I took it for granted they were in charge of transforming the sticky opium into the more compact smack—a skill many of them had brought from China when they escaped the Glorious Revolution of 1949.

Richard had been in conference in Kun San's office all afternoon; on leaving it he had been flushed with ill-concealed excitement. I didn't think it prudent to ask the reasons; I preferred just to play dumb for now. I felt helpless: I hadn't been able to share more than a couple of words with Tysee since she left us at the plane. There were urgent plans to make; she had to get into that office safe and lift that Head while I created a diversion of some kind. But every time I tried to attract her attention, she just sent me scooting, too busy with food preparations to talk.

Everyone noticed me, but was visibly keeping some distance—including Richard, the guest of honor, who I suspected had divulged enough information about me to return me to my former suspect position. I hesitantly stepped forward just the same and presented my gift to the host. It wasn't necessary, but I knew it wouldn't do any harm. It didn't.

"Ah! Vodka!"

Kun San didn't need an interpreter to recognize the Soviet swill. He held up the large bottle appreciatively.

"Kun San say he used to drink much of vodka before he

say he kick the bad habit out," Sea Food interpreted, a small smile on his lips, pleased with his double entendre. It wasn't lost on the assembled party, for a jocular laugh spread among them. I pretended the joke was over my head and didn't join in. But any hope I had that information about the mysterious Russian might be stimulated to flow by the vodka came to naught. Richard was left out of it altogether. Kun San, seeing our discomfort, reacted quickly.

"He thank you very much and we take here at feast."

A servant shuffled off with the bottle. Kun San whispered to an aide, who hurried off, returning a moment later with a cigar box. The warlord graciously passed it to me. On the package was a crude red-and-yellow picture of a goofy-looking duck.

"Kun San make present to you of cheroots. He say they fresh from Pegu near Rangoon where they made few days ago. It Duck Brand. Number one on market."

I accepted them graciously, lighting one from a smoldering hemp tail that had been placed nearby for that purpose. The cigar-sized cheroots, stuffed with a mixture of cut tobacco and little wooden chips from the *lathtoke* tree, were mild and sweetly aromatic.

Some minions, not in battle fatigues but in the black dress of village Shan, dragged a number of wire-mesh cages into the rear of the compound. They also set up what looked like a clothesline. The cages were full of writhing snakes: some held hooded, swaying cobras, others, banded kraits, their yellow-and-black rings shifting energetically as they came to nocturnal life. Kun San made a proud "help yourself" gesture. The men pressed forward, joking and arguing in rapid voices.

Richard was given first choice. Reluctantly, he fingered a small hooded cobra, an adolescent barely into its teens. Polite acknowledgment of his choice murmured through the crowd. Then I was drawn forward by Kun San. I fingered the largest cobra I could see, a black diamondback. Deep nods, and an octave rise in the slip and sing of voices around me, verified I had easily upstaged the pommy wimp.

It was my only hope—I had to somehow make Richard

lose face, so I could undermine his prestige among the Shan and usurp his credibility and position.

The others made their selections after much jovial bickering. Within moments an expert snake-man was hooking the selected reptiles out of their cages with a wire. One by one, he pinned each snake to the ground with his bare foot just behind its haircut, strung a looped cord around its long neck, and hung it from the line. When he had them all dangling in a row like so many neckties, he grasped the end of each snake's tail, and made six-inch slash in its soft underbelly, the incision ending just inches away from the tip. Each snake stiffened in shock, its lifeblood draining into a separate glass. From each slithery serpent he also surgically removed the small, pale-green, bean-shaped gall bladder, which he popped into each half-full glass of darkly crimson liquid.

In a few minutes the snakes were reduced to a bloody, death-writhing tangle, lamplight flickering on their wet flanks, a huge pool of blood staining the grass beneath them. The twenty or twenty-five half-full glasses of blood were topped up with mekhong whiskey and distributed. Mine was fullest of all.

Kun San made a small toast, then waited as Sea Food translated. The speech concerned Richard: he was being presented as the buyer for the syndicate in London. A glance at both Sea Food and Richard told me this was bullshit—a cover story.

"Snake blood good for circulation," Kun San said through his interpreter. "Warm the body and cleanse the blood. Good, like color of Burmese red ruby!" Then he smiled coyly before adding: "And make you want to go massage parlor!"

The Shan were already laughing by the time Richard and I heard the translation and joined in.

Richard was glowing under the looks of respect from Kun San's men, who hoisted their glasses and shot the concoctions down the slots of their mouths in neat jerks. I noticed Richard was having trouble with his—his stiff upper lip quivered slightly as he swallowed. All eyes turned to me as I knocked back the cool, thin liquid. It lightly coated my mouth and then, like water on a hot tin roof, seemed almost to evaporate, leaving no trace except for a warm feeling in my throat. Nods and betel-stained smiles greeted the look of pleasure on my face. I took a drag off the cheroot and happily blew out the smoke.

Richard, as he clattered his glass down, looked like a man who had narrowly escaped death.

Just before I set my glass aside, I caught a slightly sheepish glance from Kun San. In light of his concern about Tysee's work, I suspected it had to do with his last adlibbed remark. While the other men broke into a scramble of conversation and pressed back for seconds of snake blood, he drew me aside, waving Sea Food away when he approached to translate.

"Bok row trong-trong pben pu-ying yawng rai Tysee ny Bangkok?"

My eyebrows rose. His Thai was better than I had expected, though it was very laborious, and the syntax a little awkward. I knew what he meant when he asked what kind of girl his daughter was in Bangkok. Partly in Thai, more through gesticulation, I communicated to him that Tysee was a very good girl, that she only danced, that I was the only man she had ever left a bar with, and only then because we had known each other before and she liked me. I told him that no money had changed hands, which was a fair fib. He listened closely and with obvious concern, then turned away for a moment to soak up what I'd told him.

"Tom my?" he asked.

After hesitating—I was wondering whether or not I should tell him—I confided that the reason she worked in the bar was that she didn't feel good about her father's business being heroin, that she had seen what it did to people and what they thought of it in Europe. He nodded gravely and deeply, as if he had experienced a revelation.

"Kow my chi my dee pu-ying!" he said with relief.

No, she's not a bad girl at all, I agreed.

He looked up at me, his eyes still sharp, but now there was also a distinct spark of gratitude and a new warmth. For once they weren't looking right through me—only as far as my heart. I couldn't help but feel a twinge of warmth for him.

"Come! We eat!" the translator called to us in the same tone of voice as Kun San had used. Tysee's father drew me back into the group, then led us all to a banquet area set up under the stars. The Chinese lamps cast a soft, romantic glow around the prepared area. Mats were laid out in a large circle, with cushions; the barefooted and smiling Akha girls placed large, steaming bowls of rice and other food before us. I butted my cheroot and joined the movement forward.

"The large pieces meat, that tiger," Kun San explained expansively through Sea Food. "There crocodile and those pots, snake done nine different way. There also mongoose, bat, bear paw, lizard and *mangda,* both live and roast. We even find some turtle egg in Chiang Rai market that fly up from south Thailand . . . and here come dog!"

An approving murmur raced through the guests as two men carried in the *pièce de résistance,* the large, still-steaming canine. Skippy had been skinned, eviscerated and spit-roasted. The meat was dark, the teeth set in a fixed, fried grimace. The blank and shriveled eyes seemed to express surprise. It smelled delicious.

Richard, already uncustomarily silent, looked like a rat caught in a corner. Nervously, he pushed his glasses up on his nose. My mouth watered. I hadn't had a good home-cooked meal like this since Borneo, when I'd lived with the Penans and we'd cut into huge steaks from a twenty-foot constrictor.

Our dishes were brought in by the Akha girls and by Tysee, who was assisting. Each plate was already topped with steaming rice; another girl brought in a huge bowl heaped with still more. The brightly dressed hill-tribe girls set plates before the others; it was Tysee who brought mine. She brushed the side of my cheek with her own, and whispered a sweet nothin' into my ear, and winked. I smiled. Her father noticed, and a light, approving smile creased his lips. He glanced toward Sea Food, who had been seated between Ham-Sandwich and me for the purpose of translating. The lieutenant's eyes spat at me like a cobra's before he quickly regained his composure, and shifted then to meet Tysee's. She quickly averted hers, and I made a further note to keep my distance from him.

Kun San rose and strode meaningfully to the barbecue and began to carve the mutt with a machete. We pressed in with our plates, with me salivating like Pavlov's dog. He treated me to a cut off the shoulder, and gave Richard, as guest of honor, the head and a bear's paw. Despite the many looks of envy from the other guests the pommy looked anything but pleased with his good fortune.

"Living pretty high off the dog, aren't we?" I said as I returned to my place. I'd had to lean across Sea Food. Both shot me a bitter and spiteful look.

Soon all that remained of Rover was a ragged skeleton caught in a pose of mid-flight—of course it was obvious that he hadn't run fast enough.

Everyone dug in, although Richard acted like he had a teaspoon rather than a shovel. He also avoided the other delicacies. It was clear the boisterous crowd was extremely pleased with the quality and quantity of the fare. I took up my chopsticks, piled up my plate, and dug in. The tiger was moist and tender, as pussy should be.

"I've heard of the Chinese serving cat but this is ridiculous," I whispered to Richard, from behind Sea Food's back. I held up a light-colored piece of meat the size of a man's hand with my chopsticks. He stared blankly at the blackened head before him.

"Quit looking so finicky, Richard," I said fastidiously, as I took up a huge, skinned bat, the remains of its leathery wings spread over a foot wide, and nibbled at a scrawny shoulder. "I'm sure all the fleas are burnt off Ol' Yeller there."

Richard rolled his eyes, poked at his food, and turned even greener than before as Fido stared up at him.

"Why don't you see if Snoopy knows any tricks?" I teased, baiting him.

Richard always took things a little too seriously. But then, short people never seem to have a sense of humor. He prodded Blackie's blackened head with his knife.

"Tut-tut, Richard. If you want to play with your food, I suggest you should have done it yesterday when Spot could play back."

Sea Food caught the last joke and passed it on. Laughter rang out from all around. Glasses were raised in my direction, mekhong and vodka spilling over their edges. I was being accepted into the party.

I laughed and raised my glass as well. Glancing at Richard out of the corner of my eye, I saw that he was flushing red with anger. There was blood in that look, like he was eyeing my jugular. Kun San and the others were noticing that he hadn't joined in yet. I winked at him.

"How's Puff?"

"You son of a bitch, Rivers," Richard growled at me under his breath—the first thing he had said for a quarter-hour. "If you're so bloody hungry, why don't *you* down this hideous thing," he spat in aristocratic disgust, maneuvering the head in my direction with a knife and a chopstick through Rex's nostrils.

I slipped my plate under it just before it could land in Sea Food's lap. Kun San looked shocked. I shrugged helplessly and dug in, knifing out a very shriveled eyeball and popping it back with a shot of coconut water and mekhong. All eyes were on me as I deftly carved out the stiff tongue and placed it between my teeth so it stuck out. I leaned over to Richard.

"Woof, woof," I said.

Cascades of laughter and hoots of glee flooded down on me. I bit off a chunk, chewed it, and swallowed. I was smiling. I love dinner parties. I caught a glimpse of Tysee's mother watching me from a doorway, and noticed the approving smile on her face.

"You bastard," Richard snarled again, his green chameleoning to crimson. His eyes grew even larger. He roughly shoved his glasses up on his nose for the tenth or twelfth time.

"What's the matter, Richard—no sense of humor?" I shrugged innocently, holding up a dog-eared dog ear, then noisily crunching off a portion of the crisp, curly-edged flap. "His balls are still there if you hurry. And . . . *tsk!* . . . I just thimply *know* you'll loooove the penith!"

"The only balls I want are *yours*— and I'll have them if you're not *bloody* careful! I can read your game, Rivers!"

His hands were claws—he was angry at being made a fool, and knew what losing face means to an Oriental. Kun San held back—on the one hand, offended by Richard's crass behavior in refusing the best the house had to offer, but on the other hand, silently enjoying it.

I glanced again at Richard. He was concentrating on his rice. I dug into my dog, then sank my fangs into a charcoaled cobra.

"Help yourself to more rice!" Kun San indicated to me with a nod, passing the bowl.

I noticed it was still more than half-full. I held up my hands, then patted my stomach and smiled before pointing to the crocodile that I really wanted to sink my teeth into. I took the bowl anyway and urged it onto his two lieutenants. Both spooned out generous portions, to my pleasure. I pressed the rice bowl around until it was empty. Tysee shot me a warm, pleased smile when she took the bowl back to the kitchen for a refill.

Pleased, I reached over and fished out a couple of turtle eggs from another bowl. I peeled back the rubbery shell from two ping-pong-ball-size eggs, then held their slippery insides up to my eyes. With their translucent whites surrounding large, dark yolks, they looked like huge eyeballs.

"Hey, Richard—guess who this is. All I need are your glasses!"

He turned away. When he looked back I popped the raw eggs down with a splash of mekhong coconut. He almost spewed.

The party had downed several bottles of mekhong and most of my forty-ouncer of vodka—which is twice as strong —by the time the main-course dishes were cleared. Even Kun San, who had poured back Kloster beer almost exclusively, was laughing and gesticulating with a looseness that spoke of eased inhibitions. For myself, I had managed to spill more than I drank, and been careful to refill my glass with mostly coconut water, and only enough mekhong to color it. The increasingly slurry group was in high spirits by the time the hill-tribe girls, smiling broadly, brought out the specially prepared desserts.

They carried in a number of little benches, into which holes had been cut—they looked like the sitters in an elves' outhouse. Then two men brought in the snacks—more than a dozen baby monkeys, trussed up hand-and-foot on a long pole. They were whimpering and crying, frightened looks in their wide, darting eyes. And they had reason to be worried, though they wouldn't be worried for long.

One by one, they were strapped firmly beneath the holes so that the top thirds of their hairy little heads protruded through. A muscular Shan, a confident grin on his face, appeared with a machete that glistened in the light of the Chinese lamps. First one, then another, then all had the tops of their skulls skillfully whipped off before us. Slurred voices sloshed out with each flash of the blade. The monkeys squealed in dumb panic and struggled in their bonds as they sensed what was happening, then fell into loose fibrillations, as the proud Shan dispatched them one by one, to that great tree in the sky.

Richard's face was lime-colored as a bench with a still-convulsing monkey was placed before him. He stared at it in repulsed shock, his mouth gaping, his glasses on the end of his nose.

The other guests drunkenly dug in with knives and chopsticks, some pouring mekhong over the brains to add flavor. I never particularly cared for brains, but to be polite I carved out a few pieces. The razor-sharp knife easily slipped through the light, warm tissue. The texture was cheesy, the flavor vinegary and strong.

Out of the corner of my eye, I saw the girls carrying in baskets of papaya, rambutan, longan, mango, jack, pomelo, lychee and mangosteen.

I grinned devilishly as I spotted the one I was looking for.

Durian.

The spiky fruit was already cut open. I signaled to a servant to bring me one over.

"Richard! What tremendous luck! Look what's for dessert!"

I stuck a large piece of the mushy fruit under his nose just as he slowly turned his pale face toward me. His eyes and cheeks began to bulge. In a moment he was up and hurrying to the darkened margin of the compound. Loud, uninhibited retching, gagging and gasping rose from the dark as he puked his guts out.

Durian. For some reason it's considered the *finest* of delicacies. It smells exactly like fresh, human shit.

The sounds of his suffering brought smiles and laughter to the party, most of whom were already drowning in the river of mekhong that I made sure flowed unimpeded. Some had already retired to other mats set up near the poolside, and were unwrapping their opium pipes and paraphernalia. Some drunken guests were already heating little lumps of opium on the ends of pieces of wire, twirling them over the flames of little oil lamps. Once the black opium started smoking, they plunged the *soma* into nail-sized holes in their yo-yo-shaped pipes.

Kun San was deeply offended by the behavior of his guest of honor, but was none the less honor-bound as host to act civilly. He stumbled to his feet and signaled his two lieutenants to follow. They walked over to assist poor Richard. All three were gone for a while. I wasn't surprised.

I *was* surprised, though, at my own composure, which I was maintaining even though my heart was pounding louder than an orchestra's drum. The sweet nothin' that Tysee had whispered in my ear was this:

"You *no* eat rice in big bowl *for sure*. Understand?"

Still gasping, Richard returned to his place and reluctantly sat down. Kun San was unsmiling. From the way some guests were muttering and gesticulating, they were making remarks among themselves about the pommy's behavior. The warlord hurled a gruff order at his servants. A moment later the monkey on Richard's back had disappeared.

Time for the *coup de grâce*, I thought, reaching into the steep-sided bowl and selecting the largest live *mangda* I could find. The best of them had already been taken. The three-inch rice beetle is a particular delicacy of the north, and available only during the wet season, which had just, belatedly, come to an end. Not only do they look startlingly like large cockroaches, but so obnoxious is their flavor—to most people—that *mangda* has found its way into Thai slang as the equivalent of "pimp."

"Richard, try one of these," I said solicitously. "They'll help settle your tummy."

The large insect's arms scrambled uselessly in the air as I brought it to my mouth, bit the head off and spit it away, then chewed up the remainder with my mouth open, Shan-style.

He made a squealing sound, then barfed all over the remaining food bowls. Kun San and the guests stared in shock. When he was finally reduced to dry, bubbly gasps, he turned to me, drizzles of saliva and puke dripping from his mouth, fingers and nose. His eyes were whale-sized, but had the cold, killer look of a shark's. I knew right away I had taken things a little too far—he had lost too much face.

"You bloody *cocksucker!* I save your bloody ass by keeping mum about you being at Tengboche talking to Abbot Tengid, and this is how you bloody well repay me!" He squeezed his hand into a pudgy fist. "You can bloody well kiss my *ass* from now on!"

We were both on our feet. Others were unsteadily rising. Sea Food, sobering, hadn't missed the remark and pressed Richard to repeat it. He did, in greater detail. Sea Food shot an electric glance at me, then turned to Kun San. The warlord's face flushed and his eyes narrowed as he soggily absorbed the information. Kun San shot a few questions at Richard. The wimp blurted out still more details, his biting voice laden with spite.

In the end Kun San turned sharply to me, his burning eyes demanding an explanation.

"Look, I was just up there trekking—"

"You close up mouth!"

It was Sea Food who had spoken, a new excitement entering his wavering voice. A trace of a smile touched his cruel lips as Kun San drew his staff aside into a huddle, leaving me alone, with a pounding heart, to frantically try to come up with an extenuating lie. The other guests began to talk rapidly among themselves, unsure of what was happening.

Movement to one side caught my eye. It was Tysee, a puzzled, frightened look on her face. She glanced at me and was about to speak when Kayao staggered up from around the corner and jerked a finger at me.

I shrugged, grabbed my hat, took one last glance at her, swore at my stupidity and followed.

The house guards seized me from either side just as I stepped around the corner. An AK- 47 was jammed into my gut. A few feet into the background, beside the gate, stood Kun San and his two lieutenants. Richard was nowhere to be seen. The warlord gestured for his lieutenants to follow him and disappeared with them around the corner of the outer wall. I was hurriedly dragged forward and pulled up short before them.

"You at Tengboche," Sea Food slurred, backhanding me.

My hat flew to the ground. It was a declaration rather than a question.

"Yes, but I was up there—"

"Shut you mouth!" Kun San barked.

He nodded to a soldier, who roughly frisked me. From my pockets he pulled baht change, a box of matches, some keys.

Kayao bent down and scooped up my hat. Just as he stood erect, something fell from it. If it hadn't hit his bare, splayed toes, he probably wouldn't have noticed it. He bent down again to retrieve the object.

It took a couple of seconds, but finally it registered in his ape-like mind what it was. He tried to speak, his thick lips moving, but no sounds came out. He jabbed a finger toward his palm. Sea Food and Kun San broke off from me for a moment to stare at it.

There was no doubt—it was Kayao's talisman. The Shan goon stared up at me, his expression churning with gratitude, relief, confusion, derangement, and guileless utter hate.

"I've been meaning to tell—"

A stinging slap across my face silenced me. I shook my head to clear it, and stared, distantly, at the man who had struck me. Kun San, a man betrayed, glared at me with ill-concealed contempt. He spat out some words to his attendants, jerked his thumb behind him, and without a word, strode back toward the gate to his compound.

I think he stumbled slightly as he reached it. I wasn't sure, because a vicious blow to my solar plexus from a snarling Sea Food dropped me to my knees, gasping for breath. Rough hands tied my arms, other hands tightly gagged me—too tightly. Still wheezing for breath, I fought for consciousness.

I lost. The movie faded suddenly to black.

SEVEN

Thunderheads

CONSCIOUSNESS SEEPED BACK subtly. I don't know how long it was before I returned partway to my senses and became aware of my situation. All was still black. I slowly began to make out a large, flowing, crescent-shaped light directly in my line of vision, and thought *what's an outhouse door doing in front of me?* It took several seconds for me to realize it was the quarter-moon peeking through high foliage.

Then I felt the discomfort. I tried to shift my position on the bed—the springs were digging sharply into my back—but I couldn't, and thought I must still be dreaming, riding a nightmare. My mind flickered erratically forward, expanding in jerks toward awareness. I was bound. Bound on my back. Spread-eagled. Outside. In the dark.

Then I knew where I was and a shock of fear flashed through me, bringing me completely to my senses.

I glanced to either side. Moonlight reflected off the smooth sides of thirty-foot sprigs of bamboo. A strong and sour odor forced me to focus on what appeared to be a

small mound ten feet to my right. For a moment I knew
what I was looking at, but the reality of it didn't—couldn't
—register. When it did, panic gripped me and I fought
madly but vainly to escape my bonds.

The mound was another man, bound like me. Even in
the poor light I could see protruding, from all over his
bloating body, two-foot spears of bamboo that had grown
right through him. Those had made his body arch upward
grotesquely, and pull at the stakes at the end of his limbs.
He was long dead.

A statistic leaped into my mind.

Bamboo grows five inches a day.

I tugged and twisted at my bonds and felt young bamboo
shoots digging into my back. They'd been sharpened. . . .
At my feet lay stacked a small stand of freshly cut bamboo,
each stick about ten feet long. With a gasp, followed by a
sharp cry torn from my lips as a knife-honed stump dug
into one of my kidneys. I lay back, trying to balance myself
evenly over the razor-sharp shoots, across which I was
stretched like a beaver pelt. I felt a wet stickiness as I
shifted on the barbs.

Five inches a day!

I fought back my panic, my urge to scream, and tried to
calm my heavy breathing, which was forcing my back
down on the inch-high spears. Flashes of Ham-Sandwich's
fury, Kun San's viperous eyes and Sea Food's vicious sneer
flickered across my mind like snakes' tongues.

Like a cold wind through an open door, an objective
calm flowed into me and I began to assess my situation. It
didn't look good. My breathing was shallow and rapid, and
a shiver ran through me. I wasn't sure it if was the damp
cold or the fear. Probably both.

A shuffling noise to my left made me jerk my head that
way. It was from a nearby stand of bamboo. The knowledge that those were a favorite nesting spot for cobras sent
more shivers slithering down my spine. Leaves rustled
again, then stopped as from somewhere else in the jungle
came the snap of a twig. Then another. The new sound
drew closer, until I begain to hear the intermittent footfall
of some animal. A tiger come to feed? My breathing tightened and the wall of panic closed back in. Tears burst into
my eyes.

"Lee . . . ?" a frightened voice softly called.

"Tysee!"

My voice was a gasp.

In a moment she was at my side, her hand on my cheek, her flashlight glancing over my features. She sawed through the hemp bonds with a knife. A moment later, we were away from the nauseating stench of the rotting body and in each other's arms, unsure now who was shaking more. We waited until our breathing settled before speaking.

"How did you find me?"

She hesitated before she explained.

"Just before Chung Si Fu go sleep, when he really drowsy, he brag," she said, pulling her hand off my back and shining the light on it. There was a small bloody patch on her palm.

"How did you get that out of him?"

She didn't answer.

"That son of a bitch was your lover once, wasn't he?"

"He first man. But he no good man. Papa try to make me marry him but I want to go London instead. I say no. Since then Papa and I no get along much." She was whispering, strain showing in her voice. "But you no worry. This time he no get everything."

"Well, thank God for that."

"I bring back something of his—for you."

She slipped it into my hand. It was the gold talisman.

"Good stuff," I said, clenching it in my fist and managing a smile.

"Shhhhhh. Here, take. I bring you gun and bullets too. We go. Dawn come soon."

———— • ————

Tysee slowly coaxed open the door of her father's office and peeked through the crack. I remained back, in the shadows of the house and out of sight, my senses sparking, the small Walther in my moist palm. A deep, low snore drifted out. She turned and beckoned me forward, opening the door just enough for us to slip through. I quickly slid forward. The scene before us would have brought a smile to Caligula's lips.

A single coal-oil lamp still flickered, its yellow light casting wide shadows that swayed and danced against the polished teak walls. Kayao was slouched deep and awkwardly in his plantation chair, the gold pendant on his chest rising and falling in quiet rhythm. The son of a bitch was wearing my hat. I took it back. One of the cronies sat at his desk, his head facedown in a plate of rice beetles beside a spilled glass of mekhong, his arms dangling so his knuckles almost touched the floor. Beside him was a large cellophane package containing at least a pound of white powder and beside that, a well-used syringe—one of the larger, older types—and a darkened rubber tube.

Ham-Sandwich lay sprawled on the floor beside an overturned chair, half on his back, his mouth open and loose like a beached grouper. He had been sick again and was covered in barf. Cheroots from a spilled box lay beside him.

The low snore was rising from Kun San. He was sprawled on his belly on the floor near the safe, an army-issue Colt .45 in his hand. It looked like he had become alarmed, and tried to return the object in front of him to the safe before passing out. He hadn't made it. The door was wide open, revealing stacks of currency notes, many in U.S. dollars.

Lying on the floor in the curl of his free arm was an oblong bundle the size of a soccer ball, wrapped thickly in black cloth. If it had been his intention to fire off a warning shot, he hadn't managed that either.

I stood guard while Tysee tiptoed over the sprawling figures, her back to me. She gently removed the bundle from her father's loose grip and quickly unwrapped it for a quick inspection. The glint of a ruby eye on a yellow background caught my eye. She deftly rewrapped it—clearly, the object was heavy. In a moment she was beside me, her eyes gleaming. She nodded happily—too happily—and I hoped she wasn't treating this like a game. If so, it was too deadly a one.

Just the same, I stepped over to the betel-mouthed Shan sagging loosely in the chair and, with my Swiss army knife, slashed the cord to his pendant and shoved it quickly in my pocket. Then I scooped up a cheroot and stuck it in his mouth.

While I looked at Richard, a powerful urge to feed him

his teeth with my foot swept over me, but half out of fear of the noise it would create, half out of respect for the passed-out, I did the next best thing; I chose the largest *mangda* I could find on the desktop, snapped off its head, squished its guts loose, and shoved the mess into his mouth. I fluffed my fingers, smiling slightly, then turned from him.

We tiptoed to the front door and stepped out. I peeked around the corner of the building and saw, silhouetted in the moonlight, the bodies of the guests, all lying crumpled around the pool where they had drifted off, none of them the wiser for the heroin, opium, cheroots and Thai-stick smoking they had apparently taken up in earnest after I was taken away to check out a more deadly variety of local grass.

"How did you manage to take care of the guards?" I whispered, after we had passed through the gate, stepping over a number of prone figures in the process, and reached the shadows at the end of the wall.

"You no worry. Not like Chung Si Fu," she said, making me wish he *had* been in the office. *Him* I would have kicked—down or not. "They very happy when I come around and offer them rice and beer of Papa," she whispered. "I tell them it wild rice—they find out how wild. Servants eat after, too. Nobody wake up long time." Then she added as an afterthought. "And I no think of idea until I start to help Mama, so you no get angry at me."

I shook my head with amazement, and wondered if I should take the package. But she was holding it confidently, which freed me for action. I don't think she would have let me handle it anyway. There was a possessive and otherworldly look in her eye that I suspected came from holding the actual skull of her Lord Buddha. At the same time, her happy smile was fading as she faced the seriousness of our situation.

"I hope you extended your hospitality to the guards and mechanics around the airplane as well," I said.

"Of course," she said confidently, flashing a smile again.

"Shhhh. Not so loud. And you better take those bracelets off, they're tinkling. What about your mama?"

"No problem," she replied removing them. "She sleep deep as usual. I make sure she get different rice."

"Good. What'd you put in that rice to make it so, uh,

delicious?" I was whispering, and hoping the lightness of
the remark would relax us both.

But it seemed I was the only one who needed to relax;
she appeared perfectly calm, holding the wrapped bundle
like a favorite doll. I was worried that maybe she didn't
understand how dangerous our situation was—at least for
me. *She* might get away with a spanking. Yet her confidence was contagious.

"It kind of ground root we have here and use put monkey sleep with old-kind blowgun. It have no taste. I mix
only one bamboo-cup juice into rice so it not be too strong,
so take little time. No want them suspicious."

I raised my eyebrows.

"You're a fine cook. Gourmet."

"Thanking you."

I checked the time, surprised they hadn't relieved me of
my watch. But then they probably found it more fun to rob
the dead. Dawn would be breaking over the hills in a half-
hour.

"Okay. Follow me."

We strolled as casually as we could from the compound,
toward the landing strip a short distance away, keeping as
close to the edge of the buildings as we could, the morning's thick jungle mist helping to hide us.

The field was silent as we came to the edge of the runway. For a moment panic stabbed me when I couldn't see
the plane, but then Tysee led me to the very end of the
runway. It had been pulled back under the partial protection of a lean-to covered with jungle camouflage, though it
was still in full view of the sentry hut only sixty feet away
on the pilot's side. It was quiet. I hoped the occupants had
been very hungry.

Moonlight knifed through the netting and glistened off
canvas skin, giving the plane's spottled look a spottled
look. It was still pointing downfield. I looked at it and
began to think that perhaps I had chomped off more than I
could chew. The plane had begun to look sinister in its
innocence—not unlike a coffin.

We crouched down beside a banana tree and shivered
from the cold and from fear—both were real. We would
have to wait for the first flickers of light. The waning but
still-bright moon made silhouettes, like shadow puppet

scenes, of the undulating hills, which rose above the low, swirling mist that settled into the bowls of the valleys like gray, always-shifting whipped cream. The sky was a translucent blue, the moon's silver crescent hung lopsided like a great, bright beacon, the stars around it scintillating in the clear, tropical sky like diamonds surrounding a moonstone. At any other time I would have thought it was beautiful. Instead I thought it was a lousy place to die.

I needed the break to try to recall everything I had ever known about flying. It had been years since my uncle had given me flying lessons but I'd been in a lot of small aircraft flying to remote collecting sites around the Far East. And, enjoying flying, I'd always paid attention to the mechanics of it all. Somehow it had never seemed that difficult to me, as long as the instruments were fairly standard.

A rooster, getting the jump on his brothers, arrogantly announced the morning. It was still dark, with the vaguest hint of sunrise far off to the east. The scarlet-feathered alarm clock would soon have people up, packing their lunch-buckets and heading out to punch the clock. Women would shortly be lighting hearths. Daughters would be going to fetch water.

Guards would be changing.

The first oil lamp flickered to life in a bamboo hut on the edge of town.

"Damn it," I whispered.

Tysee looked at me for guidance, her eyes on mine. There was still no movement from the sentry box.

"Come on. Around to the passenger side," I said quickly.

We stole around to the opposite side and I quietly unlatched the door. The metal hinge squeaked quietly.

"Hang here just a minute," I whispered. Then I carefully removed the wheel chocks and checked for tie-downs.

There were none. I crouched my way back to the passenger side and stepped on a strut to climb into the plane. It creaked and complained like one of the Lion's old barmaids being laid as I clambered across the cramped cockpit to the pilot's seat. This is certainly no 747, I thought, as I squeezed in, my hat tumbling somewhere behind me. Tysee climbed in and sat down, the bundle securely in her lap. Reaching across her, I eased the door shut.

"Do up your seat belt. Tight."

I squinted at the unfamiliar instruments before me, the illuminating moon through the netting just bright enough for me to gradually locate the artificial horizon, air speed indicator and, more important, the key.

"Whew," I said, mostly to myself. It had been a long time since I had hot-wired the ignition on my old '48 Fleetwood back in high school.

The throttle was easy to find. Next to it was another control for regulating fuel richness; I shoved it in to the hilt. It began to dawn on me that I just might be able to pull it off. I placed the Walther on my lap and cinched myself in tight, though I really didn't know what difference it would make; even if I survived the crash, I knew I wouldn't survive the rescue. But there was no other way out. Our neat plan of gaining Kun San's confidence, and offering to flog the piece for him was hardly in ascendance anymore. Operation Snatch *was*.

I squinted out the open window of the pilot's door, toward the sentry's shack. Still no movement. Behind it more lamps were beginning to flicker through chinks in the houses. A dog barked somewhere in the rising mists. The sound of men hawking phlegm from deep in their throats began to mix with the rising chorus of roosters.

Reaching around through the window, I wiped the film of dew off the front of my side of the windshield—Tysee followed my lead on her side—then looked ahead at the dark runway. It disappeared into gloom and low fog. The horizon was visible, though barely, the first hints of light touching the hilltops.

"Ready?" I whispered hoarsely, feeling death already rattling in my throat.

I looked her directly in the eye, hoping to offer encouragement. Her own eyes shone back with excitement, then her hand gripped my thigh and she nodded rapidly. I placed the gun on my lap and hoped its jarring around wouldn't blow my balls or Tysee's boobs off.

My trembling hand moved to the key. I fingered it, then retrieved my hand to pump the throttle a couple of times. I gripped the key again.

Here goes everything, I thought, turning it to the right.

My heart leapt to my throat. I tried it again. Right to the end. Waves of anxiety flooded over me. I fought them back.

Nothing had happened.

I glanced out the window. There was still no movement in the sentry hut. The loud, clear sound of a man clearing his throat just behind the lean-to hangar jarred me. I raked the instrument panel with my eyes.

"I think start switch here," Tysee whispered, pointing to a protuberance on the dash in the shadow of some instrument.

I let out a deep breath I didn't know I had been holding. My finger found it. Jury-rigged. A whir began. The propeller be to rotate slowly, faster, then faster. The engine began to sputter and cough, catch, sputter and cough again. Then it grabbed, and the propeller became a blur before us as it revved up into a roar that scared the shit out of me. The tiny plane shook and beat up and down like a horny bantam rooster. I knew the whole town could hear.

"Eiiiiiiii!" came a scream from somewhere near the sentry box.

I heard the sound of more anxious cries and imagined the sound of running feet. I rammed the throttle in to the hilt. The cold engine coughed, sputtered sickeningly and almost died. I quickly pulled the throttle back. After a loud hack that threatened to still it once and for all, it slowly caught again.

"Lee!" Tysee cried, pointing out my window.

I turned just in time to see two soldiers running toward us. The guard in front was swinging an AK-47 down from its port position to jam through the window. Just before he succeeded, a slug from my Walther caught him full in the face. His head jerked back but his body continued forward, slamming against the fuselage, shaking the entire plane violently before falling in a lifeless heap to the ground. Frantically, I looked for the other guard, and was surprised to see that he too was sprawled writhing on the ground, his M-16 away from his body.

Farther back beside the hut, a large shadow moved. I pressed off another shot. The figure disappeared in a dive behind a wall.

With the side of the gun butt, I carefully fed the throttle forward again. The engine roared to full life and the little plane began to bounce down the rough runway. A burst of automatic fire sent up a line of geysers in the dirt to one side of us. More automatic rifles joined in.

The plane's roar couldn't mask the sound of shouting and shooting as we picked up speed and hurled down the black runway, dark mist swirling behind and obliterating the easy target we were. We began to drift to the left. I jerked off a couple of quick shots out the window, hoping that would scare them off. It didn't. Bullets made little nipping sounds as they ripped through the thin skin of the plane. One shattered the window beside Tysee but she said nothing—she didn't even move. It flashed in my mind that she must be in shock.

We were drifting more to the left, careening down the homemade strip. The struts began to snap off twigs. The wingtip ripped away on overhanging banana frond. Something my uncle had told me years before about takeoffs flashed through my mind, and just in time I kicked in a bit of right rudder.

"Lee!" Tysee screamed.

The end of the runway suddenly loomed out of the gloom ahead, rushing up at us, its lip giving steep way to the jungle below.

I nudged the yoke forward slightly to get our ass off the ground, then pulled it back just as we reached the end of the road.

We leapt out into nothingness.

Another nip, as a bullet whipped through the wing a foot from my head. I quickly checked for damage—as far as I could tell nothing vital had been shot through. The gas gauge—I hadn't checked it before—showed full. We hadn't blown up: we weren't in heaven, or Patpong, whichever comes first, and Tysee hadn't been reincarnated as a panther or some kind of exotic bird.

"Hey! Hey!" I shouted. *"We made it!"*

I suddenly realized I was thoroughly enjoying myself.

Tysee was silent. I looked over at her as we wobbled like a drunken sailor through the dawning skies, my trying to milk altitude and keep more or less level at the same time. Her eyes were wide open and she was smiling happily, still clutching the bundle like it was a teddy bear. I couldn't see any blood.

"You okay?" I said in a happy shout over the roar of the

engine, glancing at the nonexistent window glass beside her.

Her voice was calm and clear.

"I okay. The Buddha protect us."

"Well, he's doing a good job so far." I laughed, flicking the safety on the Walther and shoving it in my pocket.

Then I realized the reason for her complete confidence: she was no less superstitious than any other Asian I had ever met. If a Buddha amulet carried around the neck was supposed to offer protection—think of how much you would have if you held His actual Head! Fine. I hooted and shook her knee gleefully, then broke out singing the happiest version of Peter, Paul and Mary's old "Leavin' on a Jet Plane" ever heard in the skies over The Golden Triangle.

I figured out how to coordinate the foot pedals with the yoke in a few minutes and made a sloppy turn to keep the rising sun on my left, slipping a hundred feet in altitude doing so. I pulled back on the stick and regained this and more, then eased back on the throttle until the rpm needle rested over an area marked green. That cut the roar of the engine back to a loud purr. I didn't even bother trying to figure out the trim controls. Wherever they were.

I sang on, high as a Malaysian kite. The only thing in the world I needed to be completely happy was someplace to land. And to somehow do that without smudging the landscape, the Buddha's protection or no.

———— • ————

"I no think this Thailand," Tysce shouted, peering out her window into the heavy monsoon.

"What? I can't hear you," I shouted back over the engine, as the wind whistled through the broken window, and the rain pounded on the plane's skin. I was flying below the clouds, scud-running 400 feet above the deck.

"*I said, I no think this Thailand!*" she shouted.

"Come on, what else could it be? Albania?"

But I wasn't so sure myself. We had found the navigation charts and calculated a compass heading that would take us as close to Bangkok as we dared go. After plotting our course, calculating our ETA wasn't too difficult; the map gave distances, and the air speed indicator showed a steady 90 knots. I just wasn't quite sure what in hell a knot was—whether it was the same as or different than a sailor's knot. At least I knew we had enough petrol; while fetching my hat we had learned that an extra tank had been rigged up behind us, which explained the plane's ability to leap-frog to Assam, then into Nepal—no doubt dropping down at smuggler's strips all along the way.

"I think this Burma."

"Why? Why do you think it's Burma?"

"Because of paddy field."

"So what the hell's the matter with them? There's paddy fields all the way to Bangkok once we leave the hills, and we already left the hills." Though I was arguing, I knew in my heart that something was definitely amiss.

There were freighters in the Chao Phrya—there shouldn't have been, not this far upstream. Not only that but the bloody river below us was about four times as wide as it was supposed to be.

"See how many field brown and deserted? Not like Thailand. Papa tell me paddy field in Burma once like Thailand —very rich—but when army take over in 1962 *coop de tet*, they make everything belong to government and try goofy —that Papa word he get from English and he like—style of socialism on country. Everyone become equal—all poor. No one want to work field because all money go big general. So field deserted."

I opened my side window and did a Lindbergh, sticking my head out into the slipstream so I could see where the hell we were going. The rain lashed me in the face. I immediately pulled it back in, my face and hair completely matted. I swore under my breath. I had to admit it—she was right.

"Papa say he hope Burmese no smarten up," she shouted in my ear, "because as long as poor people no can work for selfs, country stay poor and no have enough money to get big enough army to fight Papa. Papa say that why Shan so strong behind Papa, and want to make Shan State real country like Thailand—because he let them make money. He no like Burmese government, but he laugh and say if government let people vote that he would give money to government campaign."

Then I knew she was right. A city was looming up on the

right side of the river. And it was more than two hours before Bangkok was due.

"What the hell is that compass heading?" I shouted, irritated.

Rain hammered louder against the craft as we bounced through a squall. I began to make our buildings ahead, in British Victorian style, from out of another time. Then I recognized one of them, an imposing old edifice with huge white pillars. It was unmistakable.

"Oh shit, the Strand Hotel—it's bloody *Rangoon*," I mumbled half to myself.

We passed over an old passenger steamer beating across the flooded Rangoon River.

"See? This no Bangkok," she called, pointing to the right, not having heard me.

"Of course not!" I shouted. "There's no smog. It's Rangoon!" I was about to tell her to get the chart out again when I spotted three Harvard trainers cranking toward us in formation. "Oh, Christ—the Royal Burmese Air Farce. The airport must have picked us up on their radar."

I pulled up immediately and easily lost them in a maze of clouds just before they could pull around and wax our ass.

"I just hope we don't hit a rock in all of this," I said to no one in particular, as we punched holes in small cloudettes, me catching just enough glimpses of the horizon to keep us level. More or less. The sound of the hammering rain rapidly diminished with our ascent, making conversation easier.

"There no rock in these," Tysee replied, looking at me funny.

"I was just joking," I said, trying to check our instruments to see if we were level. One cloud was showing signs of not having another side. Just in time, we popped out the other end, only to find we were practically standing on our wingtip, and banking off to the north. I kicked the pedals and quickly corrected our drift, and started trying to go around the clouds rather than through them.

"It too wet. Maybe there be whale instead."

We looked at each other and laughed, but then the seriousness of our plight quickly rushed back to me, washing all humor away with it. I took a general southeast heading and dipsy-doodled around the clouds, confident it would be hard for the aging fighters to find me. I knew that ahead of us, for at least an hour, there would be only open water. We calculated our new heading and this time, since we were able to keep the plane more or less in the direction we wanted to go, we triple-checked. But despite both of us having double-checked before, when we left Kwan Mae, I knew I should have noticed that we couldn't be going south by southeast when the compass said south by southwest.

"Damned whiskey compasses," I said sheepishly when I realized my role in the error.

———— • ————

Every conceivable kind of cloud at every conceivable altitude filled the sky, from happy, white popcorn cumulus to strips of cirrus and everywhere tumbling cotton candy, feathers and rose gardens making the sky look like the inside of the most exquisite of gems. Hints of rainbow were everywhere, sprinkling colors among the already-soft pinks and reds, against the ever-changing cornflower blue of the sky. Foothills of clouds bubbled higher and higher, rising into flying buttresses supporting massive thunderheads, rising like mighty but graceful columns thousands of feet into the air, where only 747 eagles dare to roam. It was peaceful, seraphically beautiful.

And it was suddenly broken by an explosion of sound and fury.

"What the *hell* was that!" I shouted, as our plane bucked in the turbulence of an F-16 fighter I could see only too well.

It had just buzzed us, and was now immediately ahead and climbing into the sky like a raging bull, leaving a deafening roar behind. It began to turn in a wide arc to prepare another pass, disappearing into a huge white cumulus.

We had done so well to this point, at least since having banked out of Rangoon into the right direction. Flying over the ridge of mountains that separates the plains of Burma from those of Thailand had worried me; I knew we couldn't avoid radar detection here, so had my knowing nothing about flight corridors, except that they didn't have rooms off like a Bangkok massage parlor; and so had my knowing we were making for a country that was as security conscious, because of its particular geographic position, which is that of a domino surrounded by questionable neighbors on all but one side, and they Islamic. Knowing all that, I also knew there had to be trouble ahead, an alert out on us. I was only surprised that it had been so long coming; it had to be because we'd flown like a cruise missile, at at three hundred or four hundred feet, which is below detection level, after barely clearing the border hills by a handful of feet.

We had to be just outside visual recognition range of Bangkok, though any view of that city would be muddied considerably by huge clouds dumping rain on the area and creating a humidity as thick as a steam bath.

Then I knew how we had been picked up. After shoving the throttle to the hilt, we cut through a small cumulus to see looming ahead and slightly to our right, a flat-topped pile of gray.

"Bangkok," I whispered to myself. "Home smoggy home."

It must have been the defense radar at nearby Don Muang Military Airport that had detected us. Spotting the city couldn't have come at a more propitious time; our sightseeing tour of Burma had guzzled a lot of gas. We needed a place to land—and soon. Tysee, who knew more about the plane that she let on, wasn't unaware of that.

"Where we land?" she asked.

She was still cradling the bundle lovingly on her lap. She hadn't set it down for even a moment. She hadn't put forward any second thoughts about the venture, either.

Don Muang was out of the question, simply because there'd be *too* many questions. I was sure they wouldn't appreciate this mosquito landing on one of their two parallel runways reserved for jumbos and other leviathans of the air.

"We're going to a small airport I know on the east side of town in Thon Buri," I called to her, "unless you have a better idea. But the first thing we have to do is ditch that chopper, if we can."

A military Huey was sweeping up from out of nowhere in our direction.

I pressed the throttle forward as far as it would go, another eighth of an inch. The air speed strained forward slightly, to a little over 125 knots. I turned and pulled back on the yoke while at the same time pressing on a foot pedal, causing the plane to bank and climb into a cloud. We disappeared into it just as the helicopter, now only a few hundred yards away, suddenly leaned over on its side and dropped away, as if giving up the chase. I hoped the cloud wasn't huge; without that visual horizon, I knew we could very well come out of it upside down.

We broke out into a huge, cotton-candy valley with fluffy, brilliant-white thunderheads rising like mountains all around us, the dazzling blue sky above. We were more or less level. I banked around one column, then another, then still another, then flew under an enormous arch and across a fluffy valley into an opening in the wall, threading the needle out into nothingness. Suddenly we were suspended in space, the green floor of the Thai delta far below us. Then we flew right into another wall of white, expecting to smash into a zillion pieces only to pop through to the other side, tendrils of cloud swirling behind us. We swept into another magic world of white, a huge and heavenly landscape on which I could envision angels resting, and naked, cherubic children bouncing and playing.

It was into this enchanting escape that the long-silvery body of a Thai Air jumbo jet suddenly burst in an ascending incline from out of a wall of white. It cut directly across our path. Visions of angels disappeared as I rammed the yoke forward and we nosed into a near-dive. The shocked faces of passengers all along the fuselage were visible as we dipped just under an enormous wing, the turbulence of its huge engines almost flicking us away like a used cigarette.

"Jesus Christ!" I swore, fighting for control, amazed we hadn't had a wing ripped off, at least. "We're over bloody Don Muang! How the hell did we get going in that direction?"

I checked the compass. It said we were *not* going east. We were supposed to be going east-southeast. I cranked the crate around. It didn't connect that the jumbo was the reason the chopper had pulled off.

Hearing nothing from Tysee, I glanced at her. Her calmness was pissing me off. I pushed the yoke down and we dropped below the clouds. Not far away was the muddy Chao Phrya snaking through the twin cities of Bangkok and Thon Buri, toward the distant Gulf of Thailand. Disappearing behind us, I noted with a shudder, was Don Muang.

"We have to follow the river till we come to the airport," I said, trying to sound reassuring despite my trembling voice. "It's practically on the bank on the other side of the city."

But she wasn't listening. Her eyes were closed and she seemed to be praying. At last I knew the Buddha Head was in good hands; she was gripping it too tightly for anyone to take it away—even the ambulance attendants who might later have to cut and scrape us out of this wreck. Despite His divine protection.

"Damn," I swore again, just as we crossed the city limits. The gunship was back, pulling up to our port side, the pilot trying to establish radio contact, giving me incomprehensible hand signals. I fumbled for the microphone and held it up as if to say *it doesn't work.* I was buying time. For all I knew, it didn't work—I hadn't tried it.

I saw movement in the open bay door of the ship; just in time I covered the side of my face with my hand as a soldier in green khakis began shooting pictures. Another soldier beside him manned the machine gun, beading it directly on us. Peeking through my fingers, I recognized it as an M-60. It could blow us out of the sky like a can off a fencepost. It looked hopeless. He wobbled the dragonfly back and forth. I shrugged and gave the thumbs-up sign— our wings were already wobbling as it was, it being the only way I knew to fly the ship. It was returned with a nod and another thumbs-up sign. The nimble helicopter pulled in front of us and banked to the left.

I banked to the right, diving for the river through a cloud and its attendant rain squall, hoping he would lose visual contact. It was a moment before the chopper realized he had been ditched and in that space of time I almost lost the game of hide-and-seek. Our air speed indicator was pushing 150 when I pulled back on the yoke and leveled off mere feet above the fast-flowing river, shooting over startled commuters on long-tail boats and just missing the higher, whale-backed rice barges lumbering upstream.

I glanced quickly at Tysee as we approached a large bridge. Her eyes opened momentarily. We swept under it and through to the other side. Her eyelids slammed shut hard enough to shake the plane. Her confidence in the Head's protection was not, I could see, total.

It was after we began to follow the wide curve of the broad river toward the heart of the city that I realized we would never make the airport. The first sputter of the engine came before we reached the grounds of the Royal Palace.

I checked the gas gauge. It was well past the prominent E and into the red zone.

"Oh *shiiiit!*" I shouted in a rising voice as I pulled back on the yoke, scratching for altitude as the plane's momentum rapidly disappeared. The motor sucked in the last mouthfuls of gas, then the last thimblefuls, sputtering and gasping like a wino on his last bottle.

But it was a toss-up whether the lack of fuel or the gunship would knock us out of the sky first.

"Oh *shiiiiiiiit!*" I shouted in a higher octave as the big chopper whipped up directly alongside and above us, off our port wing again. They were so close we could see the yellows of their eyes. They wasted no time.

With several hundred yards of water to absorb any misses, the gunner carefully aimed his big cannon and sent a burst slamming into the engine. The small plane jerked like a target at a carnival turkey-shoot as the armor-piercing shells sought its heart. The motor exploded, a piston shooting through the top of the engine housing, rivulets of oil spreading all across the windshield as the engine seized. Just as suddenly silence overwhelmed the plane, the only sound the swish of wind in the ailerons. And me.

"Oh *shiiiiiiiiiiiiiiit!*" I wailed in soprano before sticking my head out the window to see where we were going. Ahead to our left I spotted the riverside patio of my house. There wasn't room.

"Tysee! *Wheredoweland!*"

"*Wat,*" she replied calmly, making a gesture to the right.

"I said *Wherethehelldoweland!!!?*"

We were already beginning to drift down. This was no glider—I had only been able to gain perhaps 300 feet and had to push the nose down to avoid a stall.

"Wat Arun. To right. Over there."

Her eyes were bright yet peaceful, her faith in the Buddha's protection had returned. I couldn't understand it, but then, she was a woman, and if a Western woman is next to impossible to figure out, an Oriental is light years worse. I jerked my head toward the tall phallic-shaped monument to the Buddha at Wat Arun, across the river and a bit downstream. I locked in on it and hit the rudder pedals, turning the wheel sharply to starboard.

"Ifwehitthewater,youforgetaboutthatHeadandgetthe helloutasfastasyoucan!" I shouted. *"Infact, throwitinthe backrightnowsoyourhandsarefree!!"*

There was no Chuck Yeager in my voice. But it turns out I could have whispered; the only sound was the chopper, which had pulled to watch the wounded duck's feathers fly all over the sky.

Hearing nothing from Tysee, I jerked around to glance at her. She was staring at me calmly and holding the Head more protectively than ever.

"We make it," she said in an indignant voice. "We have Buddha. He protect *us* because we protect *Him.*"

I had no time to discuss metaphysics. We were dropping rapidly toward the *wat* while I maneuvered the craft into some kind of landing position. Before us was the large Temple of Dawn, at the very edge of the river. I hoped all the flowers and offerings Po had placed before our spirit house had been noted. A vertical stone embankment rose from the river's edge to about three feet above ground level. We'd have to hurdle it. Leading toward the temple was a wide walkway that ended abruptly at a small, block-built building. It had to be too narrow for this, and besides it was lined by a short wrought-iron fence. And besides that, the runway at Wat Arun International ran back only about seventy-five feet.

Not long enough.

I pushed the horn to warn the few monks and tourists that we were parking. Of course there wasn't one, but I could see them scattering helter-skelter anyway. It didn't matter in any case—it didn't look like we would clear the reinforced quay as we dropped out of the sky at forty knots and slowing.

And we didn't—the stone ridge sheared off the wheel

struts. Everything turned into a loud, rasping, spinning blur as the plane belly flopped onto the walkway, the fence ripping off its wings and struts like they were fly's wings as we skidded sickeningly down the length of the walk, sparks flying every which way, us banging around inside the cockpit like a beans in a child's rattle. Finally, we came to a stop inches away from an enormous and tranquil stone Buddha holding His palm up to us.

"The eagle has landed," a voice in space said, sounding vaguely like mine. Then, for the second time in twenty-four hours, everything went as black as the dark side of the moon.

———— • ————

Tysee was wrong about reincarnation. But there certainly is a heaven. What else could explain this angel hovering over me? Then I came to my senses and realized that for better or worse I was still alive, and that Tysee was trying frantically to unstrap me from my seat. Something burning reached up into my nostrils.

Fire!

My head cleared rapidly. I fought with the seat-belt catch. It was jammed. Pulling out my knife, I quickly cut through the restraining strap. The door was jammed too. Jabbering men on the outside were fighting with it. Tysee tumbled out through her door as a rescuer yanked it open. I clambered over the seat after her. Almost forgetting, I reached back in and grabbed my hat.

She looked at me expectantly, the bundle in her arms. A crowd was rapidly gathering—monks, locals, a few bleached, overweight tourists. Children and dogs were running in from every direction. Flames were beginning to eat up from the undercarriage. There wasn't much to burn, but empty tanks are more explosive than full ones.

"*Toy lung!*" I shouted, urging the crowd. "*Com lung ra-berd!*"

They quickly began to scatter.

The loud *wap* of chopper blades grew near, sending sand flying. The Huey was flaring back to land on the river quay.

I grabbed Tysee by the hand and we ran out a side entrance in the wall, then down a path that ran parallel to it. Teetering teak-slat houses grew up in a jumble beside us. Banana trees with garbage at their bases were scattered about.

The sound of the explosion when the empty tanks blew hurried us across a narrow footbridge over a small *klong*, the first of many canals that crisscross Thon Buri in a maze. Ahead was the first of the larger *klongs*, half-jammed with small sampans selling vegetables, noodles and flowers. It was late in the morning but the floating market was still in action.

Turning, I could see soldiers with M-16s double-timing down the trail we had just come up. They'd quickly maneuvered around the burning wreckage. Before us was a small quay. An old Thai woman was stepping from it into a long-tailed boat operated by a young man. He stood at the back beside a four-cylinder car motor mounted so that it balanced on a fulcrum at the stern. His hand was on a handle protruding from the front of the engine; out of the rear dipped the ten-foot-long drive shaft, a small propeller at the end.

"Pom chow reu-ub!" I shouted, shoving my pocketful of mostly purple bills at him. *"Coon pby! Coon pby!"* I added, before new passengers could embark.

He stared in wonder at the windfall of 500-baht notes I was pressing into his hand, but made no move to leave his beloved boat.

"They close!" cried Tysee beside me, looking back.

I jammed my hand into my pocket and yanked out the gun. His eyes turned from saucers to plates and he quickly scrambled onto the dock. A second later we roared away, startling commuters and frustrating the soldiers who impotently waved their guns. In moments we were skimming at thirty miles an hour down the narrow canal, our wake flipping sampans left and right, and dumping their contents and captains into the sticky water. Lampshade hats bobbed behind us in our wake.

We careened out of the *soi klong* and onto a main artery. Other long-tailed passenger boats like ours were skimming up and down at fast idle. I spotted some passengers at a quay, pulled in and took them on, ignoring their curious stares at seeing a *farang* at the throttle, then gunned out into midstream again. I pulled off my shirt and hat and

shoved them under the seat, then offered my last bill, a
500-baht note, to an old Thai couple sitting just in front of
me. They smiled and made many *wais* of gratitude, and
handed over their lampshade hats. With my constant tan, I
might be able to pass for a tall Thai. Tysee's black outfit
already blended well, but she quickly stuffed her long hair
beneath her blouse and donned one of the hats.

I couldn't have done it sooner. The helicopter flapped
low down the *soi klong* we had just left behind, hesitated
at the intersection, and turned up the main *klong* in our
direction. The dragonfly beat slowly down the wide canal,
flying so low the draft from its big blades slapped the
choppy water smooth and silvery. Passengers in our boat
pointed and looked up, hanging onto their hats as the
downblast from the big bird flapped through their clothing
like a typhoon.

I ignored the bird, having a job to do and no time for
sightseeing. I had rice to put on the table. Another day,
another baht. I maneuvered the long boat up to the next
quay, dropped off the old passengers, took on new. Tysee
collected the fares, just whatever was handed to her.

We reached the mouth of the canal, where it merged
with the mighty Chao Phrya, and nudged up to a wide
quay. The eggbeater pulled out over the river a few yards,
looked both ways hesitantly, then turned and began another slow sweep back up the main *klong,* flattening the
water below it once again. Angered vendors shook their
fists and screamed out in shrill voices.

"Set lao Bangkok!" I called out, taking on a huddle of
old, shuffling Chinese with many bags of produce, having
to wait a moment while an old lady in her lampshade
danced up to us with a fully laden *bap,* two baskets bobbing and balancing from either end of a shoulder yoke.

Tysee clutched her package as firmly as ever. Then the
newly named *Chinatown Express* roared into high gear
and out into the flotilla of boats, speeding across the
choppy river to its destination.

EIGHT

Teahouse of the Setting Sun

"THIS REAL . . . GROTTY. How come you know place look like . . . this?" Tysee asked suspiciously as I closed and carefully locked the door to the little room. She was holding the bundle even more protectively than she had on the plane.

We were above one of the ubiquitous, ramshackle teahouses of Chinatown that front for cheap, three-dollar-a-throw brothels. Outside the room we'd rented was a complex of narrow halls with doors off either side every ten feet that led into cubicles just large enough to accommodate a double bed, a small table with a tiny hot plate for making tea, a spittoon and two feet of foot space. Slouching and lounging in the doorways were the girls, some as young as fifteen and sixteen, many of them pretty. Fortunately, we were in a deluxe, a little away from the main action. Ours had been an unusual request, but my very last 500—the one Tysee had given me and which I had stuck in a special crease in my wallet—had quickly persuaded the wizened old pimp to rent us a room in his whorehouse, it being enough to order in at least six of his inventory, if we so wished. The problem was it now left me with only the small amount of change generated by our water-taxi business.

After abandoning the boat we had quickly lost ourselves in the Casbahtic maze of narrow, twisting streets—a kaleidoscope of strange smells and clashing colors, jammed with shuffling crowds with singsong voices. We had peeled off to take shortcuts through the back doors of restaurants and shops selling everything from smoked duck Frisbee to rhino horn to paper houses for use by the dead in their next life.

"It's not grotty," I told her for now. "It's just grungy. A *friend* of mine told me about this place," I half-lied. "His name is, ah, ah, Snake. Yeah! Snake! Perhaps you'll meet him someday."

"I not know if I want to," she replied skeptically. "Why we come *here?* I no like way dirty old man wink at us."

She looked around as if the place was crawling. An enormous cockroach scurried out from under the bed, didn't like what it saw either, and disappeared back under.

"Security," I explained. "Guards the place. A watch-roach. Comes with the room at no extra charge." That didn't convince her.

From next door issued the crunching squeak of bed-springs being exercised, the sound increasing in tempo, and making me wince again. Fortunately he finished seconds later—a premature ejaculator.

"Listen, we don't dare go to my place and we need rest —we haven't slept for two days. We can order up food from downstairs. A regular hotel wouldn't be as safe. They'll never think of looking for us here. We can lie low for a while until we figure what to do next."

"Well . . . this certainly *low,*" she replied, resigning herself to the logic, fingering the red-vinyl mattress and the threadbare set of sheets I had talked the old man into giving us. I knew, because, ah, Snake had told me, that sheets weren't normally provided.

She disdainfully peered around. The walls were landlord green, the floor cracked and chipped linoleum, but there *was* a toilet, of sorts—a hole in the floor flanked by two porcelain footpads. In place of a roll of toilet paper there

was water dripping from a tap into a rusty tin can. The bog
was fine with me and her. With no contact between bottom and top, so to speak, it was more hygienic.

In the bedroom, there was a window with a view of
rusting tin roofs, the nearest of them, I noted, only six feet
below the window. I pulled the floppy wooden shutters
fast and flicked on the bare, low-cal light bulb. An ancient
ceiling fan shunted the hot, sweaty air around.

"Now, let's have a look at the treasure," I whispered
expectantly, trying to ignore the sounds of springs warming up in the other adjoining bedroom.

She listened for a moment to the thumping action next
door, shook her head with silent disgust and carefully
placed the bundle down on the middle of the bed. She
pressed her hands together in a reverent *wai*, then began
to carefully unwrap the black bindings. The neighbors
reached a crescendo next door, then fell still. I was about to
speak when the welcome silence was broken by a loud fart
through the same wall. Tysee screwed up her face in dis-
taste and anger, but kept at her task.

She peeled away a corner of the rough Tibetan cotton,
revealing soft, yellowing linens. Underneath those was the
innermost silk wrapping, on which was painted an ancient
thankya. She lifted back another corner.

It revealed a glistening, golden cheek.

Another corner slipped away. A shiny, carefully formed
golden ear revealed itself. Then the final two corners fell
away and the Buddha Head, lying on its side, lay exposed
before us.

We both gasped at the same time.

Unconsciously, we knelt beside it for a better look, with
Tysee consciously keeping her head below the level of it, in
Buddhist fashion, now that her work was done.

"Jesus Christ . . ." I muttered in disbelief, the sounds
from the other room forgotten.

"No. Buddha!" Tysee said, turning sharply to me.

"Same-same thing," I said, feeling embarrassed about
the blasphemy. "The real McCoy. . . ."

"McCoy . . . ?"

"Yeah. Like . . . forget it. It's really not important. But,
by God! Look at it!"

It was smaller than I had expected. Its surface showed

the exquisitely sculpted and highly polished features of a very old man, in the yellower, purer gold of the time. The artist, clearly a master, must have studied the Enlightened One personally to have captured so many intimate details, to have read the spiritual contours of the Being beyond and behind the mere physical ones. Whoever he was, he had captured his subject with a love and passion and understanding beyond brilliance.

I gently shifted the Head to let the beam of light from the crack in the shutters pierce the hollow cranium. The bone was yellowing; at the very top of the skull was an unmistakable bulge that found expression on the exterior. In today's world, the bulge would have been considered a slight, but noticeable, cranial deformation; in the Buddha's time, because of his enlightenment, it had been seen as the seat of His godliness.

"I wonder what happened here?" I asked, pointing to a spot near the base where a wedge of bone had been cut out, leaving the gold behind.

Tysee didn't seem to notice, she was so caught up in her rapture. Delicately, I placed the Head upright again.

The Buddha's features exuded opposites that should have clashed irreconcilably but instead were in harmony and peace, their juxtaposition creating a power beyond all limits. The violence and painful suffering of human life blended with the deepest tranquillity and pleasure in a way that transported a witness beyond either. The beauty of youth; the perpetual cycle of death and transfiguration; and the process of beginning to die from the moment you were born, only to be born again from the instant of death, which is not a death at all but a new beginning into another form of life, one that is all-spiritual, all-material, all-eternal —these things were mirrored on His timeless face.

Yet His features were, in themselves quite nondescript. His lips were strong but gentle, His chin ordinary, His nose plain and hooking slightly with age. The slightly prominent cheekbones hinted at His race in particular; His narrow eyes, slightly upcurled at the corners, spoke of it in general. The Buddha evidently had kept His hair strong and healthy into His eighth decade, as the gold showed it to be tightly curled. The elongated earlobes hung gracefully down in golden loops, much thinner that has been depicted in sculpture since.

Yet it was the eyes that commanded the greatest attention; they acted as magnets to one's own. Planted in their sockets were two large and absolutely flawless pigeon-blood rubies, the finest gems I had ever seen, that burned with a life and sagacity that lifted them beyond mere stones.

I felt Tysee's light touch on my arm. How long we had knelt hypnotized before the sacred relic, I don't know—time and existence had for the moment lost all meaning. I only knew I was moved to the roots of my soul, and ashamed that I had even entertained thoughts, no matter how false, along Wolfgang's line. Even my foolhardy risk of life and limb seemed to explain itself in some mysterious way. Even the possible loss of Patpong seemed to pale to insignificance. But then it had anyway since that first night with her.

Tysee began reverently to wrap the Head. The sparkle in its mysterious, all-seeing eyes hardly faded as she covered them delicately with silk.

A heavy exhaustion from two vigorous days without sleep began to meld with the rich emotions I felt. With both of us beginning to feel the lumps and bumps from the one-point landing, we spontaneously and wordlessly crawled out of our clothes. We curled up together on the solid, industrial-strength bed, oblivious to the grunts of pleasure issuing from through the walls, the Buddha Head lying protectively between us, and slept.

———— • ————

"Oh God . . . well, I'm not surprised," I said flatly, after flipping over the folded Bangkok *Post* and scanning the front-page headlines.

The old pimp had brought it up with our very late breakfast, given us another leering wink, then shuffled off.

"What is it?" Tysee asked, chopsticking rice.

"It's on the front page, thankfully not headlined. See? The whole story is here . . . *everything.* Here's a picture taken from the helicopter, with my hand over my face. They even have a description of us, damn it. Oh, my God . . . listen to this."

And I read for her:

> The single-engine plane was identified from
> photos as being an aircraft drug kingpin Kun San
> is believed to have owned, and has kept at his
> Kwan Mae hideaway for some years.
>
> Military and police spokesmen say they can of-
> fer no logical reason why Kun San's plane would
> be flying so blatantly into Thai air space.
>
> Speculation about the reason for the mysterious
> flight and elusive behavior of the two occupants,
> one a white male and the other a young Thai
> woman is rife.
>
> The investigation is continuing.

"What do we do now? How we get Head back to monastery?"

"Well, the first thing we have to do is get some money.
I'm broke. And what little you have won't take us very
far."

I stuffed in some sticky rice.

"How we do that?"

"I'll phone Nog and Po and see if it's safe to go over to
the house. We've slept practically twenty-four hours. It'll
be dark soon and it's only walking distance. I'll also try to
phone François and the Wolf. I know Wolfgang is supposed
to handle communications, but frankly I don't trust him. I
think he'd like to sell it."

"Wolfgang want to sell?"

I described my conversations with him. She looked troubled, and held the Head closer to her breast.

"Getting this Head back may be more trouble that we
realize. We just can't fly up to Kathmandu."

"Why no?"

"Security. Particularly at Tribhuvan Airport in Kathmandu. They're always looking for people smuggling gold
in and artifacts out. Security is so tough there they search
you just as carefully going in as out. Toughest airport in
Asia. But we've done our bit—I just want to get this into
the proper hands as quickly as possible. And we have to get
out of here. If we read the paper, the old buzzard with the
gimpy eye possibly does too, though I don't think he's the
type to put one and one together—except for his business,

of course. As for my hat, I'm sorry to say, but it'll have to go. Too easily recognizable."

Reluctantly, I picked up the battered old chapeau that had been with me through countless jungles and tossed it into the corner.

"What I do?"

"You stay right here and take care of the home front. Putter around the house, sit and watch the soaps—that sort of thing. But don't leave the room. *Don't* even answer the door unless I knock twice, pause, then knock twice again. That's our signal. I'll take the key in any case. Do you think you'll be all right?"

She looked at me and nodded with determination. I knew no one was going to get the Head away from her without one hell of a fight.

"You be *careful,"* was the last thing she said.

———— • ————

"Sawadee ca."

It was Po's voice. It sounded normal.

"It's me. Everything okay around the house?"

"Ah! I so happy you phone, Mr. River! Just now Mr. Stambuck come visit and I say you no here. He about to leave," she said in English.

Brock? What the hell would he be dropping by for? I wasn't in any mood for houseguests.

"Is it social or what?"

"No. He say much important he talk to you. He going to leave his number. What I tell him? You want talk?"

I pondered for a moment. I was only a couple of blocks away.

"No," I replied. "Tell him I'll be there in a few minutes."

I hung up, and headed out of the smelly phone booth and down the rabbit warren of narrow streets to my home. The twisting alleys were empty and dry as I rounded the final corner to the house, the monsoon finally giving strong indications it was breaking once and for all.

I was looking at the soft shadows the moon and stars were casting on the brown teak of the bordering shacks, when I heard a tuk-tuk backfire twice. It startled me. I wouldn't have given it a second thought except that it had come from within my courtyard. I certainly don't own a *samlor,* and there's no room for one when my car is there.

I quickly blended into the shadows across from the large swinging doors, then drew my pistol and waited, listening. A bent-over old man with straggly white whiskers hobbled by one way; a young woman with a jug of water on her hip strolled by the other. No one paid attention to the reports but me.

Nothing happened. I began to think that the sound was probably some long-tailed boat on the river just beyond. Yeah, that's it, I decided, shoving the gun back into my belt. They backfire too.

I slipped across the street to the spirit house in the shadow of the recessed courtyard entrance and reached through the small door with my finger, feeling for the key.

In a second, I had my back pressed to the wall and the Walther in my hand again. It wasn't a noise, or a moving shadow, or even a strange smell that had suddenly primed my attention. It was the key—it wasn't there.

I glanced at the door. It was closed. I padded closer. My hand found the latch and gave it a careful turn.

It responded. The courtyard door wasn't locked. It was always locked.

I listened a moment, heard nothing, then very quietly opened the door a fraction, keeping to one side, behind the concrete wall. The distant mutter of rising and falling voices seemed to indicate the door wasn't being watched. I slipped through and quietly closed it behind me, then crouched behind my car. The birds were nervous in their cages, shunting back and forth on their bars.

Lights were on inside the house. Through the shutters I could see a tall, very thin man in a dark suit. He was haranguing someone below him on the floor, though that was hidden from me, the windowsill being too high and too distant. The man clearly wasn't Brock.

I began to creep forward. My foot hit something soft and I almost tripped. I bent down. It was Raffles. He was limp. The odor of almonds rose from his dead body. A piece of meat lay beside his head. Cyanide.

Those bastards, I swore to myself, my teeth clenching. My fear disappeared in the wake of the outrage I now felt.

I crept forward like a cat, crouching from flowerpot to

divan, drawing closer to the building. The man shouted at her to shut up and she began to wail. It was Po. From somewhere deeper in their living quarters rose another wail, that of Pac, the baby.

"Do not make a move! Let it cry!" the voice barked viciously, in an accent I couldn't catch for a moment.

Slipping up the stone steps onto the veranda, I crept to just below and beside the window. The other voice became clearer, more familiar. It was a voice in pain.

"I don't know where the guy is, I tell you," it gasped. "I just got here myself."

"Bullshit, Brock Stambuck," said a voice as taut as a bent steel band, and made even more menacing by what I now recognized as a thick, Slavic accent. "I believe you just about as much as I believe you are with the Drug Enforcement Agency. We know who you are. You know the rules. Tell me what I want to know and I give you a clean death. A bullet in the brain. No pain. Just like the one you give here to Abul and—"

I didn't hear the last name—it was lost in a gasp of pain from Brock as someone delivered him a vicious kick.

Where was Nog? I peeked over the edge of the sill, through a tangle of orchids that grew out of a flower box. Three bodies lay scattered on the floor, Po in hysterics over one of them. The tall intruder was half-facing me, and gesticulating angrily over another figure, who lay partially on my sofa. The tall man was tamping his bleeding mouth with a handkerchief and was murderously angry. In his other hand was a .22 revolver, a large silencer exaggerating its size. He turned my way. I ducked. He changed position, his long shadow nervously shifting on the wall.

"The Head—where it is?" the voice spat in the thick accent. "This be your last chance. I have no patience."

My ears perked.

"I don't know what you're talking about."

Another kick. This time the gasp was more like a deep, deathly groan. Brock fought for breath. I moved my head up again.

"I no have time to work on you like I enjoy with *Americans,*" he said, as if shitting on the word. "Maybe I can get more out of you if I go work on the woman. I show you what it look like to shoot a Thai whore in the guts."

Pac was now screaming somewhere in the background, frightened even more by Po's hysterics. The intruder swung his gun around to aim at Po.

The sound of her wailing almost covered the report of my pistol. The tall man jerked with surprise, then instinctively whirled, still dangerous. My second shot slammed dead center into his chest, sending him tumbling backward over a pedestal table displaying a Ming Dynasty teapot I had saved after a treasure diving escapade with Snake. The rare porcelain smashed to pieces on the floor.

"Shit," I swore under my breath as I covered the room, my trigger finger twitching.

"Lee? That you?" groaned the body on the couch.

"Yeah," I snapped in high tension.

"Good man," he wheezed. "I *thought* I recognized the sound of my old kraut slammer. Get in here. They're all dead. And I'm half that way."

I hurried into the room, kicked the three guns I could see away from the sprawled intruders, and surveyed the room. It looked like a slaughterhouse floor. There were four bodies splayed out among the knocked-over furniture. Blood was everywhere.

I stared at Brock. He was slowly bending over to pick up his Magnum. He carefully set it beside him on the sofa, then raised one of his porterhouse-sized hands to a wet, red shoulder. Blood dribbled from the edge of his lip. He wiped it off with his free hand, looked at it, then groped for a pillow and pressed it against the larger wound.

I heard a sob and jerked my head in Po's direction. She was in shock, her entire body shuddering, her eyes wide, her hands on Nog's back. I quickly checked him. He was lying facedown, limp. Blood was oozing out his side and across the floor.

"Check his heart," Brock said. "He may not be dead. He took one but I think it was his banging his head that knocked him out. It made a helluva noise against that coffee table."

I did that, after quickly straightening the table and setting my pistol down within easy reach. I put my ear to his back. There was a strong beat. A quick inspection revealed a swelling black-and-blue bruise on one temple. I tried to assure Po that he was all right but it didn't seem to sink in.

Then she finally heard Pac and rushed off, returning a moment later, still pale and wide-eyed, and rapidly rocking the infant, as it pressed its gumless teeth to her breast.

I turned my attention momentarily to Brock.

"Don't worry about me, I've had worse," he wheezed, his eyes showing suppressed pain. "This is just a skinned knee in this business. Make sure your friend is okay. He's pretty brave. Pretty effective too."

I rushed into the bathroom and grabbed some towels and tape. Gently, I rolled Nog over on his back. Po's hand went to her head when she saw the blood. I pressed a towel against the point of entry on the side of his waist—a flesh wound. Calmed by my familiar presence, Po returned to rocking the baby and crying. When I was finished, I turned to attend Brock's wounds. I helped him pull his sports coat off. He had taken one through the meaty portion of his shoulder. The wound was clean but bleeding copiously. He might have some broken ribs from the kicking but it was going to take the eyes of an X-ray to see that.

"Sorry about your sofa and all that," he apologized while I ripped his shirt apart and pressed the shreds and some folded facecloths against the entry hole, then taped them on. "Pretty fast boy, that Nog. They got here right after you phoned. You were pretty lucky you didn't arrive much sooner. I was just coming out of the can when they burst in. The lady saw the guns and went hysterical. The skinny guy knocked her to the floor. He shouldn't have done that. Nog just let loose with his foot and caught the bastard in the mug, which was quite a feat, considering how tall he was. Nog put him out of action for a second but one of the other sons of bitches here touched him. Still, it gave me a break and I yanked out my bean shooter and did him and the other fucker in. But before I could do the tall mother, he numbered me from the floor. It happened very fast, but then it always does." His voice seized for a moment from a stab of pain.

His ribs *were* in rough shape.

"And fortunately you didn't turn out to be a pansy yourself," he added. "Hey! What are you doing?"

"Phoning an ambulance, of course. What the hell do you think—a pizza joint?"

"Put it down. We have people who'll take care of all this.

Set me up with the best medical attention. Clean up the joint after these bloody Bulgarians and leave it as good as new. Take care of Po and the kid in a safe house. Keep the cops out of it, if they even find out. And it won't get in the papers. Let me give you a number."

We stared at each other, the receiver still in my hand. "Who the hell is 'we'? And how do you know these guys are Bulgarian?"

"I'll tell you later. Just make the fucking call first, okay?" He recited a number from memory.

"Now, when they answer, just tell them this: say you're a friend of Harry's calling and that there's five letters over here, three of them are canceled and two need stamps. And when you give them the address, reverse the numbers. Also tell them we need a janitor. You got it?"

I stared at him for another moment, then punched the buttons on the phone. A cool, neutral male voice answered with a simple hello. I passed him the information. The voice said, "Right, thank you," very courteously, and hung up. I looked into the buzzing earpiece for a moment before setting the receiver back in its cradle.

"Some of the boys in the shoe department will take care of these suckers," Brock said, surveying the carnage.

Blood was oozing into my Kashmiri carpets, into the sofas.

"Shoe department?"

"Yeah. As in concrete flippers. We got some wops working in Shoes. They're not really wops but we call them that." He forced a laugh, then winced violently, the pain overwhelming him.

"Who the hell are these guys?" I asked, my voice high.

"Why don't you check? They got pockets, you know."

One lay in a heap in the center of the floor, half on his side, staring vacantly at the Chinese paintings on the ceiling, obviously not enjoying them. He had the kind of mug that has a five o'clock shadow by nine in the morning. At first glance I had taken him for Mediterranean, but on second I saw he was too big-boned and thick. Brock had said Bulgarian. A second body lay flopped on its face like a big, blond ragdoll. He wasn't as messy. I rolled him over. And froze.

"Jesus Christ, it's the Tass man!" I exclaimed, staring in

surprise into the wide-open but equally vacant eyes of the local Red rag man. I had been introduced to him at the Foreign Correspondents' Club one time.

"*Tass* my sweet little ass," Brock grunted. "He's fucking KGB like all their so-called journalists are. And his name isn't Jesus Christ—he's Russian, not Puerto Rican. It's Yuri Denisovich Drapakov."

A Siberian chill ran through my body. What was this talk of the KGB? Bulgarians? What the hell had I gotten myself involved in?

"What is he doing here?"

"The Tasshole here who you should be damned glad that I just sent to the great gulag in the sky was just helping the tall guy and his friend make sure they got the right guy, is my guess. It also means you probably weren't meant to live since you would have had to have seen him."

I let it sink in a minute. I didn't like this dead feeling. Too cold. Stiff.

"What the hell do they want to recognize me for?"

"That's what I'm here to find out."

"What the hell exactly *are* you doing here, Brock?" I demanded. "You're supposed to be a drug cop!"

"Well, you should be damned glad I *am* here. And no I'm not, really—a drug cop, that is. It's just a dandy cover to get me into strange places with a minimum of suspicion and a maximum of local support. I always liked your cover better, though. More romantic. Jungle collector."

"It isn't a cover, and I don't collect jungles," I said, putting my arm around Po's shoulder and holding her. She was calming down as Nog began to groan and show vital signs, though it still looked like he wasn't about to come around for awhile.

"Well, you know what I mean. It'd be damned good cover for someone in *my* business. And I think you've probably guessed what it is. I *do* punch a clock for the government, just not the DEA. "

"The CIA . . . ?"

"A star on the wall for the kid with the beard."

"Jesus Christ," I said in amazement. Everything was going too fast for me.

"There you go again. *My* name isn't Jesus Christ either." He pointed to the tall, skinny guy I had dropped. He lay there like some kind of dead spider, the backs of his hairy hands reminded me of tarantulas. He must have been six-foot-five, but couldn't have weighed over 150.

"His name sure the hell isn't Jesus Christ either. Go on, check 'em out. You might recognize him from the newspapers. I can tell you who he is but the news isn't good."

"I've never seen him before in my life," I said, leaving Po and moving over to the body littering my living room floor.

"Haven't you? Then you don't pay much attention to the pictures they print in the papers. You just blasted one of the biggies. Remember the Pope thing a while ago? When the Turk tried to knock him off in St. Peter's Square? Remember the Agca guy pointed to a Bulgarian so-called diplomat as being behind it? This tall guy is him. His name is Major Fazidar Amur and the other bloody mess was his top lieutenant, Abul Muskad. Muskad here was in the crowd at St. Peter's in case Agca missed. Agca got in the first shot though, and this guy ran away but someone spotted him and got a picture of him from behind. Later, Agca admitted he wasn't alone and fingered them both out of rogue's gallery we in Western Intelligence share. The guy above them, the real biggie who managed to stay out of the papers—but we got his number anyway, a Colonel Theodore Skibinsky—is here in Bangkok and is going to be fairly pissed when he learns what happened to his top guns. We know he was meeting with the local KGB chief, we've been keeping track of them. These boys arrived a day after Skibinsky, about three days ago. All three work— I suppose 'worked' is the proper word to describe it—for the Bulgarian Secret Service, but they're just a branch plant of Moscow. This happily dead tall son of a bitch was a genuine sadist. He was head of the Bulgarian team's hit squad, which is really the KGB assassination team. I don't think his mother or wife will weep when he doesn't come home for dinner."

"KGB *assassination* team . . . ?"

I shook my head, then started to go through the tall Bulgarian's pockets. He had a billfold crammed with large-denomination American bills. I also found Bulgarian and international driver's licenses in his name, along with other identification, the same, dark, stern face glaring out from each item. In other pockets were Visa, gold American Express, and yellow Aloha Travel Club cards. And a number of business cards giving various names and professions, all from the same printer and in the same style. There were papers connected with the Bulgarian Foreign Service, including a well-used diplomatic passport. I skimmed through it and saw stamps for Hong Kong, Tripoli, Athens, Damascus, New Delhi, Colombo. A number for Karachi and Kabul. Manila. A lot for Hanoi and Ho Chi Minh City. I pocketed the bills and threw the passport to Brock. In another pocket I found three more passports, all with his picture, none with the same name. Thick folders of unsigned American Express traveler's checks in denominations of 100 filled another pocket. I stuffed all the currencies into my own pockets.

When I didn't say anything, Brock went on.

"Amur here had proven his stuff. Remember the Bulgarian writer in London back in '78 or so who got 'accidentally' poked with an umbrella while he was walking across Waterloo Bridge and croaked a few days later? No? Georgi Markov was his name. He wrote nasty things about his old home. We're pretty sure it was this guy who did the hit. After that, the KGB recommended and the Bulgarians followed and put him in charge of the hit squad. He did okay till the Pope thing, then to lower his profile they assigned him to the Far East."

"You're kidding," I said, pulling a handful of stuff out of his back pocket. His comb was greasy, the toothpicks and Kleenex both used.

Overcoming my hesitation, I turned to the Tass man's pockets, and found the usual. Wallet with press cards. Change. Business cards. Pen and scraps of paper. Then I noticed a slight bulge in his breast pocket—the key to my gate, with its chain.

"How the *hell* would they know this key was in the spirit house?" I asked, holding it up.

Po was sniffing, holding Nog's hand and rocking back and forth with the baby.

"Don't be surprised at *nothing.* They probably got a dossier on you. You're suspect, you know—ex-Military Intelligence, hanging around. The Lion's Den, and you know what kind of a crowd *that* is. Like I say, it sounds like a good cover, jungle collecting and all that, getting into places that are off the beaten track and with a good excuse. You've probably been shadowed off and on for some time. They probably found you were more or less legit, but they still knew your habits. And where you put things, like spare keys and so on."

"Oh, that's great. Makes one feel secure in one's own home."

"What have you got there, Jungle Boy?" His voice was hoarse with pain.

I was weighing in my hand a package of Marlboros I had taken out of Muskad's pocket. It was much too heavy.

"I don't know," I said, flipping open the top.

None of the cigarettes had been smoked. I tugged at a filter: they all came out in one section—but only the filters. They'd been glued together to hide something black and heavy. When I turned the package over a tiny pistol fell into my palm. I held it up for Brock to see. He stared at it in equal surprise.

"Well, I'll be damned," he exclaimed. "I've only seen one of them before in my life, back during training. It's a Khokhlov Special!"

"A . . . what?"

"Khokhlov. He was a KGB hitman in the fifties who defected. He brought a gun like that with him."

"Never heard of him," I said.

"People forget. You were too young. It runs on batteries and shoots two poison pellets. I didn't know they still used those things. Must have modified it a little." He reached for the Tinkertoy pistol as best he could.

While Brock examined it, I continued fishing in the Bulgarian's pockets. I pulled in his passport, also diplomatic, and flipped through it.

"Christ, this guy got around as much as the tall guy! Lots for Hanoi and Ho Chi Minh City again. Manila. Seoul. Kabul. A couple or three for New Delhi. Karachi. Colombo. Jakarta. All over the bloody Far East."

"Well, it makes sense."

"What makes sense?"

Brock paused while he shifted his weight on the sofa. I finished rifling Muskad's pockets. There was also a slew of duplicate passports with false names, some baht, and change from a variety of countries, together with buck knife. I pocketed the money.

I took up my Walther from the coffee table and plugged the clip with fresh shells. On a whim, I grabbed the buck knife and the Khokhlov that Brock had set down and shoved them in my pockets. He looked at me skeptically but said nothing.

"What makes sense?" I asked, repeating the question.

"The passport stamps. Wherever there's trouble those bozos are there, like supplying arms and support money to the Tamils trying to break away in Sri Lanka. The Russians would love to have access to the port at Trincomalee. You probably didn't know that the Sinhalese government quietly expelled eight Soviets five days after the initial flare-up there back in '83. They have contacts with the New People's Army in the Philippines as well. And when they divert their heavies from games like that it means you must have something important they want. What is it?"

"I really have no idea."

"Bullshit," he said firmly and flatly.

I recalled that a CIA man had briefed François. It was no use being completely coy.

"What do *you* know about it all?"

He looked at me straight on, then shook his head slightly. He knew I held the cards.

"We intercepted some traffic from their embassies, here in Bangkok and in Kathmandu. They were using their double codes, the ones they save for top-priority stuff, that we haven't been able to completely unscramble yet. But we know that it's got to do with a telephone call from Kathmandu to New York about some kind of 'head.' Today we deciphered something about this 'head' supposedly being here in Bangkok. And I didn't miss that the late major here asked about it too."

He rested, breathing laboriously for a few seconds waiting for me to say something. I didn't.

"Whatever it is," he went on, "those bohunks in the Kremlin are taking it very seriously. How they get all their information, we don't know."

"So what's this all have to do with me?" I asked, knowing full well what he was going to say.

"About a week ago, and then again today, your name

came down the wire. Believe me, I was surprised as hell when they told me, since I know you. This one today, there was also mention of Kun San."

He scrutinized me, looking for a reaction. He got one. François had said that he had given my name to Abbot Tengid. I fell back in an armchair, flabbergasted, and surveyed the carnage before me.

"The KGB *have my* name? They're interested in *me?* What the hell for?"

"You tell me. For your own good, you tell me. Did that airplane crash over at Wat Arun have anything to do with you? There was also something about a stolen plane in the message today. I see your clothes are a little ripped up and you're a bit banged up. You loosely fit the description. You're *farang.* While we're at it, if you're involved, so who's the broad?"

I didn't answer, stunned that so much was known. Even the Kun San connection!

"I'll tell you something," Brock said, getting exasperated. "It's top-priority KGB business. It's causing a bigger flurry of transmissions than anything we've ever seen here. Anything the KGB are interested in, *we're* interested in. You're one of our people. We're here to protect you and protect our people back home. Whatever you have appears to be of some kind of vital importance to them. That means it is to us, too. If you don't tell me now, we'll learn about it sooner or later. And it's better *sooner* than later. Now, what the hell is it?"

I thought about it for a second. It obviously wasn't going to remain a secret very long. And I certainly didn't want to take on the KGB alone. I nodded my head, took a deep breath, and spilled out everything I knew, though I kept one detail in reserve—where the Head was. Brock listened, ears wide open, his wound seemingly forgotten. When I was through, he nodded slowly and deeply.

"It makes sense. Yeah, it makes damned good sense."

"What does? Why would they want the Buddha Head?"

"It's quite simple, really. One of the most important movers and motivators of man is religion. Gorbachev might be talking religion a little more but the Reds are still damned cautious about it despite all this *glasnost* stuff. They know very intimately how much trouble religious revivals can be, in fact they have one going on in their belly right now, with the Moslems in south-central Russia upset about the invasion of Afghanistan. The last thing they want is a Buddhist revival on their Far East flank—or anywhere in the world for that matter. Buddhists all over the world would be fired up if the head of Buddha appeared. There's still a lot of thin ice around, despite the Great Thaw—just ask someone in the gulag how much *glasnost* is affecting him. The KGB is still bigger than all the Western agencies combined, and their methods haven't changed. You just don't hear about them—because they're secret, of course."

I nodded. His reasoning was sound. In fact it was obvious.

"But *how* would they know about me grabbing the Head in Kwan Mae? I haven't been close to a phone since I was up there. They couldn't have tapped me!"

Brock thought for a moment, fatigue showing more and more on his sweaty face. Po was still tending to her husband, fluttering over him like a butterfly.

"This is an outside chance, but I'd never put it past the bastards. We know for a fact that the KGB has been encouraging many countries—their client states is the right lingo —that are into drug-dealing. That hasn't changed since *glasnost* either. There's the Bulgarians again, who openly allow heroin to cross their territory on its way to Europe from Turkey. And we know the Russkies have been up in the Triangle, giving support to the various so-called liberation groups. And we also know that they were up at Kun San's some years ago. Apparently he booted them out a few years later, but it's entirely in keeping with their nature to leave microphones wired to whatever electrical source there is so they can keep tabs on things. That, or else they've got paid informers to keep an ear to the ground for them. Probably both."

I nodded slowly as I remembered the mysterious *farang* I had seen in Kwan Mae years before. Tysee had said he was Russian. I was beginning to feel the full impact of what was coming down on me.

"My God. What should I do?" I said, almost to myself.

"I'd suggest turning the Head you told me about over to

us. We'll get it back to where it belongs. And it'll be all hush-hush."

It didn't sound like a bad idea. I'd wanted to unload it before it burned my fingers. And I did want to make sure it got back to where it was supposed to be, though I wondered if it would be safe there anymore. Brock looked at me expectantly.

But then I thought of my arrangements with François. And I thought of Tysee.

I shook my head.

"What the hell do you mean by that?" he demanded.

"I can't give it over, Brock. At least not yet. It's not just my decision."

He stared at me like I was some kind of crackpot.

"You dumb shithead! Do you have any *idea* what you're up against?"

"Watch your fucking language. You're a guest in my house," I said, and then I headed for my room.

I spun the dials of my wall safe, filled my pockets with more money, then hurriedly shoveled toilet gear and clothes into a small knapsack. As an afterthought, I threw in my Instamatic and some rolls of special passport film, a bottle of peroxide, and all the forgotten makeup from all the forgotten girls that was lying around. On a whim, I stuffed in the cobra bikini Tysee had left behind. I headed for the laundry room and crammed in some of Po's washing. Seeing some Aussie T-shirts in a neat pile with a ball cap on top—some of Snake's hand-me-downs that Nog treasured so much—I stuffed them in too. Anything I thought we could possibly use.

I returned to the living room, knapsack in hand. Brock lay back, white-faced, the pain draining him. I checked my watch. Where was that damned ambulance, or whatever it was? Just then the bell attached to a button out at the gate rang in two little sets of jingles. I grabbed my gun.

"Relax, it's *our* people," Brock said. "Haven't you heard? The postman always rings twice."

———— • ————

The phone rang on the other end for the fifteenth time.

"Damn," I mumbled. The Wolf was obviously not at his door.

I cast an eye out of the booth. Although the telephone building, next to the main General Post Office on New Road, was only a few blocks from the house. I had taken considerably longer to reach it to be sure I wasn't coat-tailed. Brock hadn't looked too pleased when I suddenly left him with his friends, all of them dressed like vacationing *farangs*. I had been past their nondescript Toyota van and disappearing into the dark before they and their stretchers could even make it to the house.

On the twentieth ring I reluctantly collected my baht from the return slot, then plugged it back in. If anyone knew where Wolfgang was, it would be the old man with the smoky-hills breeze in his voice.

"Yeaaah?" the voice drawled.

"Lion, it's me. How are you doing?"

"Well, if it ain't. Ya know some of the boys were a bit pissed at you for the fucken stunt you pulled the last time you was here—leavin' without pickin' up the tab fer that dead bug. Just thought I should let you know."

"Ah, they enjoyed reliving old times. The hell with them. Lion, I'm trying to get ahold of the one-armed bandit."

"I figured so. Matter of fact he's trying to fucken git ahold of you too—he was in here jist awhile ago. Left ya a fucken message. Says fer ya to call him right fucken away or to go straight over to his goddamned place, because he'll be there till ya do. Sounded awfully fucken important. He jist stayed fer one schnapps, then left about . . . ah, goddamned fucken son of a bitch *all to hell!*"

"What's the matter?"

"Talkin' about fucken krauts, it's thet goddamned Brussels kraut. He jist came in with a goddamned Nazi flag wrapped around his goddamned fat naked disgusting body and the fistfucker is drunk as usual. I gotta go."

"Hang on a minute, Lion. What time did he leave?"

"It was about . . . *Kurt! Get yer Nazi ass outa this here fucken bar!* . . . about three, four hours ago . . . *Kurt! Put thet goddamned fucken* FLAG *back on!* . . . I gotta go!"

The next call was through to New York. Less than five minutes later, a familiar and elegantly curled voice thick with sleep bounced off a satellite and into my ear.

"It's me," I said into the mouthpiece.

"*Ah! . . . Tres bon! Un moment!*" the voice said, springing to life. "I'll just crawl out of bed . . . sorry, Bree dear, go back to sleep . . . and sliiiiiip into my robe and . . . thank goodness for these cordless phones . . . transport myself down the hall . . . here . . . to my office where I won't bother the queen again . . . and . . . throw open the curtains. Ah, the sun is just starting to come up and, *mon Dieu,* it's snowing in the park!"

"That's all I have to hear. You know how much that cheers me," I said flatly. "Here, it's hot. In fact it's very, very hot."

"*Oui,* but isn't Bangkok always the hottest of cities? I don't know how you can stand to live there, really!"

"I won't be . . . living . . . here much longer unless I get rid of this . . . headache I picked up in the jungle. And damned quick."

There was a pause while he absorbed that. When he spoke again, the sleep was gone from his voice.

"A real heat wave?" he asked, his tone clear and sharp. "It is *that* bad, *oui?*"

"*Oui.* Worst I've ever seen. It could kill a guy if he didn't keep out of the sun."

"The monsoon has broken then, has it?"

"Yeah, it finally blew out but this hot front is blasting down from the direction of Russia, despite the time of year. It's surprising as hell, believe me. I'd head up into the mountains to escape the heat and . . . clear my head but getting out of here is pretty difficult right now with my . . . health being a little touchy. I'm not really sure going up there would be the wisest thing anyway. It'll probably be the same up there—in fact I'm sure of it. I really don't know what to do."

"Have you spoken to our mutual friend? I'm sure he has a remedy."

"Just like when you want a cop, he's not to be found. I just tried to phone him."

"*Comment!*" he exclaimed. "I just spoke to him a few hours ago before retiring. He told me he'd be puttering around the house for the next few days and didn't plan to leave. He mentioned he was expecting an important visitor he didn't want to miss." He paused to let it sink in.

"Perhaps he just can't hear the ring. I would suggest you try again. I'm sure he's there."

"Okay. I'll keep trying."

"*Bon!* In any case, I have a diplomat friend who is planning to do some trekking on his vacation. He's been in the Far East a very long time and I'm sure he would be of some help too . . . with your headache. But it will be a few days. I'll try to put you in touch with him."

A diplomat. Good. Access to the diplomatic pouch.

"Good one. Thanks. I appreciate it. When?"

"Well . . . I don't really *know* at this point. But I'll let you know at the earliest possible time. But I understand how bad a migraine can be and I'll do my best to make it as soon as possible."

"The sooner the better. It's killing me."

NINE

Chinatown

A LIGHT WAS burning through a shuttered window of Wolfgang's ramshackle house on Soi 52, off Sukhumvit, as I stepped down from a tuk-tuk, took up my small knapsack with the things from my place, and handed the driver some baht. As the *samlor* roared away, I faded back into the shadows and looked around. All seemed silent.

Wolfgang's house was a tumbledown structure of Thai design, teak like most were, and probably built a half-century ago. Like many in the area, it didn't have the usual Bangkokian compound, but opened directly onto the narrow *soi*. Beside its front door was an electric buzzer, the only modern innovation to the otherwise archaic structure. I slipped over and pressed it. From inside came the high ring of a bell.

Nervously waiting a few moments and not hearing anything more, I tried again. The house responded with a thundering silence equal to the first. Knitting my brows, I reached for the door handle. It turned easily in my hand. It wasn't locked.

I stepped inside, slipped out the Walther, and quietly locked the door behind me. Tiptoeing into the small living room, gun at ready, synapses snapping, I peered around. Just a small desk lamp was on, reflecting off framed news clippings that decorated the walls. Piles of moldy magazines he should have thrown out years ago were stacked here and there. The room was brown with disuse, the air stale, and I wondered, as I had many times before, how Wolfgang could live like this. It didn't encourage anyone to call around too often—and in all the years I had known him I doubted if I'd visited more than a half-dozen times, the last having been at least six years before. I was surprised to see the house hadn't changed at all, down to the stacks of the same magazines.

I peered into the kitchen. Water dripped from a brass faucet, forming a discolored ring at the bottom of the ancient porcelain sink. There was only one other room, the bedroom, and into this I silently moved. All was silent. No one was home.

I dropped the pistol to my side. Had he gone out for a moment? But no one steps out in Bangkok—it's like any other city—without locking their door.

On a whim, I pulled open a drawer in his dresser. The odor of mothballs rose from the neatly folded shirts and pants. I fingered them—they felt slightly damp. A patch of mildew was on a sock. I checked another drawer. A cockroach scurried back into a corner. The yellowing sheets inside were speckled with tiny droppings.

The one luxury the tiny home had was a small walk-in closet running about five feet back, which I opened and peered into. On either side hung old suits, slacks, and shirts, all fairly high with mothballs. I was about to close it and walk out when something caught my eye—a narrow shaft of light emanating from the floor near the back, where there was a break in the hanging clothes. I stepped inside, my Walther once again at the ready.

I bent down. The band of light was slashing out of a partially open trapdoor, its edges disguised to blend in, when closed, with the other joins in the plank floor. In what looked like a knot was a tiny hole just large enough to

fit a key. I swung the heavy door up and open. Light filled
the closet, and a cool, air-conditioned breeze swept up and
over my face. Carpeted stairs led downward.

Puzzled, I padded down to the bottom. Ahead was a
long, narrow tunnel, the sides moisture-paneled with some
kind of plastic, the floor neat and carpeted. I pulled the
trapdoor shut behind me and noticed it locked securely
from the bottom with a bolt. I set my pack to one side and
began to make my way down the long corridor.

Something on the pathway ahead caught my eye. I bent
down and picked it up. A cheroot. The tiny label on the
neck read DUCK BRAND.

Tossing it aside, I continued to the end. A padded, circular staircase rose to what I guessed was two stories above
ground level. Halfway up I could see that the door at the
top was open, the room beyond it lit. Quietly I crept upward in a silent crouch, my grip sweaty on the Walther.
Just below the final level I paused, listening for sounds.
Hearing none, I peeked over the top of the final step.
Before me was an opulent desk, on which sat a bonsai tree
planted in what looked like a pure gold box about a foot
square. Behind the desk, paintings hung all over the walls.
I inched forward. More of the room came into view. In a
moment I was inside. No one was there.

It was a large study, and obviously designed for the absolute and exclusive use of its owner. A room like this was not
to be advertised. There was another door at the far end.
Besides thick, heavy, leatherbound furniture and a desk, it
was loaded with art, often three paintings high—and what
art! I recognized a couple of Van Goghs, from both his
earlier potato-eater and later southern France periods; a
Frans Hals of a laughing, drunken tavern wench, the sort
of woman Snake would have unwound his boa for; a couple
of Vermeers and another that could have been an Aver-
camp but was certainly of the Vermeer school; a da Vinci
Madonna and diaper-dumper; some of Rubens's slobs; a
Raphael and a Van Dyck; three Rembrandts, one a red-
faced, obviously hung-over self-portrait; a couple of ankle-
biters by both the younger and elder Cranachs; and finally
—my eyes fixed on it in amazement—two identical
Brueghels of a wintery, village scene, both describing in

portrait a number of contemporary parables, one done by the father, the other by the son.

And there were more, many more, all by artists identifiable at a glance. I was so taken aback I almost bumped backward into a large, marble sculpture, perhaps unfinished, of a man trying to free himself from the raw rock that imprisoned him—unmistakably a Michelangelo. Nearby was a life-size bronze of a stiff-backed athlete about to throw a javelin. On a pedestal nearby was a foothigh Gupta-period Sitting Buddha displaying the circlefingered A-OK scuba diving *mudra*.

I was stunned. There was millions' worth of art treasures in this single room—a private gallery with some of the most priceless works in the world. That it was Wolfgang Kreuger's there could be no doubt. His personal memorabilia was everywhere. A picture of the young Wolf in a Luftwaffe uniform standing proudly beside a Messerschmitt 109 verified the rumor that he had been in the last war.

There was also a Renaissance sideboard that held many other pictures of him—some as a cub with all four paws, another taken beside a stream with a large, handsome woman, yet another with a well-tailored man. Both father and son were standing with one foot resting on the running board of a large Mercedes touring saloon. In the background was a palatial country house that bespoke of a great deal of aristocratic money.

But there were three other frames that grabbed my attention more; they were lined up in a small recess in the wall between two paintings of the Dutch School—obviously a position of particular honor.

The first was a five-by-seven, sepia-toned black-and-white with a younger, handsome though by then one-armed Wolfgang. It had been taken on a broad lawn in front of a grand country lodge of Scandinavian design. He was wearing casual clothes and was laughing, as if caught in the middle of a joke. A flicker of blond hair fell over his forehead. Beside him was the vast bulk of a man dressed in knee britches and a pompadour shirt. A half-grown lioness was standing on its hind legs, trying to lick his face. My head jerked back slightly in recognition.

The man was Field Marshal Hermann Goering.

Below it was some writing which, being in kraut, I couldn't understand. I did the signature, though. Not "Field Marshal" or "Reichsmarschall Hermann Goering." Just: "Hermann Goering."

Beside this was a second photograph of the two, though the setting was much more formal. The field marshal, in full peacock uniform, was pinning a medal on Wolfgang's tunic. In the background were rows of pilots standing stiffly at attention, more rows of Messerschmitts behind them. This one carried a more formal inscription: "Reichsmarschall H. Goering."

The third frame in the trilogy held not a photograph but the medal itself, a Zahring Lion with Swords.

"Jesus . . . ," I said under my breath.

I glanced around in disbelief, then headed for the next door. It opened onto a walk-in wardrobe—one, I noted, that would be invisible if you closed its door, which I didn't. Tiptoeing through the mostly empty closet, I emerged into another master bedroom. The endtable lamp was on beside an enormous, canopied bed. The room was decorated in an aristocratic style, with settees and French Provincial furniture and all the comforts of a minor Versailles. The colors were light pastels. Full of curiosity, I peeked and poked around. The spotlit paintings on the walls were fine, though not so fine as those in the room behind me; many of the artists' names were unfamiliar to me. Objets d'art were everywhere, and many of them, I noted, were Tantric Buddhist.

The bedroom door opened onto an upper balcony over the main hall of the mini-mansion. Again, all the lights were on. I padded along the wool-carpeted upper level, gun always at ready, peering into the lateral rooms: one a study, another a spare bedroom, a third for storage, many others holding unopened crates of weathered wood. Through broad windows I saw carefully manicured lawns and gardens bathed in indirect lighting and surrounded by a twelve-foot wall.

Quietly, I pussyfooted down a broad, sweeping staircase. It led into a huge foyer lined with paintings, furniture, and ornately bordered mirrors, all of the finest Oriental design.

To the right, off the semi-open foyer, was an enormous salon set with more exquisitely carved Oriental furniture, and filled with elaborate wall hangings, jade and ivory ornaments, great copper and porcelain vessels, and sculptures, in both marble and stone, of various Far Eastern idols from all periods and places. I recognized a large Mathura-period Buddha, a Five Dynasties five-foot porcelain and a *thankya* at least as old.

To the left was a dining room, again superbly decorated in an Oriental motif. Tall silver candelabra and porcelain vases decorated a long, carved table. An elaborate crystal chandelier hung from the high ceiling.

A cat meowed nearby, making me jump. It was a crisp, eager type of meow that echoed through the silent house. I had hardly taken a step in its direction when a Siamese blue point slipped out from under a chesterfield and hurried quickly into the dining room.

I followed, just in time to catch it slipping through a cat door into what was obviously the kitchen. I was about to press against one of the two swing doors when I suddenly stopped.

The lingering aroma of cheroots tickled my nostrils. My hand tightened around the Walther. I peeked through the crack between the doors—the light was on. But there was no movement. No sound.

Crouching, I pushed one of the doors open and crept in, senses crisp, reactions at ready. The kitchen was a vast, square room with a well-used chopping block and battered preparation islands. Brass pots and pans hung on the walls. Along one stretched a huge gas stove.

The cat meowed again, obviously ravenous—I could hear the rapid *slip-slip-slip* of its lapping tongue. That came from near a heavy wooden door that led into a large walk-in freezer. I crept closer and peered around a counter. The blue point stared up at me with longing eyes. Something red flecked her moustache, which she hungrily licked before returning to her windfall meal.

It was a trickle of red coming out of the corner of the partially open freezer door. Wolfgang's meerschaum lay on the floor beside it. A whiff of something unpleasant mixed with the cheroot smell reached my nostrils.

Cautiously, I pulled the heavy door open and peeked inside. The light from the kitchen penetrated part way, outlining the figure of a man. I jumped back, jerking my gun hand forward.

A split second before I pulled the trigger, I stiffened. The figure wasn't moving. It didn't even seem to be dressed.

The cat scrambled away with a high-pitched *scrowl* as I ankled it aside. Fumbling with my free hand, I found the inside light switch. Then I looked up—and froze.

Wolfgang was hanging from a meat hook on the end wall, his toes inches off the wooden floor. He was naked. Nickel-sized burns from cheroot butts now littering the floor covered his body. A bamboo reed protruded from one eye. Into his mouth had been stuffed his genitals, another reed still projecting from the end of the dangling, uncircumcised penis. His large belly had been slashed diagonally, his still-steaming guts had spilled out in a red-green mass almost to his knees. On his black- and blue-mottled chest had been carved an eight-inch-high outline of a Shan good luck amulet.

The stench hit me and I reeled backwards, vomiting in horror until I was puking dry, and even then my abdominal muscles convulsed inexorably inward, leaving me gasping for breath.

——— • ———

The girls were having a busy night, I noticed, as I trudged up the stairs and past the caged entrance to the teahouse/whorehouse. Middle-aged, working-class Thai men lounged on benches, smoking, chatting and sipping tea brought to them by a dumpy Chinese woman, before taking their pick and pleasure. I slipped the arthritic old pimp a few more red baht notes and tried to avoid both his breath and another of his obscene winks. I tried to give the girls a friendly smile as I trudged by, but somehow my mouth and mood wouldn't cooperate. Some girls giggled, a few looked on with hostility, most just stared at me with incomprehension.

So the postman always rings twice, I thought wearily as I knocked on the door with our prearranged signal. There was no answer. I put my ear to the door. Silence.

I rapped again, slightly louder.

Still not a sound.

Fear and apprehension welled up in my chest as I

dropped my bag and groped for the key, yanking out the gun at the same time, holding it close to my belly so no one happening down the hallway would see it. The rusty skeleton key fumbled noisily in the hole. I swung the door wide open and stepped to the side, shielding myself with the wall. I reached around and found the light switch, then burst into the room.

Tysee sprang bolt upright in bed and stared with horror down the gun barrel, a scream caught in her throat.

"Oh God," I said, relaxing, my gun hand going limp. "I thought you were in trouble. Or worse. Gone."

I fetched my bag and locked the door behind me.

"I sorry," she said, her hand drifting to the wrapped bulge beside her. "I fall asleep."

"That's fine my Siamese pussycat. Go back to it. I'll join you in a minute."

She sat back on her elbows and watched me as I slipped out of my clothes. I disappeared into the bathroom with my toilet kit and turned on the water. It was luke-cold as usual.

"How it go tonight?" she called in a concerned voice. "You look *mahk-mahk* tense and white."

"No problem," I said. "I got money and things we need. It's just been a hard day at the office, dear, that's all." I leaned out of the can. "Turn out the light and go to sleep. I'll tell you about it tomorrow."

A frown crossed her brow, but she rolled over and went back to sleep.

———— • ————

It was my turn to wake up to the sight of a gun barrel staring me between the eyes. I blinked. It was *my* gun. Gripping it from behind was Tysee. The bare bulb was on. Sunlight snuck through the ratty shutters.

"What the hell are you doing?" I asked sitting up on my elbow.

"You say that again," she snapped.

I shook my head in disbelief.

"I said, 'What the hell are you doing?' "

She lowered the gun and sat on the edge of the bed.

"You scare me when I wake up and see you. I not know

for sure who you are. I turn light on. But it would like you. Swear *mahk-mahk.*"

I raised my hand to scratch my beard. Then I understood. It wasn't there.

"I shaved last night," I said, managing a laugh. "And cut and peroxided my hair. Don't you like it?"

"You look different man. Hair even yellow now. I guess I have to get used to you."

"We'll have to do the same to you."

"I no have beard to cut," she replied, protectively stroking the long hair that fell down over one shoulder.

"I know," I said, forcing a smile as I crawled out of bed. "And don't worry. We don't cut that gorgeous hair of yours. Gorgeous."

I felt considerably better though the dark, horrible image of Wolfgang's death scene still consumed my mental vision. I had to tell her, so tell her I did, though I left out the grislier details. She took it well, though not without an air of sadness. It was clear that news of that sort wasn't alien to her unconventional background. I also showed her the buck knife and the Lilliputian KGB pistol, which we figured out how to work.

"Yes, that Shan way," she said quietly. "I sorry to hear about Mr. Krueger. I know him long time . . . but we in trouble for sure. I think you right. I need disguise also. How I do?"

One idea seemed perfect. It took about half an hour to rig everything up and apply the makeup. Finally, with wads of toilet tissue shoved under her lips and into her nose to distort her face, she was ready.

"Okay, rogues' gallery time," I said, attaching the flash to my camera and loading the passport film inside. "Sit on this chair with your back to the wall and look at the birdie. And mumble something like, 'I make-a him an offa he can't refuse.' "

———— • ————

The Crack of Noon Club at The Lion's Den had just finished rolling dice for the daily short-time as I took a deep breath and slouched through the door and into the air-conditioning. It took my eyes a moment to adjust and as

they did I made out, among others, a few ex-Special Forces
boys and a couple of journalists I knew. The Lion and Hal
Lawson, apparently arguing over the latest batch of tabs,
looked up at me for a moment, and I stiffened. But neither
gave me any sign of recognition, but instead returned to
their perpetual disagreement.

The disguise flew. With my clean-shaven chops, an old
pair of jeans, a Foster's T-shirt of Snake's that fit so loose
that it flopped over the small bulge in the side of my belt, a
battered ball cap with a Four XXXX beer label, Indian
buffalo-hide sandals, and my gut pressed out, I was a different person. Just another one of what always seemed like
thousands of horny, beer-swilling Aussies shuffling around
Southeast Asia. Being a born-again Down-underer made
me as thirsty as a dingo in the desert for a cold brew.

The man I was looking for was leaning like a crane over
the jukebox. We called him the Wizard, short for the Wizard of ID. He dealt in identification. I walked over to him,
pulled out the pictures of Tysee I'd taken, and the ones
she'd taken of me, and I asked him to make me up kits of
Aussie ID.

Ten minutes later, after making an appointment to meet
him in a restaurant can at the Oriental Hotel down by the
river, I exited The Lion's Den and almost ran into a splay-
toed Shan making use of a two-fingered handkerchief
standing directly in front of the door. In fact, I almost
knocked him over. The worst part was I recognized him:
the guard at Kun San's house.

"Excuse me, mate!" I said in my best kangaroo, pulling
myself together into a slouch with my gut out as far as it
would go.

He seemed as surprised as me, and I hoped it wasn't
because he recognized me. Then he grinned sheepishly
and his eyes softened. He was embarrassed—the hick
country kid in the big city.

I waved my hand at him good-naturedly, turned on my
heels, and sluffed off down the street, praying he wasn't on
my trail. A block down I cut into the traffic, which gave me
a chance to glance back. He was still prowling around The
Lion's Den. I breathed a sigh of relief.

Patpong was off-limits, I realized with a jolt—it was sure

to be hotter than ever. Ham-Sandwich knew my habits. Kun San would have his men all over it looking for me. I cut into the nearest massage parlor. Some of the day shift, not exactly prime-time players, were lounging on the bleachers behind the windows, watching TV. The choice was lousy but all I wanted was a massage to kill some time while avoiding getting killed myself. I read off the number of the first girl who looked like she wouldn't chew my leg completely through. She rolled over and sat up when she was called.

Two-and-a-half hours later I was in a cubicle crapper at the Oriental inspecting the ID that had just been passed to me under the partition. Quickly leafing through the passports, I learned that my name was Martin Thomas, that I was thirty-two and Kiwi. Fine. Everyone knows New Zealand is just across that bridge from Australia anyway. My wife's name as Pranee. Flipping through the back pages, I learned that we'd both been to Hong Kong before reaching Bangkok. I checked our pictures on the stolen, doctored documents carefully. The government seals blended perfectly—the man was a pro. But although there was a Thai marriage license and what-have-you, he hadn't managed to package up driver's licenses for either of us. We'd have to use public transportation. There was not time to argue. Pocketing my disappointment with the new identities, I slipped him several thousand baht and cut over to New Road. There I flagged down a 125cc Honda— a motorcycle harder to chase than even a tuk-tuk and used for transportation around Bangkok—and jumped onto the pillion. My pockets bulged not only with new fake passports and support documents for both of us, but also with matching wedding bands that I had picked up in a jewelry shop inside.

"Hua Lampong," I said, naming the main railway station on the edge of Chinatown, just a short walk from our cozy little whorehouse. If we didn't have the papers to rent a car, we would have to take the train.

———— • ————

The lineup to the ticket window for heading south was long, and I tried to cover my nervousness by flipping through a copy of the Bangkok *Post* I had purchased. Although there was the usual heavy swirl of humanity in the European-style station, I knew that as a *farang*, I would still stand out.

I hadn't been in line more than a minute before I began to feel distinctly uncomfortable. Instinctively I knew someone, somewhere, was watching me—I could feel the unmistakable weight of a gaze.

Flipping through to the comics, I tried to concentrate on Robotman. But the naked feeling grew more intense— someone was sifting my image through his memory. I could only hope that I would be chaff in the separator of his mind.

With my peripheral vision, I tried to determine who was causing that naked feeling. All I could see were a couple of Indians, one of whom seemed to be looking at me intently. He swept a dark fall of hair away from his eyes, then turned away.

The feeling didn't retreat, and it didn't take me long to discover the source. Glancing nonchalantly up at the station clock, I spotted him. He was standing at the end of the long tier of ticket wickets. My heart skipped through a tattoo of beats, and beads of sweat sprang to my forehead.

It was Kayao. He was dressed in ill-fitting jeans and a black T-shirt. And he was looking directly at me.

He began to walk toward me, his eyes riveted to my face. I made sure my gut was sticking out and sloped back my shoulders slightly more. I gave him my profile, not wanting him to see my teeth or eyes, and I fought to relax, wondering if I should go for my gun if he tried anything.

He stopped ten feet away, ostensibly to light a cheroot, then moved closer. I could feel the full force of his stare, on the untanned regions where my beard had used to be. The sweet smell of his cheroot wafted over, reminding me of Wolfgang, and for a moment I shuddered. I concentrated on Blondie. The boss was kicking ass. Just as he came abreast, he shot me a penetrating look. Then he just as quickly turned away and I watched his stocky, black T-shirted back move off. From the corner of my eye I saw him turn his attention to a new *farang* who had just entered the station. I breathed easier. The line inched forward. A Thai family fell in behind me.

I finally reached the head of the imperceptibly moving line and pushed several 500-baht notes through the wicket, enough for two First Class Compartment tickets through to Singapore. I would have to phone Snake at the earliest opportunity, and hope he was around—I wasn't due for a couple of weeks yet for our diving expedition. Tickets in hand, I stuck the paper in my back pocket and headed for the arched entrance.

That was when I made the fatal mistake.

My heightened senses told me that the Shan lieutenant was off to my left, keeping an eye on the Tourist Information Counter at the head of the huge station foyer. Out of curiosity or stupidity or both, I snuck a glance. His head was turning in my direction just as I did so. One second more either way and I would have been safe.

But our eyes met, and although they held for only the briefest of flickers, it was enough. In that brief flash I saw the blandness and boredom disappear from his face and a spark of recognition ignite behind those dark orbs. As I turned away, I saw his mouth open, his red gums and black teeth flashing a malevolent grin.

When I reached the entrance I saw another Shan ahead of me perk up and fasten his eyes on me. He'd been signaled.

I cursed bitterly through clenched teeth as I skipped down the steps. There were no motorcycles in sight—my only real hope. Grabbing the nearest taxi, I ordered the driver into Chinatown. By positioning myself directly behind him, I could lean slightly forward and see a corner of the rearview mirror. Another beat-up blue Datsun cab with two shadows in the rear was directly behind us.

Telling the driver to hurry in Bangkok's horrific traffic was a waste of words. Through luck, we managed to put two car lengths between us and them, and to swing down in one clean sweep to the big traffic circle at the head of Yawarat, which curls like a dragon's tail through the heart of Chinatown. But it was there that we hit our first red light. My jaws were working. My whole body fidgeted. My hand kept moving to touch the comforting bulge in my belt.

Then my eyes opened wide, as through the rearview

mirror I saw both side doors of the blue Datsun suddenly swing open.

In a flash I was out of the cab and dipsy-doodling through the shuffling crowds on the sidewalk, the angry shouts of my unpaid driver receding behind me. I cut into a side alley and sprinted half its length, cut through a restaurant and back through the messy kitchen, where I knocked an old woman carrying a large pot of steaming rice flying, which sent us both sprawling in a loud clatter of pots and pans and crashing porcelain. In a moment I was on my feet and out the front door, back down a narrow alley full of wicker baskets overloaded with garbage spilling out onto the concrete, through a small shop, in the back of which two monks sat cross-legged on the floor reverently watching "Dallas" on TV, hardly shifting their gaze as I scrambled through. I spotted the back windows of our teahouse not far ahead and slowed along the mostly deserted narrow lanes, my chest heaving, hoping one moment, sure the next, that I had ditched my followers.

Wiping sweat from my eyes, I walked around a dog-legged corner and almost knocked a man over. I started, but just as quickly relaxed when I saw it was an Indian.

"Pardon me," I said, as I began to move around him.

His chest was heaving as much as mine, and sweat was dripping down his forehead, over which hung a shock of black hair. He looked vaguely familiar . . .

Then I recognized him.

But it was too late. A broad, thin smile spread across his bony features, revealing sparkling white teeth against dark brown skin. He had been at the railway station.

I groped for my gun, but to my horror it had slipped down into my shorts during the chase. His hand came up evenly. In it was a pistol. It was no use reaching for the buck knife in my pocket. His smile grew wider and thinner.

"We are wanting the Head," he said menacingly, wobbling his head back and forth.

"Well, you came to the wrong country, I'm afraid," I replied hoarsely, stalling for time. "You'll have to go to the Philippines for that. I know a couple of places there where they can suck the color right out of your hair."

It went right over his head but his grin widened just the same. It flashed on me that he wouldn't risk shooting to kill —he needed me as much as the Shan, as much as anybody. I glanced to one side as a prelude to cutting.

It was not to be.

I'd turned half-around before I stopped. Approaching me from behind, gun in hand, was the other Hindu. He wasn't smiling. I jerked my head both ways, desperate, a cat in a corner.

Instinctively, my foot lashed out in a roundhouse, sending Thin Lips's gun clattering. I dropped my kicking foot at an angle and spun around with a swinging back-kick, the heel of my foot hammering into his temple, driving him splayed against the wall with a thudding, clumping sound.

Before he had dropped to the ground like a sack of curry, the other wog was on me, the downward arc of his pistol butt just grazing my shoulder. I wiggled aside, driving a fast fist into his kidney. He grunted sharply but was back on his feet within a second, expertly blocking a front kick I'd aimed at his balls. But then my fisted backhand sent him sprawling, giving me an opportunity to scramble for Thin Lips's loose gun.

It took a moment to find, being half under the unconscious Hindu. As I grappled for it, I heard something firm and angry in Hindi. I looked up. the second one was on his knees, staring at me, spitting out the words along with blood and teeth, his black eyes a raging storm of malice. Deliberately and steadily, he raised his pistol with both hands. There were no thoughts of caring about any Buddhist Head in his head just then, as he lined up mine squarely in his sights while a smile began to spread across his cracked and bloody lips.

Whether or not he was going to pull the trigger, I'll never know, for just then one of his eyes exploded in a mass of blood and brains, with the light going out of the other at the same instant. He collapsed straight forward onto the smooth concrete before me, landing with a dull thud. I scrambled forward to him. In the back of his head was a neat hole. The only sound had been a *punk* as the bullet drove through his skull.

I quickly looked around, but could see no one. I ran the

twenty feet to the end of the alley then around the dog-legged corner, only to trip heavily over something large and soft. My eyes bulged in surprise.

Beneath me, on his back, his arms splayed out and with one leg crossed over the other from the way he had spun to the ground, lay Kayao. His cold eyes were empty, his betel-reddened mouth open and hideous. Blood dribbled out of a neat hole in the middle of his forehead.

The body of another Shan lay five feet away, a large pool of blood forming around his crumpled body. Their weapons lay scattered beside them.

I stood and jogged down the alley, then suddenly stopped as something caught my eye. Bending down, I dipped my finger into it and brought it up. Blood. One of the Shan must have gotten a lick in before getting it himself.

Now in a half-run, I followed the bloody trail to the main thoroughfare until it disappeared beneath the feet of hundreds of thousands of noisy Chinese shuffling about their daily business on the busy streets of Chinatown.

———— • ————

"Tysee? What's the matter?" I asked, closing the door behind me and hurrying to her side.

Her sobs had been audible before I had even turned the key in the lock. Her face was buried in the crumpled bed sheets, her hair completely disheveled. The Thai newspaper I had brought up when I fetched breakfast that morning lay scattered across the bed. She clutched a portion of the front page in her little hand. I took the paper from her. Tysee stumbled into the bathroom. The sound of water dribbled from the tap could be heard between her sobs.

The lead story had a photograph of a village. It had obviously been devastated in some kind of attack.

The village had been Kwan Mae.

Front and center was a large photo of a man dead lying on the ground, on his back, his shirt blown open, his head to one side. A dark stain ran down from his neck. There was no question about it.

It was Kun San.

Throwing it down, I remembered my *Post.* I slapped my back pocket—somehow it was still there. The headline struck out at me in huge letters. How the hell could I have missed it!:

KUN SAN DEAD

I gripped the paper closer to my eyes and moved under the bare bulb.

> Heroin and opium drug kingpin and warlord Kun San was killed yesterday in a surprise air raid on his Kwan Mae headquarters. The attack was launched out of Rangoon by the Burmese Air Force.
>
> No official report on the highly unexpected move was given, but sources close to the Burmese military say it was in retaliation for the brazen act of Kun San's private airplane violating airspace over Rangoon only the day previous . . .

My heart began to beat like a kettledrum: the Royal Burmese Air Farce wasn't a complete joke after all. I know I turned white as my eyes rolled down the page. In the middle of it was a blowup of an old visa photograph of myself.

> It is this same plane which crash-landed onto the grounds of Wat Arun, causing 300,000 baht damage. The two member crew, identified as 37 year old American Lee Rivers and 21 year old Tysee San, escaped and are the subject of a nationwide police and military search. Miss San is the only daughter of the slain Shan leader.
>
> Rivers's riverfront home was found abandoned by police.
>
> A reward of one million baht has been posted by an anonymous donor for the capture of Rivers. This same donor reportedly hinted that Rivers, an internationally recognized collector of antiquities and anthropological items for museums, may have discovered an important relic relating to the roots of Buddhism and is trying to export it . . .

It was like my eyes had hit a brick wall at ninety miles an hour. Who the hell put a reward on my head—Kun San? could he be that vindictive to his only daughter? I returned to the scene of the accident and read the paragraph again. Then, having hit, I ran.

> If this is the case, this would fall under this country's strict Cultural Properties laws, which prohibit the export of any and all Buddhist relics and statues. Thailand excludes antiquity thieves from being able to take advantage of the international prisoner exchange program.
>
> Authorities state they are taking the matter very seriously.
>
> The latest developments raise speculation as to the reason or reasons the plane flew down from the Golden Triangle into Burma's capital, then inexplicably crossed the mountains into Thailand where it was shot down by the Thai Air Force later the same day.
>
> Reports of the dead and wounded in Kwan Mae are difficult to fix, but it was reported by the Shan who smuggled these pictures out of the town that up to 40 were killed with scores more injured. Among the survivors was Kun San's wife.

I heard a loud sniffle and looked up from the paper. Tysee had just shuffled slowly out of the bathroom, and was staring downcast and red-eyed at the curling linoleum like a little girl waking from a nightmare. Her matted hair half-covered her face, wet strands sticking to her cheeks. Po's plain, oversize clothes hung on her drooping shoulders as if on a lost or discarded doll's.

"Hold me," she whispered in the tiniest of voices. "Please hold me till it's better. He my papa and he often bad man but he still my papa."

I gently took her into my arms and held her, rocking her limp form slowly back and forth while huge, wet sobs broke against my shoulder. Somehow I found my voice.

"There, there," I said. "I love you. Papa loves you. Papa loves you."

———— • ————

I stopped halfway down the final creaking set of stairs that led into the teahouse itself. Something was wrong. Over the topless partition that partially hid me and the stairs from the teahouse, I could see into the restaurant.

But it wasn't something in the teahouse that had attracted my attention. It was just beyond, outside the open-fronted café, on the noisy Chinatown street. Standing in a small circle like the calm at the eye of a cyclone, while the storm of humanity whirled around them, was a huddle of military police. In their center, gesticulating wildly and waving a Thai newspaper, was the old man who ran the brothel. As he spoke, he repeatedly jabbed his bony finger in the direction of the teahouse, causing some of his khaki-clad company to glance curiously inside. Just then another mini-truckload of police braked to a rapid and rude halt in front of the teahouse and began disgorging its brown-uniformed load.

I wasted no time—I triple-stepped back up the stairs to our room, locked the door, and jammed an old chair under the handle.

"You no find rice and Coke?" Tysee asked blandly. She sat on the bed, her face puffy, her eyes still red. Noticing my haste, she grew alarmed.

"What you do that for?" she asked, her voice filling out.

"We have to check out of here. And fast. There's cops downstairs. The old man ratted on us." The words came out like slugs from a 50-caliber machine gun.

I crammed our few things into a bag and headed for the window. She swept up the bundle from the bed. Already the hammer of boots could be heard thumping in double time up the rickety stairs.

Throwing back the peeling shutters, I looked down to the tin roof below. I turned to Tysee—her eyes, though crimson, were alert and locked to mine.

The heavy pounding of police boots grew louder as the squad marched in noisy disorder down the gloomy hallway.

After the briefest of nods, Tysee led the way out, the round bundle under her arm. The clatter of her slamming onto the warped and rusting tin roof drowned out the loud banging at the door, and was only surpassed seconds later by my greater weight crashing down after her.

Cries of alarm rose from beneath our feet as we scrambled noisily over the nearly flat gable. Just before we jumped to the lower roof of a neighboring house, we heard the smashing of timber that meant our door and chair had given way. By the time we had leapt to a third, lower rooftop, loud and excited shouts were echoing out from the open window. I heard the loud explosion of a pistol, followed by more shouts and the crash of heavy bodies leaping from the window onto the roof.

Frantically, we leapt from tin rooftop to tin rooftop, hoping we were staying out of sight, knowing they could follow us by our sound. We were searching desperately for a way down from the irregular mountain range of brown metal.

Then we found it—a smaller house. It took a five-foot leap over a narrow alley onto a lower shed. A moment after that we had scrambled down onto a tall, covered crock, and dropped the final few feet into the small garden of our startled host. Chickens scattered and clucked in indignation.

Wasting no time for introductions, we ran past excited, angry residents waving their hands in the air, and quickly disappeared into the maze of narrow streets. Within a few minutes we were out of the pandemonium and slowing our pace to a quick walk past drying clothes and bare-bottomed children.

"Where we go?" Tysee whispered, out of breath and glancing behind us.

"Railway station," I panted back.

I pulled her into a small alcove where clothes hung on a clothesline.

"We'll have to go a little early but it's our only chance. Here's your passport. And wedding ring. Congratulations. You're knocked up and we have to get married. Your name if Pranee Thomas. I'm Martin. Can you remember that?"

She looked puzzled, then momentarily pleased, as I slipped the ring onto her third finger. Unfortunately there was no time to consummate the nuptials.

"Okay, get into your disguise," I ordered, checking our flanks with my Walther.

It didn't take her long. In a moment the Head was underneath Po's oversize dress and lodged in the special sling Tysee had hooked up. Within the same time she had gone from being single to married to seven months gone. With her puffy eyes and matted hair hastily tied into a bun, she looked the picture of uncomfortable pregnancy.

I pulled out my wad of money and flipped through it. Few of the bills were new and I gulped as I selected the least greasy ones. But this was no time to be acting like Richard Haimes-Sandwich. We quickly chewed them up and pressed the wads into our cheeks. They felt like hell. They tasted worse.

From the clothesline, I stripped off a plain pair of wrinkled pants and a floppy unironed cotton shirt. These I exchanged for Nog's Foster's T-shirt, jeans and cap. Suddenly we were the picture of a typical sloppily dressed *farang* and his dumpy-looking, pregnant Thai wife.

I nodded and she waddled off ahead of me, one hand on her back to feign lower back pain, the other clutching our bundle of few belongings. I shook my head in admiration, adjusted my gun so it wouldn't slip into my crotch again, and quickly followed.

———   •   ———

Just maybe we had a chance—a narrow one, but a chance.

I was counting on there not being many, if any, Shan left in the station. I had little confidence in my disguise anymore, and surely Tysee would be recognized by anyone who knew her. We hadn't had time to apply any of the makeup I had brought from the house for her. As for any other thugs, I hoped that the ones who had recognized us had already been taken care of in the alleys of Chinatown by the mysterious guardian angel I hadn't even had time to tell Tysee about.

My apprehension rose as we approached Rama IV. We stared at the black storm clouds of smoke spewing from the belching river of traffic, unable to see across the multi lane boulevard.

"Well, it can't be much more dangerous than anything else we've done lately," I said, taking Tysee by the hand. "The Buddha will have to help us through this one."

We dipped our feet into the river of traffic and wended our way across, jumping from break to break among the hurtling vehicles. Miraculously, we reached the center divider, where we had a better opportunity to survey the station front.

I didn't see any Shan, and was about to leap into the traffic again when Tysee gripped my arm and froze.

There, directly ahead of us across the traffic, was Chung Si Fu.

Sea Food was standing in front of a taxi in high agitation. He waved frantically toward the station, then looked at a newspaper in his other hand, as if he couldn't quite believe what he had read, then waved some more. Two Shan I hadn't seen were hurrying toward him.

He looked up and we stiffened. He stared right at us but didn't recognize us—his mind was far away, his face betraying both panic and greed. In a moment, he had herded his men into the taxi, clambered in behind, and roared off with them, hurtling into the turbulent rapids of traffic.

"Whew! That's a bit of good luck," I said, both of us letting out our breath. "Now just keep on waddling, my little duckie, and let's see if we can get out of here in one or two pieces."

We crossed the street, mounted the steps and entered the crowded, cavernous hall. It appeared there were no Shan left. Even better, there were more *farangs* in the station, giving me something to blend in with.

"With any luck one of those might be our train up ahead and we can board early. It's supposed to leave at 4:10 p.m. It's only 3:00 now . . . ah, good, there's the schedule. Track three. Terrific. There's our train."

My feeling of extended luck dissolved when I saw that another layer of security had been laid on since I'd last left. Police checkpoints had been set up at each entrance to the boarding platform. I gulped and cleared my throat, frozen in forward motion. It was too late to retreat. The soldiers' eyes were already locked on to us, interest igniting their dark little pupils as we approached—a white male and a Thai female, just what they had been ordered to watch out for. A guard with an M- 16 moved to block the way; a stubby, lower-echelon officer stood up from a grubby little desk and raised his callused claw authoritatively. The greasy butt of a .38 stuck out of a fast-draw police holster secured to his belt, his ample gut almost obliterating it. I feigned modest surprise.

"Passport," he demanded. Then he scowled under his breath as he noted Tysee's bulging abdomen.

Her hand was on her hip again, her body arched to straighten her aching back. I passed him the papers. He sat down on the edge of a dirty little chair and flipped them open with his thick, dirty fingers. Carefully, he compared the pictures with a set of others he carried in a soiled and well-fingered folder.

My heart sank when I recognized the pictures in his folder—a passport photo of Tysee and the publicized visa shot of myself. But from a photograph there was little chance that a stranger would recognize Tysee, not with her swollen face and belly. I just didn't want him to notice the partially tanned areas where my beard had been.

"Where you stay?" he grunted.

"Ah, the Oriental," I replied, instantly worried that we were dressed a little too down-market for the best hotel in Asia.

His eyes roamed over my body, stopping at belt level. I prayed that the overflowing shirt covered the bulge created by the small Walther. The tiny gun felt like Henry VIII's huge cannon at Dover Castle just then, the buck knife in my pocket like a broadsword.

"What you do for living?"

"I'm a dentist. I have a license to stick my tool in people's mouths. Heh-heh-heh."

Tysee looked at me disapprovingly. Any points I had hoped to gain by the joke or by awing him with my position, were lost when it went over his head.

"Where you luggage? All you got it little bag."

"Well, we got all our stuff ripped off after just arriving here," I said. "We got out of a taxi in front of the hotel and went in for just a minute and the bleedin' driver just took off! Can you imagine that? All me wife's things were in there, and as you can see, the little lady needs her stuff." I was talking in Kiwinian, trying to play the role of the dumb *farang.* "It's a good thing I had me money on me or me sheila and I would have been broke!"

He mulled that over for a moment, then looked at Tysee, unconvinced. My heart hurdled a few beats—the scenario I'd made up was weak and we had been thrown into the bearpit with only a buck knife. I knew it would take a lot of skill to carve ourselves out of this one.

"Why do you do that? Leave in taxi?" he asked with the cynicism only a cop can muster, his eyes full on Tysee.

"I'm sick," she said greenly in Thai. "I had to go to toilet very badly. My husband helped. When we come out, taxi gone."

"She's somewhat pregnant as you can see. We shouldn't even be traveling in her condition." I added as an afterthought, "Mate."

"Why you do it then?" he asked carefully, eyes glinting suspiciously at me.

"Her mother here in Thailand is very, very sick, mate," I said, slipping some compassion into my voice. "Very sick indeed, I'm afraid. She might even kick th' . . . ah, die. It just wasn't a good time to leave Auckland at all."

"Where you ticket?" he demanded without a pause, though I could see him softening a little.

He checked the entry dates in our passports while I dug those out. Behind us I could hear a lineup forming. He scrutinized the chits.

"This say Singapore," he said accusingly, his voice and manner cooling again. He waved them before Tysee. "You mother live Singapore?"

"Hat Yai," she said, naming the major city in the south, near the Malaysian border.

I knew the train stopped there. But then I remembered that special ticketing arrangements had to be made for stopovers. My show of confidence began to dissolve into visible panic—we were talking ourselves into a corner. I groped desperately for another lie to lie on top of the last lie.

"We're going to stop in Hat Yai just briefly before going on to Singapore," I mumbled. "My wife is having complications with her pregnancy. There's a special gynecologist down there, a Doctor, ah, Wang, who has been recommended."

He glanced down the growing lineup behind us. I thought I could see a glimmer of interest forming in his reptilian eyes, and for a moment the tickets in his hand moved down. Turning, I saw a tall, dark-haired *farang* about my age and size falling in several people behind us. Even better, he had a pretty Thai girlfriend with long hair.

A slight groan from Tysee turned my attention. She was

looking ill. Beads of sweat had formed along her brow and over her lips. She lightly clutched her protruding stomach. Instantly concerned, I gripped her elbow.

"Are you all right, mate? I mean, Pranee dear?" I whispered solicitously.

"I must sit down, Mah-tin. No feel very good."

"May I have your chair for my wife for a moment?" I half-asked, half-ordered the cop.

He didn't move, but just stared unsympathetically at her protruding abdomen, trying to see through the cotton, an inscrutable expression on his face. But then he tossed the passports and tickets before us and waved us dismissively through. His attention turned to the couple down the line as we wobbled through the gate and found our car.

Just before we boarded, I glanced back to the gate. Both the tall *farang* and his girlfriend were up against the wall, being frisked.

"Are you okay?" I asked shakily as we walked down the corridor checking the numbers on the compartment doors against those on our tickets.

That had been a tight call.

"I okay," she replied, the previous sadness returning to her voice. "I just tired of waiting for little fat man."

We found the door and Tysee quickly stepped inside. I was about to follow when something caught my eye on the floor of the corridor directly in front of our compartment. I reached down and touched it. It was wet. I drew back my finger and looked at it.

Blood.

TEN

The New Orient Express

"BREAKFAST THIS MORNING before come quick. I wonder when steward man bring our dinner. We no eat since noon and I hungry."

"I don't know. I should have asked him what the delay he told us about was all about."

Our vintage compartment with its plush, thirties-style seating, rich wood paneling, porcelain vestibule and tiny WC would have brought the big salts to the eyes of Somerset Maugham. Out the window, black smoke from the big steam engine up ahead drifted over the flat, lushly verdant landscape of southern Thailand as we chugged along at about thirty miles an hour. Here and there, large hillocks rose inexplicably up from the paddy fields, jungle topping their peaks and falling down their shaggy limestone sides like toussled hair.

Tysee looked up at me from across the tiny table attached to the windowsill. I could see from the pain on her face that she was still dwelling on her father. I nodded understandingly and leaned across, taking and squeezing her hand.

"It was my fault," I said, looking down. "I should have been more careful with that compass."

"No," she said after a pause, squeezing my hand back. "He do it to himself. Lord Buddha angry at him. It his fault."

Then we held each other in a long gaze, silently, reflectively, our hands locked lightly together, the arrhythmic click-clicketty-clack of the steel wheels on rail rising from below us. Behind the intelligence in her eyes was growing a tentative acceptance. I wasn't going to argue with her conclusions. As she had told me previously I, after all, wasn't a Buddhist.

"He my papa but maybe it best," she said in a quiet voice. "There much bad in him. He have Mr. Krueger killed like mafia man. He try kill you—he steal and try sell Buddha Head," she added in a whisper. Then she paused as a trickle of tears flowed down her cheeks once again. "And I think it he who put big reward on you and tell paper about me."

She quickly fought back the light flow of tears, and looked lovingly up at the Head. We'd secured it on the hat rack. I could see the strength and comfort it gave her. I squeezed her hand again.

"I feel sad for Mama too, for now she alone."

I was relieved that she was adjusting so quickly. But then, Buddhists accept death in a different way than Occidentals do. Even so, I recognized her strength, and realized that I not only truly loved her—I admired her as well. She was, to me, an extremely rare and exotic bird.

"How *you* feel? You have to kill man. You friend killed. We in big trouble all time."

Her eyes were open, sympathetic, no longer thinking of herself.

"No one likes killing," I said, trying to dismiss that deed with a shrug. "But it felt like in Vietnam—it was war. Them or me. I'm happy to be here. I have a lessened sympathy for anyone who tries to off me. Or you. Or anyone innocent."

The memory of Wolfgang hanging from the meat hook was quite another thing, and it quickly sobered me. It had been horrible. Particularly since I had known the man so well, and owed so much to him. Why Wolfgang? Somehow the Shan must have thought he was involved directly in the snatch. But why? Because we knew each other? Did it have anything to do with the bruises he'd had the day I returned from the Phillippines trip? Kun San and his men *had* reacted strangely when I told them about the Wolf having been mugged. Why had they so hideously tortured him, and left the Shan amulet image on him? Surely as a message to me . . . ? If so, it was one I read only too clearly.

We were in serious trouble. A million-baht reward on my head! And who had taken care of the Hindu, and Kayao and his friend, in the Chinatown alley? Tysee had been just as puzzled when I told her about the guardian angel. And I swore that I had only nailed one Shan up in Kwan Mae. This was getting more tangled up than a nocturnal epileptic under a mosquito net. I was already regretting not having given the Buddha Head to Brock Stambuck, but it had been a spur-of-the-moment decision. If Tysee hadn't approved handing it over, I'm sure François would have.

I tried to explain all this to Tysee, though I left out the parts about Wolfgang cooling his heels, and the drops of blood outside our compartment. I knew that normally she could have handled it, but for now she'd had enough. There was no use adding to her pain and grief. For any other problems, I was keeping my Walther and the buck knife handy under a cushion.

"You good man," she said quietly, a sure sincerity in her voice, after I had finally finished speaking.

She kept her eyes open and unswerving on mine, and I could feel the strong bond that had grown between us. It happened so fast, no doubt hastened by the rough roads we had traveled together thus far. It reminded me of my Nam days, when soldiers in combat forged bonds just as quickly. Tysee and I had been in combat together.

I had almost forgotten how beautiful she was. I hadn't forgotten how long it had been since we last made love. But this certainly wasn't the time.

"I think we going to stop," she said.

She was right. The train slowed and pulled onto a siding in the middle of nowhere, jungle pressing in on either side of the tracks. I had been at the border at Padang Basar a couple of times, but the train had never done this before. In fact, I was sure we weren't even at the border yet.

Whatever was happening, I didn't like the way the universe was unfolding. Soldiers had begun to appear—outside the window must have been a battalion of them, or so it seemed. The train ground to a halt with a final lurch and wheeze, and had hardly stopped before officers were coming aboard, ordering everyone off with their luggage.

We looked at each other and quickly stuffed wads of tissue paper into our mouths.

"Here. You give me you gun and knife. I put with Head. They may search you."

I didn't have time to argue—I grabbed the weapons out from under the pillow. A moment later, Mr. Thomas was solicitously helping his hobbling, pregnant wife, Pranee, down the steps.

The confused, mingling passengers were being herded into two groups, the *farangs* in one set of lineups, the Asians in another. Tysee stayed with me.

My heart sank. Everyone was being searched, baggage and body. The women were being taken inside a tent, outside of which stood two uniformed women.

Farang tempers—often short at the best of times in the Far East with its heat, slower pace and numerous delays— quickly reached the ends of their fuses. The grim-faced soldiers, doing their duty, absorbed the verbal punishment from raging, ignorant white travelers.

Tysee and I remained silent, trying to be invisible, while my eyes scanned for an avenue of escape. Soldiers were everywhere—we were trapped.

Just in front of us was a particularly obnoxious tourist. That he was a kraut didn't surprise me. When it came his turn to be searched, he raised such a hue and cry, swearing and gesticulating angrily, demanding in his arrogant, teutonic manner to know what the hell was going on, that the harried soldiers were visibly disappointed that they could find nothing incriminating in his luggage. I jerked my thumb toward the sauerkraut's back as it disappeared onto the train and put on a disgusted expression.

"Bah-bah-bah-bo," I said. Crazy.

They looked visibly relieved. Not only was the next

farang not another *farang* asshole, but he spoke Thai. It was no use asking what they were looking for—the jumping jerry hadn't been able to find out.

Without waiting to be told, we opened our bit of gear, explaining apologetically in simple, sad terms how we had been robbed back in Bangkok. The inspector's assistant smiled warmly and understandingly. Before his superior could ask for our papers, I offered them. With them were two 100-baht notes.

He looked up in surprise, a trace of a happy smile on his lips.

I pulled my Buddhist amulet out from under my shirt and put my finger to my lips. Although the law was on the books about not being able to take Thai Buddhist images out of the country, it was rarely, if ever, applied to *petits objets.* The inspector and his assistant smiled brightly and looked at me like I was a fool. It was the easiest money they had ever made. It was also the cheapest diversion I had ever bought. Next, I had to work on getting by the physical search.

"Oh, *mon Dieu!*" a man's voice next to us exclaimed in anguish.

All of us turned. Soldiers had lifted a *farang's* shirt halfway up his trunk, exposing the flat, cellophane bags of white powder that he'd taped to his body. There was a stunned, sick look on his swarthy face. The cops were smiling and laughing, their day made. The police made a great show of handcuffing the frog and continuing a minute search of his belongings, in no hurry to bring an end to their pleasure by tossing the pond-plopper into the first slammer of the many he would be seeing for the next quarter-century.

When our inquisitors returned their attention to us, I put on another strong, disapproving look and shook my head firmly.

"*Jet wan nee,*" the inspector said, shaking his head and frowning.

The seventh today. Business was good. But not for the smack smugglers.

Stepping forward, I offered myself for inspection. Although it proved to be only cursory for me, Tysee wouldn't be treated any differently than anyone else in the tent that now loomed ahead.

While my panic rose inside me, the happy smile on the assistant's face dropped. I turned while they were inspecting me and saw Tysee doubling forward slightly, her trunk bobbing slowly up and down. I was at her side in a moment.

"I okay, Mah-tin. It just little cramp," she said bravely, then she stepped in the direction of the tent and doubled over again. She hadn't even been called forward yet for the body search.

The inspectors' faces both registered concern. The leader glanced behind him. The female inspectors were busy inside the tent. I quickly slipped out another couple of red baht notes and secreted them on him.

"*Pby, Pby,*" he said, dismissing us rapidly.

The green-faced frog was finally being led away.

"Ah, *cup coon cup! Cup coon cup!*" I said, thanking them profusely and helping my dear wife back to the train.

"Jesus! That was *close!*" I said as we both collapsed into our compartment. "Oldest trick in the book but it worked again. I'll tell ya, we make some pair!"

"Buddha, He take care of us before, He take care of us now," she said simply, the sad look back on her face.

I could only nod. I was drained.

"You worry too much."

"I hope you're right," I said, still tense and worried, "because we still have the border ahead of us."

———— • ————

It was dark a half-hour later when the train shunted up to the border itself—a loading platform in the middle of nowhere, surrounded close in by a high, rusting fence and barbed wire, and beyond by more jungle. Everything was lit up by powerful spotlights. At first I was shocked to see as many military as at our last stop, and by the familiar long lineups of passengers being searched. I thought we were going to be inspected again, but then our train started moving in a different direction, and I realized the reason for the previous stop: the border itself couldn't handle all the trains coming through, not with the extra delay caused by the heightened inspections, so another stop had been laid on. We had already passed our border search.

Customs were cursory for our train—both the exit formalities with the Thais and the entry ones with the Malaysians, the latter being, as usual, only casual. Soon we were past the narrowed neck of the gauntlet and picking up speed. I felt safe. These Moslems would have no interest in a Buddha Head, I was sure.

"That's hard to take, without food in the stomach," I said. "With the delay, we won't arrive in Butterworth till nine tonight. That's less than an hour away. Then I think we have a three-hour wait on board before we pull out for Singapore. Let's see if they're serving now."

I pressed the polished porcelain button that summoned the steward. A few moments later there was a light knock at the door. We quickly packed the wadding into our mouths—it was formed like some orthodontist's molds by then—while I palmed the Bulgarian's open-bladed buck knife under a pillow, just in case. The gun's noise, I had realized upon reflection, would cause many more problems than it would solve. Tysee still had the Head in the sling, and only had to put on her best pregnant look.

The now-familiar old Malay politely took our order of orange juice, *nasi goring* for myself, and a fruit-and-vegetable salad for Tysee. After a small but distinct bow, he was gone.

I sat back opposite Tysee and we held hands loosely again, our heads turned to the window, our darkened reflections jerking and bouncing gently with the click and clack of the old railway line. I'd opened my mouth to say something when there was a low rap at the door.

"Well, that didn't take him long," I said, palming the knife again. "Perhaps he brought the orange juice first."

I flipped up the lock and turned the handle. It was the old Malay with a pot of tea on his tray.

"Ah, we didn't order tea, mate. We want . . ." Then I started at the look of terror on his face.

It was too late.

A huge Sikh wearing an enormous black turban pushed the steward violently into the small compartment. He crashed across the table like a sack of old bones, tea splattering ahead of him. In the Sikh's black, hairy fist was a .22

pistol made much more threatening by its five-inch silencer. Immediately behind him was his companion, my size, pulling a large, curve-bladed *kirpan* from under his coat.

I could only bring the buck knife off the seat a foot before the pistol was against my temple. The gunman disarmed me, then crisply and efficiently pushed the old man to the floor and under the seat, where he gasped and rattled in fear. At the same time and as rapidly, the *kirpan*-waving Sikh shut and locked the door, and roughly searched me until he found the gun. He took it and pushed me back down on the seat. He closed the buck knife and pocketed both weapons. No one spoke while they quickly searched the small room.

Finding nothing, they turned to us, their faces knotting with tension and frustration. Their black eyes fell on Tysee's protruding stomach. The one with the *kirpan* tapped it with his knife, then woggled his head back and forth, a broad smile spreading across his bearded face.

"It must be a boy baby," he said. "He is going to be velly, velly strong. His muscles are already velly, velly hard." He laughed roughly.

"You are called Lee Rivers," said the bigger of the two, the one with the gun massaging my temple. "You know what our purpose is here. Give it to us the Buddha Head and there will be no problem. No, no problem at all. Or else we will gladly kill you."

He nodded his turban toward Tysee. If any man had eyes like a tiger, he did.

She looked at me, her eyes wide with panic, the Buddha evidently having stepped out for the moment. There was no use arguing. There was nothing to barter with.

"Well, Sikh and ye shall find. I think you'd better give it to them, Tysee."

She stood and reluctantly reached under her dress. After a brief fumble, the round relic appeared, still swaddled in its protective layers of cloth. Pushing the tray and teapot aside, she set it down on the table between us. Their eyes fixed on the bundle, fascination and excitement lighting their cold, professional stares. The larger of the two, standing beside Tysee, rattled something off in Sikharian. Without even a nod, the other pulled up a stool and sat down just to my right, placing the shiny blade of the *kirpan* beside the bundle. He began to unwrap it. The broad blade was less than two feet from me. A sudden flash of large, white teeth dared me to move for it; he brought up the buck knife, snapping it open and waving it menacingly before my eyes. I turned away, looking into the reflections in the darkened window, while he silently turned to his business.

Among the dancing images in the glass was one of Tysee slowly, conspicuously reaching into a fold in her skirt. The long pistol unhesitatingly swung over to her, the barrel inches from her head, inches from sending her to eternity. With a brave smile, she brought up the package of Marlboros and indicated with a helpless shrug that she'd like one. Her hand trembled. His eyes glinted with suspicion until she flipped up the top.

"Would you like cigarette?" she asked, holding out the open pack to both of them.

I almost leaded my breeches.

The big Sikh smirked, not condescending to answer. The long barrel of his .22 gravitated back to me. Tysee closed the package and set it down in front of her.

The other Sikh used the point of the Bulgarian's knife to lift off the coverings, as if touching them with his bare hands would contaminate him.

There was little time. Once they had confirmed that it was indeed the Head, we'd lose ours. The tension, the danger was thick and hard, the air almost as dense as steel. The old steam locomotive blew its whistle once, then twice.

Tysee fumbled in the folds of her dress for a match, distressed she had none. There were some provided in a receptacle before us. I slowly reached for them and passed them to her; our fingers touched, lingering for a moment. The Sikh's gun tracked me carefully the entire way.

The big Sikh, his face set as steely as the air, kept an open corner of one black eye on us as he grew increasingly interested in the unveiling. He was now down to the last layers. Tysee picked up the package of cigarettes. I crossed my arms. looking beaten, harmless, and made the strongest fist with my right hand that I could.

The Sikh threw off a corner of the innermost protective

cloth. A golden cheek appeared. Tysee moved to re-open the flip-top Marlboro package. The knife's shiny point lifted a second corner away, revealing the knobby-topped, golden Head. Tysee flipped back the top, her hands still trembling slightly. The Sikhs' eyes fastened in wonder on the revealed Head as the final corners slipped away. She fingered a cigarette. The big Sikh, an arrogant smirk cracking open his dark-bearded features, made a sarcastic comment to his partner, who smirked back in kind. With deft skill, the subordinate flipped the strong knife over in his hand so that it landed point down, in stabbing position. Tysee froze. Both fixed their eyes on her and guffawed.

"Smoke your cigarette," the big one said sardonically. "But have you not heard that smoking causes early death?"

They both laughed darkly, the gun dipping slightly.

Tysee shakily moved her hands below the level of the table. The big Sikh standing next to her noticed but said nothing. An evil and hateful look surfaced on the smaller Sikh's face as he gripped the knife with both hands. I tensed, ready to spring. He raised it high above the table.

Then drove it straight down into the top of the Head.

At the same moment Tysee's hand came up over the tabletop. The dull *thunk* of the knife lodging in a golden curl hid the little *ptew* sound from the Khokhlov Special as it spat its poisonous, silent bullet into the big Sikh's chest. For a moment he didn't move, but then he collapsed backward, his silenced gun discharging wildly in the confined room with the sound of a champagne cork, the slug slamming into the windowsill inches from my head.

The hammerhead of my right backfist slammed into the sitting Sikh, smashing his nose and driving him off the stool and onto the convulsing body of his partner, the buck knife's blade snapping off in the Head.

Instantly I was on him, driving my fist with all my might again and again until his face was a red, pulpy mass. I need not have bothered—he was probably unconscious after the first blow.

I stood up, panting and heaving.

"Good stuff, Tysee. But, Jesus! Did you have to *offer* him one of the goddamned cigarettes? What if he'd taken it!"

"Sikhs no smoke—you know that," she replied, sounding

more upset than unsteady. She replaced the tiny pistol in the pack.

I shook my head, still panting, and looked around.

"You know, you're bloody incredible! Do you know that!"

But her attention was totally on the Head. Tears sprang to her eyes as she inspected the scar. I glanced at it. The top of the knife was firmly embedded in the top, behind the right eye. Tysee looked for a moment like she was going to fall apart.

"Best get it wrapped. We'll have to . . . what . . . ?"

I was interrupted by a croaking sound below me. It was the old steward. I had forgotten about him. I pulled the terrified old man to his feet—he was shaking so violently I thought he was going to fall apart—and set him on a seat with instructions not to move. The big Sikh was still twitching. A slight odor of almonds rose from his body.

I retrieved my Walther from the big Sikh's pocket and dug through the rest of their clothes, checking their papers, aware that this was getting to be a habit. The big dead one was Arat Singh, and his smaller buddy, Awithur Singh. Other identification confirmed that they lived in Amritsar in the Punjab, the home of the Golden Temple. In a breast pocket I found an airplane ticket—Aeroflot from Bombay to Bangkok direct just the day before. The fare was marked FOC. Free Of Charge. There were other papers.

"My God, look at this!" I said in surprise. "Here's how they spotted us!"

They were pictures. Some were clipped from my old high-school and university yearbooks, and had been taken before I had a beard.

"These *aren't* Xeroxed! They're *original!* Clipped right out of the bloody books. And look at *these!*"

There were others, of me walking down Bangkok streets. I'd never noticed anyone photographing me. From what I was wearing I knew some of the snaps had been taken years ago. Brock was unquestionably right—I *had* been dossiered. I pocketed them all. I wasn't sure if Tysee even heard me while she wrapped the Head.

After she was finished, I stood and unlatched the little table and flipped it down to its rest position. Reaching up, I unsnapped the brass latch above the wooden sill and yanked the window up. Hot, humid air blew into the compartment along with bits of ash and the coal-dust smell from the huffing locomotive. I stuffed the gun into the big man's pocket, and the broken, now useless buck knife into the other's.

It took me a moment to draw Tysee away from where she was rocking the Head in her comforting arms. Without a word, we manhandled the two heavy men up. We raised the first one and draped him over the windowsill, his arms flopping out uselessly until we tumbled him into the dark, the gravel and the jungly track side. Then the other. . . . The frightened little steward made a little gasp like a baby bird each time.

I turned to hastily wash the blood off when I heard something move behind me. It was the old man, terror written all over his face, making a dash for the door. I grabbed him by the collar. He made a strangled squeal as I pushed him back down. I handed him a glass of water to calm his whimpering, but his shaking hands spilled most of it.

"Christ, you drink like I do on Patpong," I joked, trying to put him at ease. I could have saved my voice. He had no idea what the hell I was talking about.

"Take off your jacket and shirt. And your belt."

He looked at me with saucer eyes and began to shake like a wet dog.

"Don't worry," I said, as gently as I could. "I'm going to tie you up. If I wanted to give you flying lessons, you'd be out the window already."

He nodded rapidly and complied with my request. The engine blew its whistle again. I glanced out the window. We were approaching the outskirts of Butterworth and the train was beginning to slow. Tearing strips from his shirt, I gagged and tied him up, then secured him in the bog—a suitable place for the old geezer, since he looked like he was going to crap his drawers any minute, if he hadn't done it already.

I hung his watch on a prong in front of him and left the light on.

"Don't make a sound until a full hour after we arrive in the station or you'll be joining the Sikhs, do you understand?" I growled with the fiercest look I could conjure, destroying whatever little confidence I had built up in him.

His eyes looked like a scared puppy's as I closed the door, and just in time—I thought I caught the scent of something unpleasant.

"What we do?" Tysee asked listlessly. "We no can stay on train."

"That's for damned sure. Best get the Head into the sling. We'll have to get lost in Penang for now." I was whispering, and wishing she'd snap out of it. At least we still had the Head. And our lives. "Don't worry. Something always turns up. There is . . . always a way," I added, my choice of phrases reminding me of Wolfgang again.

My brave voice didn't match my words. Tysee looked grim. Once the steward was free, the heat would really be on. And we were already long past the frying-pan stage.

The train huffed down to a crawl and the glow of starlight and what moon there was reflected off the tops of other railway tracks outside, creating graceful, gleaming ribbons of light. These split into more and more branches as we slowly clattered and clacked into Butterworth railyard. A few minutes more and the tired old train jerked to a stop. Escaping steam hissed loudly as we joined the noisy, chaotic crowd breaking off to catch the connecting ferry to Georgetown on Penang Island.

We quickly made ourselves lost in the thick, scurrying glow of dusky Malays, stiff-walking Indians, shuffling Chinese and young, backpacking travelers, all hurrying onto the large, old ferry at the dock adjoining the station. Tysee and I made it just as the final whistle blew for this shunt. A few minutes later the creaking old boat pulled away from the battered dock and began to shudder across the narrow strait.

We wriggled our way through the crowd to the front to be one of the first off, knowing it wouldn't be long before a furnace blast of heat blew down on us. It wasn't only the old steward who would soon be chattering his teeth to the cops. With two bodies littering the rail allowance, there would soon be a major effort by the Malaysians to nab us—in addition to everyone else in the bloody universe. At least I expected they'd find two bodies—I didn't think the other Sikh would have survived the fall, despite his cushioning ragtop.

The same, unmistakable feeling I'd had back at the railway station, that eyes were burning into my back, overwhelmed me again. I expected a gun in my back any moment. Unable to control the acutely uncomfortable feeling, I swung around and surveyed the thick crowd. But there were too many people, too many eyes. I hoped I as just being paranoid.

My spirits sank lower as I turned back and leaned against the railing to study our position. I watched the low, dark, rounded island approaching, the flickering oil lights on sampans and tramp steamers all around us unable to prettify the scene. The Pearl of the Orient was tarnished and clouded that night.

We were in more serious trouble than I thought, it slowly began to occur to me. We'd be trapped on the island, though Butterworth would have been even worse, there being no tourists to blend in with. That's why I'd instinctively chosen the island. But certainly every ferry out would soon be carefully watched. As would be the airport. If the Thai reward was broadcast, I could bet that before long some observant Chinese, and they make up most of the population of Penang, would be cashing in. Suddenly Singapore, once the light at the end of the tunnel, took on the image of a blown-out candle.

A deep depression descended on me as I pulled Tysee close and we leaned against the rail to watch the dock looming, several hundred yards distant. On top of everything else, we still hadn't eaten. My vision was so tunneled by my gloom that I didn't pay any notice at first to a long, white sailboat gliding across the bow of the ferry. It barely escaped being cut in two. Frantic warning blasts from the ferry seemed to bring me back closer to reality.

"Why don't you watch where you're fuckin' goin', you goddamned son of a bitch! I ha' the fuckin' right of way!" a figure draped in white at the back of the sleek craft screamed drunkenly. His arm suddenly seemed to wave. Seconds later a mostly full bottle of beer hit the ferry's metal side and disintegrated.

Then the graceful smaller craft, its running lights not on, was swallowed up by the gloom behind us.

I looked at Tysee in disbelief.
It was Snake.

———— • ————

"Is that him? Come in little boat?"

"Huh?" I mumbled, struggling from a disquieting dream in which crocodiles were chasing me and my legs were like lead, unresponsive.

Raising myself on an elbow, I took in the tiny, dollar-a-day beach hut we had rented at Batu Ferringi, an hour up the island's coast from the city. I knew that would be Snake's destination. If he made it that far.

"There! In little rubber boat," Tysee exclaimed, pointing through the slat door of the raised shack.

I squinted into the bright morning, the sun reflecting off the calm waters. My heart leapt and I was instantly awake. Sure enough, Snake was rowing his Zodiac toward shore. The *Riquer* lay anchored alone behind him. He would be coming in for supplies—probably beer. He'd no doubt depleted his stores the previous night.

"Right! Good stuff!" I said excitedly, giving her a hug and a quick kiss on the cheek, then jumping to my feet and whacking my head on the low crossbeam.

Snake fumbled out of the rubber boat into knee-deep water, then his bloodshot eyes widened as he turned and saw me reaching for the rope with one hand, still holding my head with the other. Without the mouthplugs, my disguise hadn't fooled him long.

"Well, I'll be goosed by a cross-eyed kangaroo," he said in his Tasmaniac accent, his voice graveled and thick, as he stuck out an enormous hand in my direction. "I've heard you can see some pretty ugly things on the DT s but this is ridiculous. And *you* look ridiculous. How are ya, mate?"

"Oh, I can probably complain, but I'll do that later. Christ, your eyes look like a road map for the entire Communist world!"

I'd always liked that about him, his eyes. They were normally a vivid, bright blue, and even when completely whipped they remained anchored solidly in his head—eyes you could trust. I had known Snake practically as long as I'd been in the Orient, meeting him, interestingly enough, way back in the jungles of Palawan in the Philippines. I had been in the area of the Tabon Caves, where the skull of Tabon Man was found, looking for the Tao't Bato tribe, whose basketry is among the most attractive in the Far East.

He had been there collecting animals for zoos. A black-palmed cockatoo he could pick up in the jungle of Indonesia or Papua New Guinea for five dollars, he could flog for two thousand in Europe or the States; a three-foot red arowana, a particularly rare fish, would fetch the same price in Japan. Birds did particularly well. Rhinoceros hornbills, mynas, birds of paradise, sacred ibis, orange-bellied leafbirds and parrots were always in demand. But his real interest was snakes, mainly because they didn't have to be fed much and didn't leave a mess. Thus, his nickname. Singapore, because it had long been at the heart of the black market in exotic animals, had been his home for years.

He had done well enough to buy a small boat and dive headfirst into treasure hunting. He had a knack for finding old pottery wrecks—so much so that he was as familiar with the auction houses of Amsterdam as I was. He could often be found there, flogging his finds. I'd augmented my income on a few dives with him as well.

He had done well enough after one particularly good discovery to pay cash for the sixty-foot *Riquer,* named after an eighteenth-century Mediterranean pirate whose statue he once saw standing in the main square at Ibiza.

Mike Cheevers, his real name, is one of those tall, good-looking Aussies with a thick tousle of sun-bleached hair. Atop his was usually perched a yachting cap with a patch displaying, appropriately enough, a skull and crossbones. He was also huge—six-foot-six and weighing in at a solid 260. None of it was fat, despite the voluminous amounts of beer he poured back.

"Thanks. You don't look unlike the bottom of my bilge either. What the hell are you doing here, mate? And what's with the hair?"

"I'll explain later. But you gotta get us out of here. And fast."

My voice was calm but he caught the urgency in it.

"There's no time to pick up some beer? That's what I'm coming in for. I've only got three or four cases left."

He stared at his half-smoked cigarillo with a worried look.

I shook my head and looked back over my shoulder, scanning the mostly empty beach. May it stay that way. He shrugged and raised a large finger.

"This *better* be urgent. And I sure the bloody hell better not run outa beer. Christ, everything else has gone wrong since that damned Pen . . . hey! I say, mate, who's this?" he asked, his voice expanding as he noticed Tysee for the first time.

His eyes lit up as he took her in. She was standing just on the edge of the sand. With the bundle under her arm, she looked like a little girl who had run away from home—perhaps because she just had. I introduced them, and he waded over, flipped away his cigarillo butt, leaned down and took her hand in his. I could see the familiar leer that substituted for a smile spread across his face.

"Nice to meet you. You speakee English?"

"Yes. How do you do . . . ah . . . Snake?" she replied, the name uncomfortable on her lips. "Lee tell me some thing about you," she said, the coolness in her voice not lost on him.

"I'm sure anything Lee would say about me would be the unadulterated truth," he said, casting a narrow glance at me. "I'm sure I can tell you all kinds of interesting stories about him as well."

I shifted nervously, then jerked my head toward the sea. He took the cue.

"Right! If we hafta shove off, let's shove off! All aboard that's goin' aboard!"

We clambered into the stern, with him rowing.

"Now, you still haven't told me what the hell you're doing out here, mate," he repeated, leaning into the oars. "You heading down early to meet me in Singapore for that dive we got planned? At least we're all stocked up for it, except for the beer, that is."

"I'll tell you when we get to the boat. You won't believe it unless you see it."

Snake's eyes dropped to the bundle Tysee held under her arm, a glimmer of interest forming for the first tine in his red winkers.

"What are *you* doing here?" I added.

No one was following. The beach was still empty except for a couple of strollers. Relief mixed with excitement to produce a feeling of guarded euphoria.

His face clouded.

"Aah, that damned Pen. She talked me into sailing up here so she could visit her folks, and then jumped ship. That was yesterday. Damn. Solid as a brick shithouse too," he added remorsefully, between long pulls on the oars.

"If she's anything like your other girlfriends," I said, "I'd say she was probably more like a brick sewage disposal plant." The first smile in days cracked my face. His taste in women was appalling. "What happened?"

"Aah, it was nothing. Just some little thing I picked up off some bimbo down in Jakarta and passed on to 'er. Bloody sheilas, I'll never understand them—they get upset about the silliest things. Too bad. I'm gonna miss the way she used to give me head when I was at the tiller and cuttin' a force five. Christ, she used to blow me until my ears popped. Somebody should have written a song about it, it was so beautiful."

"Somebody did. 'Blowin' in the Wind'," I said, laughing.

Tysee looked diplomatically away for a moment. I couldn't read the expression on her face. Though normally one of the least inscrutable Orientals I had ever met, she hadn't lost the ability to look deadpan at will.

I felt my smile broadening. That's what I liked about Snake—he always brought out the worst in me. He gloomily checked over his shoulder and concentrated on his rowing, his bulging arms pulling the little rubber boat through the water with no apparent difficulty.

"Where'd you meet the little lady?" he asked, leering at her again. "Not often I like one of your broads. A bit skinny, but nice eyes."

Tysee turned away again.

"I'll tell you about her, too," I replied, "once we're aboard. It's a *long* story, believe me."

We pulled alongside the yacht. I climbed aboard first. Tysee stood and began to pass me the Head.

"You be careful. This isn't the most steady . . . oops!" Snake called, as a wave came in from out of nowhere and rocked the rubber boat.

Tysee lost her footing and began to fall backward. In an

instant Snake was up. With one hand gripping the side of the *Riquer,* he scooped her up in his free arm before she and the Head tumbled into the Andaman Sea. She fumbled the Head closer to her breasts, panic in her eyes, while Snake pulled her securely to his side.

"Here, here, here little lady, it's okay," he said, holding her tightly. "You gotta be careful in these things. You never been in a boat before?"

She shook her head rapidly.

"Thank you," she said to him, deep gratitude showing in her eyes, not so much for herself as for the Head.

"Think nothing of it, little lady," he said gallantly. "Any friend of the polluted Rivers here is a friend of mine. Now let's get you aboard proper."

In a moment she was safely on deck. She looked back at him, her gratitude still plain. She held the Head tightly with both arms, unsure of the lightly bobbing deck below her. Snake leered back to her in a friendly way and tipped his sailor's hat gallantly.

"Now come on, mate, gimme a hand with this thing."

While we on hoisted the Zodiac aboard and into place, Tysee collected herself and began to look over the boat, a world obviously unfamiliar to her.

"Why you have Molotov cocktails?" she asked, once the rubber boat was stowed.

She was pointing at a mekhong bottle filled with two liquids—an amber one that took up the bottom two-thirds, and a milk-white layer above it. The nozzle was stuffed with a rag, and covered with a cellophane wrap, rubber-banded down, to keep it dry. The cocktail was carefully secured with tape to an inside corner of the cockpit, at foot level.

It was clear from her voice that her attitude toward Snake had already changed. She probably thought Snake's saving her from a dunking was divine intervention, a sign.

"Oh! So you know what it is?"

"Oh yes," she said matter-of-factly. "We make when children and play with them, building little hut and burning it down. But what white stuff above gasoline?"

Snake stopped what he was doing, unlocked the door to the main saloon, and raised his eyes. He stared at her as if she was some kind of exotic species of snake.

"Well, I'll just have to hear about this childhood of yours, that's bloody *certain,*" he said, fumbling the key in the lock. "That's liquid laundry soap at the top. Gets at those hard-to-get-at stains and dirt, and helps the gas stick to whatever it splashes on. There's three of 'em on board. Here, and taped to the mainmast, and beside the fore hatch. Lee'll be familiar with them but it's best if you check them out too—like, know where they are. It seems I don't have to tell you how to use them. There's a Bic lighter beside each one of them. Blows up first time, every time."

He swung the door open and shoved the keys back in his pocket.

"Why you have . . . ?" she asked in all innocence.

"Well, Terry's gone but these waters are still full of his pirates, me dear. The bastards are even taking down freighters in the Straits of Malacca these days. Lee'll show you the armory below, too. There's a couple of pistols, a Riot Remington 12-gauge, an M-16 and a Savage 30-30 with a scope for long range. Hell of a lot better protection than Ban or Arrid."

She pulled her pack of Marlboros out of a pocket, flipped off the top, and dropped out the midget pistol. Snake stared at it, wondering what to think.

"You still play with toys?"

"No toy. But I know how use other guns too."

"She saved our lives with that. It fires poison bullets."

Snake pushed his cap back on his head.

"Well, I'll be bloody dammned!" he said. "You *will* have to tell me all about your childhood, little lady." Then he turned to check a line. "Okay, now what's so important that I can't get stocked up on beer? Who's the bogeyman you got after you, mate?"

"Come on below. We'll show you something," I said, stepping down the companionway.

A moment later we were standing around the small galley table in the good-sized cabin. None of us moved.

"Well?" Snake said, his voice still thick with hangover.

Tysee looked to me. I nodded.

Quietly and smoothly, she placed the bundle on top of the chart table. She delicately and deliberately removed the layers of covering until the last corner fell away and

the Head lay alone in front of us. She slipped to her knees
and held her hands in a *wai*, unmoving but clearly moved.
A shaft of sunlight beaming through a porthole lit up one
rubied eye and caressed the smooth, golden features.
Snake's eyes fastened on the red gleam from the unblink-
ing corundum orb.

"What . . . ! What *is* it?" he finally said, though his
voice betrayed that he knew.

"It's the Rumor, my friend."

"Jesus Christ—"

"No! *Buddha!*" Tysee said sharply.

"Sorry. Same thing. You mean after all this time, there is
truth to it?" he exclaimed, fixing his eyes on mine, his voice
full of little boy's wonder. "You're joking, right, mate? I *do*
have the DTs."

I bit my bottom lip and slowly, firmly shook my head.

He looked down at Tysee, then at me. What he saw left
him with no doubts.

"So it *is* true. The bloody thing *does* exist!"

"It's true. And it seems like the whole world is after us
right now, trying to get it. I guess you haven't read a paper
lately."

He shook his head.

"I listen to the news on Radio Aussie every day for the
cricket scores," he said, "but there's been nothin' on *this!*
Where'd you cop it?"

"François Giscard put me onto it. You remember meeting him a couple of years ago, when he came through
Singapore and we visited him on the *QEII?*"

"Yeah. The animated frog who took us to dinner. Go on."

"Swiss, actually," I corrected him. Then I told him everything else, less the gorier details. When I was finished
he nodded his large head slowly, and bent down to inspect
the rubies more closely.

"It's got eyes the same color as yours a lot of the time,
you know that? And a head as thick and hard as yours, too."
He couldn't resist a joke, though his voice was serious. "My
God, but those gems are *unbelievable!* Bloody *perfect!* The
entire thing is perfect, except for this knife scar that Sikh
put into it. Too bad about that, all right."

Tysee had spotted the first aid kit on the wall. A moment
later she was lovingly applying peroxide and a Band-Aid to

the gash. Snake and I looked obliquely at each other. I shrugged so only he could see. He grinned, pushed his cap back again, and scratched his head.

"Yep, little lady, I'm sure that should take care of it," he said, winking at me. "Now, where we goin'?"

"I need to make a phone call to François in New York."

He thought for a moment, scratching his day-old beard.

"Georgetown out of the question?"

"Completely."

"I can only think of Singapore, then."

"It'll have to do." I shrugged, holding up a palm. "And then?"

"I'll find out from that call. Maybe that's it."

Tysee made a *wai* again and began to carefully rewrap the Head. Snake's eyes lingered on the bundle long after it had disappeared beneath the layers of cloth.

"And Kun San's daughter. Bloody incredible," he said, looking at her with increasing admiration.

A hint of sorrow passed over Tysee's lovely face.

"Snake," I said nervously, knowing we'd talked long enough. "Let's pull those panties up and get the hell out of here."

As he keyed onto the old sailing joke between us, the leer suddenly returned to his face and his eyes danced the way they did whenever there was excitement around.

"They're not bloody *panties!* How many goddamned times do I have to tell you? Seems we Aussies have to give you damned Yanks another lesson in sailing. *Drapes!* Now get your ass up on deck or I'll keelhaul ya. Semen Last Class. And one more thing," he added, rummaging around in a drawer and fishing up a plaque from among the junk. "With that whinging Pen gone, it's back to life as normal!"

He removed a second plaque from the wall and looked at it fondly for a moment. I glanced over his shoulder and read it.

PRESENTED TO
PEN YUEN
THE SNAKE HIGH ACHIEVEMENT AWARD
FOR
BEST FREE FORM FUCK

Snake unceremoniously tossed it out the porthole. He replaced it with the one he'd dug out of the drawer, then stepped back to admire it.

> *If it burns, smoke it.*
> *If it flows, drink it.*
> *If it moves, fuck it.*

Then he turned, gave Tysee a wink and agilely charged up the companionway and out on deck.

———— • ————

"Are you *sure* they're not on duty right now?"

I was nervous as Snake calmly glided the *Riquer* into Changi Yacht Club. It had taken five days to sail down the coast, Snake insisting we tie up every night because of the concentrated tanker and freighter traffic. Tonight, because we were so close to Singapore, we continued on. It was late evening, near 11:00 p.m., and our running lights were on. The yellow quarantine flag we were required to raise up was purposely stowed below so it would look like we had just been on a cruise around the island. So was the Head, safely ensconced in the small cabin Tysee and I shared.

"Quit your bleedin' whingin', Lee. Customs has gone home, I tell ya. We'll berth the lady and you can slip ashore and make that phone call, then we'll be gone."

Cabin lights in many of the yachts at anchor in the small, enclosed bay glowed through rounded portholes. The club itself was dim.

I helped Snake tie the boat up, then fixed fresh mouth wads in place and wobbled on my sea legs toward the clubhouse. I was wearing some of Snake's yachting clothes, which Tysee had altered, and my pockets were full of Singapore dollars Snake had provided. To my disappointment, the door was locked. An armed guard behind it politely waved me away, then pointed at his watch. Cursing to myself, I walked back to the boat.

"I have to go into town," I said dejectedly.

Snake's eyebrows rose. He checked his watch, then shrugged. He was alone, slouched in the cockpit, sucking on a cigarillo and a can of beer. Tysee was stowed out of sight. I turned toward the quay.

"Don't forget the cigarillos, mate," he called after me as

I headed down the wharf. "And the Singapore Tigers. This is my last one."

I indicated in sign language to the guard at the gate that I would be back, and tried not to flinch as he memorized my face. A cab was handy, and when the Chinese driver asked me my destination, I thought for only a moment before replying.

"Raffles."

The hotel I had named my dog after. My late pet.

The car whizzed down the smooth, winding highway toward city center, past glimpses in the dark of the luxuriously manicured landscape bordering. I looked the other way when we whisked past Changri Prison.

A half-hour later we pulled up in front of the old hotel.

"Wait," I told the driver.

It was nearly midnight when I walked into the colonial foyer with its potted palms and lingering aromas of Kipling and Conrad. The place was quiet, which was fine with me. Rounding the corner to the left, I wandered into the Long Bar and chose a table off to the side, behind a large, overhanging palm. The place was not entirely empty; a number of patrons still hovered in the ornate old lounge. One was a Sikh, and a couple of others were clearly Moslem— all non-drinkers, and all, so it felt, scrutinizing me with a less-than-casual air that put me on guard. My disguise seemed to be working this time, perhaps because five days in the sun had tanned my complexion considerably, leaving no telltale white shadow. But I hadn't forgotten how the two Sikhs on the train had penetrated it.

I ordered a Sling, a telephone, and the *Straits Times*. A waiter brought them all to me on the same silver tray.

"Collect call to New York please, operator. For François Giscard. Just tell him Brook is calling."

I gave the hotel operator the number and set down the receiver. Minutes later it rang. A nervous twitch of a shoulder here, a shuffle of a newspaper there, seemed to betray a stir of interest among my bar companions. I hoped I was being paranoid.

The anxiety in François's voice was obvious.

"*Comment allez-vous?* I have been so worried!" he exclaimed, a large measure of his relief escaping down the long but perfectly clear connection.

"So have I, *mon ami*. And I think more so than you."

"Our assistant? Did you find him?"

"Yes—sort of . . . ," I said, not knowing how to put it. Not wanting to.

"I have not heard from him—is he okay?"

"He's keeping well. Just has a bit of a cold," I replied, regretting my choice of words again. I couldn't tell him my old friend was dead. Not on the phone.

"Talking about the temperature, has the weather improved?"

"Terrible. Getting worse all the time."

"You sound different . . . a little garbly—"

"I'm chewing gum," I said. I couldn't mention the lip plugs.

"Are you still keeping . . . your head up?"

"No problem, as they say in India, which means that it's very much of a problem indeed. I wouldn't mind putting it behind me as quickly as possible, if you know what I mean."

"Oui. Je fait. The operator says you are in Singapore. Where?"

"Sipping on a Singapore Sling," I answered.

François had to know it had been invented here, in this very bar at the Raffles. He always stayed here when in town.

There was a pause. Then he let out a long aaaaaaaah.

"Your friend with the embassy?" I asked impatiently.

He was silent for a moment replying.

"I'm afraid some problems have arisen."

"Jesus Christ, François! I'm going crazy—" I started to spit through clenched teeth before he interrupted me.

"Calm down! Calm down! It is just temporary. I am doing my best. It is not easy. Can you wait a few days?"

"I can wait till eternity. But if I stick around here that's *exactly* where I'll be—eternity."

"Hmmmmmmm. . . .There is only one other thing I can think of, though it is difficult. Is there *any* possibility you can find your way to somewhere you can sling back a sunset?"

"Sunset?"

Then I understood. The Manila Hotel's specialty is a soft, colorfully delicious drink called the Manila Sunset.

"Yes," I replied strongly.

"But how?"

"I have run into a friend of mine you met once. He's in the . . . Zoo's Who."

There was another pause while he flipped through his mind's card catalogue.

"Perhaps he is the Flying Dutchman, who is not Dutch? *Oui?*"

"Right, mate. We all had dinner on the *QEII* together once. Now, how do I meet your man when I get there?"

"There's a plane you always catch when you're there. See the pilot. He will know what to do."

It took me a minute to figure that one out.

"You don't mean 'The Fastest Place in Town'?"

"That's it."

I knew he meant the Boeing 69 Club, a bar down on del Pilar in the heart of the Ermita tourist belt. But how did he know I hung out there a lot when I was in Manila? I'd always tried to keep my generally decadent life private from him. But this was no time to ask.

"Okay. We're on our way."

"And Brook . . . be careful."

"I'm doing my best."

"Au revoir."

"Oh reservoir to you too."

I replaced the receiver on the antique telephone and took up the *Strait Times.* An item on page 2 caught my attention. It was about succession battles raging in the Golden Triangle between competing would-be warlords. It appeared Chung Si Fu was already consolidating his power over Kun San's old empire. In the meantime, the paper reported, heroin prices had taken a rise due to the unsettled supply. I made a note to pass the information along to Tysee.

So as not to appear rushed, I flipped through the pages, until page 6 . . . where a headline knocked the breath out of me.

BUDDHA HEAD FOUND?

I flinched when I saw the wire photo of the downed plane, and the visa picture of me. In the corner was a bespeckled shot of the Dalai Lama. I bit my lip and scanned the copy.

It said that "rumors continue to grow that the actual

skull of the Buddha exists and has been found." It speculated that the Dalai Lama had planted it at Tengboche during the crisis of 1959. A report from Kathmandu confirmed that a robbery had taken place at the monastery; another, from travelers, stated that a monk had recently been cremated, though no reporters had as yet reached the remote monastery. Worst of all, Tysee and myself were still named as the prime suspects, with the police centering their search on the Penang area, where we had been seen leaving the ferry and boarding a pedaled rickshaw—the last reported sighting of us.

I carefully read what the old steward had to say about the "violent encounter" in our compartment.

> He claimed two Sikhs held himself, Mr. Rivers and Miss San captive at gunpoint but that the Indians were overcome after a struggle. Their bodies were subsequently thrown from the window of the moving train.
>
> The steward, wishing to remain anonymous, said a round bundle was the object of their attention but that he did not have a clear view of exactly what it was.
>
> A search of the rail allowance has turned up only one body, identified as one Arat Singh. He had been shot with a small caliber gun.

"Huh . . . !" I mumbled. Just one? Maybe the animals got the other. Indian food. My eyes rolled down to the paragraph concerning the Dalai Lama.

> Despite the great amount of interest generated in the Buddhist world, the office of the Dalai Lama in Dharamsala refuses to comment, saying only that to do so would be to fan the flames of the rumor. His Holiness has gone into seclusion, frustrating the efforts of reporters.

The next paragraph was like a boot in the eye.

> A huge explosion took place near the home of Mr. Rivers in Bangkok two days ago. A large area of houses was flattened by a car bomb attack. It is speculated that the Jains, a minority Indian sect

who have claimed responsibility for the bombing, were operating with the incorrect address. At least 25 people were killed and numerous injured in the explosion. Little damage occurred to the residence itself.

Then followed a report on the mysterious long trail of bodies. The story ended by stating that Interpol was involved, and reiterating that a mysterious one-million-baht reward had been placed on my head.

Depression and anxiety descended. The only thing I could be thankful for was that they hadn't pinned Wolfgang's murder on me. Presumably they hadn't discovered his body yet. That might take a while; I had locked the trapdoor behind me.

I folded the paper, slung back my drink, left a reasonable tip, and headed for the door, aware, as I left, of a chair creaking away from a table and the slow click of heels behind me. I quickly crawled into the back of my waiting cab and we sped off. Through the rear window I saw one of the Sikhs standing on the steps of the grand old hotel, staring after us, thoughtfully scratching his shaggy chin.

The trip back to the club felt longer than the one out to Raffles. I sat in the back, fidgeting. There was no doubt: I was caught between a Head and a hard place.

Almost forgetting, I ordered the driver to stop at a grog shop, where we piled the trunk and back seat to the brim with cigarillos and beer. Half an hour later we were back at Changri. I unloaded the cab, paid the driver off, and hustled down the floating wharf to the boat.

I was a boat's length away from the *Riquer* when I first heard the laughter. The lights were on below deck. Curious, I peeked through a porthole where one of the blinds had been carelessly drawn. They were sitting across from each other at the cabin table. Snake was holding one of Tysee's hands and pointing to something on her palm. Her head was thrown back in laughter at something he was saying. I watched as he added something else I couldn't hear, that too-familiar leer on his face. More cascades of laughter burst from her lips, and her eyes flashed with glee, mourning thoughts of her father, or worries about me being in danger, apparently far from her mind.

The laughter stopped abruptly as the weight of my foot-steps hit the deck. They were no longer holding hands when I slid down the companionway into the cabin. Tysee's long, tapered fingers were straightening her hair, and she avoided my look. Snake was already on his feet, looking serious.

"Come on," I said coolly, my voice trembling slightly. I slapped the newspaper down on the table with the story folded faceup. "I've made the call. Your beer is at the gate. Let's get it and get those fucking drapes or whatever the hell you call them up, and get the hell out of here."

ELEVEN

The South China Sea

"YOU KNOW," I said softly, "if you watch really carefully the very last split second before the sun disappears, it'll flash a bright, iridescent green— brighter than the brightest emerald."

We were sitting on cushions amidships, watching the great orange ball boiling down into the South China Sea off the stern. Sailing was perfect—a force three or four was blowing, but at one of those magic moments when the sea is relaxed and languid, the swells wide and gentle. The jib and mainsail were full and taut, the bright genoa billowing out the side as the sixty-foot lady gracefully sliced through the lazy seas. Lounging in the cockpit was Snake, comfortably drawing on a cigarillo and sipping from a can of beer, occasionally monitoring the compass and keeping an ear to the chatter on channel 16, letting the hydro-vane do the work of steering. Now and again he cast unhurried glances at the gathering spectacle behind him.

"No! Does it really do that?" Tysee replied.

"Sometimes. Maybe we'll be lucky tonight."

She snuggled a little closer, her head settling softly against my shoulder, her long hair caressing our cheeks in the trades, and squeezed my hand. I was happy to feel her spirits reviving so quickly. That was partly due to Snake—to the warm, joking camaraderie he had so quickly established with her after her initial hesitation—and partly the result of her Oriental way of putting on a good face, then growing into it—the millennium-old psychocybernetics of the Far East.

Mostly it was because of the sea and its vast emptiness, which relegates all earthly trials, tribulations and traumas as far into the horizon of one's mind as they are left behind over the real horizon. And for once, we had a horizon free of enemies, real or imagined, and could begin to relax for the first time since Kwan Mae. She had adjusted well, feeling few symptoms of seasickness, despite handling all the galley duties, usually the first person to go to the rail.

Our eyes swept up along the scintillating carpet of diamonds cast on the neon water to the huge sphere sinking before us.

"The flash is so small and brief that it's important not to even blink those last couple of seconds. Remember that now."

Only the top quarter was showing. Snake returned our smiles with a slight but relaxed nod and a lazy half-wink with both eyes, and shifted so he could watch as well. The daily ritual and reward of life at sea. Sunset.

Less than a quarter of the burning red arc now showed.

"Now, don't even blink or you'll miss it," I added. "It's that fast."

She squeezed my hand again in heightened concentration.

"Now!" I exclaimed.

The sun's very tip suddenly flashed a vibrant, brilliant green, then faded away, all in a shave of a second. The sun was gone with it.

She looked at me, her eyes wide with delight.

"So-ay mahk-mahk! Very beautiful! What it called? It have name?"

I thought for a long moment before answering.

"Yes," I replied. "It does now. It's called the Tysee Effect."

She laughed freely, hugged me, and gave me a full, moist kiss on the cheek. I could smell the freshness of her hair and breath mixing with the freshness of the sea.

With the sun out of the picture, the sky began to glow with indelible beauty, from horizon to horizon to horizon above the shimmering sea. Colors of every hue passed across clouds of every shape. It was soon a panorama that only Walt Disney in his spare time in the heavens could have produced. He moved through his entire, magical spectrum of colors, then—a pro to the end—began the most subtle of fades. But the show was far from over. The cartoons were just ending.

Delicate tones were still tracing the edges of some cumuli, when the main feature began, the multihued curtains dissolved to present the vast, tropical night sky. It began with some god's handful of diamonds being tossed out into eternity, and soon became a sparkling show of the finest facets in infinity, each trying to outflash, outwink, outsparkle the others, the visual music of their merriment creating a vast, universal orchestra of dancing light.

The insignificance of ourselves, specks on the broad sea below, and it a speck on the much broader sea above, was awesome—the Grand Mystery was awesome. We could feel our hearts beating in time with each other and with the rhythm of the living universe.

Her breath was moist on my cheek, her hair caressive as the wind played it gently across my face.

"Lee . . ." Tysee whispered, her voice now husky.

And it was all she had to say.

——— • ———

"Lee!"

The urgency in Snake's call was unmistakable.

I turned from where I was finishing up reefing the mainsail. There was a heavy roll to the sea and the possibility of a squall, the sky having boxed in a couple of days before. He was waving me frantically back to the cockpit.

Hurriedly, I made my way back along the pitching, wildly angled deck. He was tapping his ear but by the time I crawled down to the cockpit, he was shaking his head.

"Too late," he shouted over the mounting gale, pointing to the radio's waterproof exterior speaker and dials. It was spitting static. "It's Radio Aussie. Damned thing keeps fading in and out. They just said that the trail seems to lead back to Kwan Mae. They just had your friend Ham-Sandwich on. He described how he was recruited to go there, ostensibly to look at a piece. He says he had no idea it was the Buddha Head, that Kun San offered him twenty-five percent of the profits if he would flog it. Ham-Sandwich said there was no way he could do it, being as it was the Head and all."

"What crap. Any more of that and I'll be joining Tysee barfing in the bilge below."

Her stomach had finally caught up with her when she tried to read a book on anthropology in Snake's small library. A boat ain't no place to read.

"He also described how you drugged everyone. He says that you duped that little lady of yours into going along with it."

"Oh, God. Gag me with a shovel."

"And that you stole the plane, of course. He said the next day, when they came to, that five people were dead." Snake was shouting, concentrating on the helm. "We're going to have to haul down a little more of the drapes here in a sec I'm afraid, mate."

"Dead! What? From the food?" I said, shocked.

"No, mate. From gunshot wounds. Claims you had to be the man."

"Five . . . ?" I asked blankly. I only knew about the one for sure and the mystery about the other. It had to be Ham-Sandwich bullshitting again.

Snake looked grim and kept an eye on the tautness of the sails.

"Just a minute, Lee. I think it's coming back," he said, as the crackling static faded and an arrogant Brit voice surged out of the speaker. To my surprise it was Ham-Sandwich himself, being interviewed.

". . . arrived I was to see Lee Rivers in the village as well. Rivers is somewhat known in the collecting community—though most would agree, I'm sure, as an opportunist whose illegal antiquities-smuggling practices leave many things to be desired."

"That sleaze-bag, hypocritical son of a bitch," I swore under my breath, having to grip the hatch sill to keep steady in the bucking boat.

The moderator's voice interrupted Richard.

> . . . Mr. Haimes-Sandwich subsequently asked Kun San where he had found such an object:
> "Well, he was somewhat coy about answering at first, only saying that it had come into his possession recently, but when I pressed him if it had anything to do with the mysterious burglary at Tengboche Monastery, he became quite frank with me and freely admitted it, saying his plane had been used."

My ear grew even keener as the broadcaster's dulcet tones bridged the next break in Richard Haimes-Sandwich's testimony.

> One of the other mysteries in this story made up of so many, is the source of the one-million-baht reward, which an anonymous donor has placed in trust with the Bangkok *Post*, and which has fueled a great deal of interest. The late Kun San himself is widely suspected as having been behind it.
> That amount is something just a little in excess of 50,000 dollars Australian, or 40,000 American. The *Post* itself, which has been the first to publish a number of important leads in the story, says only that it was placed in a blind trust, with them holding the keys to its disbursement to the eventual captors of Lee Rivers. Numerous bounty hunters and would-be bounty hunters have joined . . .

"Ah, sorry mate, there it goes again," Snake said, rolling the dial on the set back to 16, the open channel. Neither of us said anything for a long time. We just rode, with the rocking boat crashing through the whitecaps and sending sheets of spray flying up like wings on either side. Snake's powerful hands worked the helm, keeping us hauled as tight into the northeaster as he could tack.

"Gettin' exciting, aye?" he shouted unenthusiastically.

"It's growing. Like the blob."

"Yeah. You'll be pleased to know there's been rumored sightings of you and Tysee in Mombasa, Madras and even Perth."

"May they continue to be so observant."

"I do have a bit of other good news I can pass on, though, if it'll help cheer you up."

"Yeah?" I said, hanging on as a surge of water swept over the side of the cockpit.

He drained the last few drops from his can of beer and tossed it over the stern. A fifteen-foot shark that had adopted us earlier in the day rose from our wake, rolled onto its side, and swallowed it, adding it to the rapidly growing pile of crumpled aluminum in its stomach.

"Ol' Walter's still with us. Seen lots of porpoises do this, but never a chomper. Must know I'm Aussie. The Great Australian Byte. Their favorite food. Probably a tiger shark. Sure likes the stuff anyway."

Snake pulled another Singapore Tiger from his small portable cooler and flipped off the snap-top. Walter ignored the tiny prize.

"Just what we need," I mumbled. "A shark at the door."

———— • ————

I didn't like the sound of the laughter from below. It had been going on for too long. Just like this watch, which fortunately was coming to an end.

All along the coast of Sarawak we had been changing shifts every four hours, running, at night, with only the mainsail up and an eye to the radarscope. The little snatches of sleep weren't enough, and after only six days, irritations were setting in, at least with me. Snake was more used to the crazy hours of life at sea. And Tysee, despite that one night as a bilge bunny, was back to taking sailing like a flying fish.

The muffled laughter from below was blowing up into a gale every bit as big as the one threatening to form outside. The wind had suddenly surged up to force five or even six, and was gusty, forcing me to yank down a lot of the panties with our electric winches, and wrestle with the helm, all of that while warm spray constantly stung my eyes. Normally

I love the thrills and spills of plowing through the hay-stacks; now I was concerned about the laughter and muf-fled voices from below. I didn't like to admit it, and I like to feel it even less, but jealousy was rearing its horned, green little head again. I didn't mind her *liking* Snake, but she was enjoying his company more than *I* liked. She'd been spending almost as much time with him as with me since we left Singapore. And I knew when Snake was attracted to a girl, and he was attracted to Tysee, despite her not being his usual type.

The final seconds eventually numbered off on my watch. I unlatched the door and, controlling my voice, shouted down the watch. I didn't want to repeat my entrance at Changri, though I was still keeping an eye on their forming relationship.

Five minutes later, Snake's huge bulk filled the compan-ionway as he clambered out in his squall gear, a can of Tiger and a cigarillo in hand. He was still chuckling at some joke he had shared with Tysee, and his mood was exuberant. He took up a good bit of the available room in the cockpit.

"How's Ol' Walt?" he shouted cheerfully, stepping back to look over the stern, hanging on to a guy wire for sup-port. The sight of the now-familiar fin made him smile like a boy home from school. "Now that I've got the little bug-ger fetchin' so well, I'm hoping to teach him to bark. Hey! Walt! How ya doin' boy?"

Walter didn't respond. Snake shrugged but kept chuck-ling. He tried to take a drag but his cigarillo was already soggy. He tossed it over the stern. Walter rose for it. Snake leered happily.

He checked the single G-string I had up and looked at the clouded sky.

"Jesus, I've seen more canvas on a Patpong dancer than *you* have up," he said boisterously. "Fair dinkum breeze blowing. What's happened to the bloody weather, then?"

"Blowing hot. Just like the wind below deck."

I hated myself for saying it the moment I did. Snake's happy leer abruptly disappeared and he glanced at me out of the corner of his eye. I turned away, pretending to check the compass.

"Hey, hey, hey! What's this then, mate?" he half-joked,

punching me in the shoulder. "Look and listen, *Semen Last Class*—I have to admit for a skinny little broad she's pretty attractive, but you know I like them with more meat on them, so they don't rattle apart when I give them a good pounding. She's also quick and has a great sense of humor. Good company all around. But in the end, I have to say that I only *like* your sheila, and I have to stress the *your* part. She's *your* sheila."

I turned and spat overboard. It was a reflex and I wished I hadn't done that either. I was acting like a goofy four-teen-year-old. I spun the wheel to correct a drift, but overcorrected and had to spin back. Snake noticed but said nothing.

"Well, have it your way," he said resigned, taking a sip and picking up the cellophane-wrapped Admiralty Chart tied to the compass. "I never figured you for one to still be green behind the balls—if you still have them. It sounds to me like perhaps she's wearing them for earrings."

"I wish I never would have met her," I said lamely, still in a funk and blathering. I needed a good night's sleep to straighten me out.

Snake chortled and pushed me aside, taking the helm.

"Christ, are you ever full of it now. My God! The hired help you have to take aboard these days. Can't steer a bloody boat and whines more than a whingin pommy."

He stuck a fresh cigarillo into his mouth but a gust of spray soaked it down. He tossed it back over the stern, pulled out the pack again and stuck the last one in his mouth, flipping the empty pack overboard. Walter took each of them in turn.

"Hmmmmmn. Gotta talk to that boy. Chain-smokin'. Gonna stunt his growth. Could get cancer."

I knew I had to say something that made sense before I left.

"Snake," I said, a trace of a smile feathering my lips, "I know I'm acting nutty. I've just never met a woman like her before. She's knocked me right off my feet. I don't even think of Patpong anymore."

He made a gesture like he was throwing up.

"Oh Christ! He's really got the bloody disease now, doesn't he? Now I'm *sure* that's where I saw your balls—danglin' from her ears. She'll be using your prick as a

fountain pen to sign your name to checks next. I think you
better get down there and get them back."

He leered at me as if I was the compleat fool and I knew
it and I knew he knew it but we also both knew we were
good friends so he could do it. I shook my head and tapped
my forefinger to my temple as if to say, I'm a little touched,
then shrugged helplessly.

"Ah, good. We're both agreed you're bloody insane,
which I knew anyway, but hopefully this new strain is
temporary. Now, what's new up here what I should know
about?"

"I've talked to a couple of freighters and they say things
are worse up the channel," I said, referring to the Palawan
Passage, a heavily traveled area between the long, narrow
Philippine island and an oceanic no-man's-land, hundreds
of miles across, that was dotted with reefs and atolls.

"Ha!" he snorted, looking up at the sky. "I've heard that
before from those big bastards. We don't get there for a
couple or three days anyway. It'll all be blown away by
then. How far till we're abreast of Brunei? Anything to
watch out for?"

"No. Clear water. Just Walter."

I pointed out our position on the chart. He noted it, then
glanced back at the marauder skimming just below the
surface on our tail, his fin slicing through the water like
the fin on a '59 Caddie. Snake leered wickedly back into
the wind and spray.

"God, after four hours of being close to such nice quiff,
it's gonna be awfully damned *hard* to take four hours of
this," he said. "Wait'll you see how she's *dressed*," he
added, with theatrical lust in his voice.

"Fuck you," I said, a sheepish grin on my face, as I
reached for the cabin door.

Tysee was in the cobra-skin bikini I had bought her and
was sitting on the couch. Her smooth tummy was still
palpitating with giggles as I reached for the coffeepot, my
heart beating too loudly.

"What's so funny?" I asked. "We don't get a chance to
enjoy life so much up on deck." I was trying to sound cool,
hearing and hating the edge that persisted in my voice. I
was clearly beside myself.

"Oh," she said between laughs, "Snake is funny."

Still giggling, she looked at me. I rummaged around for a coffee cup. That they were all dirty irritated me more.

"And how did he do that?" I demanded. "Undo his fly and show you his duckbilled platypus?" I chuckled. I liked my own joke. Inane as it was.

"No," she said, jumping up and giving me a hug and snapping a kiss to my cheek. We both leaned against the table, the boat rolling with the heavier weather. "He tell me about when he first meet you on Palawan Island."

I reacted like a dumb kid whose mother has instantly soothed an imagined hurt with a soft word and a kiss: I didn't return her affection, pretending not to care. I knew I was pouting and hated myself for it. And over a girl young enough to be my fucking daughter.

"I could tell *you* a few funny things about him and that trip," I said, disengaging myself. I dumped a cigarillo out of a cup, stuck it under the tap, swirled it around and dumped it out. "What'd he say about it?"

"He say you in area where Tabon Man found in cave." She hugged me and laughed again.

"Yeah. So what's so funny about that?"

"I no understand him and think he say *Tampon* Man!" She squealed, bursting into cascades of giggles again, her eyes watering.

I had to hold her up to keep her from collapsing with laughter. I felt myself loosening up and started to chuckle. That wasn't bad.

"Tampon man!" she squealed again, seized with the giggles.

I felt the icicles break and fall away. A minute later we were leaning against each other, both weak with laughter, in my case partly out of relief. An idea sparked to mind.

"Hey! Do you want to see Java Man?"

She looked up at me wondering, then nodded rapidly, her eyes and teeth sparkling.

"Okay. Stand back."

She did, holding herself steady in the unsteady craft. I hunched down like a gorilla, grabbed the coffeepot with my free hand and held it out before me, and then began beating the cup against my chest.

"Unga, unga. Java Man," I grunted, making a face.

Her mouth and eyes opened wider with glee and she

screamed so hard with laughter that tears began to flow down her cheeks. I was spilling coffee from the pot all over the floor.

"Now, hey you! You want . . . want see . . . Peking Man?" she asked, between sobs of laughter. "Oh, my cheeks sore from laughing!"

I took a "show me" attitude. Slyly, and with the most wicked grin possible, she moved her fingers to one of the triangles that covered a breast. With a quick motion she popped the top of it down, then back up.

"You Peking Man because you *peek!*"

She did it with the other boob and we collapsed into each other's arms again. Our laughter had hardly died down when she noticed the front of my cutoffs moving. Her laughter grew softer and sexier but was every bit as happy as she pressed herself to me.

"It's my turn now. How about if I show you *Homo erectus?*" I said, my voice growing husky. "You be Lucy and I'll jump on your bones."

"You know why caveman he drag woman around by hair?" she asked, giggling. "Because if he drag by leg he get pebbles and sticks in she pussy!"

I laughed so hard I almost lost my grip on her. My hand slipped down to caress a tight bun.

"Mmmmmmmmmmm. Cavewoman like feel of you club," she said, lustily unzipping my fly and reaching in. That now-familiar gleam was back in her eyes.

". . . you Asian women," I whispered hotly as she shined my *lingam.*

"Ohhhhhhhhhh, you cock-Asian men," she whispered back.

I knew just how she spelled it by the way she squeezed me. Ol' Thunder clamped on a bayonet. She smiled wickedly and guided me by the blade into our tiny cabin. An erratic wave came up just then, almost causing her to yank it right off except I tumbled with her onto the cot instead. I wrestled my wet gear off while she slipped out of her bikini. No sooner were we in each other's arms. Ol' Thunder happily between her thighs, than another wave almost dumped us right over the bed's cribbing onto the floor. I grabbed a storm rail only just in time.

"This is going to be like trying to make love in a washing

machine," I complained, holding her securely until the boat lurched over to the other side, rolling us against the bulkhead. "I think if we try to bang in this weather we're really going to get banged up," I added, recognizing with regret the facts of the matter.

Without a word, she wiggled out of my arms, making me wonder if I had said something wrong. I had already learned she didn't like being said no to. While I tried to think of something to say, she flipped open a drawer and withdrew the four lengths of rope she had shyly presented me with a few nights before.

"Hey! Great idea! That'll hold you steady!" I exclaimed, reaching for the cords.

She shook her head and held them back away from me, excitement flashing in her eyes and smile.

"No. You too heavy and it my turn anyway. Maybe boat throw you around and hurt me. I always dream to do this." Then she looped the rope around one of my wrists.

I let her truss me up and spread-eagle me on my back across the bed. She could have tied Ol' Glory to Ol' Thunder, my flagpole was flying so high.

Kneeling between my open legs, she bent forward, I thought she was going to practice a new tune on the flute, but instead she lowered the firm, silky orbs of her breasts till I was between their smooth valley, the boat's heavy motion making her sway back and forth, caressing my turgid tentacle as it slipped from firm hilltop to smooth valley to firm hilltop. It didn't take long before I wanted to feel myself sinking deeply into the warmth and love and snugness of her and her incredible pussy.

But she was enjoying teasing me, and in no hurry, taunting me the way I had taunted her just a few nights before. Bracing herself with one hand, she used her free one to lightly stroke and nestle the raging beast between her breasts. I met her gently rocking motion and felt my swollen cock jerk involuntarily. I tried to reach for her but my wrists could only jerk forward a few inches.

"Oh . . . please . . . now . . . ," I whispered, my voice full and hot in my ears. "I want to be inside of you, Tysee."

She looked up and smile impishly, her eyes shining, and slowly, deliberately shook her head. Instead, she drifted up on me slightly, sliding her smooth, silky tummy back and forth against me.

I wanted her. I wanted to be in her now. I tried to pull at my bonds, to free myself, to draw her down onto me. It was no use.

She slowly slid back until she was again kneeling between my legs, hanging on to one of my thighs to steady herself. She began to lightly stroke me, carefully studying my painfully rigid prick like it was a new toy she had never seen before. Her silver bracelets jingled faster and faster as she stroked. Now, she would link her eyes with mine, reading in them and in my helpless squirms when I could take no more and was about to blow the deck off the boat. Then she would slow, or pause to caress my chest, only to continue sensuously as soon as the wave had passed, keeping me, with her finely tuned sensitivity, on the edge of exploding.

Finally, when I could plead no more, she smiled slightly, as if to herself, and slid up into position over me in the bucking, bouncing boat, hanging on to the rail for support. I thrust my hips up to meet her as she slowly slipped down on me, that incredible, warm, wet, comforting pussy surrounding me like a tailor-made glove vibrating with sex and love and life, and I knew my stupid jealousies were for naught.

We lay with our bodies linked, our eyes locked, neither of us having to move, the heavy motions of the boat rocking us around.

It was then that I saw something new enter her dark, deep, intelligent eyes—something that hadn't been there before. As we shared our open-eyed ecstasy, I saw it flowing into her eyes from deep within, as if a dam had burst somewhere inside her. I don't know if it was something she saw in mine that had stimulated it, but the excitement in hers had given way to a passion that was past sexual arousal. Her glistening pupils filled her irises and I felt like I could see and feel her to her depths, feel in my blood the circular flow of communication that passed from our eyes to our bodies and back through our eyes again.

My emotions surged up to meet hers. All we had been through, the many dangers and close calls, had cemented that strong bond between us and we both knew it. It didn't have to be said.

"I know . . . even when little girl . . . that you right man for me," she said hotly. "I just know."

Our bodies began to tighten and quiver and pulsate at the agonizing apex of our ecstasy. Just as she collapsed onto my trussed body, the words gushed simultaneously from our hearts and lips in a rich, involuntary gush that sounded like it would go on forever.

"I love you."

—— • ——

"I'm afraid it's reached Voice Against Russia."

That was Snake's name for Voice of America. I cringed. Regional shortwave was one thing. The VOA was another.

"What is it?" I called, clambering down into the cockpit, where he was working the helm, Tysee keeping him company. She looked unhappy.

"I have to go make food—but there not much left," she said, standing and making for the companionway. Snake gently reached for her as she worked her way by, giving her a warm, one-armed hug.

"Don't you worry, little lady," he said quietly. "Everything will work out for the best."

She put her head to his chest for a moment, then freed herself, opened the hatch door, and slipped down the companionway.

"What the hell was that all about?" I asked, bewildered.

I couldn't figure that woman out. Then I remembered why I had avoided relationships for so long—the fucking hassles weren't worth it. But it was too late now—like it or not. I was locked into one.

"Not much. She's a damned good girl, that Tysee. A real sweetheart. She was telling me about how she felt so bad about being Kun San's daughter and how she wants to be an anthropologist so she can record her people's background. She's upset because she doesn't think she'll ever be able to go back to Kwan Mae to do it."

Snake returned to looking as gloomy as the weather. At least the wind had cut back so we could make good time with all the panties up.

"Come on, damn it," I repeated impatiently, my hair up

a little. It was hard to get used to a woman who was so damned open with her affections for everyone she liked, even when she wasn't interested in nailing them. Or was she? "You said there was something on the radio I missed. I'm tired of having to haul things out of you every time something new comes over."

"Sorry, mate. I just hate passing on bad news. This thing is opening up like a Chinese puzzle box, and what's inside ain't much good. Tysee heard it too and it added to her depression."

"What is it?"

"Jist a sec," he said, cranking the volume up. "I think there's an editorial coming on."

Rumors are spreading like lotus blossoms that the Enlightened One's supposed Head has reappeared after all these years. Can it be true? So little is known at this point that one can only comment on the interest—and tremendous it is in the region, and growing around the world. All we have is an unsubstantiated rumor, but in only a matter of weeks, nay days, it has swept and riveted the imagination of the Buddhist world like nothing before in.

Monks from Sri Lanka to Nepal to Thailand report food and monasterial offerings up. The number of initiates in these Buddhist Belt countries has trebled virtually overnight and shows indications of going even higher. Police in all Buddhist countries report a sudden drop in crime at all levels.

If the rumor is found to be true, there can only be greater rejoicing in the Buddhist realm. And as true as this should be of the world as a whole, alas it is not so. Every silver lining has its dark cloud—and this one is threatening to be backed by a forming typhoon.

True, Pope John Paul II is generous in his description of the Buddha. He has said, and I quote: "The Buddha was a man of peace who had much in common with our own Savior, the Lord Jesus Christ. We understand the importance of relics, and if the rediscovery of this most important of all is a fact, then it can only work toward greater peace and understanding in the world, which all the great religions must work toward today."

But the Pope often seems to be a voice crying out in the wilderness. One of the strongest and most immediate backlashes is coming from another Christian sect, the fundamentalists, and one of their foremost leaders. Bat Rabidson, who denounces the possible discovery of the Buddha Head with these words: ". . . as the work of the devil in his most wicked form, enticing millions to a fiery eternity, for did not Jesus Himself say in John 14:6 that 'I am the way, the truth and the life. No man comes to the Father except through me'? Is it not written in John 3:3 that 'unless a man is born again, he cannot see the Kingdom of God'?'"

Moslem leaders are no more tolerant, denouncing the Buddha as a heretic. In a rather more receptive vein, Hindu leaders in India are saying that they have peacefully shared the same land with fifteen million Buddhists for centuries and it is hoped that relationship will continue. Sikh leaders at the Golden Temple in Amritsar say they have no fight with Buddhism, nor do they wish one, but that, and I quote: "Buddhists will be free to continue living in the new Sikh nation of Khalistan when it is created."

Response from national governments has ranged from silence, in the case of Russia, to hope, in the United States and Britain, to excitement, most notably in the Buddhist countries. Generally, reaction to the supposed discovery has been mixed, and at best cautiously optimistic. One must hope that this latter contingent will grow in strength to the detriment of the detractors.

We believe that the appearance of the Buddha Head can only augur well for the peace

and future of the planet, for this is a world that
needs a reawakening of spirituality—whatever
the source. And in the end, aren't all the
prophets, messiahs, yogis, gurus—whatever their
guise—spiritual leaders talking about the same
thing? About unity with each other and with
God? Aren't we all just part of the same Family
of Man? Perhaps He has sent this Head back as
a message, or an omen.

It may be just what this beleaguered planet
needs right now. This is the Voice of America.

"The blob is growing," I said. "Sounds like it's just oozing
out of the movie theater. Damn it. Now, what's this other
bad news?"

"It has to do with your house."

"What about it?" I asked, anxiety creeping into my
voice.

He paused again, shifted uncomfortably, and corrected
for a wave surge on the calming sea. Light rain splattered
the deck.

"I'm afraid it doesn't exist anymore."

"What the hell do you mean it doesn't *exist* anymore!"

"Someone firebombed it. Apparently there was quite a
shoot-out. They got one of them. I didn't catch the name.
Hiviz or Hafaz or something—a Paki. I guess he got the
idea from the other Eastern injuns who tried to blow it and
blew it. No pun intended, mate."

"Oh, Jesus. Just great," I groaned, feeling a deep depression coming on. My masks. My birds. My collections. My
home. I hoped Nog and Po were still at that safe house.

"No. Buddha . . . as Tysee keeps reminding us. And
there's worse news."

"Oh God, what could possibly be worse?"

"Wally's just about outa beer," he said, tossing another
empty overboard.

Walter dutifully rose, and rolled and snapped his enormous jaws down on it, then retreated just below the surface, his dorsal fin cutting through the water with us, knot
for knot.

"We'll pull in to some fishing village on Balabac," he said,
naming the fairly large island at the bottom tip of Palawan.

"We'll stock up on some fresh food, fruit and water for the little lady so she can keep herself pretty for you. We wouldn't want her to get dirty behind the balls—your balls," he chuckled.

"Very funny."

"And we'll see if Waldo likes San Miguels as much as he does Tigers. I'm looking forward to his opinion."

———— • ————

The sound of the shotgun blast blew me out of a much-needed sleep. I sat bolt upright in the gloom. For a moment I wasn't sure if I hadn't been jerked from one dream to another, but if so Tysee must have been in it with me, because she was sitting up just as rigidly, her eyes wide and fixed straight ahead.

The rude jackhammering of automatic weapons above us, frantic shouts in some foreign language, and the sound of bullets smashing along the top of the deck followed by another blast from the Riot Remington, told us we had awakened into a nightmare. I was on my feet in a split second, fumbling for my Walther and the M-16.

I hit the cockpit and the pandemonium on deck just in time to see a dark figure, on a seventy-five-foot wooden fishing scow forming a T with our bow, jerk backward as another blast from Snake's shotgun roared out. Behind the intruding vessel hovered the vague outline of the secluded, coconut-lined lagoon where we had anchored after stocking up. We had decided to wait out this latest stretch of bad weather—it had gotten worse again while we were entering the Palawan Passage. Because of the clouds, it was almost pitch-black.

Catching sight of something moving on our foredeck. I raked the bow with the M-16 on automatic. Another dark figured hurtled backward into the water. Two identical flaming tongues of staccato automatic fire licked out from two positions on the scow, and we ducked down into the cockpit as chips of wood and fiberglass spat up around us.

Snake held the shotgun by its pistol grip, the flip stock thrown forward. He crammed more shells into it. We looked at each other.

"Christ, don't you know how to dress properly when people drop over?" he rasped.

I was still naked.

There was a heavy thump as a body landed on the fore-deck and scrambled for cover. Our reaction was instantaneous—we both popped up at the same time, guns blazing. But we were too late, and saw nothing. The automatic guns began to spit death again from the high prow of the scow, forcing us to drop quickly again.

At least I did. Snake was too late. He jerked sideways with a grunt, half-crashing onto me where I crouched on the cockpit floor. He didn't move for a moment and I feared he was dead, but then he suddenly began to disengage himself. While he did, the thump of another set of feet landed foredecks. I leapt up and let off a burst. Just as quickly the return fire forced me back down.

Snake shifted around, leaned back against the seat, and calmly stared at his bloody arm.

"You okay?" I spat hoarsely.

"No. I've just been shot, asshole," he croaked.

Without stopping to bandage the wound, he picked up the shotgun like a pistol in his big mitt, then rose slightly, taking advantage of the darkness, and blasted off another shot. The barrel kicked upward to almost vertical. A hysterical scream of pain from the scow told us he had connected.

The two invaders quickly advanced to mid-deck, scuttling like cockroaches, hiding behind the Zodiac and the raised cabin, forcing the gunners on the scow to hold fire. I squinted in the dark down the port side. If anything moved I'd have a clear shot at it.

"You see that?" I whispered.

"Huh?"

"I thought I just saw a third one up at our bow. Just below the jib."

I saw a glint of something again. Taking careful aim. I locked my sights in as best I could. Another glint confirmed I was on target. I was about to squeeze off a burst when a wave came in out of nowhere, lifting and rocking the boat, causing Snake to bump into me. The gun went off but I had clearly missed. The glint disappeared, the opportunity lost.

Gunfire suddenly resumed from the scow, most of the bullets kicking up the water behind us.

"They're providing cover fire. Getting ready to rush us," I whispered quickly.

Even in the near pitch-black the pain on his face was obvious. As was the dark, sticky mass widening on his entire left side.

Something hard struck fiberglass ahead of us. Movement. We glanced at each other. His eyes were burning. We knew what we had to do.

We jumped up at the same time, just in time to see a flash of light at the bow, followed by an arc of flames flying up toward the scow. A huge *whoosh* followed as the Molotov Cocktail smashed against the cabin of the invading boat, its sticky contents smearing in a rage of fire across the deck and up the side of the wheelhouse. A hideous scream followed as a loinclothed figure, its bare back in flames, stood and began to jump around like a Sri Lankan devil dancer, arms waving frantically. The living torch leapt onto the edge of the boat and into the water before either of us could get off a proper shot. A moment later he screamed again, even more hideously, then all was silent. The red light from the flames reflected off a large dorsal fin and swirling water.

I saw a silhouetted figure amidships on the port side rise to his knees and turn to look back at the blazing scow. He carried a rifle and wore only a loincloth as well. He was also trapped, exposed by the roaring pyre of his vessel. He stood and began to run back to his boat. He never made it. A burst from my M-16 kicked his legs out from under him, splaying him facedown onto the deck. Wounded, he tried to escape by yanking himself under the safety ropes and into the lagoon. There was a little splash. A moment later the water was boiling.

"There's still another one," croaked Snake. "On the starboard."

He lay back, breathing heavily, holding his left side just under his armpit. His eyes were reptilian slits. The crippled boat, pilotless now, flames licking higher as they quickly swallowed the dry wheelhouse, began to drift aimlessly away from the *Riquer*.

A new figure we hadn't seen before began trying frantically to extinguish the fire, but was stopped short by a long dragon's breath of fire licking out from the Remington. It threw him into the flames, his personal Viking pyre. Snake was down but certainly not out.

A silhouetted figure on the foredeck poked its head around the jib boom. I swung the M-16 quickly into place, sighted, and pulled the trigger. Nothing happened. Jammed. I swore out loud, threw the gun down, and pulled out my Walther.

The figure at mid-deck on the starboard side stood and began to run for the bow. Before I could pull the trigger, he suddenly jerked and swung around slightly to the left as if hit, though I had heard nothing. The reflection of fire-light on metal, as his pistol flew and then splashed uselessly into the sea, was clear. The figure stumbled, steadied itself, then continued.

Raising my Walther with both hands, I squeezed off a shot at the lone, wobbling figure. He dropped, but not like I had hit him.

A high-pitched scream brought me to my feet. Female. From the bow.

Tysee!

In a split second, I had run down the side of the yacht, oblivious to all else. Two figures were wrestling, one seminaked above the other and facing me, with its hand raised. Something glinted in it. My instep, powered by white-hot adrenaline, slammed him full on the face. It threw the squat shape like a sack of copra backward onto the tip of the bow, where it half-dangled over the side. His head must have been cast-iron, because he wasn't out, and his dark, sinuous figure quickly scrambled over the edge into the water. I snapped off another shot that kicked up a jet of water harmlessly beyond the bow.

I need not have wasted a bullet. The last thing I saw of him was the wild look in his eyes as he was suddenly hoisted straight up out of the water and jerked abruptly three feet to one side. Then he disappeared altogether in a wild thrashing as Walter and his dinner guests moved in for the next course. Large fins slashed back and forth through the water in frenzied motion, illuminated by the raging fire.

"Are you okay?" I gasped to Tysee, dropping to her side, my knee hitting something hard—the Khokhlov Special. It slipped over the edge and into the water. She had wounded the attacker with it but apparently that shell hadn't been loaded with cyanide.

I helped her sit up. Her face was in her hands as she sobbed. The flat fore-deck hatch she had crawled through, just out of sight of the pirates in the scow's high, sweeping bow, was still thrown open.

She reached for and clung to me, shaking like a tin roof in a typhoon, her sharp fingernails digging into my neck and back. I held her, my eyes fanning the deck, then the scow, for any stragglers, the Walther at ready.

Snake made his way gingerly up the starboard, shotgun in hand, left arm tight against his side. He had already applied a compress.

"Here, Wally! Come on, boy! Chow time!" he called.

A splash followed as he kicked a remaining body overboard. The water began to surge as Wally and some late arrivals dug into dessert, ripping and tearing at the body.

"Now, Walter," he scolded, "how many times have I told you not to play with your food."

The tide had carried the now-raging scow off a good distance. We could see no life aboard. The flames lit up the entire lagoon, casting long, menacing shadows from the wildly threshing fins. More were arriving all the time.

"What happened?" I shot at him, his face clear in the reddish, flickering glow. He had been on watch.

The crackle of wood carried across the still waters.

"Hate to say it, mate, but I fell asleep," he replied in a small voice. "I only woke up when their boat bumped against ours." For a moment he didn't look so big anymore. "Sorry," he added a moment later.

"How bad did they get you?"

"Not so bad," he said bravely, the pain in his voice impossible to disguise. "Fortunately, it's in my spare beer arm."

"Who the hell were they, I wonder."

I was rocking Tysee back and forth, holding her close, trying to still her terror. My terror. Her faith in the Buddha's protection had clearly suffered a severe lapse this time—it had been too close a call.

"I don't know. From the shape of the boat though . . ."

He nodded in the direction of the huge blaze, which took that moment's opportunity to explode in a huge fireball that shook all of us. Pieces of the boat flew high in the air as if in slow motion, speckling the still waters of the lagoon with splashes of debris in a wide circle. A host of fins excitedly zigzagged through the water, searching for tidbits.

"Toothpicks for the boys," Snake eventually muttered. "Well, the size of that explosion kind of explains it—that's one group of fishermen that won't be screwing up the coral, dynamiting for fish anymore."

With the bottom and sides mostly blown out, the scow rapidly sank, the flames sizzling out in the sea with the doomed boat. The water churned in a stir of shark fins for several minutes more near the point where it went down. Then all was silence and darkness once again.

"It was a Moslem boat, the kind you find in the Sulu Sea just south of here. I've seen a lot of them around Zamboanga," he said, naming the city on southwestern Mindanao, at the very tip of the long, drooping phallus that is that huge island's main peninsula.

"Coincidence?"

"Probably. The bastards are no different than those damned Thai fishermen, hoisting their lines whenever they spot a scow full of Vietnamese refugees. Possibly spotted us at that village where we picked up supplies. Bloody pirates is all."

I turned my attention to Tysee, continuing to hold her close, rocking her. Her breathing began to slow down along with mine.

"It was her who saved out butts, wasn't it?" Snake asked soberly, leaning down, wiping the blood from his hand onto his pants before placing it gently on her arm.

She seized his hand with one of hers and held it tightly, one arm still firmly around my neck. My eyes widened as a bit of light glinted off the silver bangles she wore on her wrists.

"It sure was. . . . It sure was. . . ." I said. "She seems to make a habit of it."

I stared at the bangles. It suddenly occurred to me that I had come within a split curly from blasting her once, if not twice. I tried to push the horrifying thought from my mind. I couldn't.

"Are you okay, mate?" Snake asked, looking across at

me. The three of us huddled on deck like frightened monkeys. "Your face is as white as a shark's tooth."

"I'm okay," I replied, my voice high and breaking. "Just not used to being on call at all kinds of crazy hours. But we have mouths to feed. Walter's a growing boy." I said, trying to joke it away.

I saw a remote, familiar gleam in his eye, and a flicker of his usual leer on his lip.

"No table manners though, that boy. We're spoiling him."

"How's the boat? Anything vital damaged?" I asked, still trying to push the thought out of my mind that'd I'd almost tapped Tysee.

"From what I can see, not good. I don't know if we can go on."

"What'd they hit?" I asked, anxiety rising in my voice. "Something in the steering mechanism?"

"No. Bloody lot worse than that, mate. A bullet smashed me bloody opener in the cockpit."

———— • ————

"Lee! Tysee! Get below! Quick!"

We did as we were told, slipping down the forehatch. Snake continued to tack the *Riquer* to the starboard of the approaching freighter, spinning the wheel with his one good arm, holding the other close to his side. There were a lot of ships now—we were in almost constant sight of one or another near the north end of the Palawan Passage— and I didn't see how this one was much different from the others.

It was a full quarter of an hour before he rapped on the door and we ventured up the cockpit. There was a worried look on his face.

"Damn it all to hell!" he swore. "And it had to be a *Commie* Russian vessel!" He checked the sky—it had finally cleared up the day before, and the sea was settling. The world at least *looked* beautiful again. "I didn't notice until too late that they had binoculars on us."

"Ah, come on," I said. "They were probably just admiring a yacht that they won't admit that only capitalism can produce." Yet I knew that whatever was on Snake's mind was serious.

He was unusually edgy. A definite strange mood. Tysee noticed too.

"I'm not so bloody sure, mate. Here. Take over."

I did. His hand was shaking as he pulled the last cigarillo from his pack. Besides the air-conditioned hull left from the shoot-out with the pirates—if indeed that's what they were—we had a shattered port hole that was drawing waves, cracked and chipped spars, a severed metal guide, and splintered wood paneling. The riddled Zodiac was as limp as a used condom, so we had flushed it down our wake. Even the mainsail looked, at least to Snake, like one of those paper cutout snowflakes. The electrical system was semi on the blink, kicking in and out at will, crippling the radar and depth sounder, making running at night chancy and—but worse to Snake—providing only luke-cool beer from the fridge. Even that curse of sailors everywhere, the boat's head, had packed in, and we were back to bucket and chucket. The cabin had been turned into a saltwater shower, fed by waves slipping over the deck and running down the bullet holes, single and in rows. Fortunately, the Buddha Head in our cabin had escaped unscathed.

"What's the matter?" I asked, quickly running my eyes along the full complement of billowing, snapping panties. Off our starboard stern was a cluster of islands—the Calamian Group. Another day and we'd be sighting Mindoro and Luzon. Snake and I were tense and on edge, knowing our two-week hiatus was soon to end, with what seemed like the entire world after our asses. Only Tysee somehow managed to keep her relative equanimity.

She looked at him with large, open eyes full of concern. His were distant, lost in some dark forest of thought, the pupils traced for the first time with fear.

"I heard it about an hour ago when you guys were napping or screwing or doing whatever you do down there, but I couldn't bring myself to tell you. News flash over Voice Against Russia—they have my name," he said flatly. "They think you're with me. They even got the name of the boat right. The *Riquer*. Now how the hell did they put that all together?"

"*What!* You gotta be kidding."

"I wish I was," he said, pausing to light his cigarillo. "And there's a *lot* more on Voice Against Russia. There's been a bloody typhoon of bad news today. This story hasn't just broken—it's bloody well exploded! Apparently the media has been on that abbot's back up in Nepal but he has been refusing to say anything. At least until yesterday. Then he said that he couldn't talk because of a 'three-decade-old oath of silence' he made to the Dalai Lama."

"That makes sense."

"Yeah? Then why did the Dalai Lama announce today that there's absolutely no basis in fact to the Head's existence?"

"Well, that's what He said He'd say," I explained, reminding him of His original letter of 1959 to Abbot Lobsang at Tengboche.

"Yeah, that's right. But all that should clear up in about six days. The Dalai Lama has agreed to make a statement and appear on Ted Koppel's 'Nightline.' It'll take that long to hook up the satellite feeds to Dharamsala. It's going to be picked up by the VOA."

"That be interesting," Tysee interjected. "There anything more?"

"Lots. You wouldn't believe what's been happening in the world. It's bloody incredible! Communal fighting has broken out in central India and Kashmir, where most of the Indian Buddhists live. Delhi's called in troops. That's all they need—to add to the trouble the Hindus already have with the Sikhs and Muslims. In Sri Lanka, the gloves have come off completely between the Buddhists and the Hindu Tamils in the north. Even those ignorant fucking Iranian mullahs are foaming into their beards about some kind of holy war, no less. They're promising to do to the Buddhists what they did to the Baha'is, and worse."

"Jesus . . . sounds like the good old days of religious wars," I said, keeping the yacht on an even keel.

"No kidding. Get this: The doily-heads in Israel have even officially announced the they *do* have the Bomb! The big one they've been coy about for the last few years. It's not the Buddhists they're worried about, its those carpet-beaters around them who might go on a general rampage. The Moslems are the ones most up in arms. And the fundamentalists in the States are getting an even bigger hard-on.

That southern preacher Bat Rabidson's at the head of it as usual. There was even a bit from The Golden Triangle."

"What that?" Tysee asked quickly.

"There's some guy there . . . I didn't quite catch the name . . . Chung Sea Weed or something—" Snake said, looking up to check the rigging.

"Chung Si Fu?" she asked helpfully.

Snake shrugged. "Something like that. Sea Weed. Sea Food. Whatever. He got Hal Lawson—he's a journalist we know, Tysee—up there to interview him. Sea Food said that he was very sorry about the robbery at the monastery but blamed it on your dad. He said he didn't want to have anything to do with it, of course, but had no choice. Sea Food gave Lawson some masks and a bronze Buddha, or something or other that was stolen at Tengboche, to have delivered back. *And* he made a 100,000-baht donation to Tengboche."

"Chung very smart," Tysee reminded us with a perspicacious nod. "It stop Burma and Thai people from making war against him about this."

"Bright boy," I agreed, having to admire the son of a bitch. "It not only gives him some space to consolidate his gains, but announces to the world that he's the one to deal with up there."

"Did they say anything else about Golden Triangle?" Tysee asked.

"Yeah. This was interesting and maybe you can fill me in. Sea Food claimed that that old kraut, Wolfgang Krueger, brought the entire project to Kun San in the first place."

"*What!*" I was flabbergasted.

"You don't need to spit, Semen Last Class. I've had enough spray in the face the last days to last me a lifetime. Yeah. Apparently Krueger learned about the Head being in Tengboche from someone on the Dalai Lama's staff. He offered Kun San fifteen percent of the profits. Sea Food says Kun San sent two men in from Kathmandu by foot and then had a plane rendezvous with them."

I was still incredulous. *Wolfgang?*

"Did they say if they found him or not?" I asked, again visualizing him hanging in the meat locker.

"No. They just say he disappeared some time ago. They're looking for him, though."

I scratched the thick stubble on my chin. Reporters would soon be flocking around his shack with all the sensitivity of a bleacher full of well-lagered Liverpool soccer fans. I wondered if they'd manage to find that trapdoor.

"You wanna hear more?" Snake asked, blowing smoke in the direction of the blue sky so that it immediately swept back of the bow and dissipated. He didn't wait for us to answer. "Finally, Lee, they had your buddy Ham-Sandwich on again. He reiterated your dubious reputation as an antiquities smuggler—a thief stealing from thieves, is what he called you. But then we've always known you were a bit of a douche-bag anyway."

I felt my face flush with anger, and gripped the helm tightly.

"I'll get that fat motherfucker some day. Mark my words."

"And it doesn't help your plummeting reputation much, being the boyfriend of Kun San's daughter, a shady relationship with all kinds of connections to heroin to be sure. You, little lady, have been described as a former exotic dancer and prostitute in, get this, 'Bangkok's notorious red-light area.' Isn't that enough to make you spew?" he added sarcastically.

Anger flashed in her eyes for a moment.

"What about you, Snake?" she asked. "What they say about you?"

"Me? Oh, I've been mauled over as a onetime zoo and pet shop collector who once dealt in rare and prohibited species, smuggling them from one country to another. So we're all in the same boat, quite literally. That it's true, I don't give a damn about. Fuck 'em. But they're sure shoveling the bullshit into our graves."

"I no think it good to listen to radio. It make us unhappy."

"Wait—there's even more," he said dramatically, thoughts of impending doom tainting his voice. "I've saved the worst for last."

"Come on. Spit it out."

"Wally's left us," he said ruefully, tossing the empty cigarillo pack and a San Miguel beer can over the sterns. "I guess he didn't like Filipino food and beer as much as I thought. . . ."

The familiar shape failed to rise to the bait, and the bobbing flotsam soon disappeared in the whirls of foamy wake behind us. The fire had burned down in Snake's eyes, and I saw in them then what he already knew: that the comfortable world he had put together at great risk was being pulled apart at the seams.

"I'm sorry to have gotten you involved in all of this, Snake," I said, "I'll make it up to you somehow."

He was my best friend and I was responsible for ruining him. Snake tried to force a leer onto his face.

"Forget it, mate. The way you and I live, we have to be prepared to lose everything as easily as we won it. Besides, tomorrow is another day and we'll be arriving at the Philippines proper. Things can't get any worse there, can they?"

TWELVE

Manila

"SO THAT'S WHAT you think we should do, eh, mate?"

The old, bald mountains of the island of Mindoro loomed closer, already dried to a reddish brown. Cape Calavite at its north end and its attending Calavite Passage was just ahead, opening into the greater Verde Island Passage, a giant tongue of water that licks into the central Visayan group of the Philippines' 7,107 islands.

"Yeah. I think it's the best idea." I was in a pair of trunks already.

"Sounds fair dinkum to me. Fine with you, Tysee?"

She looked troubled, the thought of being parted from her much-beloved Head was causing her new anxiety.

"Come, on Tysee. We're marked men, woman and boat. We'll be spotted and searched sooner or later, by officials or bounty hunters. Until we make contact with François's man so we can make arrangements for the transfer, it's best if we hide it."

She looked down and nodded her head.

"Chi," she said sadly, agreeing. "We must leave it for short time. It best."

"Short-time—that's what I could use right now," Snake mumbled to me, looking longingly toward Luzon's still, green shape. Farther off to the northeast, across the channel. Manila and her bars—well-navigated by Snake—waited just beyond. Neither of us laughed. "Then maybe you can tell us a bit about this diplomat you're supposed to meet," he added. "You'll be phoning him at the embassy, is that right?"

"No. You'll be surprised to hear where François told me to go. It's— . . ."

"Sorry to interrupt you but I think you better hustle forward and get the drapes down. I want to use the engines for this close-in stuff and we're getting close."

I glanced ahead. We weren't that far off the site. I had already told Tysee about a small sunken freighter Snake and I had discovered a few years before, while underwater sledding, looking for wrecks. It hadn't yielded anything of value but it had been interesting to dive on. Judging the hole in its side, it had been sent to the bottom by a sub in the last war. It was an old metal-hulled job in 120 feet of water, just on the edge of a drop-off to the dark depths. Upright and still in fairly good condition, it was in an area where other divers rarely went—if they ever did—because of the wicked currents that surge in and out of the passage behind. It was also just off as isolated a piece of coast as you can find in the Philippines.

"Right," I replied, snapping to it.

A quarter of an hour later the panties were down to the masts' ankles and Snake had kicked in the diesels.

"Now I think you better get that dive gear up here. I'm not entirely sure if I have any of the tanks filled or not and if they're not, that's going to take a bit of time."

I slipped down the companionway into the main saloon and made my way to the equipment locker. Four 80s were strapped to a bulkhead. One had a lick of tape over the K valve. I ripped it off, attached a regulator, and cranked the bottle open—2,500 pounds. Good. I always had a spare mask and fins aboard, and these I dug out. I scrambled together a vest, weight belt, gloves, depth gauge, light and knife. Leaving the snorkel behind, I hauled the gear back to the cockpit.

It was clear that Snake had been calming Tysee's fears about the plan.

"Okay, little lady," Snake told her. "I think it's about time we got it wrapped. You'll find a big, waterproof bag in the hatch to the left of the sink. That's the ideal thing. No use getting our man wet." He was trying to be light as he helmed us around the cape and along the coastline, the chop shorter and calmer here than in the open sea.

Tysee slipped down the hatch and reluctantly began preparing the Head for its baptism.

"Here. Stick this in there too, please," I said to her, bending through the hatch door and passing her the Walther. "It's best if we keep one with it. You never know. The box of ammo is in that drawer by our bed."

"It was about here, wasn't it, mate?" Snake asked. "Remember we used to line up that promontory with that big boulder? Hard to see through all this goddamned morning mist, though."

I checked our position against the landmarks. Then I leaned over the edge. Forty feet down, coral heads were coming into view. I nodded. Close enough.

Snake threw the engine into reverse while I ran forward to huck the hook. In a few minutes I was back. Tysee and Snake were sitting together on the edge of the cockpit, facing landward, their backs to the sea, the plastic-encased bundle in her lap. I glanced around the horizon. Good. Not a boat of any size within sight.

I geared up, looped the dive light around my wrist, spit into my mask, rubbed it around, rinsed it out. After checking my gauges and kicking the regulator a couple of times to make sure it was clear, I was ready.

I nodded. Tysee apprehensive, now holding the precious bundle with the Head and gun inside like it was her first-born child that she had to give up. The look intensified as she gingerly passed it across to me.

"Be careful," she said in a quiet, unsure voice. I wasn't entirely sure if she meant it for me, or for the Head.

I pulled down my mask, popped in the reg, held the bundle firmly to my body, and gave them the *vitarka mudra*. When Snake returned it, I gripped my reg and mask securely in place with my free hand and took a deep breath.

The last thing I saw before falling over backward into the water was Snake and Tysee sitting side by side, her hand raised in a frightened half-wave.

The flurry of bubbles and confusion of entry quickly cleared as I straightened. I began descending immediately, not having pumped any air into the vest. I set the timing dial on my Rolex submariner; I would have a quarter-hour on the basement floor before having to surface. Just right. To stay any longer would entail a decompression stop during the ascent. The Head and gun were light in the water and easy to handle, and the snap-top bag kept both dry. Tysee had bundled them in thick towels to keep them from bashing each other, or anything else.

Periodically clearing my ears, I searched for familiar landmarks on the downward-sloping seascape. Above me, the reflecting surface was freckled with fluid patterns, and the streamlined hull of the *Riquer,* with its long, white keel, settled solidly into the clear water.

After spotting a huge, familiar fan-coral, I had my directions. Bright, multicolored fish of all shapes and descriptions gently lazed around the fifteen-foot-high, Cousteauvian coral heads. A green turtle stiffly flew out from behind a mushroom coral and through the liquid air, disappearing into the fog at the outer limit of my vision a hundred feet away. Kicking on, I bypassed a three-foot-diameter jellyfish undulating rhythmically through the water in slow, pulsating motions like an aging whale's orgasm.

The downward slope steepened, the coral heads gave way to desert. I finned down the incline, the colors fading as I passed sixty, then eighty feet. Ahead and below me I began to make out the dark shape of the freighter lying alongside the edge of the reef, leaning slightly to landward.

Moments later I had glided over the wreck to the other side. It was like flying over the edge of a cliff, for here the reef dove straight down hundreds of feet into blackness and oblivion. I cleared my ears again, and drifted down along the hull on the drop-off side to a large, gaping hole torn open like the seat of a postman's pants. Kicking a couple of hits of air into my buoyancy compensator, I hung suspended in space. Inside the hull there was nothing but blackness. I flicked on the flashlight. The beam poked a hole through the thin plankton into the gloomy interior. A couple of lazy groupers eyed me with curiosity.

Luckily we had arrived over the site just between tides so the current was weak, and giving me little trouble—in a couple of hours it would surge like a windstorm through here, strongly enough to blow a diver away like an old newspaper. So I was startled when I felt a pull, a sucking sensation, as I kicked toward the gaping hole. When I reached it I had to grip a torn shard of hull to keep from being pulled *up*. I saw a large shadow rise over me, its reflection also moving *up* the side of the freighter.

I turned, expecting to see one of the harmless, sixty-foot whale sharks that occasionally drift along Philippine drop-offs, lazily letting the current drift food into their cavernous maws. I had ridden piggyback on the gentle giants before, and wouldn't have been too startled to see one now.

But I was by what I *did* see.

It was almost enough to make me spit my reg; a gargantuan, gray, menacing, atomic submarine, barely a hundred feet away and half-blending with the mist at the edge of my visual range, was rapidly rising, its conning tower no doubt already breaking the surface. The suction of the huge vessel flagged me out and up from the freighter wreck. The sunken ship began to wobble slightly back and forth. Large chunks of coral broke off the lip of the drop-off and slowly tumbled into the deep.

The surge was too strong. It pulled me loose and began to tumble me up through the water. Desperately, I closed my grip around the bundle; if I dropped it now, only Alvin, the mini-sub, would be able to reach it.

The huge swirls began to abate as the cigar-shaped monster settled at the surface. I had been sucked upward more than fifty feet. No sooner had I gotten my bearings, still stunned by its monstrous size, than I saw something hit the surface next to it—a rubber raft.

My bubbles!

Frantically I kicked downward, emptying my lungs and dumping the air in the vest to speed the descent, till I found the hole in the freighter's side and clawed my way inside, pausing to catch my breath. Jabbing the light beam around, I saw I was on the cabin deck and in the interior of a silt-covered stateroom cluttered with Japanese furniture. The door was open and I finned out into the hallway. The passageway leaned to one side like the vessel itself. My stubby beam of light probed and punched through the deadly, silent darkness as I ventured down the hall, oblivious to the clouds of silt being kicked up behind me. The doors to most of the rooms had long been rusted shut, but the third one down was wide open. Not thinking to check for small rays, morays, lions, snakes, scorpions or stones, I pulled myself into the room. A small octopus startled me by squirting by my mask and out the foot-wide porthole, leaving a trail of ink behind. I could hear my loud breathing, and my hammering heart, and my eyes felt wide open. Once I'd recovered, I probed with the light. Silt-covered radio equipment sat on a desk.

I looked up. My bubbles were running along the still-secure ceiling to the highest corner, collecting in a pocket with a shimmering, quicksilver bottom. I hoped they hadn't seen any of my bubbles before I could to trap them all down here. I forced myself to think clearly. If they had been watching us by periscope, it's just possible that they hadn't seen me fall over the side, because the early morning mist hadn't burned away yet, and Snake and Tysee had been screening me. Whose sub it was I had no idea—I just knew I wasn't about to take a chance and surface to find out.

I checked my depth gauge—118 feet. My watch told me I'd been in the hot water only nine minutes. Another six to go. I had 1,900 pounds of air left, but I was gulping it in my excitement and exertion, and the depth would make it go even faster. I might have to breathe air out of the corner pocket when it was large enough, if I had to save some for decompression stops later. I consciously forced myself to relax and calmed my breathing down to long, slow, deep pulls.

I waited nervously, my face at the porthole, my mind raging. If they sent down divers I wouldn't have a chance, but I knew Snake and Tysee wouldn't reveal that I was in the lake, and the submariners wouldn't have much time to push any interrogation; I doubted they would want to remain on the surface any longer than was absolutely necessary to do whatever it was they planned to do.

I unhooked my knife from the sheath around my calf, then felt silly as I imagined the amount of firepower residing in the massive machine before me. I could only to see one huge, gray section before the rest disappeared in the gloom.

Minutes went by. Five. Ten. Then fifteen. Just when I was making the decision to begin breathing in the corner, my air already down to 900 pounds, I felt a movement in the freighter. I stared out the porthole—the sub had begun a rapid vertical dive, and the freighter began to wobble dangerously. I heard grinding sounds. Silt drifted down from shelves. I held my breath, closed my eyes, pressed the Head to me and, for the first time in years, prayed.

I guess it had been too long since I had last used the connection or I had gotten a wrong number, because when I opened my eyes, the freighter was rocking back and forth in wider swings. Too many more and it would be upright, then pulled over and down. I had to get out. Fast.

I jabbed the light behind me. The silt was blinding. I feared I would get lost in the wreck and not make it out. I turned back to the porthole. The huge machine was level with me and beginning to move forward, picking up speed like a freight train, the silence and sheer size of it menacing. I stared as if mesmerized as its plain, elongated lines glided past me. It seemed to take forever—the sub was clearly hundreds of feet long.

As the submarine tapered down to the stern two sights appeared. Both almost made me spit my reg again.

The first was a red star painted just ahead of the two huge props.

The second was the *Riquer*.

It was being towed behind, attached by a cable. The Swan was still upright, and looked for all the world like it was sailing into this subaquatic domain, its keel cutting downward like some kind of white shark's fin. Huge bubbles of air ballooned out from its open companionway, feeding a long scatter of clothes, cushions and other debris behind the streamlined, boat-napped yacht.

I watched it disappear into the gloom. In moments it had

left me in silence, the only sound that of my deep, hyper-
ventilating breathing—and the grinding of iron against the
coral beneath me.

As soon as my shock had diminished, I knew I had to get
out of there. I kicked toward the door and groped along
the hallway. The moment I found the stateroom, the
freighter, with a low crunch and rumble, began to slowly
roll over the lip of the drop-off.

I kicked with all my might to get out from under the
tumbling hulk, through the hole, clawing upward along
the outer side of the hull that was now falling over onto
me. Just as the freighter fell on its side, the water suspended it for a moment, and I reached the deck. With my
free hand I pulled myself along it as it began to continue its
slow-motion tumble. I reached the far edge and kicked off
just as it separated from the disintegrating lip of the reef.

But I wasn't free. As the freighter fell in slow motion into
the depths, it began to suck me down. I yanked the cord
attached to my emergency CO_2 cartridge. Nothing happened. Rusted shut. I hammered the button on my vest,
pumping it up to the max. I held my breath. Fumbled for
my weight belt, held it out from me, let it go. Ripped off
the heavy flashlight. Kicked upward.

It did no good. My depth gauge showed me rapidly
being drawn down by the boat's wake to a watery grave.
My eyes fastened to the depth gauge like an octopus's paw.
I willed it to stop. 140 feet. 150 . . . 160 . . .

I fought panic, and swore I'd be good for the rest of my
life. I'd swear off whores and mekhong. I'd shake a tam-
bourine on Patpong.

I needed to unload more weight.

The Buddha Head.

I fought with the decision. 165. . . . I looked at it. It
could make the difference. I held it out from my body.

An eight-foot white-tip glided in out of the gloom, boring into me with a cold, emotionless eye. Self-protectively,
I pulled the Head close in to my body. The shark turned
slightly, without appearing to move its body, and glided
just as smoothly back into the fog.

I yanked the gauge up to my mask again. 167. I was
slowing.

I kicked upward. 165. . . . The freighter was disap-

pearing into the gloom below me. Chunks of coral, huge
and small, still drifted and sifted down and around me. 160
. . . 150 . . . 140 . . . I began to pick up speed.

But my air reading was just touching the red—500
pounds to go. I checked my watch—it read 27 minutes.

My chest tightened in shock—I was a goner. At a quick
calculation from memory using 120 feet—even discount-
ing the quick bounce to 165—I needed about fifteen minutes decom to give time for the nitrogen bubbles squeezed
into my joints and blood to dissolve—to avoid the bends.
Despite having been sucked up for a moment by the sub, I
didn't see how I had enough air. My life was bent out of
shape enough as it was; when I was forced to the surface I
was going to be tangled up like a ball of wet yarn.

I was drifting up rapidly now because of the inflated
buoyancy vest, and switched to breathing out of it to husband what little remained in the tank.

The trail of litter was easy to find. I followed the lazily
drifting arc upward, schools of multicolored fish attacking
the rice and other food that had been scattered into the
sea. At ten feet I leveled off to decompress. My remaining
air would last much longer at this shallow depth, I knew.
The fluid silvery reflection of the surface sparkled just
above me. Reachable. Beautiful. Deadly.

Recognizing something, I pulled Tysee's cobra bikini
bottoms to me, crunched them up and shoved them into
the pocket of my vest. Close by were my pants. I finned
slowly toward them, exerting myself as little as possible.
Squeezing the pockets, I could feel my necessities—phony
passport, American Express card, roll of money, soggy but
still-unsigned traveler's checks. Elsewhere drifted a shirt.
Flip-flops. For better or worse I gathered them together.

The minutes went by. Five. Ten. Then twelve. The needle was pressed against the pin, forcing me to suck the last
scraps of air out of that tank.

Then it was empty. Fifteen minutes. On the lean side of
the line, but there was no choice. Dropping the tank with
my vest, I drifted to the surface with the last of the air.

Breaking through the liquid sky, I jerked myself around
in the water, riding each successive crest of wave to shoot
off a glance in each direction. There was nothing but flotsam from the boat. And no one but me. And no telltale

tingling in the joints and extremities. Maybe one of the gods had heard my prayer after all.

———— • ————

It took me three hours to pick my way over barnacled rocks and through mango trees, keeping as far out of sight of the sea as possible, before reaching a tiny fishing village, much of it leaning on tall, bent bamboo stilts over the water. From here, I knew, a lone jeepney dared the potted, rocky road once a week, to bring in supplies for this end-of-the-line outpost.

A flea-bitten, bony old bitch all but drained of her vitality by her clumsy of puppies tried valiantly to bark, but gave up after one weak *woof.* Naked children with runny noses and the baked, wrinkled feet of old men ran up to me, quiet and curious, and old women with breasts like too-ripe papayas momentarily raised their prunish heads from the collective drudgery of their existence to stare with blank eyes at the white visitor and his strange bundle, before going back to preparing betel in the Filipino fashion—chopping the mixture up in little bamboo containers.

A few dried-out men in dirty loincloths, old before their time, hurried up, asking questions in Tagalog, but I could only shrug uncomprehendingly. When they continued jabbering, as if in doing so I might begin to understand, I began to press through them toward the road. But they stopped me, changing tactics, now gesticulating, pointing in the direction I'd come from and looking puzzled. Eyes full of guileless curiosity or acquisitiveness settled on my bundle. I pretended I didn't understand, and instead made motions as if I was driving and pointed down the narrow trail that served as the village's road link with civilization.

Green immediately flashed into the eldest one's eyes, and I wasn't at all surprised when he shook his head as if to say, there's no jeepney, there never was a jeepney, and there will never, ever be a jeepney. I was even less surprised when he pointed to a worn-out old *banca*, a double-outrigged canoe. I scanned the rocky, garbage-laden beach. It was the only one in sight.

Resigned to it, I bartered a deal in sign language with him for a ride to Puerto Galera, a nearby travelers' resort on a bay where Spanish galleons used to shelter during time of storms. The sum we agreed on was astronomical for the man, who knew he had me by the coconuts. It was 200 pesos. About ten dollars.

The *banca* was a narrow job, hand-carved out of a single tree. It took almost a half-hour, but eventually he was able to yank the single-stroke engine to near life, it coughing and hacking like a terminal tuberculosis patient. We pushed off, with me having to constantly bail out the oily bottom, and with the engine sinking into a coma every fifteen or twenty minutes. So oblivious was he to everything but his good fortune that he paid no further attention to my belongings. Nor did it occur to him that I was lying in a highly unusual and uncomfortable position, deep down in the narrow hold, out of sight of any periscopes that might be poking about. Snake was tough, but I couldn't judge how long it would take them to drag the truth from him—that they had just missed me and the Head. I'm sure they had ways to make a stone talk. I sensed Tysee would be a tougher rock to crack than Snake, so protective was she of the relic.

Snake had been right about the Russian freighter—it *had* spotted us, and no doubt surveillance satellites, blinded until only a couple or three days before, had picked us out of the sea and radioed a heading, giving their sub just enough time to cross our bow. I shouldn't have bitched about the bad weather on the trip, I realized; it had protected us from the spies in the sky. Without it, they could have come up on us in the middle of nowhere, and all four heads of ours would have disappeared forever. It came as a chiller to realize that nabbing the Head was so important to them that they had risked entering a sovereign country's waters. It was one thing to pour Whiskey-class sub on the rocks in Sweden, but quite another to serve up the stronger brew of an atomic submarine.

The sun was sinking when we sputtered into the western channel leading into Puerto Galera. I booked a small room just off the pier, overlooking the picturesque little bay, and collapsed for the night, still in semi-shock at the sudden turn of events.

Bright and early the next morning, I caught the early ferry to Batangas on Luzon, keeping well to the center of the crowd the entire crossing, feeling quite inconspicuous with my crumpled clothes and near-beard, knowing I had to look just like hundreds of Aussies with hangovers and beautiful rent-a-Filipinas on their arms. At the same time, I got more than a few looks because of the dark roots growing into my blond hair.

At the end of the dock were the waiting air-conditioned buses and I grabbed the first one to Manila.

I knew exactly where I was going. And I knew exactly what I was going to do. I never thought I would—or could —ever do such a thing. If you had asked me just the day before, I would have scoffed in disgust. But now there was no question about it—the only amazing thing was how little it had taken to make the decision.

———— • ————

It was my lucky day. The call went through. If you take the Philippine telephone service for granted, it's safe to presume it's going to drive you insane.

The voice on the other end of the buzzing line was male, his English book-learned but clear, his tone neutral.

"Embassy of the United Soviet Socialist Republic."

"I want to speak to the ambassador."

"Who is making the call?" the voice asked flatly, displaying neither manners nor emotion.

"Tell the son of a bitch that Lee Rivers is on the phone."

There was a reflective pause.

"Who . . . ?" the voice asked again, unperturbed.

"Lee . . . Rivers. R-i-v-e-r-s," I repeated in clearly enunciated English, finding it difficult to camouflage my anger.

There was another pause before the voice on the weak line replied.

"You will wait one minute."

The line went dead. I looked out of the phone booth and glanced down Santa Monica, a short side street, to Mabini where my pension stood. The cacophony of diesel motors and horns was constant as the passenger jeepneys weaved and juggled for position in the bumper-to-bumper flow. I had left the Head safely in my room, the door secured by my own padlock. A five-star hotel would have been too conspicuous.

"The ambassador is ready to speak with you," the same book-learned voice said.

I heard a click as the call was transferred.

"You say you are Lee Rivers? Is that correct?" a new voice asked, the caution obvious. If I had expected a voice as thick as the Berlin Wall—I was mistaken. His English was almost fully articulate, his accent flawless but for a trace of Slav.

"Yeah. And you're the fucking Russian ambassador to the Philippines, right?"

There was a pause. Jeepney horns and the roar of traffic almost deafened me to my own voice.

"Well?" I repeated. "Are you . . . or are you not the fucking Russian ambassador to the Philippines?"

"Yes. I am ambassador Dmitri Dimikarto," he stated firmly, suppressing his anger, his tone rising a half-octave.

"Okay, asshole. I have what you want. You have what I want. What do we do about it?"

"I do not know what it is that you mean," the older voice said, now displaying all the emotion of a T-34 tank.

"I have the Head. You have my friends."

"I have *your* friends? I do not even know who you or your friends are. And why should I even care?" The voice was strong, its owner used to wielding authority.

"Sure, and you always take calls from everyone who picks up a phone and asks for you," I said sarcastically. "You've heard of me. And you have them."

"I *don't* know what you mean. That I have *them*," he said, sounding sincere.

"Come on, Rasputin. One of your atomic submarines just dragged the boat we were on to Davy Jones's bloody basement. I saw it. But I've still got the Head. And your sub still has—"

"Just a moment," he said, cutting me off, his voice suddenly tinged with paranoia. "Perhaps we can make a meeting, no? It is better than to talk on the telephone—not the most private medium."

"Well, I'm sure you would know much more about that than me. What would you suggest?"

"Can you come to the Soviet Embassy?" he said, without so much as a pause.

I guffawed out loud.

"You can blow that one out your babushka. I trust you just about as far as I can throw Lenin's Tomb. You'll have to think of something else."

"What else can we do? Can one of my staff—or I—meet you at a place of your choosing?"

I thought about it for a minute.

"What good would it do?"

"You are the one who is making this call."

"And talking on the phone is what we are going to stay doing," I said just as cautiously. "We can get just as much accomplished this way for the moment. I have nothing to hide and anything I say can be said on the telephone."

"So be it," he said, after a leaden pause. "But should *other* groups come to interfere with any arrangements we should make about any subject, I can not be held to blame. I am merely trying to protect both our interests. I will have to have a little time to find out what can be done. Can I call you back?"

I thought for a moment.

"I'll call *you* back in an hour."

"Please. Give me two."

I didn't wait for an answer but just hung up.

———— • ————

I stepped away from the pay phone and surveyed the area around me.

It was early afternoon and the narrow, one-way street of del Pilar by the infamous Raymond's Fast Foods, normally a drunken pandemonium of whores and blaring jukeboxes, was quiet. A few street-sweepers in their bright yellow T-shirts were lazily sweeping the gutters of last night's cigarette butts, beer cans and barf with home-made twig brooms, shuffling it into piles of garbage that permanently decorate the street—a Patpong this ain't. A few bored bar girls slouched in bar doorways, making less-than-half-hearted attempts at enticing the few tourists wandering the strip into the dark bar interiors. Elsewhere, a few hookers of both sexes and either persuasion stood around waiting for some afternoon short-time action.

Later in the evening, the entire Ermita area would transform itself into an enormous, drunken party, with thousands of eager, laughing a-go-go girls, but right now I was pleased it was relatively tranquil. As things were, there was an inordinate number of Arabs, Sikhs and Indians around, all of whom seemed to be staring at me. It wasn't my paranoia—I had planned it that way. I was market-testing my new disguise.

If a strong defense is a strong offense, I was offensive enough that Attila the Hun would have hired me as his chief of staff. Thanks, Lady Clairol—you did wonders for my looks. Her and a few safety pins and studs to go with the black clothes I had picked up at a sidewalk sale, along with a weird haircut-and-shave job, that had scraped everything away except for one-inch squares all over my face which I had dyed green, and lip plugs—only under my bottom lip, so as not to interfere with my talking as much as before. I positioned myself so I could catch the reflection of my now spiked and chartreuse hair in the chrome edge of the phone booth. I was pleased. I looked like an escapee from Leicester Square.

I glanced at my next destination, the bar on the corner opposite: The Boeing 69 Club. It bothered me. François would be much more familiar with the Manila Hotel's Champagne Room than with this girlie bar in Ermita, and I could have misinterpreted him. Why the hell would a diplomat be connected with a semi-sleazy a-go-go bar?

I shrugged, took advantage of a brief lull between the grumbling jeepneys, and hurried across the street and into the dark confines of the most popular watering hole in Ermita.

The joint wasn't jumpin'. It was mostly empty, with only a couple of lushes at the bar, hands draped protectively around frosty glasses of San Miguel. A single, third-string a-go-go dancer in a bikini that had YOUR PUSSY TONIGHT? embroidered on the ass slowly shuffled her overweight body around on the stage, a half-beat behind the music of the cheap sound system.

"I want to speak to the manager," I said to the hostess who had taken my elbow and was starting to guide me to a bar stool.

She looked at me questioningly for a moment, then nodded her head.

"Come," she said.

There were all kinds of things I could have done with a

lead line like that but I wasn't in the mood. She led me through a greasy, beaded curtain and down a narrow hallway. Just opposite the unisex toilets was a door on the right. She rapped on it twice, paused, then rapped one more time. A signal. A voice grunted me in.

The office was rectangular, but cramped with the usual filing cabinets, a Remington manual on a work desk, and stacks of drink receipts stuck here, there and everywhere. At the end was a plain office desk. Behind it sat a broad-shouldered man in a sports jacket, leaning over the bottom drawer of a filing cabinet with his back to me. The stench of cigar smoke was as thick as a burning barricade of old rubber tires.

"My name is Lee Rivers," I said.

"Yeah. I heard of the name," the man said quietly, closing the drawer slowly spinning around on a swivel chair. He took one look at my hair and his eyebrows bobbed. "Christ, Jungle Boy, did someone barf all over your head after eating a pizza with everything?"

It was a moment before I could reply.

". . . B . . . *Brock Stambuck!* What the hell are *you* doing here?"

"Sit down and I'll tell you. Sorry we don't have any mekhong but would you care for a beer? It's the national sport here, you know."

He didn't wait for an answer, but reached into a small refrigerator and pulled out a can of San Mig. In front of him was a half-empty glass of whiskey, beside it a half-full bottle of Old Crow. He dug into the freezer, grabbed a small handful of ice, and dropped it in his glass. I sank into the ratty armchair opposite him and popped the top off the can.

"*Mabuhay,*" he said, raising his glass.

I shook my head in disbelief, hoping it would clear. I removed the lip plugs.

"That's better," he chortled. "You almost had me fooled. You were uglier than all the Rolling Stones put together there for a moment."

I took a sip. Specks of foam dribbled down the side of the can.

"I suppose you know why I'm here."

"I have a pretty good idea," he replied, pulling out an eight-inch Manila cigar and lighting it.

"You know François?" I said.

"The Swiss frog?" he asked, shaking out the match.

I nodded slightly.

"I do now. Sort of. By way of this and that."

"How do you mean?"

"He contacted us. Or actually, he contacted one of our men, a guy with our embassy here. Peter Melville. This Melville apparently was supposed to do a favor, pick up the Head from you and return it to Nepal."

"What happened? Where is he? Why are *you* here?"

He was still favoring his right arm, I could see. There was a slight bulge from the bandages under his sports jacket. He noticed me looking.

"It's okay. I'm gonna live. The post office in Bangkok sent me out First Class. Nog and Po are in good hands too. Don't worry about them."

The information came as a relief.

"Can you answer my question? I'm a little beat."

He leaned forward confidentially, pushing his glass aside.

"Well, this thing got all outa hand to such a degree that what started out to be basically a minor favor for a friend got our man Melville a little concerned. Your name is in every newspaper in the world right now! That sort of favor could have directly affected his career with who comes first, and that's the United States of America. Melville got cold feet and went back to this François Giscard Swiss guy who has the connection with the abbot in that monastery in Tem . . . Temp. . . ." He slowed, stumbling for the word.

"Tengboche."

"Yeah. Tengbotchy. . . . And he explained the problem —that it was too big and too important. Well, this François guy by that time saw the seriousness of it all himself, and thought about it and finally figured out that it would be best if we got involved. A friend of his apparently is one of the big boys in the Agency. What held the frog back was he said he had to contact the abbot first, because he felt honor-bound to his agreement to keep quiet or something like that."

"By 'we,' you mean the CIA?"

Brock nodded.

"That's why he told you to come here. I was on the case and knew your MO—bars and bimbos and that sort of thing. This bar is run by one of our people as a cover joint. We don't like so many of our men working out of embassies anymore. That damned Iranian thing taught us a lesson."

". . . I'd been wondering how François would know about a place like this. . . ."

"Yeah. He's with us—let us know right away you called from Singapore. Raffles, right?"

It was my turn to nod.

"Why didn't he just put me in touch with your office in Singapore? It would have been a hell of a lot safer. The voyage was no Sunday row on the pond."

"Yeah, I wish that too. But the Swiss frog hadn't contacted the abbot at that point and he wasn't sure if Hizzoner, or whatever his name is, would go for it, though he was pretty sure. So he had to phone some friend or another of his in Kathmandu and have him fly to this Tengbotchy, then take the old guy back to Kathmandu so he could call New York. Took a lot of time. And money. This guy must be loaded." He rubbed two thick fingers together. "And that's why he told you to come here. Both he and we knew you just couldn't be left hanging."

"What did Abbot Tengid say?"

"The old guy said yeah. So the Swiss frog said we should get involved and that he would cooperate with us."

I nodded slowly, letting it all sink in.

"Now, I'm sure you agree that all of this has gotten a little out of hand and I presume that you're going to be happy to get the Head off your back and put it under the protection of the United States Government?"

He chuckled, presumably at his little pun.

I didn't think so. Although I'd been eager to give up the Head only a day before, everything had changed.

"For one thing, I'll have to talk to François about this."

He grabbed the phone with a big mitt and jammed it down in front of me.

"Help yourself. You'll find I'm not tossing the gears to you."

"Brock, it takes hours to get through from a private phone in this town. This country is a mess."

"Not on this phone. In addition to our special postal department we have our own wire-pullers. We have scramblers that secure it from this end. Dial direct. I have the number here if you forgot it."

I looked at it. As near as I could recall, it was François phone number. The call took only a couple of minutes to go through. His wife, Breenda, answered the phone.

"Lee! *Alors!* Where are you?"

"Where I can get a good Sunset. Though I'm on a plane there," I answered. "I have to speak to François."

"Oh, Lee, I'm so sorry," she said, her voice bleeding. "He's meeting with the Brooklyn Museum. They're negotiating an acquisition of some of Fran's Etruscan collection. They went out for dinner somewhere in the Village. It's awfully late and they should be back by now but they're not. May I help?"

"Maybe. You know the whole story, right?"

"*Oui,* of course."

"Is it true? He wants me to give it over to the CIA for protection? Brock Stambuck is with me."

"If at all possible, *oui,*" she said. "Fran spoke to Abbot Tengid by phone and the abbot says to do whatever is most secure to get it back. We think Tengid is secretly trying to make some arrangements with the Dalai Lama to take direct responsibility for it again." Then she added, with frustration showing in her voice, "Oh, I wish François was here!"

"Okay. That's all I wanted to know. Thanks, Breenda. Tell François I'll be in touch."

I hung up.

"Okay. Good enough? Now, you'll give us the Head this time?"

I looked at him straight on. Then shook my head.

"I'm afraid I can't do that."

Brock's face flushed with anger. He jerked the cigar to one side. Before he could speak, I did.

"Now hold it, Brock! I don't want another of your crazy speeches about how dangerous this all is. *I know!*"

"Well, if you *know,* why the hell don't you give it over? You've got the Head, don't you?"

I had to tell him—I needed all the help I could get. Most importantly I needed quiet but powerful diplomatic pressure, which is why I had come here. Like the diplomat I had hoped to see, he had the connections. I was worried he might order a muscle job on me but I had to take that chance.

"I still have the Head," I said cautiously.

"Then what the hell's the matter with you? You think you can protect it? I haven't told you yet all *who* we *know* wants to pluck your short ones, and how close they are, because I don't want to scare you, you being just a simple jungle collector and all that. You're going to need protection, bodyguards for some time."

"I can't give it to you, Brock. There's—"

But before I could explain he interrupted angrily.

"God damn it, Rivers! How many times do I have to tell you! That thing is vital to the interests of Buddhism! If it's not safely returned to them it's going to reflect damned bad on the USA—and don't forget you're an *American citizen!*" he snapped while he ground out the cigar he'd barely begun. "Christ, we're not going to *do* anything with it but get it safely back! What the hell do you think we are?"

"Brock, it's not that. I trust the Agency. I know you're working in the best interests of the Head and all that. It's *not* that!"

"Then what the hell is it?"

"It's the only tangible thing I have to get Tysee and Snake back—the *only* thing. And until they're back, the Head is *mine*, because I know you'll sacrifice them for it." I slammed my beer down on the table. More foam bubbled up and ran down the side of the can.

"What the hell are you talking about *now?*"

"If you'll shut your fucking face up and *listen* for a minute, I'll tell you!"

Surprised, he quickly sat back and rapidly nodded his head. I blew the foam off the can and took a long, cool pull, which gave me time to calm down a little. Then I told him about the Russian submarine. His anger and irritation disappeared as the story unfolded. He was looking incredulous by the time I'd finished.

"You're crapping me—aren't you, Jungle Boy?"

I shook my head.

He yanked the telephone off its cradle and quickly hammered three numbers.

"How's the fishing?" he spat into the phone. "Sighted any whales in the general area?"

A moment later he nodded and grunted and nodded some more, his final grunt one of confirmed fact. He slammed the phone down, then looked up at me, his eyes like landmines.

"Well, those rotten bastards! You *weren't* shovelin' it outa the barn. Our satellite sea-surveillance division reports a whale sighting in the Calavite Passage. A big gray Russkie whale. Typhoon-class yet. This changes everything. There'll be big rumblings about this stateside," he finished, half to himself.

"That's why I can't give you the Head. Tysee and Snake are aboard. It's my only bargaining tool."

"You'd *trade* the Head for the two of them?" he asked in disbelief.

"I remember reading something to the effect that if he had to choose between his country and his friend, he hoped to God he could choose his friend." I paused for a moment, feeling myself being torn apart. "The choice was hypothetical to him. It's not, to me. I don't want to give them the Buddha Head, but. . . ."

My voice trailed off.

"So you'd trade the Head for them? For one little pussy? And Kun San's kid no less? Her and this Snake? And fuck the rest of the world, huh? Fuck Buddhism? Fuck the U.S.A. too? Sounds to me more like Benedict Arnold wrote that one."

I could have nodded. I didn't. I knew it was a horrible thing to even consider. I also knew there was no choice.

"She means a *lot* to me. And Snake's my best friend."

"You want to know what I think? I think you're a dumb fucking asshole to even consider it. Why do you even tell me when you know I'm going to have to stop you?"

"Because I need your help. There has to be something we can do through official channels—put diplomatic pressure on the Russians to cough them up. They've created what could turn into a major international incident—kidnapping two Westerners—something I'm sure they don't want right now, with public opinion shifting toward them lately. If they're told about it quietly, maybe they'll see the wisdom in avoiding a confrontation, and just release them. I don't want to be forced to make the exchange—it's only my last resort—and I won't if something can be done otherwise, but meanwhile I'm hanging onto every card I have." I took a drink, then plunged on. "And I should tell you, I've already talked to the Russian ambassador—and he certainly knows who I am, and that I'm in the Philippines. He's presumably contacting Moscow now. I'm calling him back soon."

"You *what?*" Brock sputtered, looking astonished again.

"You heard me."

He shook his head. His expression said I was mad. Maybe I was.

"*Don't* under *any* circumstances meet him or any of his colleagues anywhere, anytime without contacting me, or you'll be seeing the sunset over Manila Bay from *under* it. You realize that?" His voice was charged up, his thick finger jabbing at me like a machine gun. "World opinion may have changed, but their covert actions haven't."

"Don't worry. I told him roughly the same thing."

"Where did you make that call from?"

"The phone booth just across the street."

"Oh, great," Brock said sarcastically. "In case they ever learn we're here and start tapping it, we *never* use it."

I shrugged. It was too late.

"Will you help? Get the State Department on it?"

He thought about it for a minute, then nodded imperceptibly.

"It might work. You have a point there. So the bastards are going to this extent . . . incredible. . . . But that's all the more reason to *give* it to us, for Christ's sake."

He saw his last effort was getting no further.

"Well, have it your way," he said, resignedly. "But I better tell you a few things I didn't want to mention about just how bad things are for you. And the longer you keep the Head the worse they're going to get, until you're either slapped on a slab or are catching that watery sunset. You say you know something about the jungle? Well, there's not just headhunters *there*— there's headhunters *everywhere* right now. And they want two heads—the Buddha

Head, and yours for the big reward. Christ, if they got your friend Richard Haimes-Sandwich, who as far as I can see is well out of the picture, you can be damned sure they're after you."

"Hold it—for one thing, he's *not* my friend. But what are you talking about? Who got him? What happened?"

"Don't you read the papers?" he said, tossing a folded edition of the *Bulletin Today* over to me. "Right here on page 5. Near the bottom, in a corner."

My eyes hit the copy.

> UPI—A new twist has been added to the search for the so-called Buddha Head. It was reported from new Delhi yesterday that Richard Haimes-Sandwich, one of the principals involved, was kidnaped in broad daylight while emerging from his hotel in Connaught Circus. He was apparently there on business.
>
> Witnesses described Haimes-Sandwich as having been forced into the back of an automobile by an armed group of men identified only as European.
>
> Little else is known about the incident, but police are following all leads.
>
> Meanwhile, the hunt goes on for Lee Rivers, rumored to be on his way to the Philippines, and his accomplice, Tysee San, daughter of the notorious and late opium warlord, Kun San, allegedly the man who directed the burglary at Tengboche Monastery.
>
> A number of vessels plying the South China Sea have reported a yacht similar to that owned by Michael Cheevers, an Australian national, to be heading in this direction. It is believed Rivers and San are aboard. The Philippine Constabulary have been put on alert.

It went on to describe Haimes-Sandwich's involvement, and a bit of familiar background. A date was announced for the Dalai Lama's statement. It was only three days away.

"Who the hell would want the Ham-Sandwich?" I asked, looking up in surprise.

"Your guess is as good as anyone's. We're baffled. But I

suppose the point is this. If they snatch a guy like this, who is out of the picture, think of the interest there must be in *you*. And, as of this date, we know of about a half-dozen different agencies looking for you, including the Mossad. Have you read what the Moslems have been talking about? A holy war? And it's *you* who's going to be made holey, as in full of holes. Just wait until the Dalai Lama gives that speech in a few days. Whatever he says, all hell is going to break loose. I might add that there's more than a few Buddhists pissed at you too, for not coughing it up as well."

Brock's frown deepened as a small wave of pain brought his hand up to his shoulder. Just as quickly he ignored it. He took another quick drink, slammed down the glass, and continued.

"Every religion in the world is after you. We even got a report out of Madrid that something called the Society of the New Inquisition has just been formed and they're out here. We only have so many men and we can't keep track of it all."

"You're still not going to get it. Not yet. But find out what can be done. Find out what the president will try to do. I won't do anything rash unless you fail me."

Brock shook his big head back and forth, staring at me like he was looking down into a casket.

"I'll tell you more. Remember me telling you about Colonel Theodore Skibinsky?"

"Who?" I said, taking a sip. The beer was almost empty.

"You've got a memory like a fish. It was after you air-conditioned his boy, Major Fazidar Amur, at your place."

It came back to me. I nodded. The KGB connection.

He narrowed his eyes as he took another sip of his Old Crow, emptying the glass. He didn't pour another.

"He had his passport stamped at Manila International two days ago after a JAL flight from Bangkok. His diplomatic bag looked damned heavy, according to our people with contacts with Customs. And yesterday, four Bulgarians flew in on separate flights, two of them from Bangkok, two from Sofia. 'Diplomats.' We've traced them to various hotels from Makati to here in Ermita and we have them covered as best as we can, but we're shorthanded, as I say, and these guys are pros. They've already ditched our men a couple of times. And they're here looking for you, make no mistake. Everyone is converging here. You should get a medal from the government here for doing so much to advance tourism in the Philippines. Now, what do you say? Still want to play marbles alone?"

"I told you already. I have no choice. It's all I got. And I also said I want *help.*"

"I'll see what I can do. But if you *are* offering him a trade, you're pulling the rug out from under us already."

"I can lead them on until we see what you can do," I said, winging it. "If it looks at all promising, I can put them on hold. But I had to act quickly—diplomatic channels can take time. I had to make sure the Reds have a good reason for keeping Tysee and Snake alive. They won't want them debriefed by our side, not after giving them a ride in a Soviet submarine."

He nodded. His frustration was showing.

"I'll see what I can do."

"Good. Thanks."

I began to insert the mouth plugs. Brock leaned back to watch me, then sighed deeply, shaking his head in resignation.

"What kind of flowers would you prefer I bring to your funeral? We may as well make the arrangements now. Bougainvillea is popular here."

I stood up to leave.

"How many spooks you got out there that are going to follow me?"

He looked down and chuckled.

"A few."

"But, as you say, you're shorthanded."

He wobbled his head as if to say, go ahead. *Try.*

"And don't *you* try anything," I said, my hand patting the Walther in my pocket.

He held his hands up defensively.

"But you hang onto that gun. You don't know just how much protection that little thing is to you. And here," he said, taking up a pen and scribbling on the back of a card. "Just in case you lose my boys, despite you looking like a walking neon factory, here's my number. Call me tomorrow and I'll see what I got for you. And call me when you need help. You noticed I say *when* and not *if* you need help?"

He pushed the slip of paper across to me. I picked it up and walked backward to the door. He made no move to stop me. I pulled open the door and was halfway through it when he called after me.

"Hey! One last thing. If you're going to give me all this trouble, can you at least make one small concession that'll save the nation a great deal of embarrassment?"

"What's that?"

"How about doing your fly up."

THIRTEEN

City of Angels

I FLEW OUT of the Boeing 69 Club, followed too obviously by one of the slouches at the bar. The decoy was easy to ditch. His partners, who were more invisible, were difficult. It took several jeepney changes, followed by a couple of taxi rides down Roxas Boulevard and around Rizal Park, where I ordered a number of sudden U-turns that thoroughly confused the drivers, followed by my disembarking and jumping two more jeepneys, thoroughly confusing me, followed by a fast walk through the thick, midday shopping crowd at Harrison Plaza, followed by a couple more cabs, before I was confident I had done the job. I figured the only reason Brock had let me go was he was confident his men could tag me. He should have known better.

I finally slipped into a small Filipino restaurant, where I found a corner table, ordered some chicken adobo slopped onto rice, and waited until the two hours were up. Then I slipped into a phone booth just around the corner.

I was luckier this time. Not only did I get through—and in thirty seconds—but the line was reasonably clear.

"This is Ambassador Dimikarto," the voice said stolidly.

"And this is Lee Rivers," I said, mimicking the stolidity.

"You are a rude man, Mr. Rivers," he said after a pause, his tone bunkering down, and lightly etched with malice. "Consider that we are trying to do business on the basis of equality and mutual respect."

I snorted in reply.

"Also consider that there is the possibility that we may be able to provide you with what you want. I have been brought up to date on the most recent developments. They are very interesting."

"What do the big bohunks have to say?"

"Pardon? Who?"

"The big perogi and the Bohunkburo—the cabbage rolls that run the Kremlin. What have they decided?"

There was a long pause full of heavy, constricted breathing.

"We would like to talk," he finally replied, each word with the weight of a cast-iron borscht bowl.

"That's just what we're doing right now. Talking."

"I have said before that the telephone, as you must realize, is not the best and most reliable way to communicate. There are groups working not in the best interests of either of us that could be listening. You will not meet us? Not even at, say, the lobby of the Manila Hotel? You would be secure there."

"Sorry. Not yet." I also needed time for Brock to try to get the State Department to put some pressure on them.

"That makes this very, very difficult then, Mr. Rivers. *Very* difficult. For I must tell you that there are other staps being taken to resolve this problem to our satisfaction that may not be wholly satisfactory to you."

"I know Colonel Skibinsky is in town with some of his friends."

"I don't know of any Colonel . . . Skibinsky, you say?" he replied, obviously lying. "But whatever he might mean to your health and well-being, I am speaking of other staps that are in progress. They are somewhat *more* severe and persuasive."

"Well, spit them out, these 'staps.' I know a threat when I hear one."

"I'm afraid I'm not at liberty—"

"You can say that again," I interrupted. "Listen, Dimmy, here's what we do. You first of all bring my friends back to Manila and we'll make the trade at some place completely neutral and *equally* safe." I hoped the emphasis indicated to him I still had muscle on my side. "I'll be in touch with you on the phone."

"I can see many problems in it. This is not something that can be done on a whim."

"It'll have to do. At least for now. One 'stap' at a time."

"I will have to make inquiries and learn what counter-proposals there are."

"I don't want any counters. This isn't a real-estate deal. I want my friends."

"Tomorrow, you will call at ten in the morning?"

"On the babushka."

I hung up.

———— • ————

I hadn't make it past the small registration desk in my pension before the old bag who ran the dump limped up and began berating me in Tagalog. I shrugged my shoulders uncomprehendingly. Seeing this, she looked at me sharply, then hobbled rapidly down the hall with an irritated downwave of her claw that meant I was to follow.

I did, through the small common-room area with a couple of red plastic-covered sofas, a TV set on which a pretty Filipina was lip-synching to a pop hit, and walls decorated with kitsch wall hangings of the Madonna and her rug rat, then on to the entrance for a narrow hallway. Here she stopped, and jabbed her bent, bony finger down the hall with one hand akimbo, and started jabbering again in a shrill and angry voice. I was becoming alarmed. My room was down there.

"Look, I don't speak the language, you crazy old bat, okay?" I said politely but helplessly, casting worried looks in the direction of my door. Something was clearly wrong —something bad. I was about to abandon her to her ravings when someone spoke behind me.

"Do you speak little English?" the hesitating voice said,

poking around in the air for words. "May be . . . I can be
of little help. I have been hair . . . sometime . . . and
speak the language little."

A young man a couple of months past his last haircut
stood up from a chair, where he had been sitting watching
TV. His accent sounded Dutch. His clothes strengthed the
impression—they were even wilder than mine.

"English? I speak a bit," I told him, worry tainting my
voice. "What's with the old hag?"

She was still raging shrilly.

The European asked something in a reasonable imita-
tion of Tagalog. She seemed to understand, and rattled off
a long litany of sentences, at the end of which she threw
her hands in the air, then jerked her finger in the direction
of the hall again.

"As much as I can . . . oonderstand . . . a policeman
came here from the droog . . . droog . . . how do you
say . . . ?"

"Drug?"

"Yes. From the droog squad. And searched your room.
She makes think you are a droog user and want you to
leave. I'm sorry about that."

My blood froze it its veins.

"Did she let him into my room?" I asked, *my* voice now
shrill. He sought the words out.

"Yes. She says he take . . . took . . . some droogs and
he is going to come back after to make your arrest. It is
better if you go now. I wood not want to see anyone in a
Filipino . . . monkey house."

I ran down the short hallway. My padlock lay broken on
the floor in front of the door. The door was still locked. I
fumbled for the skeleton key, my hand shaking, an icy
coldness sweeping my body. I threw the door open and I
hit the light switch twice before I found it.

There was an empty space in the corner of the bed
where I had left the Buddha Head.

——— • ———

"Lee! Hey! Lee Rivers!"

I was shaken out of my shock. I was wandering in a daze
down Mabini, hardly a block away from the pension.

"Hey Lee! God damn it, stop. Lee Rivers!"

Running steps approached me from behind and I prepared to swing around with a fisted backhand, but something in the voice stopped me. A powerful hand grabbed my arm. I turned to face my attacker, and I looked up from the hugest beer gut I had ever seen to a head full of prematurely gray hair.

It was Snow White, my friend who ran the Statue of Libertine Bar in Angeles City.

"Jesus H. Christ, Lee, what th' . . . oh! Sorry all to hell, friend," he said apologetically. "From behind you walk and look just like this buddy of mine—"

He caught himself. His perpetually red eyes dropped from my screaming, porcupine hair and stabbed deeply into my own. I saw he was suddenly unsure again. He blinked twice as he scanned my weird beard. Under different circumstances I would have laughed.

"Yeah, Snowy, it's me," I said, pulling him forward by his meaty arm and glancing behind us. "And, no, I haven't gone wacko. This is supposed to be a disguise."

"Disguise!" he exclaimed. "Christ! You looked like someone puked all over your head after eating a pizza with everything!"

"Yeah. That seems to be the popular opinion," I said, glancing around. There were a lot of people on the sidewalk. It was impossible to spot anyone who might be following.

"Just walk alongside of me like it's normal and for Christ's sake, *don't* use my name again. *Please.*"

Snow White looked stunned.

"Holy Jumpin' Jehovah! I'm completely amazed. You just leave here a month ago and the next thing you're in all the news about this Buddha Head thing! And now I run into you walking down the street! Hey, are you all right? You look downright sick."

"Listen, Snowy, I'm in trouble."

"Don't I know it! I've been listenin' to the VOA. Lette goes around telling everyone, including her new bar fines, how you used to bang her all the time. Is this thing for real? This Buddha Head?"

I nodded and glanced behind us again. There were too many people. "I wish it wasn't but it is," I said tensely. "And it's just been ripped off."

"What?"

"Yes, just now—out of my pension. A guy claiming to be a cop talked his way into my room. It's gone. And I'll be gone a hell of a lot farther unless I get off the street."

"Hmmmmmmm. . . .The old cop con trick? The Filipinos use that one all the time. Probably a fluke they happened to hit your room. Hey, do you have to walk so fast?"

I slowed down a tad.

"Where are you going, by the way?" Snow White asked, panting.

"I don't know . . . I don't know. . . ."

He suddenly stopped. I did as well but I felt open, vulnerable. And irritated. I wasn't thinking clearly. Anxiety filled my chest.

"Look, you need a place to go to the mattresses, right?"

I nodded abjectly.

"Well, why didn't you say so, buddy? What's a friend for?" He chuckled, a deep lumberjack's chortle that was his trademark. "Be great to have someone famous around!"

I looked up at him. This wasn't my idea of being famous.

"Come on, then. I have the Ratmobile just around the corner. The last couple of things I had to do in Manila can wait. Just come along."

His old and battered gray Datsun, that looked like it was built about the time MacArthur was returning, rumbled to a start of sorts.

"Now you keep down or whatever," he said, chortling again and pulling the rattling, rocking and rolling junkyard that leaned to one side like the Tower of Pisa into the liquid honk and spew of Manila's traffic jams.

———— • ————

On a hot, humid day in Angeles—and there it's always hot and humid—the smell of pussy lies thick as old cheese on the heavy air. The first whiff can be noticed as you approach along the MacArthur Highway. It becomes decidedly unmistakable by the time you turn right onto Field Street, which runs by the base itself. Bars line the strip facing the complex almost continuously for four miles. There, the aroma becomes so thick you can cut it with a filleting knife.

Welcome to Angeles City, a community with an appropriately biblical name, in that it makes Sodom and Gomorrah look like Salt Lake City, and whose angels will spread their wings at the least hint of a tiny offering, and where the blood of the patron saint of the Philippines—San Miguel—is taken in communion religiously twenty-four hours a day by its faithful congregation. Just off in the near distance is an extinct volcano named Mount Ararat; if it was Noah's mandate to encourage his flock to multiply, many have come to the right place. For coming is what this town is all about.

It was to Angeles City that Snow White had come on a three-week vacation from felling trees in Oregon, some dozen years previous. His story resembled that of many expats in the Far East: he'd taken one look around, shaken his head in ecstatic disbelief, gone back home and spent the next three months selling his house, car, business—*everything*— then come back, in his case to buy a bar—actually, three of them. There was The Gold Coast and Fanny's Retreat on ground level, and the main event, the Statue of Libertine, on the second. His harem of fifty girls was housed on the third floor of the three-story joint. All his friends were there. All the cold beer you could drink was there. And all the hot pussy you could pound was there. Snow White was genuinely a happy man.

This was also where he had met his wife. She had come up from Leyte, where many of the prettiest Filipinos come from, and worked as a cherry girl—a virgin handling bar duties—until she was ready to lay down on the job and really pack in the pesos. Snow White had taken one look at her and laid claim. Her nickname, the Dwarf, followed naturally behind. She wasn't really a dwarf, of course—just miniscule compared to Snowy, whose 240 pounds beefed out a six-foot-plus frame. Of course he had another explanation for the nomenclature; whenever you asked him which one of the seven dwarfs she was, a sly leer would cross his ruddy face and he would form a tight little aperture with his forefinger and thumb. "Tiny," he would reply wickedly. *"Tiny."* They were very happy together. Snowy hardly ever sneaking off for a short-time at any of his friends' bars.

The Statue of Libertine was mostly empty when the

Ratmobile squeaked to a lopsided stop outside. Stepping out, I looked up at the big neon of the Lady of Liberty, though there had been some license taken with her. She still wore her tiara and held the torch, but one full breast had fallen lasciviously out of a fold, and she was bent over, holding her gown hiked up over her fanny and sticking that well-rounded hind out toward Clark Air Base across the street. Her heavy, classical features were warmed into a welcoming smile, with the neon blinking so that she appeared to be winking and wiggling her fanny. Above her figure, also in neon, was the name of the joint: THE STATUE OF LIBERTINE BAR. Below it flashed the epigram: GIVE ME YOUR HAPPY AND HORNY, YOUR DRUNKEN MASSES.

We double-timed up the wooden stairs. About a half-dozen beer bellies—of a size that made those in The Lion's Den look like training tummies—were lumped against the bar. A couple more were settled into the open balcony seats that overlooked Field and the runways on Clark. Now and then their owners would glance at the F-16s and Herculeses taking off and landing.

Although it was barely four in the afternoon, there was a show on—of sorts. On a low stage behind the bar, a very shapely, totally nude teenybopper was standing under a shower rigged up with drains to take the water away. With her was an equally nude man in his forties. He was big, with a red face and arms but a dough-white body—a farmer's tan. The soap she used to lather him up must have been made of some kind of yeast, because one part of him was rising, at least tentatively. She giggled and kneaded him but, although assisted by encouraging hoots, cheers and laughs from the other half-cocked, half-crocked men at the bar, she had so far only half-succeeded. Just as she was slinking down in front of him, his eyes and mouth opening like the bay doors of a C-123, Snow White pushed me up the stairs and out of sight of the bar. His eyes were gleaming. He was back in his element.

"Ssh," he said, holding a large finger to his pouted lips, as we reached the top landing of the third floor. "Most of them are still sleeping."

The entire building vibrated as a squadron of jets across the street took off in a huge roar.

"They're used to *that*, though."

I looked around. The entire floor area was divided into what must have been sixteen open-topped, plywood-partitioned units. I glanced into one, and saw two wood-framed bunk beds standing four feet from each other, one girl to each bunk, four bunks to a unit. Home. Their few possessions—mainly cosmetics and cutouts from magazines—were spread over a small, handmade table, or taped to the rough plywood walls. Most of the girls up here were asleep, but would be up in time for another full night's action beginning at six or eight, depending on their shifts. More than a few were snoring. A couple were talking.

Snow White motioned me toward another door, which led to the roof. Part of it had been built up to make two rooms. One, the more strongly built of the two, was his office. He'd begun to lead me forward to the other when I stopped.

"What's this?" I asked, looking down. What looked like huge white letters had been painted on the black background of the roof.

"That? Says FUCK YOU RUSSIA. For their satellites."

I raised my eyebrows a little, then followed him.

Snow White opened a flimsy wooden door. Inside was a bed with an old mattress and bedding that looked relatively neat.

"Stupid place to have a short-time room anyway," he grunted. "It's all I got but you're welcome to it. I'll put a sign on the door downstairs so no one'll come up, and I'll tell the gals to take their customers to one of the short-time rooms at The Gold Coast or Fanny's. I use the office every day, so no one will suspect me coming and going. I can bring you food. Here's the keys to my office. There's some pocket books and a phone if you need it. The can's right over there so you don't hafta piss off the roof like some of these drunken assholes we get up here do."

His words were muffled by another loud roar as a jet took to the air.

"By the way, Snowy, did you get a call asking for me just after I left a month ago?" I'd recalled Wolfgang saying he had phoned here while trying to track me down.

He looked puzzled.

"Phone call? No. Did someone say they phoned here for you?"

"Yeah. A friend of mine. Guy named Wolfgang Krueger."

"You mean the guy in the news?"

"Yeah."

"No. Hell, there's no way I coulda. I only had the damned thing hooked up again last week. It was out of order for five months."

I scratched my head between the spikes.

"I really don't know what's going on," I said in a fatigued voice. Then I added thankfully, "Anyway, it's a good setup here. I appreciate it, Snowy."

"Don't mention it, buddy," he said, turning. But he just as quickly turned back, something else coming to mind. "Want me to send Lette up? She'll keep quiet. If you're worried, I'm sure you can think of something to stuff in her mouth to shut her up." He chortled at the thought.

I thought for a moment of her petite, perfect little body and happy, bright manner. It now seemed so long ago. But she was also a friend and I needed a friend right then. Anything to take my mind off the numbing situation I was in.

I nodded. Less than ten minutes later I heard the pitter-patter of little feet, followed by an urgent rapping at my door. I slipped the Walther under a newspaper where it would be handy and reached for the handle.

"Oh, you broke my plastic little heart!" she cried, half-mocking me, throwing her smooth little arms around me and pushing me onto my back.

———— • ————

I didn't call the Russian ambassador the next day. I didn't know what to say. I had lost my bargaining tool.

I spent it instead—at least most of it—with Lette kneading my back while I wondered who had stolen the Head, and how. I scoured my mind, trying to think of some way to help Tysee and Snake. With the Head gone, the Russians had no reason to keep them alive—it would serve no purpose. My nerves were shattered, dulled, deadened. Even Lette's spirits began to dip through the course of the day, because of my almost totally silent preoccupation. Then, late in the afternoon she finally sat up from where she had been working on my lower back.

"Come awwwn. Sing me your favorite song," she complained, frustrated.

"Huh?"

"You know," she said, taking up the tune. " 'You don't have to say you love me, just pull down your pants.' "

I could only turn my head, avoiding her sad gaze.

"I don't think you want me anymore," she said in a quiet voice. "You don't do *gilling-gilling* with me and I said I wouldn't charge you. You have another girlfriend."

"What gives you that idea?" I said weakly.

She reached down beside the bed and pulled up Tysee's cobra bikini bottoms, the ones I had salvaged from the wreck of the *Riquer*.

"You wear wedding ring now. And I found these sticking out of your pocket last night when you were asleep."

I took them and felt their texture. Lovingly. She rose and reached for her string bikini. I said nothing, but turned my head to the wall. After she had dressed, I sat up and drew a fifty-dollar note from my pocket roll. That was far and above her usual fee.

"I'm sorry, Lette," I said sincerely, slipping the money under her purse.

She looked at it, then at me.

"Bar girls have feelings too," she said in a tiny, hurt voice, her eyes red.

She quietly left. The money still lay on the tiny table.

"Damn it all," I said, tenderly setting Tysee's bottom aside. Hurting Lette's feelings just made me feel worse.

I had to do something. Anything. I couldn't just sit in my cell all day. A couple of half-baked ideas had formed that I had to try.

I leapt to my feet and I dug into my pockets, looking for the card with Brock's number on it. After going through my few belongings four times until I was ready to scream with frustration, I finally found it. It was in the breast pocket of my only shirt.

I crossed over to Snow White's office and picked up the telephone. It took me an hour to finally get through and when I did, the line reverberated with a high-tension hum.

"Well, I'm glad you called. I didn't think you could do it,

but you shook my men. Change your mind? Going to cooperate now?"

"I lost it, Brock, I lost it," I confessed dejectedly, heading
straight to the point.

"Huh? You *lost* it! You lost *what?*" he barked.

"The Head. It's gone." I said weakly.

"Whatdya mean it's *gone?* Gone where? What happened?"

His voice was a shout. I could hear the scrape of a chair as
he clambered to his feet.

I told him about returning to the pension. There was a
long pause at the other end while I listened to his deep
breathing.

"Well, you dumb, fucking shithead! Do you *know* what
this means! Do you have *any* idea? I should have hammered you when you were here. I didn't because I thought
my men could tag you! My goddamned career is gonna be
out the gaddamned door!"

"Brock, no one could have followed me. I'm not dumb to
those sorts of things. Before I first took the room, I spent a
couple of hours making sure I wasn't shadowed."

"Yeah? Well, what happened then?"

"I don't know . . . I don't *know,"* I said lamely. "It must
be just a regular con job."

"Yeah . . . I suppose there's that remote possibility.
Though it seems a little too coincidental to satisfy *me.* You
don't exactly look like you have a lot of money, and the guy
chose your room specifically."

"I don't *know.* I just know it's gone. I'm sorry. You have
no idea how sorry I am. . . ."

A fighter jet peeled overhead, breaking the sound barrier. I hastily covered the mouthpiece, knowing it would
do little good. The roar receded. It wouldn't take a genius
to know I was in Angeles City.

"So you're just calling to pass on this bit of good news, is
that it?"

"Not exactly. I have an idea. If it *was* a con man, it'll
probably be fenced at a local antique shop. There's about a
half-dozen or ten of them on del Pilar. Can you have your
men keep an eye on them? It's the only thing I can think
of. I know a few of them but I don't feel safe out in the

open yet. Even if I don't have . . . the Head . . . anymore."

"Yeah. That's a thought. I'll do that. What're you going to
do now?"

"I . . . don't . . . know. . . ."

"Well, when you figure it out, gimme a call, okay?" he
said harshly, no sympathy in his voice.

He hung up, not even bothering to ask where I was. By
then it was too late to make the second call. If the first one
had been difficult, the second was going to be triply so.

To help me sleep, I filled a small cooler in the corner of
the office with cold San Miguel from Snow White's refrigerator, and carried the heavy load back to my room. Later
I returned to fill it again. By midnight his fridge was empty
and I wasn't.

But I was also snoring.

————— • —————

I didn't know which had woken me up—the brilliant dag-
gers of light stabbing through the cracks in the window
and door, or the shriek of jet aircraft that slashed through
the pea soup of my hangover. I did know I was covered in
sweat and that it was stiflingly hot. I glanced at the fan. It
was dead. Another power failure? I hit the button. It rattled to life.

Easing myself into a sitting position, I gently shook my
head, hoping it would clear. It didn't. I tried to focus on my
wristwatch. One p.m.

Time to make that other call. I struggled into my pants
and stumbled across to the office. It only took me forty-five
minutes to get through though, and when I did the connection sounded like someone was using the lines for violin
strings.

I didn't know what I was going to say. I was grasping at
straws, hoping to find out in the conversation whether or
not it was the Russians who had nabbed the Head. If not,
perhaps I could somehow bluff my way forward. But I
knew even as I called that it was a straw too weak to break
even an insect's back.

"Mr. Rivers, I'm afraid it has taken you a long time to
make this call," Ambassador Dmitri Dimikarto said, his

voice preemptory, when he finally came to the phone. "You were supposed to phone me yesterday."

"I wasn't able to," I said, my voice thick with a hangover. "What do your colleagues in Moscow have to say?"

"I note a somewhat more respectful tone in your voice. That is good. But I am afraid that it is too late."

My heart sank. A phalanx of jets thundered overhead, rattling the windows. An empty beer bottle rocked and fell off the desk. I tried to cover the mouthpiece until they were gone.

"What do you mean it's too late?" I asked, trying to control my voice.

"When you did not call, the other staps that I mentioned to you were put rapidly into motion—and they are, unfortunately, irretrievable. But do not worry, Mr. Rivers. It all comes out to the same thing. We can both be assured of getting what we want."

My heart rose.

"What are those other steps, Ambassador Dimikarto?"

"You will hear of them soon enough, Mr. Rivers. Soon enough. Now, I must be going. The Dalai Lama is speaking tomorrow. That should be interesting. I will think of you then. As we shall have no further need of speaking again I wish you every success in recovering what it is you wish to recover."

He hung up and I let out a deep breath.

So at least *they* didn't seem to have the Head, and didn't know I had lost it.

But if not them—who?

———— • ————

For once, the Russians were efficient beyond their usual capabilities. I didn't have to wait very long, just till the next morning—though it was one of the longest, hardest waits of my life—to learn what those "other staps" were that the Soviet ambassador had alluded to.

The news came to me by two couriers. The first of these was Snow White.

"Hey, Lee! Wake up!" he roared excitedly. His beefy fist thumped against my door while I groggily unlatched it. His eyes were popped in amazement as he followed his beer belly through the door. He looked at me like I had just been awarded the Nobel Prize. He was waving a can of beer.

"You're still famous!"

"Water ya talkin' 'bout?" I asked, shading my eyes from the brilliant tropical sun, my voice liquid. I checked my watch. It was barely 10:00 a.m.

"I just heard it on the radio! There's been a skyjacking!"

"So? Big deal! They're a peso a dozen. Where's it going down *this* time? Beirut as usual?" I rubbed my eyes, still waking from one nightmare into another, and not sure which one I was in or preferred.

"No. *Here!* Clark Air Base!"

He couldn't suppress his glee.

"So what's that got to do with me?" I asked, sitting back on the bed, hands on its edge, looking up at him.

I was naked and felt grungy with old sweat. Still hungover from two nights ago.

"It's because of what their demand is! You'll never guess."

"Well, if they're coming here, pussy I would think," I said, scratching my tangled charteuse mop.

"Nope. Guess again."

"Come on, Snowy. I'm in no mood for games."

"They want *you!*" he exclaimed.

"Huh? You're kidding," I said, suddenly wide awake.

He slapped his big hands together in front of his beer belly. He looked like an enormous kindergarten pupil.

"I tuned into the VOA to get the latest football scores and right in the middle of it, some announcer broke in to say that a Pan Am 747 bound for New York has been hijacked in Istanbul by a bunch of Arabs calling themselves the Holy War, or something! The jumbo just finished refueling in Dubai and is on its way *here right now.*"

"You're *not* kidding?"

I knew he wasn't. After what I'd been through lately I wasn't terribly surprised.

He shook his head.

"They say they want *you*, and this Buddhist Head you don't have anymore."

"Oh . . . God . . . ," I mumbled, dropping my head. It must be Monday again.

"But that's not all—here's the *best* part. *Snake* is on the bloody plane—*Snake!*"

He almost started to jump up and down, he was so excited. My mouth suddenly turned dry as a mummy's armpit. I was on my feet in a second.

"Was there any mention of anyone else besides Snake?" I shot back, eye to eye with him.

"Uh . . . yeah," he said, momentarily taken aback. "That broad with the funny name. I never was good with these languages."

"Tysee San?"

"Yeah, that's it.

I fell back on the bed and stared blankly at the wall.

"Are you all right?"

I barely heard him. My initial flood of relief turned into anxiety that was seven on the Richter Scale. I didn't have the Head. What would the terrorists do to them when I couldn't deliver? I closed my eyes. The image of their bloodstained bodies became even clearer.

The second messenger was actually a number of messengers and, unlike Snow White, clear-eyed and trim. They announced their arrival right then with the hammer of hard boots, and authoritative voices that had to be military. Three smartly dressed MPs in white helmets and gloves had clambered efficiently onto the roof and marched directly over to us. I grabbed a towel and wrapped it around me.

One of them, a Spanish-American with major's stripes, clicked his heels before me smartly. A radio unit on his belt squawked quietly.

"Are you Lee Rivers?" he asked, his eyes solidly on mine. It was clear that he already knew. I looked at Snow White.

"I didn't say a word, honest," he flustered.

I could see he meant it. His white-stubbled chin had fallen almost to his belly. I nodded.

"My name ees Major Mendoza of Base Security," he said courteously. "We would like to ask you to please come with us."

I shook my head and reached for my clothes. There was no escaping. Within minutes I was crumpily dressed, my neon hair bristling. We marched down the steps, me in the middle, leaving an upset Snow White. I had left my gun behind, still hidden under the newspaper.

The girls on dorm level were now all awake, giggling in their nightgowns, panties and less, flashing and wiggling their fannies at four handsome and thoroughly impassive young men who were waiting there for us in freshly starched uniforms. The MPs smartly hammered down the stairs behind us. There we were joined by four more. Three military jeeps and a wagon with meshed windows waited on the street, engines idling. To my relief, I was courteously directed to a jeep.

Lette was standing motionless on the second-floor balcony, holding her blanket to her face protectively. She looked at me for a moment with large, frightened eyes, then turned away. My last sight of the Statue of Libertine.

The driver slipped the gear shift into first and we roared away in a convoy of dust into the huge air base.

FOURTEEN

Clark Air Base

THE ROOM WAS carpeted and air-conditioned, decorated in calming eggshell off-whites and with just enough tinges of blue to keep the atmosphere cool, efficient. Beside a large desk stood a large American flag; on the wall behind were a number of plaques. Before the desk sat a comfortable sofa with a glass-topped coffee table topped, spartanly, with one ashtray. Across from the sofa was a matching chair. One wall was a solid bank of windows.

That was where Brigadier-General Daniel Casey was standing when I was ushered into his office suite. He was studying the runways two stories below, through parted louvers. Major Mendoza introduced us, then retreated, leaving us to our privacy. The general smiled in an open, friendly way, casually stepped forward and extended his hand. If my electric hair gave him any pause, he hid that well. His handshake was firm, full and warm while we took each other in.

General Casey was not very tall or heavy—in fact was

average or a little smaller in many ways—and was in his
mid-fifties. His appearance, like his office, was neatly ordered and lean—comfortable with itself.

I sensed an underlying calmness in the man that immediately put me at ease. Despite his relaxed manner, the
deep intelligence behind his welcoming brown eyes didn't
hide, or attempt to hide, that he was quietly but constantly
evaluating everything that passed before him. I also sensed
that a wise choice had been made in naming him Chief of
Base Security: he *inspired* security.

"Hmmmmmmn. Did my boys rustle you out of bed?
Well, my apologies. Please . . . ," he said in a soft accent I
placed as Floridian.

He stepped to one side courteously and sprung open a
wall-blended door that led to his executive washroom.

"Be my guest," he offered. "Could I order you breakfast.
Bacon and eggs? Coffee? How would you like your eggs?"

"Scrambled, please. They'll fit in with everything else in
my life right now."

He smiled slightly, nodded, and bid me take my leave to
clean up.

I took advantage of the chance to have a hot shower—
something I hadn't seen too many of in the last couple of
months. Later, while I dulled his razor on my neck, hoping
I could get a start on my old beard again. I heard personnel
flowing in a steady stream through his office, giving information in muted tones, waiting while he evaluated it quietly, then formulated and issued orders.

When I reentered his office, feeling brisk and shiny, he
beamed hospitably and beckoned me to sit down at the
sofa to my breakfast. There were three cups and a pot of
coffee. Two cups were full.

"Please. It'll get cold," he said, seeing me hesitate.

He sat down opposite me and began to slowly stir his
coffee. He quickly wrapped me in that web of comfort he
knew how to spin, and I almost forgot there was some
purpose to all this. I had been polite in restraining myself
from asking the obvious questions, but for long enough.

"First of all, how did you know where I was?" I asked,
trying to copy his understated air but looking him straight
in the eye.

"I honestly don't know. I was just given a location, and

instructions to ask you here. But if you could wait for not a great deal of time, there'll be a gentleman arriving who has that information."

"Do I have any choice?"

"He shouldn't be too long," he replied, smoothly parrying my question. "One of our planes picked him up a quarter of an hour ago."

"I presume my being *asked* here has something to do with the Pan Am skyjacking? The bacon is delicious by the way—nice and crisp."

"Thank you. Yes, it does. We need to ask for your cooperation. I believe two of your friends are aboard?"

I nodded. The anxiety, temporarily shunted to the background, pressed forward again. I set down my knife and fork, my appetite disappearing. I looked down dejectedly.

"The hijackers want the Head. You want me because you think I have the Head. This is going to disappoint you: I guess you haven't heard yet that I *don't* have it anymore."

"We know you don't," he replied mildly. When I raised my eyes questioningly, he waved a hand. "Please go on eating. I think it's important for you to have a good breakfast. It's going to be a long day, I'm afraid."

I shook my head in slight dismay.

"What can I do without the Head?"

"That will be cleared up as soon as the third party I was speaking about arrives. It will be quite useful if we can exchange some information. We have made some tentative plans. We know who the hijackers are. My Intelligence man, Major Symons, has been very busy."

"Indeed? So who are they?" I asked, forking the egg into my mouth and following it up with a bite of toast.

"When the plane landed at Dubai to refuel, it released all the Moslem passengers, leaving 102 hostages on board. Many of those remaining are Americans—businessmen and tourists. There is also an Israeli, a number of Europeans, and a scatter of other nationals, including a few Buddhists. Pan Am provided us with the passenger list at Yesilkoy Airport in Istanbul, and it was easy to strip it down to our problem people. There are eight of them. All are traveling on false Lebanese passports—we know that from our contacts in Beirut. From information gleaned from the passengers dropped off in Dubai, it's clear that three of them are actually Iranians. The other five are Libyans. It's obvious because of the false passports that they are all trying to cover their trail, to protect their governments. The entire group claims membership in the Islamic Jihad."

"Islamic Jihad? What's that?"

"You'll know when I remind you. The name means 'Holy War.' They're presently the most extreme group of the entire fanatical lot. They're the ones involved in the truck-bomb attack in Beirut that left 63 people dead, including 17 Americans, back in 1983. The same year two suicide truck-bombers demolished the U.S. Marine and French military headquarters, killing 241 U.S. and 58 French servicemen. They're also responsible for a large number of other terrorist acts, including the kidnapping of Americans in Beirut and numerous suicide attacks on Israeli troops in southern Lebanon. In 1984 they sent another suicide bomber against the U.S. Embassy in Beirut. They're believed to be made up of Shi'ite Moslems and we're all but certain they're supported by the revolutionary government in Iran. They're the worst. There are no limits to what they'll do for their cause."

"Shi'ites . . . oh my God . . ." I shuddered—Tysee and Snake in *their* hands . . . ! I had trouble swallowing, and set my fork aside again.

"The passengers gave us a profile on them that is quite typical." The general explained in his deceptively calm manner. "They are young—early twenties—most are bearded. They probably come from poorer families and are estranged or orphaned, often as a result of violence. Which doesn't mean they're stupid; if we were able to check, we'd probably find some of them have some university education." He paused to organize his thoughts. "It seems quite clear this is another of Libya's weird alliances —Libya and Iran. Iran has been talking about launching a holy war against Buddhism. This seems to be it, and they're doing it together. It's the first instance we know of them working in concert. But it doesn't surprise us. They're both the extremes of the extreme and, particularly in this case, they have a common Islamic goal: the destruction of the Buddha Head. There's many strange questions and perhaps it's my turn to ask a few. How did this come about? How did your two friends come to find themselves on board the plane? How do the hijackers *know* you're here at Clark?"

I thought for a moment, wondering how *he* knew I was here.

"Because Libya's friends in Moscow are behind it," I said. "They must have convinced Libya to talk the otherwise anti-Soviet Iranians into joining this crusade. The Iranians couldn't turn down the offer because the Russians offered a couple of wild cards to give the skyjackers the edge in the game—Tysee and Snake. It also gives the Russians the opportunity to kill two birds with one stone: they get rid of the Buddha Head, *and* they suck up to the Islamic world, particularly the Iranians. Smart."

"How do you mean? How did the Russians help out?"

I told him about the submarine, which he apparently didn't know about either, and of my conversations with Dmitri Dimikarto, though I left out the part about trying to do a trade.

"That's why Snake and Tysee are on that plane, and how come they know I'm here," I concluded. "I was talking to the ambassador just yesterday on the telephone. Half the jets on base seemed to take that opportunity to scream over. There's only one place in the Philippines where they do that."

"Very interesting indeed," he said, his usually calm eyes betraying some amazement. He quickly recovered and got back down to business. "Now let me tell you a bit more of what we have found out so far. They checked in in two groups. The first group of four terrorists consisted of two Iranians and two Libyans, but with them there were two other people, whose names check out as false—on stolen British passports. The second group of four terrorists also had a person between them, also with a false passport. The first two are listed as Lek Malinee and Tom Welsh. The second group had a John Welsh between them. Strange that two brothers wouldn't sit together when there was ample seating room on the plane. We're almost certain that two of these three are your friends. But who is the third? The Brits say all three passports have been reported stolen in the past year. They've obviously been doctored."

I nodded my head. General Casey continued.

"The first group took seats in First Class with the two

'Brits' surrounded by their companions. The second group, with the one 'Brit,' were back in Economy. This person, again, was seated in such a manner that he was surrounded."

"Why the hell would they just walk onto the plane? Particularly Snake—that's Cheevers—he's not the most cooperative guy around."

"Obviously they must have been well-armed when they went to the airport. As well, the hostages could be slightly drugged. The terrorists probably pointed out confederates in the lounge who would take care of them if they tried anything in the public areas. They had to have been quite convinced that their only chance was to go along. We suspect that the reason the terrorists chose Istanbul over, say, Athens—which has been a sieve for these sorts for some time—is because it's in an Islamic country, and some people there could be persuaded to assist. I'm sure that's how they got around security. It's the only way they could board with so many weapons—pistols, machine guns and grenades—all of which were reported by the disembarking passengers in Dubai."

General Casey paused to pour himself another cup of coffee, and top up mine. After a quick glance at his watch, he continued.

"You can almost call it double-blackmail: your friends and fellow citizens in return for what they want from you, this Head of Buddha. That is very heavy pressure—extremely persuasive."

I pushed the half-eaten plate aside, feeling a morbidity centered in my solar plexus. At least they were still alive. At least for the moment.

A buzzer on the desk intercom made a short, soft sound. He strolled over, leaned down, and pressed a button.

"Casey."

"The gentleman is here."

"Please send him in."

———— • ————

Brock Stambuck strode through the door, followed by two burly MP s carrying an aluminum metal case a yard square with handles on either side. At a nod from the general, they eased it down carefully in the center of the carpeted floor. After snapping a salute they turned and smartly exited.

My eyes were nailed to the box. The look of shock on my face must have been obvious.

"Did the general tell you I was dropping over?" Brock asked, sinking deeply into the sofa beside me. He might have been meeting me to play tennis.

"What's in *that?*" I demanded bluntly, ignoring him, my cynicism rising with my blood.

Brock smiled. I wasn't sure if it was to cover a slight embarrassment, or because he derived some kind of pride from playing with me. The general filled the third cup with coffee. Brock waved away the offer of sugar and cream.

"You want to check and see if it's okay?" he offered slyly.

I shook my head with disgust and showed him my palm.

Agile as a cat, he slipped over to the shiny metal box and twirled the combination padlock. Within seconds, he had lifted out the familiar bundle with his beef-roast-sized mitts. He was still favoring one arm. Looking around for a clear place to set it, he spotted the general's near-empty desk. The questioning raise of his head was met with a nod from the chief of Base Security. He gently set the bundle down in the center of the desk and carefully began to fold back the various corners of the material. In a moment the familiar, tranquil, golden visage faced us. Light slanting through the window louvers sparked life into the blood-red eyes.

The general, his interest piqued, rose and walked over for a closer examination.

"Any thought I may have ever entertained about *you* being a friend of mine," I said to Brock, "were obviously *sadly* misplaced."

I felt thoroughly betrayed. Humiliated. I glared at him. When another smile began to crease his face the blood surged to my head. The next thing I knew the general and a couple of MP s were pulling me off him. They pushed me down onto the sofa.

Brock began to stagger to his feet, his hair disheveled, blood dribbling down the side of his mouth.

"You're fucking lucky—pardon the language, General— that I've got a bum arm, Jungle Boy!"

"How did you find me here?"

He sneered, but didn't condescend to answer. Instead he jerked his tie straight.

"How did you do it in Manila?" I demanded. "That *impresses* me. That *really* impresses me! I thought I'd covered my trail. And then you play this stupid cat-and-mouse game, pretending to be outraged that I lost it! You fucking prick! What the *hell* is going on? *Why* are you doing this to me?"

"Don't even ask," he barked. "Just believe me when I say that all of this is for your own good. The less you know after a certain point, the better." His voice was edged with a murderous malice I had never heard before and his eyes burned with a fierce intensity I had never seen. It cooled me. I'd got him once, but I knew that in a knock-'em-down he'd coldcock me. Agitated, he began to flip the coverings back over the Head.

"Gentlemen, please!" the general said, wiping up spilled coffee. "We have little time!"

I bored my eyes into him, then glanced at the bundle the Head was in as Brock replaced it in the box and snapped the padlock shut. I glared at him, trying to contain my temper.

"Yeah, we don't have time to dab your eyes," Brock scowled, taking a seat next to the general and glancing at his watch. "Pan Am flight 306 is due to cross into Philippine airspace in about, let's see . . . in about three quarters of an hour—if Ambassador Batten has convinced the local boys to let it enter. The government keeps telling the bastards that there's no proof that you're here, but the skyjackers insist you are, Jungle Boy."

The polite buzzer sounded.

"It's for you," the general said, holding the telephone up for the CIA man. "It's the embassy."

He stood to take the call, his broad shoulders still bristling.

"How's the situation—any changes?" he demanded, forcing himself back into a state of professionalism.

The hurried whisper of a voice could be heard from the receiver. Brock grunted several times, uh-huhed once, and finally let out a long sigh. Hooking the phone between his chin and neck, he ran a worried hand through his short-cropped, graying hair.

"Better get the State Department in Washington on this. Even the president . . . or . . . you already have? Good. Christ, it's *important enough* . . . okay . . . you know where to get me the moment you hear . . . good luck."

The big spook sat down heavily. His eyes were still narrowed when he looked my way.

"Doesn't look good, but Batten called the president—*our* president—to get him to phone Malacañang."

"Something was said about a tentative plan," I said, an image of Tysee and Snake pressing into my mind. "How about filling me in?"

Knowing the Head was back in our possession didn't ease the anxiety; I knew there was no way it would be exchanged.

"You might call it a standard plan of inaction," the general said in his calm, Florida tones, relieved we were getting back to business. "It's based on our accumulated knowledge of all the factors that come to bear on a skyjacking—particularly the psychological ones. We have to relax them, make them feel they're moving forward, try to negotiate over as many passengers and non-essential crew as we can. That gives us the chance to watch for an opportunity to act. We have commandos ready to take advantage of any break and give them the ol' Marciano—though that's the last option. We don't want a repeat of what happened to that plane in Malta a few years ago—sixty dead. Fortunately our commandos are better-trained than that. The plan is little more than that."

"*That's* the plan?" I exclaimed incredulously. "You weren't kidding when you said 'tentative.'"

He nodded his chin deferentially to one side.

"What about the Head? What are you gong to do with it? I'm sure it wasn't brought up here just to show me."

"Well, that's another thing. It's not my idea to have it here or to use it—it was Ambassador Batten's. He's also the man who ordered that you be brought here. The terrorists are demanding the Head. The ambassador feels it's best that both you and it are here, just in case a contingency should arise where either of you could be put to use safely in some capacity. I stress the 'safely' aspect—it's a last-resort option. If we have to risk every life on the plane, American or otherwise, we'll have to do it, but this Head is *not* leaving this base. The damage to American prestige, purpose and image would be manifold if we traded such an important relic for the sake of a few passengers—no matter how precious those lives are to us."

"You say this Batten ordered me to be brought here and that you want my cooperation. And the terrorists say they also want me. Just how far does this 'co-operation' extend?"

"We . . . really just need you here to provide assurance to the skyjackers that you're here—if we can even secure permission for the flight to enter Philippines airspace, which we're still working on. You know some of these people; your help will be invaluable. There is no risk involved for you."

"I'll do whatever I can. Of course."

"Good. I knew I could expect that."

"A different subject. How did they get Tysee and Snake over to Istanbul?"

"This may be more in your area than mine, Mr. Stambuck."

"From the Russkie sub—I'll tell you about this in a minute, General . . . oh, you know? Good. They were picked up at sea. We got another 'whale' sighting out in international waters not far off the other site. We speculate that a helicopter met them and took them to a Russkie aircraft carrier in the South China Sea, and from there by jet to Saigon—or Ho Chi Minh City, as the gooks call it. From there, they were probably drugged, crated and carried via Aeroflot to Istanbul. That's our speculation."

"The Dalai Lama is going to make a major statement today. Is that over yet? What did he say?" I asked.

"Another casualty. He canceled it pending the outcome of this hijacking."

The intercom light flashed. It was the call the CIA man had been waiting for. He eagerly took it. I could sense Brock's blood quicken by the way he nervously shifted from foot to foot, the phone in the crotch of his neck again, his ball-mitt-sized hand behind that slab of meat one might call a neck.

"Okay! Malacañang has granted permission. We're on!"

he said, slamming down the phone. "The carpet-beaters are on their way here."

He headed for the door, then stopped and turned to me. "Where's your gun? You got that gun?"

"I left it at The Libertine. In my room under a newspaper."

"General, can you send a man over for it? He should have a weapon he's used to, if it comes to that."

The general crossed to the small intercom, switched it on and issued the order. I wondered cynically why the hell I would need my gun if I wasn't going to be used—and used is how I still felt.

"We don't have much time before they touch down," Brock added. "I have to get my end organized. General, I know you'll need your phone so I'll grab one out here, if that's fine with you."

Casey calmly pressed the button again and issued four more quiet orders. Then he leaned back and stared noncommittally at the metal box in the middle of the floor. A moment later there was a knock, and three smartly uniformed young officers marched in and saluted.

"My staff. This is Colonel Bull Ballad, my chief of staff. Major Jose Mendoza you have met. He's in charge of Operations. And someone you should have something in common with from your Saigon days, Major Donald Symons, my Intelligence Officer."

I raised my eyebrows.

"Yes, we know a good bit about you. Computers are a wonderful aid," Casey added.

Like Mendoza, the other two were broad-shouldered and bright-eyed, radiating health and vitality. Symons was in his early thirties and intense-looking; Ballad, who was black, was short and stocky and perhaps forty. He and Symons politely shook hands with me.

"All right, gentlemen," Brigadier-General Daniel Casey said, as pleasantly as if we were going to a garden party. "Shall we be off?"

———— • ————

The giant aircraft leaned back heavily just before it touched the scorching runway, sending up small smoke bombs of burnt rubber. The bulbous nose settled to earth, then a giant roar went up, distinct even in the control tower, as Pan Am Flight 306, bound Istanbul to New York, reversed its mighty engines, finding its destination at Clark Air Base. Squinting through field glasses, we followed the monster aircraft as it slowed to a taxi, found the north end of the runway, and gracefully swung portside around to a stop, forming a T at the end of the concrete.

Through the binoculars, the heat waves that rippled wide and slow above the tarmac turned the scene unreal—dreamlike, as if the jumbo was some kind of mutant guppy in a great goldfish bowl. The line of bars on Field Street and the red-brown mountains behind shimmered and blurred like the paintings at the back of an aquarium.

I felt my heart swell and hot blood fill my chest. Incredible as it might seem, my life, my love and my other best friend were in that plane. I could feel their distinct thoughts, their hopes, in me at that very moment, just as I knew my own were in them.

Around us in the control tower, radios crackled quietly, and men with starched uniforms and neatly trimmed haircuts concentrated on large green screens. The atmosphere was clean, cool and thoroughly professional, the same as the security chief, who stood beside me now, surrounded by staff awaiting instructions. The box with the Head was being guarded in a separate room.

"Perfect . . . perfect. . . . They couldn't be positioned better," General Casey said absent-mindedly as he lowered his binoculars to his chest. "Good work, Colonel McKenzie. You got them right where I want them."

Colonel Allan McKenzie, a tall, lean man in his early forties wearing a headset, acknowledged the praise with a slight nod of his head. McKenzie was in charge of the control tower.

"So far so good," the general said. "The colonel offered them the end of the runway to park, it being the farthest away from any of our installations. They took it, thinking it's safest. Little do they know. . . ." He stopped without explaining further, and turned to me. "We're going along with their demand to ground all air activity except incoming, to help ease their anxiety about landing here. They're probably going to feel an increase in their stress and insecurity levels for a while, which will make them more edgy, unpredictable and certainly more dangerous than they already are. We have to, as gently as we can, make them feel comfortable."

"Yeah. Then we can pull the rug out from under them," Brock said.

He sat on a spare chair to one side, legs crossed, elbows on the Formica counter that circled the interior of the tower. He raised a match to a cigar. An MP promptly appeared beside him, leaned over and discreetly whispered something. With a silent growl, the CIA man extinguished the cigar on the bottom of his shoe.

"General Casey, sir, Captain Harrington commanding the Pan Am reports all systems are down and that one of the members of the, uh, Islamic Jihad wishes to speak with who is in charge." The young controller who had spoken leaned back in his chair, pushing the mouthpiece of his headset aside.

General Casey thought for a moment.

"Is it possible to have that played over the monitor so we can all hear? But with a transmitter with a button so they can only hear what we want them to hear?"

"No problem, sir."

The controller rapidly typed something into his computer. In a moment an overhead monitor crackled and stuttered. He passed a hand-held mike to the general. Casey nodded slightly toward his men—he needed all their minds wrapped around this situation. He pressed a red button at the base.

"Islamic Jihad, this is Brigadier-General Daniel Casey speaking from the control tower. How may I help you? Over."

A pulsating vein at the side of his neck was all that belied his relaxed and controlled voice.

It was a moment before there was a reply. When it did come it was shrill. And young.

"This is the Islamic Jihad! You will keep all men and equipment away from the plane! To do otherwise is to blow it up! Do you understand? We have fifteen armed men aboard!"

The crackle returned.

Major Mendoza silently formed *fifteen* with his lips.

"Iranian accent," said the other major. Symons.

"Yes. Positive. I understand fully," the general replied. "No one will approach the plane under any circumstances without your permission. May I ask to whom I am speaking? Over."

"Good! That is must be very clear! We are meaning serious biz-i-ness!" the voice shouted hysterically, ignoring the general, if he had even heard him. *"You know what it is that we want! Lee Rovers and the Head of Buddha for the lifes of the hostages!"*

Ice water poured down my spine as the crackle of static returned. The general waited for a long moment, until satisfied the voice didn't plan to continue. He exchanged a glance with his staff. Brock just shook his head despairingly and tapped a finger to his temple.

"This is Daniel Casey," the general said in a friendly voice, consciously dropping his intimidating title. "We are doing everything possible to locate Lee Rivers. We have bulletins on the local radio stations every quarter of an hour, trying to locate him. Ask Captain Harrington aboard your plane to monitor the local commercial radio stations and you will hear them. We will cooperate all we can. May I ask again to whom I am speaking? Over."

As he switched off his microphone the scream came back, but it was an unintelligible mid-sentence garble. The Iranian had tried to interrupt, but the two radios couldn't send and receive simultaneously like an ordinary telephone. Only one word stood out. That word was . . . *death.*

The temperature in the air-conditioned room seemed to suddenly drop; everyone stood or sat motionless as a manikin. The crackle of static returned to the monitor. The general twitched one shoulder nervously and tried again. His voice retained its soothing, calming quality.

"I'm sorry, Islamic Jihad. We were not able to read. You are speaking too close to the microphone. Also, we both cannot speak at the same time please. Over."

There was another pause before a different voice came on—the Virginian drawl of the 747's captain.

"Clark Control, this is Captain Harrington on Pan Am 306. I've explained the problem to him. He's gone back to consult with his hotel partners. I have been instructed to tell you that they are well-armed and have grenades and plastics. I have been shown it all. They seem to be having a little trouble deciding who is in charge—"

An angry voice and grunt was heard just before the monitor returned to static. We waited, listening to the crackling, vacant speaker. Someone cleared his throat nervously in a corner of the room.

"They's only three Iranians, right? They's the real Jihad people." Colonel Ballad's heavy voice broke the silence, just a trace of the ghetto left in his accent. "I think it's going to be clear that the five Libyans don't like playing second fiddle."

"'Hotel partners' . . . hotel . . . just a minute," interrupted Major Symons, an intense look in his eye. "Hotel means eight—Harrington's remembering military parlance. Could he mean that there's *eight* partners? Nine all together? It was an unusual thing to say. And if so, who's the ninth?"

General Casey looked at him and nodded. It was a thought.

Major Symons quickly began to separate the Xeroxed passenger lists from other papers in his black briefcase. The general moved over to him. Wordlessly, they spread one copy out on an empty console. The rest of the air controllers continued monitoring the mostly empty skies around Clark. Occasionally one would guide a plane home —a Hercules here, an aerial convoy of helicopters there— always to a distant runway so the jumbo wouldn't be disturbed.

"We've double- and triple-checked, General Casey," Symons said tensely. "Those are the *only* Islamic names on the entire list that didn't disembark at Dubai, and the *only* ones on Lebanese passports."

"Hmmmmmn. Another could have boarded at Dubai. That *might* explain that other mysterious Brit passport— there's a lot of Arabs living in London these days. But let's double-check these lists again. Everyone please run them down another time."

The Major handed out copies to the other men on staff, who began to scrutinize them.

"Here," the general said, passing a copy to me and drawing another. "You're as likely as anyone to find the missing link. You are, after all, an anthropologist."

I returned his slight smile and caught the twinkle in his eye. We all began to roll our eyes down the lists. Major Mendoza was beside me, a relaxed but ready look on his face, the walkie-talkie on his hip squawking like a constipated parrot.

The list offered a varied menu of hots dogs and hamburgers, French bread and bratwurst, roast beef and rollmops, with the one bagel and a few curries thrown in, as well as a small selection of rice dishes. Businessmen and holidayers, General Casey had said. I was going over the list for the second time when my finger stopped and moved back up a couple of names, to one that caused the faintest trickle of chemistry to dapple a far, dark pool of my memory. It had done that the first time down as well. My fingertip settled just below the name.

Awithur Singh.

Could it be . . . ?

The more I thought of it, the more I was sure. I rapped my finger on the paper, striking the countertop harder each time. The general looked up.

"This could be it, if we're reading Captain Harrington on the jumbo right. I don't know how common these names are and I can't see the association, but this may be the one. Though what a Sikh would be doing hooked up with some Moslem fanatics I'll never know."

The general, the two colonels and the two majors looked at me inquisitively.

"If you've been following the news about me you might recall a conductor saying I threw a couple of Sihks off a moving train in Malaysia, but that they could only find one body. We may have found the other."

General Casey looked at Major Symons and gave him a questioning nod. The major clicked his heels and picked up a nearby telephone.

"Is it true that he actually *saw* the Head?"

It was Colonel Ballad. I nodded.

"One of them stabbed a buck knife they took off me right into it. He was the smaller one—about my size."

"Then we just may have that mysterious so-called 'Brit' to contend with," Casey said reflectively.

Brock cleared his throat but said nothing. The general

and the colonel gave each other knowing glances. Casey allowed the colonel to continue with his line of inquiry.

"So he's the only one aboard, outside of these two friends of yours, who can independently identify it?"

I nodded.

"This could be turning into a real unholy alliance," Ballad said. "Expedience. They all want the same thing: the Head destroyed. It's quite possible they're working together. There's some evidence they have before—remember there was some conjecture that Libya was the outside influence in the Gandhi assassination? And we know from recent reports that they're causing problems in Pakistan."

Everyone nodded deeply and exchanged glances.

"Excuse me . . . I need a cigar," Brock mumbled, leaving the room.

Our attention suddenly turned to the monitor—the microphone on the plane had been opened. We could hear Arab voices in the background and the loud shuffle of a headset being attached. Then the same shrill voice screamed breathlessly out of our speakers, a voice that quivered with a mixture of fear and fanaticism, that reflected a nervous system stretched as taut as violin strings.

"We don't believe you capitalist Americans! We know is that these Lee Rovers and the Buddhist Head are here in Clark City! Why do you think we come to land here? We will not be fooling around!"

Static. Everyone looked questioningly at everyone else.

"I don't know how long we can play our 'dumb' card," said the general.

The monitor crackled to life again.

"And we demand fuel!"

"This is Daniel Casey. We have a truck standing by. We can send it right out. Over."

"There will be no trick or many will die!"

"There will be no trick. Two men are aboard. You can send a man out to watch over them if you wish. There will be no tricks. Over."

There was a pause before the speakers crackled again.

"Give us our fuel."

"It is on its way. Over," General Casey said, then nodded to Major Mendoza.

The latter spoke a few words into his radio. Almost immediately, a refueling truck parked beside the runway in front of us pulled out and headed down the center line toward the plane. We watched its progress.

"Is it a trick?" I asked a general.

"No. It's just fuel. But the driver aboard is with our Intelligence. We may learn something."

"Look, General! The back door ees opening—and the front one too!" exclaimed Major Mendoza.

Everyone raised their binoculars. The yellow emergency chute billowed out the back. A moment later two hijackers with stubby machine guns slid down to meet the truck. From the front door something seemed to be thrown down. We watched tensely as the truck slowed near a wing. The driver and his assistant exited from the cab, their hands held high. They were searched, and then carefully watched while they refueled the plane. No one in the tower spoke during the entire operation. When they were through, they loaded themselves into the truck and headed back down the runway, while the two skyjackers climbed up what appeared to be thin air to the front door. What they had thrown down was a rope ladder—difficult to see at this distance through the heat waves.

General Casey thumbed the button.

"Pan Am 306. This is Daniel Casey. You are now refueled. Is everything satisfactory? Over."

"Yes. It is good."

The voice considerably calmer.

"May I know who I am speaking to? Over," General Casey asked for what seemed like the tenth time, attempting to set up a rapport.

The voice finally replied.

"My name is Mohammed Daoud!" he boasted, his swollen pride impossible to miss. "The *leader* of the Islamic Jihad!"

"He must be using his real name. It's not one from the fake Lebanese passports," whispered Major Symons.

"Can't wait to be a hero back home," Colonel Ballad muttered sarcastically.

The gas truck was halfway back to the control tower.

"There's another danger," threw in Colonel McKenzie. "If he's prepared to give his real name, he's quite prepared to die. In fact, probably expecting it." McKenzie hadn't spoken much, having instead kept a close eye on control room operations.

The thought did little to warm the room. Now the general said into the mike in a friendly voice, seeking cooperation, "Mohammed, we want to help you as much as we can. If Lee Rivers is in the Philippines, we will do our best to locate him. But you must help us too. Over."

"You can help us by giving it to us the Buddhist Head! That is our only demand! Then you can have the hostages!"

The general glanced at me. I let out a breath of released tension.

"You only want the Head, is that correct? Over."

"That is correct! Then you can have the passengers!"

"They must have changed their minds about you," Symons whispered to me.

"Mohammed, many of those passengers you don't need to hold. There are too many for you to handle easily. There's many people of other nationalities besides American. Will you release them as a gesture of good faith? It must be very hot already in the plane. Over."

"We will *think* about," Mohammed replied, who seemed calmer after his outburst.

"Will you also allow the women, old people and children off? There will be enough men to keep your position as strong as before. Over."

But when the general switched off his microphone, it was obvious that the Islamic fanatic had already tried to interrupt. His voice was back to a hysterical scream.

"—trick us! You are trying the trick with us! We will keep everyone on the plane until we let them go! Do not think we are stupid!"

The general let out a long breath and shook his head, saying to us in the room, "It's best if we can get the youngsters off particularly. All they need is a terrified child crying and getting on their nerves."

He brought the mike back up to his lips.

"Mohammed, I am sincerely not trying to trick you. I am trying to make everything easier for you. Do you have enough food and water? Can we arrange to have a truck bring out food and water for you? We can leave it on the tarmac away from the plane and one of your men can bring it in closer. We promise not to shoot. You have my word. We just want to help to make everyone as comfortable as we can. Over."

"... *want the Head!*" was all we heard from the monitors.

"Mohammed, before we can give you the Head we have to find it ourselves. What do you plan to do with it? Over."

"*We know you have it! That you have Lee Ravers!*" the voice shouted arrogantly, mangling my name in yet another way.

A light blinked beside Major Symons and he quickly picked it up.

"Symons . . . really? . . . very interesting . . . nothing else? Okay . . . still good . . . good work."

He set the phone down and turned to the general and me.

"That was our man in Istanbul. He contacted their customs and Pan Am people. They both remember the Sikh. He stood out like a broken arm, because one was broken—he had a big cast on. That's not all that was broken—his face looked like he had been in an accident. His home is Amritsar. Does that mean anything to you?"

I nodded knowingly.

"It must be our man."

Symons was about to say something else but the light on his phone flashed again.

"Excuse me, sir," a voice behind me said. "This is yours."

I turned to see a burly MP. He handed me my Walther, grip first, the clip separate. I thanked him, checked to see if the clip was full, rammed it up the grip and shoved the gun into my pocket. Brock returned at the same time from his cigar break, found an old chair and clumped down in it. In his hand was a cup of coffee which he stirred morosely. We continued to ignore each other.

"General Casey," said Major Symons, laying down the receiver. "That was Lieutenant Murphy reporting—the driver of the gas truck. He says the terrorists were armed with Uzis and one appeared to have a Luger in his belt. Both were about twenty, bearded, in jeans and T-shirts and very, very jittery."

Casey nodded as if he knew already, then raised the mike, his voice agreeable.

"How would you suggest we make the exchange, if we should eventually find the Head, Mohammed? Over."

Coffee cups were already beginning to litter the control room table. People were settling in for a siege. But it wasn't going to take days. Or even hours. Once again the general switched off his microphone to find the young Shi'ite haranguing him.

". . . *enough of this ball shit! You have the Head! You are to bring the Head to the plane! Just one of you! The Lee Revers so we know it is not a trick! We know what he looks like!*"

The ice water pouring down my spine froze solid.

"*We will confirm if it is the real or no. If it is the real, all the passengers will go and we will fly to those destination of our choice. Until then we will shoot the passenger every hour starting in one hour.*"

"Look—there ees someone sitting down in the front doorway!" Mendoza exclaimed.

Everyone sardined forward, their binoculars rising. A figure in dark pants and a white shirt was just settling down in the doorway, his back to the jam, his knees drawn up.

"Clark Control. This is Captain Harrington on Pan Am 306." The mature tones of the plane's chief pilot drawled through the speakers. "I am to tell you that the first passenger to be, ah, shot will be, ah, a Mr. Benjamin Horowitz. Over."

Major Symons immediately began flipping through his files. He held a piece of paper up.

"It's the Israeli, General. A businessman. Lives in Tel Aviv. He's in the building trade."

"Who else?" asked Colonel Ballad rhetorically. "This is beginning to sound like a too-familiar tune already."

"We have an hour," said the general, slowly surveying the field's perimeter with his glasses. "Major Mendoza, I think you should send some men and station them along the fence. There's quite a crowd forming. Also, please send a few MPs to mix—there'll be a lot of nuts coming out of the woodwork over this. Besides, the New People's Army might try to take advantage of the situation, and we don't want someone pulling out a grenade launcher or anything. Finally, Major Symons, send a man to check on that smoke rising over by the MacArthur Highway."

Both men snapped to attention and reached for a telephone.

"Colonel Ballad," General Casey said, dropping his binoculars and turning. "I think we should—"

"Oh my God! They shot him!"

It was one of the controllers who was jumping to his feet, binoculars still pressed to his eyes. In seconds we were back at the window with our own glasses raised, squinting through the heat waves. I was just in time to see a terrorist kick the body of the limp passenger through the doorway. It fell like a rag doll filled with lead shot and landed heavily on the tarmac, where it crumpled up on its side. The terrorist bent over the lip of the door, pointed his gun down, and fired another burst, stapling the Israeli to the concrete.

None of us could speak for a moment.

"Those bastards! They said they would wait an hour!" Colonel Ballad finally swore.

"Shi'ites," Major Mendoza spat. "There's one 'i' and one 'e' too many in that word."

"What was *that?*" I interjected. Something had flashed at one of the windows forward of the First Class door. A dark hole took the window's place. Then another window flashed and turned dark.

"What's ees going on in there?"

The static suddenly cut and the speakers exploded to life. For three shock-filled seconds the room filled with the sound of screams, shouting and machine-gun fire. Just as quickly the sound of havoc cut off, plunging us back into static-filled silence.

"Oh my God—they're shooting the place up!" someone yelled.

Another window blew out. Then another.

"Mendoza!" the general barked. "Get those men in there! Quick! It's a massacre!"

Mendoza dropped his binoculars, grappled for his radio, and brought it to his face.

The speakers burst to life again. It was the shaken voice of the plane's captain.

"Don't do anything! Don't come near the plane! It's over! I repeat: do not attack the plane! Or we'll all die! They have explosives rigged up! I repeat: do not storm the plane!"

The speaker just as suddenly broke into static again. The

general gripped Major Mendoza's radio arm. His eyes spoke eloquently of his battle to reach a decision. Finally he clenched his teeth and shook his head. Torment twisting his face, he turned back to the window and raised his glasses again.

As we watched in shock, the limp body of a woman was dragged to the doorway and unceremoniously dumped out. It fell like a dishrag and landed on the body of the slain Israeli. Then another body was dragged out. And another. A terrorist casually threw out a baby's bloodied body as if it were a discarded cigarette. In growing horror we counted as twenty-one murder victims were jettisoned, creating a gory pile of tangled, bloody death at the foot of the First Class doorway. In the end, the two passengers who had been enlisted to do the dirty work were ushered to the doorway and machine-gunned, their bodies flying backward down the tarmac from the force of the bullets.

We heard a gagging sound from our right. One of the young controllers was running to the doorway, his hand on his mouth, his eyes wide with revulsion. He was quickly followed by a colleague. Someone else somewhere was weeping.

General Casey's face drained of all color. His lip trembled slightly as he slowly lowered his glasses. He was shakily reaching for the mike when the speakers crackled to life again.

"The Islamic Jiha . . . means bus . . . The . . . Israeli . . . Buddha Head . . . every hour . . . imperialist Americans . . . ," the speakers garbled.

A petite figure appeared in the doorway and was forced down into the sitting position. I clenched my glasses and tried to force the wavering vision so far down the runway to clear.

It wasn't necessary. The natural grace of the figure and the way her long, black hair blew in the wind left no doubt.

"Tysee . . ." I heard myself gasp, as my binoculars drifted down to my chest.

FIFTEEN

Tarmac

"WHO?" DEMANDED GENERAL Casey, pulling up to my side.

I managed to repeat it. He stared through his glasses for a moment, looking grim.

The static broke in again. It was Captain Harrington. He had forced his voice almost back to normal.

"I . . . I'm to inform you that the next person to be, ah, shot in one hour will be Miss Tysee San. She is being placed in the doorway. They have . . . killed . . . everyone in First Class to show that they mean business. They will kill passengers all day until the Head is brought to them. If not, at midnight, they will blow up the plane, themselves and everyone in it. They mean it. I repeat: there is no doubt they mean it. They say other planes will then be hijacked somewhere until the Head is delivered. I'm sorry but there will be no further transmissions until you have the Head. Over."

No one spoke for a long while. The general leaned over a desk, clearly taking council with himself.

Anxiety, helplessness and frustration churned in my gut.
I imagined Tysee being forced to sit in the blood and gore
that surely must lie thick by the door, and the revulsion I
felt at her being surrounded by so much grisly death began
to fuel a rage in me that sent adrenaline coursing through
my system. Unable to watch any longer, I dropped the
glasses and looked out over Angeles City. A second flume
of smoke was rising from the western area of Angeles, close
by the first.

"Mr. Stambuck," the general was saying. *"Exactly* how
far did Ambassador Batten tell you we can go with that
Head?"

"He says that if it's used in any manner, it must be placed
in a position of extreme minimum danger."

" 'Extreme . .   . minimum . . . danger' . . ."   the
general repeated gravely, glancing toward Angeles. Then
he turned abruptly to the Intelligence Officer, who was
just laying down the phone. "Major Symons. What do you
have from your man? That smoke is getting worse."

"Lieutenant Thuen is having trouble getting through,
sir. There's apparently a lot of traffic jamming the MacArthur Highway into Angeles. The bars are full. People are
coming in from every which way, but it seems mostly
under control. People seem to be in, uh, a bit of a party
mood, sir."

Casey shook his head cynically.

" 'Extreme minimum danger' . . . a rather nebulous
measurement in these circumstances. *Any* exposure sur-
passes that. All I know is that I have less then eighty innocent passengers left and I have to get them out of there.
This requires risks."

"Are you saying you have a plan?" the CIA man asked.

"I want to go halfway on an exchange. Get as many
passengers off that plane as we can before we send in the
commandos. We don't have a chance if we do that now,
according to Captain Harrington. They'll blow it up immediately."

"Jeez, I dunno, General," Brock said, worry lining his
face. "The Head is pretty damned precious."

"So are those lives, Mr. Stambuck. And that Head is our
key to getting them out."

"But, General, this is—"

"We don't have time to argue, Mr. Stambuck. This is my responsibility—*and* command. If Ambassador Batten sent it up with any thoughts that it could be used in some contingency, this is it. But don't worry—securing that Head is *also* a top priority. It's cliff-edging but we're going to have the biggest safety net under it we can. Also, this being a military base, there's ways of limiting the degree of involvement by the media. Major Mendoza, we're going to need volunteers for a dangerous assignment."

"You've got one here."

The general looked critically at the speaker.

"Mr. Rivers, I'm sorry, but you're a civilian and it's my job to protect civilians."

"Goddamn it, General! I've been in this from the start! I've seen more action in the last few weeks than all your boys have in a lifetime! Christ, I was in Nam too! You *have* my records! I'm not going to sit around while you guys just *talk!* That's my girl in the door, for Christ's sake!"

"Mr. Rivers, I'm sorry but it's quite out—"

"Just a sec, General," Brock interrupted. "I think if you're going to go so far as to use the Head, I think you should think about using Jungle Boy here too. If he goes out with it, it's going to lend a lot of credibility to the whole venture. I think you'll agree that's important—that element of trust you've been working on all along. And like he says, he ain't no slouch. And as *you* say, he isn't going to be in that much danger. He'll only be going out to the tarmac, right?"

The general glanced at me, then looked away to think about it. While he did, something out the window caught his attention. With his binoculars, he scanned the horizon to the west again.

"What the *hell* is going on out there? There's three *fires* burning now. No, there's a *fourth!*"

"General Casey," Major Symons started, "I just received a message from Lieutenant Thuen. He's made it through the traffic to MacArthur. He says, uh . . ." Then he hedged, as if unsure whether to trust the intelligence enough to pass it on.

"Well? Go on."

"Well, sir, he reports that the fires are deliberate. Apparently it's the Catholic Women's League. They're converg-

ing on Angeles City from Manila and are putting the torch
to the bars, sir. He reports that they say that since the eyes
of the world are on Angeles right now, they want the world
to know that they're not going to allow this sort of place to
carry on anymore. There's general rioting going on in the
fire areas."

The general looked incredulous. A couple of the
younger controllers looked decidedly worried.

"Contact Fire Control to lend assistance," the general
ordered.

Symons grabbed a phone. No sooner had he finished
than the light on the phone lit up. He picked it up again.

"Yes, Major Symons here . . . yes . . . *what!* . . . just
a few minutes ago? . . . the Reverend Bat Rabidson's
Lear? . . . You're *absolutely* certain? Yes . . . yes . . .
right. Thanks."

All eyes were on the major when he turned. A look of
disbelief twisted on his face. Outside, within sight, the base
fire trucks were screaming out toward the main entrance.

"That was the embassy. They just received a tip-off that
a Lear jet owned by evangelist Bat Rabidson just took off
from Manila and is headed this way. He's here on a crusade
from the States. His Lear has just been fueled up. It's the
pilot's intention to crash it into the jumbo. He apparently
thinks the Buddha Head is on board." "My God, that's all
we need!" Colonel McKenzie exclaimed, leaping into action. "What do you have on your radar?" he barked at the
controller, who was handling what little traffic there was.

"It could be this one, sir, doing 450 miles an hour . . .
flying at 2,000 feet. Headed directly this way."

"You're sure it's not this one?" the colonel snapped,
pointing at something closer on the screen.

"No, sir. That's a helicopter from the embassy, sir. It's
already on its approach. I've already cleared it for landing."

"Try contacting the Lear."

"I *have* been trying, sir. He won't answer on any of the
designated private channels."

"Scramble squadron," Colonel McKenzie spat without
hesitating.

Within moments a huge roar went up as a squadron of F-
16s leapt into the air from an adjoining runway.

"What is that you are doing! There is to be no jets!"

"Mohammed, we have had a report that a Lear jet flown by a Christian fundamentalist group is headed this way from Manila. The pilot is mad. We have learned that it is his intention to crash it into your plane. He thinks that the Buddha Head is on board. This is *not* a trick. The jets are going to intercept him. You can see they are turning south right now. I repeat: This is *not* a trick. Over."

"It better no be a trick or many die!"

The posse galloped off in a tight curl to the south.

"Have them try to make visual contact."

A minute beat by. Then two.

"He's approaching the perimeter of our air space, sir. We should be just about able to see him."

Everyone shifted from the north to the south side of the control tower. I wavered between both.

"There he is!" a controller shouted. "Coming out of that cloud!"

The Lear was a tiny speck. Because of clouds, the squadron was lost from sight for a moment. But not for longer.

"The squadron leader is abreast, sir. The pilot of the Lear refuses to acknowledge . . . *sir!* He's taking evasive action . . . he appears to be dropping . . . yes . . . 1,500 feet . . . 1,000 . . . he's veering off to the west, sir, just on the edge of our air space."

"Keep the squadron on his tail."

"He's down to 500 . . . and heading around behind Mount Ararat, sir . . . he's off my radar and too low for the dishes on top . . . we'll just have to wait a minute, sir . . . *there* he is! He's coming around! *He's turning this way, sir!"*

"I can see him! He ees low!"

The Lear swept around the dormant volcano a half-dozen miles away, rolled onto its starboard side, and began a low rush directly toward the base. Through the smoke rising off Angeles we saw its tiny silhouette grow larger, the squadron in neat formation behind and above.

"Establish visual contact again. Have the flight commander keep trying radio."

"Yes, sir. Sir, he's well within our air space now."

"Does he acknowledge?" Colonel McKenzie demanded.

"No, sir. He doesn't."

"Shoot him down," Colonel McKenzie said without a moment's pause.

We watched, glued to our binoculars, as the F-16 leader abreast of the Lear peeled away to one side. The point man from the squadron suddenly slid forward and down. A moment later a missile ignited under his right wing and he too curled off out of harm's way.

A huge explosion of yellows and reds filled the sky. Fingers of fire licked in all directions. In a moment all that was left was a black cloud and litter drifting down, the sun glinting off pieces of aluminum.

"Whew-wheeeee! That was some firecracker!" Brock exclaimed, holding a pair of binoculars to his face like they were a small child's toy.

"The squadron commander reports mission completed, sir."

"Good. Bring them home."

"What is it that that was!"

"That was the Lear being shot down, Mohammed, before it could crash into you. The jets are being returned to the ground now and will be landing on the same runway as they took off. Over."

"It better not be trick! There will be no talk until you have the Buddher Head!"

Static burst back over the speakers.

"Excuse me, Mr. Stambuck. There's a Peter Melville here to see you."

I turned in time to see Brock start. A trim, still-athletic man in his late forties entered the room. He was dressed in a Filipino barong shirt. He was also very nervous.

"Could I speak to you in private?" he asked Brock obsequiously.

"Uh, yeah, Peter my boy. But, uh, first I'd like you to meet Lee Rivers." What sounded like reluctance filled his voice. "Lee, you heard of our diplomat friend, Peter Melville, I'm sure."

The diplomat's hand was cold and clammy, his voice high-pitched and squeaky. His mind seemed as preoccupied as mine. Without more words, he and Brock disappeared through the doorway. I had no time to think about it.

"General, *when* are we going to do *something*, goddamn it?" I shouted, turning back to the business at hand.

"Mr. Rivers, you're fully aware of the danger involved, are you not? There will be some, despite what Mr. Stambuck thinks."

"General, we could be *doing* something right now besides wait for those maniacs to start shooting again. No one is in control of the plane. It's obvious that the two factions are not getting along. We have to get in there and I'm the best man to do it! Christ, even Stambuck recommends me!"

General Casey's eyes locked on to mine, trying to appraise me fully in one look. He knew he hadn't known me long enough to make a rational judgment. But I was determined I would be going, and he seemed to sense it. He nodded, more to himself than to anyone else.

"Well, everything else is being risked here already. Private, please put me through to Pan Am."

The crackle abruptly increased in volume.

"Clark Control to Pan Am 306."

He had to repeat it three times before the voice that sounded of summer verandas and frying chicken came through once again.

"Pan Am 306 to Clark Control. Waiting for instructions. Over."

"Captain Harrington, this is General Casey. First of all, we have some fires going on in Angeles. You no doubt can see the smoke. But don't worry, you're well away from any danger. We also have good news. We have located Lee Rivers and he is on his way to the base. I repeat: Lee Rivers has been located and is on his way to the base. Confirm please. Over."

There was a full minute of static before we heard the switch open and the thunder of a headset being pulled into place.

"Does Lee Rovers have the Buddhee Head with him?" the voice demanded, for once at less than a scream.

"Confirmative, Mohammed. He *does* have the Head. I repeat: He *does* have the Head. Over."

There was a pause before the Arab continued.

"You will trade it for the passengers, yes?"

"Affirmative, Mohammed. We *will* make the trade. Over."

"Good! None the less, we will continue to kill passengers each hour until such is the time as we see the Head on the running way. Tysee San is the first of the next. All deaths are the complete fault of Imperialist Americans for *lying!*" he shouted triumphantly.

The general looked at me and shook his head to one side as if it was painful.

"How do you propose we make the exchange? Over."

"He will come to the plane."

"Mohammed, that is not reasonable. We must protect our people in the same way you want protection for yours. We must be fair and respect each other's interests. Here is what I propose and please listen carefully: We will send out four men in a jeep. Three of these will be armed personnel. The fourth will be Lee Rivers with the Head. They will stop 500 meters from the plane. Lee Rivers and one of our armed men will walk forward fifty meters, carrying the Head. You can send out four men also—three of them armed. Two armed men can stop 400 meters from the plane and the other two can meet Lee Rivers in the middle to inspect the Head. Do you understand and agree? Over."

There was the usual crackling silence.

"You will repeat again," the voice demanded, not able to hide its confusion.

The general explained it a different way, in terms as simple. There was a long break of static, during which we guessed they were conferring. When Mohammed came back on the air, he was screaming again.

"We have fifteen members of the Islamic Jihad on the plane but we do no think it is so necessary to send four of them out. We will send three and you will send two. Only one of yours will be armed. You will stop 400 meters from us. That is our demand!"

General Casey looked at me. I shrugged. He made one more try.

"Mohammed, we insist upon sending two guards with Rivers. You do not have to worry. You have the hostages. We will come closer—450 meters. Over."

There was a long silence before the voice, tense, nervous, paranoid, came over the speaker again.

"It is agreed . . . but any trick and many passengers *die!*"

"Mohammed, there will be no tricks, I promise you. A jeep will drive down the runway and will make a slow circle so you can see very clearly that only three members are aboard—Lee Rivers and two armed soldiers. In the back of the jeep you will see a metal box. That box contains the Head. They will stop 450 meters from the plane and Lee Rivers will carry it forward fifty meters. He and your man who comes forward will strip to the waist and turn right around to show they have no weapons. Is that understood and agreed? Over."

There was a tense pause. Smoke was beginning to drift across the airfield.

"Agreed. We wait, General Kessey," the nervous voice finally said.

His tone was much more subdued now, expressing intense worry rather than outright hysteria. It was the first time he had used the general's name, even if he had mispronounced it.

"Major Mendoza? It's your move," said the general. "Oh, one more thing, Mr. Rivers—I should tell you that we have a dozen commandos in a bunker left over from when the Japanese controlled this airfield. Most of the bunkers were dynamited when the runways were extended after the war, but one was kept at the end. It's flush with the level of the concrete and there's a large manhole cover over it. It's probably just a few yards on the other side of the plane. They have extension ladders, explosives to blow the doors, and stun grenades as well as firearms. We want to empty the plane as much as possible before sending them in."

"General Casey, I want to volunteer to go weeth Mr. Rivers."

The general raised his eyebrows.

"It ees a very tricky situation, sir. Corporal Lunan, our top sharpshooter, has volunteered as well."

The general weighed it in his mind for a moment.

"You know I can't afford to lose you," he said to Mendoza. Then his eyes shifted to me for the briefest of moments. "As I can't afford to lose anyone."

"We don't really have time to brief a man completely on the intricacies, sir," the major politely argued.

General Casey considered for another moment, then acquiesced.

"Good luck."

"Just a sec, general," I said: "I have an idea to try to get Tysee out of that doorway. Also, we have no proof that Snake . . . I mean, ah, Cheevers is even on the damned plane. Call them up and let me speak to them. It'll assure them that I'm here, and real as well."

"Good idea," he agreed without hesitating. He reached for the mike.

Within minutes he had brought Mohammed back to the line and made his request. A minute after that the figure in the doorway stood and disappeared. Yet another minute later we heard the loud jumbling of headphones being adjusted, against a background of voices and shouts.

"Lee . . . ?" a frightened voice asked. "Are you there . . . ?"

My mouth was working but it took me a moment to get my voice out. When I did, it sounded strange to me.

"Tysee, it's me—Lee. Are you all right?"

"I am all right. Just scared."

"Please relax, sweetheart. We're doing our very best. Is Snake okay?"

The crunch of the headphone being changed filled the control room. A voice laced with arrogance and ignorance followed. It was one of the Libyans.

"That is the enough! You know who is here that is her and that we will kill her unless you give us the Head!"

My jaws clenched and I had to force my voice to stay even.

"Mike Cheevers. Now I must speak to Mike Cheevers to be sure that it is he that you have."

The crash of the headset being pulled on filled the cramped control room.

"Jesus fucking Christ almighty!"

"Snake. Are you all right?"

He was panting, his voice constricted.

"Get me outa here mate and the beer's on me for the rest of your *life!* These guys are . . ."

I heard a thud. His voice was cut off.

The insane-sounding Libyan had put the headset back on.

"Now you did hear them! They will *die* unless we get the Head!"

"They are on the way," the general said calmly, taking the mike from my clenched fish. "I repeat. They are on their way. Over."

The tactic didn't work entirely: Tysee's figure reappeared in the doorway. Behind the plane, black smoke billowed higher as more of Angeles was put to the torch. There was the hurried movement of masses of people near the fence. It hardly registered on me.

"Ready?" asked Major Mendoza, his eyes burning.

"Let's go."

We headed through the exit, me trying to cope with an avalanche of emotions.

"Just a sec," Brock said, catching me in the hallway. Peter Melville, the diplomat, was nowhere to be seen. He pulled something long and metallic out of his pocket. "I heard you're going to do the John Wayne. Gimme that gun and let me screw this on. I couldn't sell you this accessory that went with your gun but at least you might get a chance to try it out. Keep it in the jeep. You saved my life once. I owe you one."

His hand was trembling slightly as he attached the silencer. I noticed he avoided my eyes when we parted.

———— • ————

I could imagine how we looked to the men standing in the control tower, following us with their binoculars—a tiny jeep with three occupants, and a square box in the back, the entire image melting and waving with the heat waves as we slowly rolled down the center of the scorched concrete toward the even larger mirage of the American jumbo jet. To them the scene would look unreal; to me, sitting in the passenger seat, senses on such alert they were almost crackling, it *was* unreal.

The slight breeze there was acted as a gentle bellows fanning the blast furnace that was the runway, and brought with it the smoke and smell of Angeles afire. Tongues of flame were already visible above some of the

bars. The hell-blast of heat quickly formed rings under the
arms of all our shirts.

Major Mendoza stared straight ahead, calmly studying
the situation as he drove, one hand as tight on the walkie-
talkie as the other was on the wheel, his M-16 between us.
On his hip was an army-issue .45. An expressionless Corporal Lunan sat in the back, a high-powered rifle, with a
heavy scope nestled protectively between his legs. I cra-
dled my Walther in my right hand, unused to its unbal-
anced feel with the heavy silencer attached.

My eyes stay riveted to the slender, shimmering figure
in the forward hatchway. I well knew hers would be on us,
though I doubted if she could or would recognize me—at
least not yet. From the plane we would appear as little
more than three figures shimmering in the watery distor-
tions caused by the sinuous heat waves, partially hidden by
the thickening blanket of smoke. Below her on the tarmac
lay sprawled the mountain of human flesh, which all three
of us tried to avoid looking at. It was only too easy to
imagine another slender body collapsed in the hideous
indignity that was that type of death.

As the distance between us and the 747 narrowed, the
heat waves began to falter and weaken. The smoke
seemed to dissipate, then disappear altogether between
us, as if we were entering a special realm, a separate reality
that included only the monster plane, its lines now sharp
and hard and stable, and us. Beyond, all else now was
quivering in the heat—the tower, the flames and smoke
rising as more and more of Angeles took to flame, the now-
panicking crowds on Field, the dry mountains beyond. As
we entered the circle a mixture of stark fear and dread left
a new taste in my mouth.

"Okay, I'm going to make a slow swing around and let
them have a good look at us," Major Mendoza said in an
even, controlled voice, smoothly turning the wheel to the
left to begin the cul-de-sac turn.

As we curved parallel with the plane, I spotted an armed
terrorist dressed in jeans and dark T-shirt in the open rear
doorway. Nameless terrified faces pressed to the Economy
windows all along the fuselage, and the bodies on the
tarmac, the latter so close I could watch their hair and
clothing being toyed with by the breeze.

And I could see Tysee. Even at that distance, 350 yards, our eyes met. I was sure she recognized me, despite my pizza-with-trimmings hair, by the sudden way her hand darted to push her own hair aside and by the way she seemed to stare. Behind her, with a pistol to her head, was another of the terrorists. I held her face in the palms of my eyes as long as I could, until the jeep turned back down the runway.

Without changing speed or shifting from second gear, Major Mendoza rolled evenly back another 100 yards, then did a wide U-turn before gliding to a stop in the middle of the white center line, facing the plane. He turned off the engine, leaving the key in the ignition. Suddenly all was silence except for the distant sound of wildly blowing jeepney horns drifting over us in waves. All three of us wiped the sweat off our foreheads yet another time. The smoke was strong enough to irritate my nose.

No one spoke. Our three pairs of eyes locked together and I felt like I was back in Nam. We disembarked simultaneously. I left my Walther on the seat; the major stepped out with his M-16; Lunan eased off the back, snaked his arm through his rifle strap, and took up a position behind the jeep's back right corner.

While Major Mendoza walked around to the back of the jeep to take up a position beside Lunan, I stripped off my sticky T-shirt. My body seemed to breath a sigh of relief at first, but then the burning rays of the glaring tropical sun hit it and I wanted to drag the wet garment back on.

"Look," Lunan said almost laconically. "They're taking the girl away."

I turned just in time to see Tysee's back disappear into the dark of the plane's interior. A new figure appeared at the top, darkly dressed, something glinting in his hand.

"That was their move, I guess it's ours next," I said, wondering why I was whispering.

I reached around for the metal box.

"Mr. Rivers, please take eet somewhat to the left rather than straight ahead," Mendoza said, in a voice as polite as his mentor the general's, but his eyes on alert. "I want a straight line between me and them, with you out of the crossfire."

I began to carry the clumsy box in a slow walk toward

the plane, counting off the steps as I went, drifting to the left. When I had numbered off fifty, I stopped and set the box down. It was then that the horrible thought burst into my head: perhaps it was still locked. And I hadn't gotten the combination. But after a short, panic-stricken glance, I let out a sigh of relief and my heart began to beat again. Brock hadn't forgotten to unclip the lock, though the padlock still hung on the eye.

Facing the plane, I unlatched the lid, raised it, and removed the top protective layer of solid foam. There, in a hole in the middle, in its original bundle, lay the Head. I carefully gripped it and lifted it out—noting with some satisfaction that my hands were steady while I did. Cradling the Head under my left arm, I closed the lid, then set the bundle on top. I began to unwrap it. In moments the gold-encased skull of the Buddha lay glinting and gleaming on the case before the terrorists, passengers and crew of Pan Am Flight 306. Any revelers or press still not caught up in the panic in Angeles wouldn't see it; they'd be blinded by the smoke screen, even with high-power binocs. I stepped to one side, raised my arms even with my shoulders, and slowly turned a full circle, giving them full opportunity to see that I was unarmed. Defenseless.

Almost immediately a man came whisking down to the bottom of the chute. He was young, stocky, dark and bearded, and no older than twenty-five. Libyan. I could tell at a glance. He was carrying one of the Israeli machine guns.

After a moment's hesitation, another man slid down after him. His arm was in a cast and he held it protectively to himself. He wore a turban.

Awithur Singh. The Sikh. We had been right.

A movement on the left caught my attention; a terrorist now stood at the front door, machine gun in hand. The last several rungs of the rope ladder were lost in the pile of corpses.

My eyes turned again to the rear hatch. Another figure, short and rotund, in a baggy white shirt that overflowed his belt, appeared against the gloomy background. It looked like the terrorists were prodding him. Hesitantly, the figure tried to sit down on the edge of the threshold, but before he could he was given a rude shove. Arms swinging ingloriously, he landed on the chute and slid face-first to a heap at the bottom. He stood up clumsily and tried to adjust his glasses with both hands.

I couldn't believe my eyes. It had to be that mysterious third Brit.

Richard Haimes-Sandwich.

It flashed on me why he had been kidnapped: he was one of the few people who could independently identify the Head.

The terrorist prodded the limey into motion. Ham-Sandwich began to limp forward. The Sikh was also limping, but didn't seem to be receiving the same harsh treatment. The gunman walked warily behind, like a cat over thin ice. Both doors of the plane were now choked with terrorists. Passengers pressed their faces to the oval windows.

None of the three advancing toward me had stripped to the waist as agreed upon—an unnerving thought. I eyed the Sikh's bulky leisure suit warily. Broken arm or no, I didn't expect him to be defenseless.

Just when I was becoming alarmed that the three were going to advance on me as a unit, the gunman halted about thirty-five yards away. The other two continued ahead. On the Libyan's hip was a walkie-talkie. The angle was good—there was clear space between the gunman and our jeep, with the Head and myself to the left some ten feet into the no-man's-land.

Ham-Sandwich was about forty feet away when he finally recognized me. His mackerel eyes broadened; his lips tried to move, but only a tremble came out.

"Well, Pig-Sandwich," I said drolly as they pulled up before the makeshift table. I fluffed one of my hands. "You're losing your grip."

His entire body was shaking. I didn't take my eyes off either him or the Sikh.

The Ham's lips kept moving, but still nothing came out. He couldn't stop quivering, and his eyes stared straight ahead, filled with fear—a dog terrorized by the pack.

The Sikh glared at me with ill-hidden malice, though his eyes kept dropping to the treasure before us. From close up, his face was a mess.

"You look like you've had a little accident. What happened? Fall off a moving train?"

364   **JASON SCHOONOVER**

"You are lucky to be thus alive," Awithur Singh said, in a voice so low, so filled with venom, that I barely understood him. His head woggled back and forth slowly, like a cobra looking to strike.

"I'd say you're even luckier," I responded. "Good thing you landed on that pillow you wear on your head. You know, at Halloween you should dip your head in red paint and go as a used Tampax. You'd be a big hit."

He growled and impatiently nudged the catatonic Englishman into action. I stepped back and to the side to give Mendoza and Lunan a clear shot in case it was needed.

Like a shaky automaton, Ham-Sandwich stumbled forward, casting his terrified eyes up at me for a moment before stooping to do his duty. Pushing his glasses back up on his nose, he stared at the tranquil features that were so in contrast to his own, trying to concentrate, paying particular attention to the rubies, which he inspected closely with a jeweler's loop he had shakily withdrawn from his pants pocket. Seeing him like this cleared my senses and strengthened my confidence and calm readiness. I could see it was having the same effect on the Sikh, who looked quite comfortable in his skin.

With hands shaking so badly he was barely able to shove the unfolded loop back into his pocket, Richard awkwardly rolled the Head over on its side to inspect the darkened bone of the skull. He fingered the missing wedge of bone I had noticed back at the teahouse. Then, setting the Head back upright, he stood and stumbled backward, his head nodding.

"It *is* the Head, isn't it?" the Sikh asked him emphatically, disgust in his voice.

The Ham-Sandwich bobbed his head up and down in large, irregular movements. The smoke from the blazing town was beginning to sting our eyes and fog the distance between us and the plane.

"All right. You will move yourself to one side. Now I will make the look," the Sikh said, woggling his head aggressively.

Richard instinctively joined me five feet to the side of the head, seeking security.

A knife that Singh had been hiding suddenly appeared in his palm, causing me to start. The Sikh snapped it open

and waved it before me with a mock threatening motion,
just as he had done on the train, and allowed himself a
laugh at my expense.

I blinked. It had a broken blade. It was the one I had
retrieved from the dead Bulgarian at my place. The one
whose tip was embedded in the Head. The one I had
shoved in Singh's pocket before flipping him through the
train window. I quickly signaled to the jeep with an A-OK
sign and a vertical palm to hold fire.

Singh's laugh was deep and bitter enough to chill a
corpse. Then he cut it short as if with a guillotine and
turned, a snarl curling his lips. He glanced toward our jeep,
noting the two rifles trained squarely on him. He ignored
them and stepped forward aggressively to inspect the
Head. He glared at the serene features, trying to force a
recollection of his previous brief glimpse. Without a
thought, he turned it roughly around with his one good
hand, causing me to flex again. But he just guffawed. His
dark, hairy finger found the scar where the knife had done
its damage.

A self-satisfied smirk spread over his features as he saw
the still-embedded tip in the soft, golden curl behind the
right eye. With a precautionary glance at me, he stooped
over and matched the broken blade of the knife with the
embedded tip.

He suddenly stood, cutting his second sinister laugh as
short as the first. Still holding the buck knife in his hand, he
turned toward the jumbo and raised his fist in a victorious
salute.

Then his hand dropped, and instead of turning around
or walking back to the plane, he gripped himself and began shaking violently back and forth. For a fraction of a
second I thought he was having a convulsion or a heart
attack, but then the bulky plaster cast fell to the tarmac in
a soft clatter in two pieces and he spun around violently.

His arm—the supposedly *broken* arm—was rising to
strike.

In his fist was a foot-long *kirpan*. *"Raj kare ga khaka!"* he
screamed, the rallying cry of his warlike creed—"The
Sikhs Will Reign"—as he whirled on the Buddha Head.

His reign was cut very short as a fusillade of lead hammered into him from both directions—from the Uzi ahead

and from the two rifles behind the jeep. They twisted him around like a turbaned dust devil.

I hit the pavement. Richard landing beside me like a Halloween outhouse. In the whirling confusion the Sikh's body spun and collapsed half behind the metal box, his short broadsword missing the Head by inches and slamming deeply but harmlessly into the aluminum top. Something clattered between the Englishman and myself. It was the buck knife. It was hidden from the Libyan's view by Ham-Sandwich's more-than-sufficient, still-shaking body. I made no motion whatsoever, my heart in my throat. Beside me the Ham-Sandwich made pitiful scratching sounds as he tried to dig a foxhole in the concrete with his fingernails.

My eyes were on the Libyan who stood motionless, his gun barrel tip to the clouds. I slowly turned my head toward the jeep. I could only see one barrel, Mendoza's, but it was slowly rising.

Then no one moved. Even the heat waves seemed to freeze. The only sound was the Englishman sobbing. Finally, the Libyan slowly reached for the walkie-talkie on his belt and spoke a few words into it. In a moment he had his reply. He reattached it to the belt of his jeans.

The terrorist nodded coolly toward Richard.

"Come," he ordered harshly.

The limey was catatonic. I helped him to his feet. While I did, I flicked the broken-tipped buck knife closed and slipped it into his pocket. He saw me do it and his enormous eyes opened ever wider. His lips tried to form a protest.

"Shut up, Richard, for once in your stupid fucking fat life," I whispered harshly through clenched lips. "Try to get it to Snake."

I pushed him off and he stumbled and swayed like a drunk toward his tormentor. They turned and walked, one after the other, the Libyan frequently shoving the Kathmandu collector toward the rope ladder at the front hatchway. All eyes followed as they walked into the thickening smoke. Haimes-Sandwich halted before the slaughter, then turned aside and appeared to vomit. After some rough prods and many false starts he managed to pick his way through and over the bodies, and climb the ladder. At the top he was dragged into the cabin like a large, gasping fish out of water.

The now-confident terrorist turned and swaggered back toward us, stopping this time closer to fifty yards away, his machine gun in a semi-port position. I glanced toward the jeep. Both men remained behind their protective cover, with an eye on the Libyan.

I strode over to my allies, leaving the Head where it was. The Sikh's blood was forming a scarlet pool a yard across around his body. His features were still gripped by a snarl.

"Jesus, that was incredible," I said, my voice a sound I didn't recognize.

Corporal Lunan kept a constant, stern-faced guard. Major Mendoza seemed to relax slightly, though he ever lowered his M- 16.

"That boy was a skipped heartbeat away from bounding on Mohammed's knee," Mendoza said coolly about the terrorist, his eyes still fixed firmly on him. "That was very close. Too close. I must admire the bastard, though—he has guts. I guess he's out here to keep an eye on eet."

"No doubt about that. What now I wonder?" I wiped the sweat off my forehead. Droplets hung from the tips of both airmen's noses.

Mendoza's walkie-talkie squawked to life. He reached into the front seat and fetched the small unit out.

"Major Mendoza, this is General Casey. What happened out there? It's getting so smoky we can't see very clearly. The city is really starting to go up. It's clearly out of control. Is everyone okay? Over."

The tinny voice issuing from the unit showed a trace of urgency.

"We're okay, sir. No problem. The Sikh tried to pull a fast one on everybody. He tried to strike the Head weeth a large knife but both the terrorist and ourselves rendered him permanently inactive. The other terrorist is back keeping an eye on the Head. Pretty tense here for a moment though, sir. Over."

"Who was the other individual who came up? A terrorist? Over."

"I don't know, sir, but hang on and I'll see if Mr. Rivers can identify him. Over."

"It was Richard Haimes-Sandwich."

The major's eyebrows rose slightly. He passed the information down the line.

I scanned the airplane windows and the open doors. There was no sign of Tysee or Snake, though it was impossible to recognize faces from this distance, even without the smoke. It was clearly getting hotter. For the first time I noticed the sound of the holocaust drifting over—a distant hiss and crackle. Black pieces of ash were beginning to flutter down. Half the bars along Field, from MacArthur to at least The Libertine, were aflame—huge billows of smoke were rising above them—more were catching fire all the time.

"Major Mendoza," the general interrupted through the speaker, showing a trace of excitement. "They acknowledge that the Head is authentic and have agreed to allow us to load hostages. We're sending up four troop transports to receive the passengers. With them will be Major Symons with a passenger manifest to check everyone off. You are *not* to move—repeat: *not* to move—until the transports are loaded and everyone is accounted for. They'll be within firing range of the plane so we just have to play it by ear. I'm still trying to talk them out of nonessential crew but I'm not having much success. Do you read clearly? Over."

"Roger, sir. Read you very clear. Over."

"Good. The boys will be ready for a much-needed coffee break right after. Over."

"Roger General. Ten-four."

Turning to me, the major said, "That ees our code. We'll be sending in our commandos immediately after the transports are loaded. Corporal Lunan will clean out the doors first, hoping to get them before they spray the transports. I'll take out this one," he said with a deceptively casual nod, indicating the wide-stance terrorist on the tarmac.

His eyes seemed to survey an area below the belly of the plane, near the rear. For the first time I noticed what looked like a steel manhole cover. The old Jap bunker. He looked back at me and nodded conspiratorially.

Almost immediately, the first passengers appeared at the rear entrance and began, hesitatingly, to jump down the chute: a thick-hipped, middle-aged woman in a paisley dress; a family, the father holding a frightened adolescent daughter protectively under his arm; a couple of Turks in brown sports jackets and turtlenecks; a white-haired businessman; a couple, young travelers. The trickle soon turned into a flood, with people piling up at the bottom like dollars in a Vegas slot machine.

They were acting like they'd been given strict orders to proceed no farther than the end of the wingtip for they crowded together nervously, seeking security like a school of fish—a school that only attracts bigger fish to the feast. Anticipation clawed at me as I strained to pick out Tysee and Snake in the ever-widening delta spreading out at the bottom of the human waterfall.

The troop transports rumbled down the center of the runway in prearranged formation, turned, stopped, then backed up the remaining distance to show the skyjackers there were no soldiers hidden aboard. Major Symons briskly stepped out of one of the large trucks and walked around to the back, a clipboard with papers fluttering off it in one hand, a bullhorn in the other.

Efficiently, he began to organize the still-rising tide of passengers. They began to clamber aboard, the major marking off their names on his passenger list as they did so. People pressed and shoved, and more than once he had to use his bullhorn to quiet the high-blooded crowd. From our distance the sound of his amplified voice was a wavering, meaningless jumble, but it seemed to calm the pack. Many were women with their hands to their faces, or tightly holding children.

Finally, the flood slowed to a trickle, the last passenger slid down to the concrete skillet and a gunman appeared at the door.

Anticipation turned to alarm. I had seen neither Tysee, nor Snake, nor even Ham-Sandwich. Major Symons seemed to be having some kind of trouble and was leaning over his clipboard.

"General Casey, this is Major Symons. Over."

The voice spittled out of Mendoza's radio. Corporal Lunan turned his head only slightly at the sound before continuing his vigil of the aircraft, and of the terrorists at each door, who were well-positioned to hose down the backs of the transports.

"General Casey. Go ahead. Over."

"General, we're missing three passengers. Lek Malinee . . . and the two Welsh brothers. Over."

"Oh shit," I said under my breath.

Major Mendoza gave me a fast, sympathetic squint.

"Hang on for a few moments please, Major," the general replied, his cool voice crinkling out of the small, black unit we were eavesdropping with. "I'll talk to Pan Am and get back to you. Over."

The wait was agonizing. My eyes locked on the back door, trying to will the smoke aside so I could see more clearly, while I hoped, prayed—demanded—they somehow appear and find their way to safety and freedom. I nervously checked my watch every few seconds. We all stood waiting, imagining the general's cool, logical voice trying to coax the three away from the the plane, the answering voice a high-pitched, triumphant, taunting scream.

"Major Symons. This is General Casey. I can get nowhere with them. They *insist* they are holding the other three and will release them with the crew when they land in their safe country, which they refuse to name. We have no choice but to go along with them. We have to save as many as we can. Do you read? Over."

"Ten-four."

"Major Mendoza. Are you there?"

"Yes sir. Over."

"They also demand the body of the Sikh. I'm having a jeep send down a body bag and a strong rope so they can haul it up. I'll stall as long as I can, but it's a very dangerous situation with the passengers exposed. We're in a vise but we have no choice. Make sure the coffee is hot and ready to be served. I'll try to persuade them to allow the trucks away. From here it appears there's men standing in both hatches with guns aimed down on the trucks. Is that correct? The smoke is getting impossible. Over."

"Yes, sir. Both with Uzis as far as I can make out. And if the one who cut down the Sikh ees any indication, very well trained and accurate with them. Another one has grenades ready to lob—uh, sir, Mr. Rivers wishes to talk with you. Over."

"Please put him on. Over."

"This is Rivers. General, they have *no* intention of re-

leasing the final three hostages. That's why they want the
body of the Sikh. They want to destroy all human evidence. if you take that coffee break now, they're going to
get dunked. Over."

The general considered this for a moment.

"I'm aware of that. Are you suggesting some course of
action? Over."

My mind whirled and clicked, clean and sharp as a la-
ser's edge.

"General, if they're monitoring this, it's just too bad. I
have no choice. Try and get something about the size of
the Head wrapped up in black *anything.* A kid's soccer
ball, I don't care. Also, send a stun grenade down with that
body bag. I'm going to take advantage of the smoke screen
to try a switch. We'll give the box to them locked, which
will buy me a few minutes. I'm also going to try to switch
places with the Sikh in the body bag and get aboard. That
way we can get the passengers away. Then we can move
in. It'll give me a chance to create a diversion and try to
save the other hostages. Another thing—send me the biggest boys you have got down with the stuff. Huge. Over."

There was a longer pause full of snaps, crackles and pops.

"Major Mendoza? Mr. Stambuck recommends it, but
you're the man in the field. What is your assessment?
Over." the general's voice was heavy with reluctance.

"Major, I'm going into the body bag," I told him. "With
the stun grenade and my pistol with the silencer, I can
probably disable a couple of them before your men make it
up. It's going to take them at least five minutes to storm the
plane. That gives the hijackers time to blow it sky-high.
And those are my friends in there. I'm going, Major. I'm
going in. You get me that stuff!"

Major Mendoza looked pained.

"You're a civilian . . . that ess a *suicide* mission!"

"Listen, sweetheart, twenty-three civilians have already
died. If I get it, I'll just be lost in the statistics. More people
are going to die and I may be one, but goddamn it, *less* are
going to die this way! Can't you see! I'm *going!* I'm not
asking you! Get that goddamned equipment!"

He brought the speaker to his mouth with a distasteful
look.

"General Casey. This ess Major Mendoza. Please send

down everything as per requested. Also include a high-powered rifle with a scope preadjusted to 450 yards for me. Over."

There was no response for several seconds. The major was about to try again when the general came through.

"I have been able to make some progress with them. Once they have the Buddha Head and the Sikh's body at the front door and tied to their ropes, they have agreed to let all but one transport leave. Once the box is hauled up, they'll let the other go. But no luck securing the release of the stewardesses or of the other three. They insist they will be safely released at their safe port. Men are on the way in a jeep with the body bag and other essentials. Over."

"Roger, General. Ten-four."

I turned and scanned the jumbo, whole parts of it were disappearing as clouds of black smoke off Angeles crowded by. The breeze was no longer gentle and tropical, but swirling and furious from the convection currents rising from the raging city a quarter-mile beyond. The sound was a not-so-soft roar. Field Street was packed with panicking refugees fleeing the city.

"Don't worry about being overheard," Major Mendoza said to me. "We use special walkie-talkies with very high frequencies. Ordinary radios can't pick us up."

"You forgot about the Russians. That's probably who supplied them."

He nodded his head glumly. Symons had everyone packed aboard the open-backed transports.

"You're right, Mr. Rivers, it doesn't look good. They may have monitored us . . ."

The terrorist on the tarmac was in conversation on his walkie-talkie.

I said nothing. It was too late. The die was cast.

"His friends have to tell him about the body bag. That's what it has to be."

"Here it comes," Lunan said, turning briefly to watch a jeep approaching rapidly through the heat waves and waving smoke like a hallucination.

Mendoza gripped my shoulder urgently.

"We'll give you exactly five minutes once you're in. That ess all it's going to take them to open that box and find the dud—if you get away with it that far. But if we hear the

grenades or any shots, we'll be in before. I suspect half of
them will be on the flight deck and the other half on the
main."

He looked at me like I was a dead man. I was getting
used to it. I nodded my head.

"And one more thing"—he added—"here. Those bags
aren't designed to be opened from the inside." He had
passed me his commando knife. In the rush and confusion
we had almost forgotten to bring one. A mistake like that
and the bag wouldn't have been temporary. "They're
sleeping bags designed for an extra-long sleep," he added,
suddenly embarrassed at having revealed his surface
thoughts.

"Thanks. Okay. I'm going to meet the jeep at the box," I
said, walking around to the passenger side and slipping the
knife and my Walther surreptitiously into my pockets.

I had to jam the gun down, ripping the bottom seam to
get it all the way in with the silencer attached.

Then I headed briskly off toward the box, the Head and
the still body of the Sikh, my nose and eyes burning from
the smoke. The terrorist eyed me carefully but didn't
budge. He seemed to expect the move. The jeep was slowing down by the time I reached the Head.

"Okay, pull in at a forty-five-degree angle so the front
fender is half-hiding the box," I called, waving it in closer.
"Hold it. Not so far. Back up a bit, a foot, so they still have a
clear view of the Head, otherwise they'll think it's a trick.
Just as long as they can't see the Sikh's body for a moment.
Good."

The jeep angled in, its left front fender only a couple of
feet from the box. Between the two was the Sikh's bloody
body, now partially obscured from the plane.

The two soldiers in the jeep stepped out on either side,
their M-16s at ready. As requested, they both looked like
King Kong's older brothers. Enormous. Good. One had
sergeant's stripes. The other unfolded a mummy-shaped
bag. The sergeant nodded to a round shape wrapped in
black in the back well. I picked it up. It was just a bundle of
clothes but it was the right size.

"Good, Okay, Sergeant, walk in front of me over to the
box so he can't see. Right . . . good . . . okay," I said,
dropping the bundle in front of the box. "Good so far, now

go get the bag ready, then one of you will have to crouch between the box and the jeep on the outside when we do the switch of the bodies. I'll get this new head ready."

I glanced up at the Libyan. He was straining to see through the smoke, and took a few steps forward, but was clearly too intimidated by four heavily armed men to approach closer. There was no fear of being seen from the plane—the smoke was too thick. The sound of the city going up in flames was now clearly and crisply audible—it snapped and crackled like a fireplace.

In full view of the terrorist, I wrenched the still-embedded *kirpan* free and threw it aside with a clatter. After carefully wrapping the Head I was ready for the Houdini. Squatting, I lifted the Head with one hand and opened the lid with the other. To reassure the Libyan, I set the Buddha Head down by my knees and grabbed the black bundle as quickly and smoothly as I could, at the same time turning myself and the entire box around so the terrorist would have a clear side view of me and dummy head. As conspicuously as I could, I gently placed the bundle in its cradle. Closing the lid, I snapped the lock shut.

I stood up and looked at the terrorist. He was grinning triumphantly. The Head was hidden from his view behind the box.

"Okay, help me get dressed," I said. "Sergeant, kneel down there between the box and the jeep. Block his view. As long as he can see the box clear enough he should be happy." I grabbed the relic and transferred it to the private, who slipped it into the back of the jeep, both of us now hiding it with our bodies.

I rolled the Sikh over. He was completely limp, his body a sticky mass of blood. Flies were already gathering for the feast. I glanced up. The private's big body effectively hindered the terrorist's view. Quickly, I stripped off Awithur's bloody leisure jacket and pulled it on like a wet shirt, the blood gluing to me.

"Now, Private, wipe his chest clean—there's a reason." I hurriedly waved some flies away, then struggled to pull the turban off the late Awithus Singh's head without breaking the chin strap. It fit me a little loose—the Sikh had extra-long hair, which was neatly rolled up in a knot on the top of his head—but it would have to do. I scrambled into the bag and lay flat.

"Okay, Sergeant, drag the Sikh behind the jeep for a moment . . . good . . . Private, lift up the box and set it on the hood so it blocks the view of the driver's seat . . . that's right . . . now just stand there beside it. Okay, Private, can you lift that dead son of a bitch into the driver's seat? With no shirt on, with the smoke and glare off the windshield, he should pass for me. Damn that tan he was born with, though."

"No problem."

The limp corpse was hoisted up into the seat like a big doll.

"Here's a stun grenade," the sergeant said quickly. He moved to block the view while the private handed me the ordnance. "Stick it in your back pocket so it won't clunk around. For sure cover your ears tight and get behind something when you chuck it—they don't call them stun grenades for nothing."

Everyone was covered with the Sikh's blood but acting oblivious to it.

"Thanks," I said, giving him the ol' A-OK *mudra*. "And if I don't make it, do me a favor and spread my ashes on Patpong Road."

He looked at me, uncomprehending. Not having time to explain, I rolled over on my face, my pocket bulging, the knife in my left hand and Walther in my right. I heard the zipper rush up my spine just as chills ran down it, then the swish of a rope being drawn through the loop at the head of the bag, and being tied securely.

"Ready?" the sergeant asked, his voice firm.

"Dead men can't talk. Let's go. One of you drag me. The other carry the box with the Head. If that Shi'ite-head asks what happened to Rivers, tell him that he fainted from the heat because he didn't have his shirt on."

With a soft jerk, they began to drag me steadily along the runway, which now seemed as smooth as a corduroy road. My knuckles bounced on the rough surface. I struggled to keep a grip on the gun and knife and in a minute had them secured; but the stifling heat and suffocating space quickly made jelly of the air inside. I began to feel dizzy. It must be even less fun being a real corpse, I thought, and I hoped I didn't have to find out soon.

"Okay, American, you throw up rope to bag. And you tie box to this other rope by handle. Then we are letting most of the trucks go." The threatening voice was shouting down from above, still full of vibrating tension. "But bad move and you all die."

"Just a minute until we clear a path through here. Private, give me a hand."

"I want to see Head," said a voice full of suspicion. It was the terrorist on the tarmac. "I not got a good look when Head put in."

I could hear him rattling the lock.

"Look, buddy, you blow the lock off, there'll be nothing to tie the Head *to.*"

The lock rattled again. I turned cold as a corpse.

"Out my way!"

"Just a minute. You could damage the Head. You talk to your leader *first,"* the sergeant said intimidatingly, a lot of barrack-room poker in his voice.

A staccato of anxiety-ridden Arabic spat from the tarmac to the hatchway above me. There was a long pause. Then a now-familiar voice shouted down something. It was Mohammed's.

"All right—tie up!" the first terrorist said angrily, overruled from above.

If I had any breath in me I would have let it out. In five minutes it sounded like they'd cleared enough bodies away to reach the ladder. I heard one of the soldiers throw up the heavy rope once, then twice before it was caught from above. Other sounds beside me signaled that someone was tying another rope to the box containing the Head.

"Now you will be give the order for your trucks to go. But one will stay behind!" Mohammed's voice, more chilling for being so close, screamed from above.

"Major Symons. This is Sergeant Ellis. You are cleared to move all but one truck away. Over."

"Ten-four."

Heavy engines gunned to a start. The quiet sound of rubber on concrete, squeaking springs and shifting gears followed as three of the large military-green trucks slowly rolled away from the plane, one after another.

"Okay, pull up there! We'll help you get the Sikh up, then we'll be gone and you can take the box. Private, grab this dead sucker and lift him up."

Strong hands grappled me like I was a corpse. A jerk yanked me upward. The rope held me for a moment before it suddenly went limp, and I crashed down with the private still gripping me. I let out an unintentional grunt as I landed unexpectedly on something soft. A body. Immediately I bit my lip and clenched my eyes tightly together, tensing all the muscles in my face and ears, hoping I hadn't been heard. I heard another grunt—it was the private covering for me.

"You'll need help up there. The Sikh is heavy," the sergeant called.

Rapid, excited Arab voices jabbered back and forth above me, sometimes laughing, sometimes cheering. It was obvious that they were already celebrating their success. It was also obvious that they didn't have the strength to haul my weight up. Panic washed over me for a moment —they might change their minds and abandon me.

"We will help lift the body up as high as we can from down here, but get two strong men on the rope," the sergeant repeated.

More harsh jabbering, then silence. In a minute the soft thump of feet approached the edge again.

"You will help us pull the body up. Do not try anything or a horrible death will be yours."

"Don't worry mate, I need a little exercise anyway. Haven't had much these last few days."

Snake.

Strong arms from below and above raised me, the rope tautened to the sound of labored breathing, and I felt myself spinning slowly upward in laborous jerks. I held my breath. The sill banged against my face, then scraped up my chest painfully. Gritting my teeth, I pulled the weapons in a little closer so they wouldn't knock on the edge. When I was at waist level, to the foot of the door, hands gripped the side handles of the bag and roughly dragged me aboard. They dumped me facedown like a bag of feed a few feet farther inside. I took a slight breath, then held it.

"Now, back upstairs again you, Chivers. You will hurry. And you will carry this box with you," the voice growled before beginning to shout other orders in Arabic.

Between the shouting, the ebullient voices, and the sound of Snake swearing as he wedged the awkward box up the circular, First Class staircase, I heard the final truck stir to life and drive off. A moment later the voices had disappeared upstairs and all was still.

Methodically, I counted off fifteen seconds. I was about to move when I heard a grunt at the door. It was the Libyan pulling himself up the rope ladder and into the plane. A moment later, to my horror, I felt his hand fumble for the zipper at the top of my head. He found it and ripped it down about two feet. I felt eyes on the turbaned back of my head and could hear heavy breathing. All my bodily functions arrested themselves—I may as well have been dead. Not satisfied, he began to drag me over on my side. I slid the Walther upward.

A loud voice shouted in Arabic from the top of the stairs. The Libyan took his hands off me and stood, but he wasn't through with me—just before he hurried away, he kicked me viciously in the ribs. His footsteps quickly faded as he scurried up the stairs, down which a constant excited litany in Arabic was starting to flow.

I wasted no time. They could be into the box already. Rolling around, I reached out and zipped the bag open. My Walther was the first thing out. I dropped the knife to free my hands.

Strapped into the jump seat only feet from me, her face frozen in horror as she watched my blood-and-gore-dripping corpse crawl out of the body bag, was a stewardess. I put my finger to my lips and glanced around. Blood was everywhere.

She quickly gathered her wits together and glanced behind the partition into the First Class section. She crunched up her face, then silently pointed her thumb toward herself and held up one finger.

I was still slipping out of the body bag when a terrorist walked around the partition. He was ruddy-faced, had a nineteen-year-old's beard, and worn-out pants and a tank top. His eyes snapped wide open, but before he could react I ptewed two slugs into him from the silencered Walther.

One of them added another zit hole to his pockmarked face. He jerked back against a wide, First Class seat and clutched at the headrest with a clawed hand, his eyes now open even wider, his lips moving, seeking words. Then he smoothly collapsed over the arm rest like a man passing out, slipping face-first onto the seat before sliding all but noiselessly to the floor between the rows.

I was out of the bag in seconds, crouched, eyes jabbing in all directions. I looked back at the stewardess. There was blood all over her. She was frightened but cool, and nodded slightly toward the rear of the aircraft, holding up two fingers. She waved her palm downward, signaling me to keep low. Then jerked her finger urgently to her left and crinkled up her face again. I looked. In front of me was a lavatory door. I pointed questioningly at it. She nodded slightly but rapidly, her finger still jabbing at the bathroom.

"Abdul?" a voice within called.

There was a pause, then the voice called his comrade again, louder and rattled off something that seemed like a question. The voice sounded like it came from waist level. A moment later I heard a dull, heavy thud as he fell forward on the seat, his head striking the door just about where I had put a neat, round hole in it.

Time was precious.

I yanked out the stun grenade from my pocket and held it in my left hand, the pistol, four shots still left, in my right.

I signaled with the pistol that I wanted to go upstairs where the excited voices and shouts of triumph were issuing from. The lock rattled. I knew I had only splinters of seconds left before the commandos hit. I had to beat them. I looked to the air hostess for clearance. She waited a moment, signaling downward with her palm, her eyes to the rear of the plane. Seconds ticked by. I made several false starts.

She rapidly jerked her finger toward the staircase. Moving like a cat, I was halfway up the steps in a moment, pistol at ready. I paused there for a brief second to fix positions. Blood covered my arms and hands. The Walther. The grenade.

Three voices were laughing. I heard the padlock rattle again. Then a shot, and cheers. Suddenly all was quiet except for the metallic sound of the broken lock being removed. From the First Class lounge I heard a male blubbering. Ham-Sandwich.

"Will you shut up, mate! It's bloody rough on all of us! You don't see Tysee here whingin' like this!"

Angry shouts suddenly rose from the terrorists. They were in Arabic but their tone was unmistakable. Stunned, betrayed, vicious.

I yanked the pin on the grenade, counted three, and flipped it toward the flight deck.

The sound of the explosion was enormous and deafening, even with my hands protectively over my ears, and the blast wave almost knocked me back down the stairs. Suddenly a pandemonium of explosions and gunfire erupted everywhere at the same time, mixed with the screams and shouts of killing and dying men.

In a flash I was on my feet and crouched on the flight deck. Bodies lay scattered. A dark hand grappled groggily for a pistol. He grunted as my bullet tore into his chest. Another tried to stand. Another shot set him back down.

A shot behind me. I whirled. Snake, broken knife in hand, was grappling with a terrorist, whose pistol fired harmlessly into the ceiling. I started. Glimpse of Tysee huddled on a seat by the window. Eyes wide. Looking straight at me.

The hammer of feet on the staircase. Commandos charging out the cockpit door. My hands thrown in the air. A terrorist beside me suddenly stirs to life. Yanks a grenade from the folds of his shirt. Immediately blown away by a commando.

The two squads of commandos hit me from both sides. Like being caught between the L.A. Raiders and a herd of stampeding water buffalo.

Blinding blurs of vision and noise. Shouts. Shots. Wrenching pain. Face slamming against something solid. Hard.

Blackness.

SIXTEEN

Purgatory

GRAY.
    Light gray.
    Angular shadows against white.
  A room? Tubes. Large shape clumped at foot of bed. Looking. Looking. Raising head. White form appears. Rushing over. Pushing me down. Telling me to lie back. Relax.
  First thought heaves up from the darkened basement of my mind.
  Whaaat?
  Moist mist of memory. Evaporating.
  Brighter.
  Recognize.
  ". . . Broooooock . . . ?"
  Mouth feels packed with sand.
  "Well, Sleepin' Beauty is awake!" Large shape claps its hands. "Or maybe I should say Rip Van Rivers."
  "I . . . been . . . sleep . . . ?"

My head thick. Packed with same-same sand. Or a cannonball. Body feels like rubber.

"Yeah, you might call it that. Since yesterday. It's, uh, lemme see, two in the afternoon. I was just checking on you and wanted to drop off a couple of things before I flew back to Manila. Nice of you to pick now to come join the world again."

"We're in the Philippines . . . ?"

Shape look at me funny. I remember Jumbo. Shooting. Blood. I start to shudder. Nurse touches my shoulder.

"You're in the hospital at Clark Air Base. Everything is all right."

Voice gentle. Reassuring.

"T . . . T . . . T . . . Tysee? Wh . . . where Tysee? And Sssssssssnake?"

"Hey, kid, they're okay. Don't worry. Tysee and Snake are *all right*. Just relax. Hey! I brought you a few beer, when you feel up to it. I'm kind of sorry about having to trick you with that head."

"Mr. Stambuck, I'm sorry, but I don't think he'll be wanting to drink anything for at least a few days."

"Ah, we can just leave them here, lady with the lamp. This is the kind of boy that needs his medicine regularly."

Nurse's hand warm. Feel secure. Relax. Crib.

"W . . . why am I—?"

"The boys gave you a bit of a wack on the noodle when they cleaned up the plane. That's why you're goofier than usual. Mendoza told them to watch for you dressed like the Sikh but their reactions work faster than their brains, these boys. They apologize. The Frankensteins around here also got you pumped up with some drugs."

I feel bottom of face curve. Recognize it as smile. Maybe I'm going okay to be.

"Where's Tysee? And . . . Snake?"

Head clearing. Jerks. Starts.

"They're okay. The commandos only managed to keep a couple of the terrorists alive. No one else was hurt, except for being shook up and deafened a bit from that stun grenade you threw. Good stuff, Jungle Boy. You get top marks."

"Everyone . . . safe . . . ?"

"Well, practically everyone. I'm afraid I have to tell you

about your friend Richard Haimes-Sandwich. The poor
bugger had a heart attack last night. Him, me, and Casey's
boys were having a beer after the debriefing and he just
flopped over. Too fat, I guess. Couldn't handle the pressure."

"Richard . . . dead . . . ?"

"Yeah, gone to that great museum in the sky. Them's the
breaks. Croaked. On the bright side, you're now a hero.
We're having a helluva time keeping the media away from
the door."

"The Head . . . Where . . . ?"

"We're taking it back to the States, but once the abbot up
at Tengbotchy has a new place for it, it's his. If he wants it.
The Dalai Lama still hasn't said peep yet, though He's
apparently preparing another news conference."

"*Where* Tysee? And . . . S . . . Snake?"

Impatient patient. Ask many time. Smell of burnt wood.

"Well, I don't *exactly* know—"

"Whatdya mean?"

Mouth still sand pit.

"Well . . . we couldn't hold them. They refused altogether to talk to the press. They wouldn't speak to anyone.
They just insisted on leaving as soon as possible."

Wave of upset. No understand.

"Wha . . . ?"

"Yeah, I don't know how to say this . . . they got together after we got them out of the plane and they told us
to tell the press that they were immediately flying into
private exile. I think the Bolshies scared the hell out of
them. We had no choice. We immediately arranged for
passports for them with their embassies and secretly stuck
them on a friendly plane where they wanted to go.
They're free citizens. We have a couple of new passports
for you, too, so you can travel freely without hassle until
the heat is off."

Confusion.

"Wha . . . ? They . . . go . . . ?"

"If you mean *where*, the answer is Hong Kong. At least
for starters. I doubt if they're still there, though. I got the
impression they didn't want anyone to know where they
were going and that's why they chose Hong Kong. There's
hundreds of flights a day everywhere from the joint and

we can't monitor them all. Particularly if they grab themselves different false passports."

Upset wave. Slow motion. Rising higher. Curling.

"The little San broad wrote out a letter to you. It was just
one of the things I wanted to drop off. Here you are. Ah
. . . maybe I better rip it open for you . . . there you
go . . ."

Nurse helps. Propped up on pillow. Sharp pains in ribs.
Head nodding. Lines on sheets.

> Dear Lee,
>
> We hate to have to do this at time like this but
> Snake and I decided that if we got out of this
> alive we would go away the two of us. Neither
> of us expected this to happen but being throw
> together like this has shown both of us that we
> really mean something deep to each other.
>
> I know you have great shock and I hope this
> no make you condition more bad. We happy to
> say that we ok.
>
> Lee, "thank you" are such little words. They
> no can tell how much we owe you and how
> much we care for you.
>
> Please, please forgive us.
>
> Affectionately,
> Tysee

Letter drifts away. Upset waves curl down crashing
against sandy beach like white molasses rolling me inside
out.

"You okay, Jungle Boy? Let me see that piece of paper."

"I think you should go, Mr. Stambuck. Mr. Rivers needs
to rest now."

Clear. Crisp. Far, far away.

"Hmmmmn . . . I'm sorry to read this, Lee, but I was
afraid that's what it would say. I *thought* it was kind of
funny, the way she was crying on his shoulder afterwards
and the way he was holding her hand," Brock said sympa-
thetically. "Well, I have a chopper to catch myself. Oh
yeah, if you can still hear me, I'm leaving your Walther
with the Security people in the hospital. I better keep the
silencer, though—you could get in big trouble if anyone

found that on you. The Security boys here are part of
General Casey's command. You can pick it up from the
checkout counter. Best keep it close to you though.
There's still some people that could be mad at you."

Light gray.

Gray.

Black.

—— • ——

Three days after the holocaust, tendrils of smoke still
drifted out of the blackened tangles on Field Street where
bars once stood, for almost as far as the eye could see. I
picked my way down this road through hell, now nothing
but a no-man's-land of blackened ash, here and there a
brick and mortar wall or the twisted metal frame of a
water tower still standing. It looked like Nagasaki the
morning after. Survivors picked through the smoldering
ruins, scavengers on an old carcass. Crews with picks, shov-
els and wheelbarrows were steadily going about the enormous cleanup job. Long-faced servicemen strolled without
speaking along what was left of the strip.

Where the Statue of Libertine Bar once stood was a heap
of ash and collapsed walls. Snow White was standing in the
middle of what was left of it. He had managed to salvage a
can of beer from somewhere. He stared at the silent appa-
rition in front of him for several seconds before his face lit
up with recognition.

"Lee!" he exclaimed, heaving himself over some tangled
wiring and rubbish, rolling over to me and extending his
hand. "How *are* you? Jesus, I never would have recognized
you! Every time I see you, you look different! What'd they
do?"

General Casey hadn't wanted me to leave the base, and
shook his head as if I was a total fool when I'd have none of
staying. I had collected my gun from the checkout and he
had reluctantly passed me my new false ID. I just wanted to
get out of there. Get away from all of it. I did agree to a
new dye job, along with a shave and fresh haircut. Black
this time, and very short—military style—so I'd look something like a soldier on leave. That was also the only way to
cope with my checkerboard beard and the punk-style sides
of my head.

"It's so I can get by the reporters and anyone else that might be looking for me."

"You okay? You sound awfully flat. You don't mind me asking, huh? Bit long in the face, too."

"I'm okay, Snowy. Just a bit banged up, that's all." I looked down and kicked a blackened beer can. I couldn't tell him about Snake and Tysee, about my torn heart. "How's business?"

He roared and slapped me on the back. The pain was excruciating.

"Oh, sorry! Well, it was *good* for a while, thanks to you. Christ, The Libertine was packed while all of that was going on across the road. We even had a pool going on for when the commandos would move in. But then those uptight old hags from the Women's Catholic League came into town and kind of messed things up a bit, as you can see."

He surveyed the damage and somehow managed to chuckle.

"Anyone hurt? The Dwarf? The girls? Lette . . . ?"

He shook his head.

"You know, I'm sure she didn't squeal on you. She was so afraid you'd think so that she bawled for hours after they took you away. And I'd spell that b-a-w-l-e-d, not b-a-l-l-e-d."

"I don't think it was her," I said listlessly. "I wouldn't mind seeing her, though."

"Like to help you but she took off back to the provinces, like most of them. Dumb, though—the price of pussy has tripled in three days. Some of the girls are operating out of tents on the edge of town. Making a fortune, I hear. Here —you want a drink? I managed to save the cooler from the office. It's in the back of the Ratmobile—nothing could destroy that beast. Even if the fucking Russians ever decide to dig a mile-deep hole here, they'll only be able to dirty the ashtray on that heap."

Even Lette was gone out of my life.

"What are you going to do?" I asked dully. "You're awfully chipper for someone burned to the ground."

"Me? Hell! Build a new bar, of course! Going to call it The Embers. The goddamned fire did me a big favor. Killed all the cockroaches! First guy open is going to clean up. The boys on base are dry and horny as hell already. I'm already planning opening night. Going to have a 'fire sale' —pussy on at the old price, and raffles for short-times, blow jobs and long-times. How's this for a slogan: 'Hottest Pussy in Town'? I'm going to get some of them newfangled lights and a big Jacuzzi under the shower behind the bar so the next time you, uh, come back out of the jungle you can have a bath in style. Hey, here comes my bulldozer! You going to stick around?"

"No. I don't know where I'm going," I said, and then I moved to the real question I wanted to ask. "Say, you haven't seen Snake at all since the skyjacking by any chance?"

Snow White shook his head.

"Damned glad to hear he made it okay. Don't know why the SOB didn't drop around for a beer after. I was damned surprised. *Nothing* usually stops Snake from comin' here for a beer when he's in town. But then I guess that's 'cause there *wasn't* no bar."

He finished his can of beer, threw it into the smoldering mass and waved the bulldozer over.

———— • ————

"Lion?"

"Is this who I fucken *think* it is?" the gravelly voice said, those sharp old eyes penetrating the thin disguise.

I hardly cared anymore. Even the Christmas decorations around the bar depressed me. But then they always did.

"Yeah. It's me."

"Well, I'll be damned—I never woulda guessed," he exclaimed before lowering his voice conspiratorially, taking me by the arm, and leading me quickly through the curtains to a back room. "It's a good fucken thing it's still early in the day. Unless you want to get mobbed by the newsboys, or worst. In here you'll keep outa goddamned sight."

He led me into his small, cluttered office, piled high with bills and receipts, dust covering everything that an elbow hadn't wiped clean. He pointed at some still-open traveling bags on a cracked leatherette chair.

"Jist move that fucken junk and siddown."

I did as he said, placing it all beside the well-worn armchair. The Lion looked me over from across his battered desk. I said nothing, waiting. I could wait forever. Nothing moved anymore. Least of all time.

"Are you okay, kid?" he asked, not unkindly. "Your voice sounds kind of far away and, well, you look pretty far away yerself is the only way I can fucken describe you."

"Nah, I'm okay, Lion. Just a little at loose ends." That didn't convince him. I couldn't tell him that my best friend had slithered off with my girl. Classic. A Snake in the grass.

"Well, if there's any fucken thing I can do to help, you just tell me," he drawled. "You've had a pretty rough time lately."

"Can you watch out for Snake? I'm looking for him. Sooner or later he'll be coming through here. But *don't* tell him I'm trying to find him, okay?"

The old head nodded slowly and carefully. He knew he wasn't being told everything. I couldn't hide the steely edge in my voice. Though it softened as I continued.

"There's a small possibility that a girl may be looking for me. That's a different story. Please find out where she can be reached."

It was impossible to hide anything from the Lion.

"That broad you're talkin' about," he rasped quietly, "that's the San girl, ain't it?"

I looked down and nodded. I couldn't say her name. I knew it would crackle dry in my throat.

"I'll keep an eye open an' an ear up. Anything else? You just fucken name it," he said kindly, leaning on an elbow closer to me.

"Don't let anyone know I'm in town. I'm going to lie low for a while, until the heat is down."

"I think that's a good idea! I certainly wouldn't fucken recommend you coming around *here* just yet. All kinds of people have been coming in, including too many fucken Eastern Europeans. I sold more vodka in the last month than the last year. Too many fucken Arabs too, which hasn't pleased the Middle East construction boys much, I'll tell ya. Been a few fights, with those asshole bandits gettin' the worst of it. Things are quietin' down now of course. The government here took their heat off you. But just the same, I'd advise you to keep on your fucken toes. And keep your head even lower. Some of these guys are heavy. You got a goddamned gun or anything?"

I plopped my Walther on desk. I was about to tell him how I had smuggled it back into Thailand in a radio when one of the old maids appeared at the door. I quickly shuffled some paper over the pistol.

"It Brussels Kraut, Lion. He want see you."

Lion's face turned vermilion.

"Tell that fucken cock . . . what the fuck are you fucken doin' here?" the Lion growled, clambering to his feet as the tall goose-stepper squeezed through the door, his hand on his heart.

"Lion! I come to make the apology for last night. I wass drunk wiss too much schnapps! I promise I will never do that again! *Never!*"

"You're fucken telling me you won't!" the Lion roared. "Kurt, how many sons of bitchin's times do I hafta tell you that you're *not* fucken welcome in this bar! You got your own bar! Why don't you goddamned well stay there and ruin your own fucken business?"

He slammed his fist down on the desk. Dust and paper rose, including the sheet covering the Walther. I quickly shuffled paper back over it. Kurt's eyebrows rose for a moment. He glanced my way. Then his eyes popped, and he instinctively waved a low-elbowed Nazi salute.

"Achtung!" he exclaimed, completely ignoring the Lion. "It iss the hero! I follow all of the newss, especially at Clark Field! It reminds me of the time with Otto Skorzeny when we rescued Il Duce!"

He pumped my hand up and down, then took a seat. I was rapidly losing faith in my new disguise. The Lion had flopped back in his seat, dejectedly shaking his head, defeated. It was easier to get rid of AIDS than Kurt the Kraut.

"And, ah, what iss this?" he asked, pushing the papers aside to expose the gun.

"My ol' seven-shot Walther," I replied. There was no use hiding it.

He looked at me strangely. I let it pass. Usually I enjoyed the Brussels Kraut's antics and stories—at least he was entertaining—but today I wasn't in the mood. I just wasn't in the mood for *anything.* And besides, he could be trusted to drop into every ear in Bangkok that he had seen me.

"I drop by looking for Wolfgang . . . you don't know where he iss, do you?"

"No idea," I lied, feeling my stomach tighten. Wolfgang, for some reason, was the only person who'd ever had a great deal of time for Kurt.

Kurt looked worried for a minute but his face quickly cleared.

"What'd you do now to piss the Lion off?" I asked.

"I try to teach everyone to sing some of our old Cherman drinking songs when I wass wiss the Waffen ss," he said, his eyes glossing over as his mind leapt back to the good ol' days, where he was he still stuck. "But please, tell me about this gun again. What did you call it?"

I looked at him. There was a strange look in his eye.

"A Walther. It's a kraut gun. You should recognize it," I said apathetically.

"*Ja,* I know. Himmler presented me wiss one when I wass his bodyguard. Mein Fuehrer used one to commit suicide wiss in his bunker. What iss the other part you say?"

"What other part?"

"How many shells you say it iss holding?"

"Seven," I repeated, wearying of the conversation rapidly.

"There iss no such thing."

"What do you mean there's no such thing?" I said. "I should know." I was mildly irritated—the first emotion I had felt since leaving Clark.

"*Nein.* Walther does *not* hold seven shells. It holds nine."

I tossed a hand up in mild frustration.

"I only know," I said wearily, "that mine holds seven. Maybe it's a different model."

He picked up the compact pistol and studied it in his palm. The Lion looked decidedly uneasy. Fondly, the Brussels Kraut turned it over in his hand and ran a finger sensuously along the barrel. He snapped out the clip with a flourish and held it up to the light. It was full. He nodded knowingly, then laid it in the palm of his hand, holding it out to me.

"And what iss this?" he asked, looking from the clip to me and back down to the clip.

"That iss za clip," I said.

"No—this," he said, not even noticing that I had mimicked him. *"This."*

I leaned forward. His fingernail rested on a small, rectangular box attached to the base inside the clip. The spring that kept the bullets pressed forward was attached to it.

"It's the bottom of the bloody clip, I presume," I said, my impatience growing, though I had noticed the slight bulky base before and had vaguely wondered what purpose it served. It was the size of about two bullets side by side.

Without a word, the Brussels Kraut emptied the tightly full clip of its cartridges, which made the Lion relax a little. He slowly poked his finger at the bullets, each in its turn. Seven. He took up a jeweler's loop from among the litter on the Lion's desk, wiped it clean on his shirt, and held the clip up to the light.

"Jawohl!" he exclaimed.

He set down the loop, took up a pair of needle-nose pliers and a screwdriver, and began to attack the clip.

"I tell ya, Lee, he's gonna screw your gun up, sure as shit!"

"Kurt, just what the . . . oh Christ, now you've done it."

He had deftly wiggled the rectangular little box until it was free of its base. Now he slid it out, the spring that forced the shells up still attached. Kurt glanced inside it for a moment, then tapped it on the desk.

A compact jumble of electronic components tumbled out onto the desk top.

"Wha . . . !"

All three of us instinctively leaned forward. There were four tiny, round batteries, a microchip and microcircuiting, all tightly packed together.

". . . Wha . . . what *is* it?" I asked again, the unexpected find making my voice break.

I fingered the mysterious pieces. All three of us were inches apart, the Lion's swampy breath mixing with the garlic and stale beer of the Brussels' Kraut's.

"Ja, didn't I tell you there iss no such thing as a seven-shot Walther? This hass been taking up the space of two bullets!"

"Looks like some kinda fucken transmitter to me. Not the kind that sends your voice—jist a tone."

"But what's it for?" I asked, baffled, picking it up in my fingers and looking at it closely.

"I think it would be good if someone wass trying to know where the gun iss. It could be used in triangulation to determine the location. In za war, we used them much to track down illegal transmitters."

"Where'd you git this fucken gun anyhow?"

The door swung open unexpectedly. We all started. I closed my left fist around the tiny transmitter.

"Oh! Sorry, eh? I was just going to grab my bags and head . . . *well!* If it isn't Mr. Newsmaker himself! Love your disguise. Save it for Halloween. You can go out tricking and treating as a felt pen."

Hal Lawson beamed and stuck out a hand. I took it. He was holding a copy of the Bangkok *Post* in the other.

"Hmmmmmn. Playin' with guns, eh? Be careful," he said, moving closer. I knew what he was going to say next. "Look, Lee, I'm supposed to be catching a plane to Saigon. After all these years Charlie is inviting me back for a few days on a 'nostalgic' tour, hoping to get some favorable copy. They've promised me an interview with some of the Politburo. But I'll drop that all right now if you'll give your ol' buddy an exclusive on the story of the decade. How about it, eh?"

I shook my head. A determined look came into his eye and I knew I wasn't going to get away that easy.

"I've got a few things to straighten out first. But I'll give it to you then, I promise."

"Sure. and when *you're* ready, who knows where *I'll* be and I'll miss the scoop, eh?"

"No, don't worry," I said. "It's yours." I held up three fingers. Scout's honor.

"All right," he agreed. "I'm counting on you. But for now can you help me with one thing, eh? No one can find the Wolf. It's a total mystery. He's disappeared completely. It's been a month now. Indications are that *he's* behind all of this. So tell me," he asked checking his watch nervously, "where and when did you last see him?"

"Ah, Wolfgang!" the Brussels Kraut interrupted. "I am looking for him too. I am very worried about him."

"Kurt," Hal pressed. "You seem to get along well with

him. What *is* his background? It seems all his records were
destroyed during the war."

"I can not say. If he wass dead it would be a different
thing. But years ago he asked me not to talk about his
contribution to Germany."

"Contribution . . . ?" *"Ja,"* Kurt replied, but it was
clear he would say no more.

Hal looked a little pissed.

"Lee? What about Wolfgang?"

Despite all the blood I'd seen in the last few weeks, my
memory of the Wolf hanging by the meat hook was the one
that most haunted me. It was time someone found him.
That no one yet had was a testimony to how securely he
controlled the secrets in his life.

"I know more than that, Hal. I can tell you where—"

"Wait! This is scoop material. For private ears only.
Would you mind telling me out in the hallway, eh?" he
asked, trying not to look at Kurt directly.

Kurt was looking upset. I shrugged. We stepped outside.
"Well?"

"You've been to his place?"

"That garbage dump off Sukhumvit? Many times. He's
never home. The cops even broke in and let us roam
around. Nothing."

"Can you get back in?"

"Where there's a crowbar, there's a way." He grinned.

"Well, take that crowbar into the bedroom closet. You'll
find a hidden trapdoor. It leads to Wolfgang's *real* home.
You'll find him in the . . . freezer where I found him right
after I got back from Kun San's with the Head. It won't be
pretty, even though I turned the freezer on high. The
Shan really made a mess of him. And keep your source
private, right?"

The Canuck nodded seriously, absorbing each bit of information. He gave me a solid thumbs-up.

"So he can keep a bit, you say, eh?"

"He'll be hanging around the house, I'm sure," I said,
wincing at my turn of phrase.

Hal nodded.

"This interview with the Politburo is too rare to miss. I'll
never get another chance. I wonder if I can have my pussy
and eat it too. . . . I think so. I'll try."

We stepped back into the office.

"I have to get going," Hal said, slapping the folded *Post* down and beginning to zip up his luggage.

I glanced at the paper. Under the headline about some emergency closed-door OPEC meeting being held in New York, a small article caught my attention. I skimmed over it, then closed my eyes for a moment.

"Are you all right?" Hal asked.

"No. I mean, I'm fine. Just tired from the flight from Manila."

I didn't think there was any purpose in telling them I had just read about a well-known American diplomat with a long service record in the Far East, including a recent posting in Manila, who had just died unexpectedly of a heart attack at the Waldorf-Astoria the day before. His name was Peter Melville. I was starting to feel like a jinx—the Angel of Death.

"Lads, I have to run." Hal announced. "Lee, you have a mekhong on me, eh? Just put it on my tab."

The Lion scowled, shaking his mane despairingly.

"Talkin' about that goddamned tab, it's already startin' to look like the fucken Sunday edition of the *L.A. Times* agin. Just when the hell . . . aaaaaaah, that son of a bitch. Fucks off every time I brings up the subject."

"Lion, I have to split too," I said, relieved to see that the pressure from the shells kept the dislodged base in place when I packed the bullets back into the clip. I shoved the gun in my pocket, stood and pulled open the door.

"Thanks, Lion. I'll be in touch. And Kurt—thanks to you too. I don't know what this means, but it's starting to explain some things."

"It iss my pleasure. But if you know anything about Wolfgang, you could return the favor."

"Just hang on awhile. It'll out in a few days."

He looked disappointed but didn't press it. He was well used to being told to fuck off. In a minute I was standing on Suriwong, surrounded by the comforting heat, noise and swirl of Bangkok's all-day rush hour. Hearing a roar that somehow managed to be louder than that on the street, I looked up at the sky. A 707 was streaking from Don Muang. Another like it would soon be heading for Ho Chi Minh City.

I wondered if Hal Lawson would notice that I had slipped the tiny transmitter into his open luggage.

———— • ————

The ceiling of my room in the century-old Railway Hotel at the resort town of Hua Hin was a very off-white. The threads of long-abandoned spiderwebs waved and shimmied as the old ceiling fan slowly revolved, each swing of its blades relentlessly beating off another small eternity of my life. The high-ceiled room with its peeling walls and ancient four-poster bed spoke of the past—a time that was gone with the typhoon and would never return, a time of gaiety and good times. Of loves won.

And loves lost.

For days I lay on my back, staring motionless up at the fan, envying it for its purpose—something I no longer possessed. Life had lost all meaning, had been replaced with a total and absolute angst, with an ennui that filled me with emptiness and, worst of all, hopelessness. I could see no use in any of it, this being born, living, dying, all this shitting and pissing. And for what? *What!* Life appeared in its stark, bottom-line form: ludicrous. Some kind of ridiculous joke played on us by greater beings, trapping us in these limited, limiting bodies with these limited, limiting senses.

Flies gathered to roomservice feasts I didn't touch. My head was still thick from the concussion, my thoughts like molasses, my emotions dull when not racked by almost incessant pain, both mental and physical. Whenever I pulled myself weakly off that large, empty bed in the larger, even more empty room, it was only to go for long, lonely walks along the deserted beach.

Then I'd drag myself back and stare up at the fan that haughtily, arrogantly spun above me until I hated it and hated God and hated everything that had torn my love and life away from me.

Time stopped. Each excruciating, painful moment seemed eternal—the seconds like hours, the hours like days. Sleep was fitful, dreams haunting. Always there was the picture of Tysee floating before me, her hair blowing in slow motion in an intangible breeze. My heart swelled to the bursting point, till I couldn't understand how it could go on beating, such was the awful, terrifying pain that I felt, spreading out into every cell of my body, each cell surging with the same aching love and desire and want and intense, absolute, anguished pain.

I'd thought it would never—*could* never—happen to me again. Not this time. Not after so long. Not with this perfect woman, who seemed to love me as much as I did her. But I knew the dragon's ways, and knew it was too late again. I knew I was back to being mashed in the monster's molars.

Each day I would phone Snake's old haunts, until they got sick of hearing from me. The Changi Yacht Club. The Hong Kong Bar in Penang. The Crazy Horse. But he was never at any of them. Every day I called the Lion, until he started to growl—he'd always hated phones—and I stopped.

It was an impossible search and ultimately purposeless. If they had decided to make a life together, there was nothing I could do. Nothing.

To try to fight off the monstrous images, I tried to concentrate on the many mysteries, such as why Brock Stambuck had hidden the transmitter in the clip. For it had to have been him. My knowing that much lifted some of the mystery. It explained how he had found my pension in Manila and nabbed the Head. And how my hideout in Snow White's bar had been discovered. And why he always seemed to encourage me to hang on to it. Was it he who had numbered Kayao and the other Shan and the Indian in the Chinatown alley? And was the trail of blood there, his? He *had* been nailed at my place just the day before.

But there was always the bigger questions: *why?*

For days I stared at the fan. And the days slowly stretched into a week, and the week into the New Year. I almost forgot to send a belated Christmas card and telegram to my folks in Phoenix, to let them know I was all right. I didn't want to talk to them on the phone. I didn't want to talk to anyone. It was well into the second week of January before my head began to clear, my body began to heal, and my spirits began to drift up out of the mire.

Thoughts of restarting work on documenting the Ifugao collection stirred in me, and I saw that as a good sign, a sign that I was returning to life. Even with that I would have to start from scratch, my loose notes no doubt having been destroyed in the explosion at my house.

"Patpong," I finally said. "That'll be the beginning of the beginning."

My voice sounded a little wobbly, but there was hope returning to it.

The last thing I did before I checked out of the room was turn off the ceiling fan.

——— • ———

Patpong.

Patpong. I love you.

Patpong. I trust you. Lust for you.

You're going to greet me with your open ways, open arms, open lays. You're going to tickle me and giggle me and have your sexy, silk-skinned girls fiddle me. You're going to pick me up as I lay you down and then after the sex and the sights you're going to leave me with a laugh and no lies.

I turned the corner off Silom and glided into the welcoming, passionate embrace of Patpong. Happy crowds strolled the flashing strip. Music, the lights and the lilt of laughter immediately began to dissolve my cares and woes.

My step took on a purpose. I had a goal in life. Once again I knew where I was going.

The Crazy Horse.

I strode by the many open doors, bikini-clad dancers with tummies tight as snare drums rocking to the roll that boomed and blasted from each with a clear, clean energy. Everywhere were girls, sexy girls, smiling girls, laughing Thai girls. I ran my hand through my fresh haircut. Felt the sensuous caress of a new silk shirt.

A smile, the first in weeks, began to crack and chip at my granite lips as my spirits trembled into flight, then tentatively began to soar. A sexy girl in a nothing bikini reached out for me from a bar door, grabbed my arm, and laughingly tried to tug me into her bar. We had a playful tug-of-war but I broke away, pleasingly startled to hear a tentative laugh breaking from me. I strode on, picking up speed, other sirens trying to lead me onto their soft but firm rocks. My step grew lighter, more confident, my face brighter. Patpong had never failed me, had never betrayed me. I began to let out long, deep sighs of relief, and felt the tension flowing from my body like magic. I wondered why I had taken so long to return to her loyal, always dependable, passionate embrace. She was always there. Was still there. Would always be there. Instantly forgiving me for throwing her over for another.

I glanced into the reflective windows of the bookstore in the middle of the strip, hoping to catch my image, the new me, the phoenix rising from the ashes.

What I saw sent my freshly flying spirits auguring in at mach two. In that single glimpse, all thoughts of pounding the pretty pussy of Patpong went permanently *poof.*

In the window was a display of *Time* magazines, neatly spread over a large area. From each cover the full, frontal features of the Buddha Head stared serenely out at me, the bright yellow of its gold and the blood-red of its ruby eyes standing out sharply against a black background. It wasn't the sight of the Head that had jolted me back to a far less happy reality.

It was the headline in gold above:

THE BUDDHA HEAD HOAX

Hoax . . . !

I pressed through the door, ripped a copy off a rack, and zipped furiously through to the cover story article: ". . . a major investigation by our special team of investigative reporters."

I blinked. The subhead read: *The lead in the gold*

My eyes pogo-sticked over familiar pictures of the many principals: Kun San, Sea Food, Ham-Sandwich. A modern shot of Abbot Tengid, and a blurry black-and-white of his predecessor, Abbot Lobsang. There were photos of the Dalai Lama, and a couple of Tengboche Monastery, with Everest or Ama Dablum in the background, and the familiar visa shot of myself.

But most prominent were the blowups of Wolfgang Krueger. Some had been taken recently, with Thai government leaders at some reception or another. Others gripped my attention more. One was the photograph I'd seen in his study, of the Wolf receiving a medal from Her-

mann Goering. The other was a frontal shot of his mansion.
The cutline set my eyelids blinking.

A PRIVATE GALLERY OF LOOTED WORLD WAR II ART TREASURES

I looked up, recognizing the startled face reflected in
the darkened window as mine. The vision of his awesome
collection burned bright in my mind's eye.

My eyes raced down the columns. I read as one possessed by an Asiatic demon. The story described how permission had been sought by the Americans from the Dalai
Lama to allow experts to examine the Head. He had issued
two statements to the world press. The first stated that U.S.
scientists ". . . could do what studies were necessary to
determine once and for all the authenticity or otherwise of
the so-called Buddha Head." In the second, he denied
once again any knowledge of the Head's existence, or of
the supposed events of 1959.

The reason for this rapidly became apparent as my eyes
burned into the copy.

> . . . All the experts called in to examine the
> Head have concluded it is a brilliant, expensive
> fake—an instant antique of magnificent propor-
> tions.
>
> A Carbon 14 dating done at the Smithsonian in
> Washington DC of a portion of skull material sets
> the age of the skull at no more than 500 years.
>
> Physical anthropologists at the Institute have
> determined that the Head is of Malay rather than
> Indo-Tibetan genealogical stock and that, judging
> from the weathering and the presence of microor-
> ganisms, it appears to have been exposed to the air
> for a considerable time, perhaps centuries.
>
> They also conclude, from the amount of wear on
> the teeth, that the Head is probably that of a fe-
> male, between 25 and 30 years old. The sex deter-
> mination was based on the size of the skull. The
> protuberance at the top was probably caused by a
> genetic defect.
>
> Pollen analysis done by the Science Faculty at

> Harvard University has determined that the Head
> is from the Philippines.
>
> Goldsmiths from Vincent Van Klee on Fifth Av-
> enue in New York City, while acknowledging that
> the craftsmanship ranks with the most brilliant of
> the brilliant, have concluded that the alloys used
> to secure the gems to the eye sockets are of a type
> used only since the Renaissance, when the science
> of metallurgy began to grow past its early, more
> primitive beginnings.

My throat went dry with shock as my eyes drifted up to
catch my reflection in the window again. Quickly recovering, I rammed my nose back into the magazine.

The subtitle of the article notwithstanding, the gold was
real; they guessed there to be about five pounds of it, all 24-
karat.

The pigeon-blood corundums were judged to have come
from Mogop in Burma, where the world's finest rubies are
found. The gemologist, not having been allowed to remove the stones, had rigged up a light source within the
skull to study their interiors and make an estimate of their
weight—40 karats each. Unlike the goldsmithing, which
was more recent, the gems appeared to have been cut by
hand centuries ago. The value of the gems and gold alone,
less their artistic and historical value, was placed in the six-
or perhaps seven-figure range.

I gripped the magazine closer as I reached the section
describing how Wolfgang's frozen and mutilated body had
been found in the freezer by Hal Lawson. As the instigator
of the most elaborate hoax of the century, all roads led to
Rome. Sea Food admitted that Wolfgang had been the one
to bring the idea of stealing the Head to Kun San, and that
the robbery had taken place as planned. They quoted Kun
San's one-time lieutenant:

> "The trouble started after the robbery. Kun San
> changed his mind about sharing the Head. There
> was a great argument between Wolfgang Krueger
> and Kun San. In the end Krueger was beaten and
> forced to leave."

I recalled with a jolt Wolfgang's injuries from his so-called mugging. Sea Food had more to say:

"Later, when Lee Rivers came and stole the Head from us, we suspected that Krueger was behind it. It is true that Kun San issued orders to have Wolfgang Krueger murdered, but these orders did not have time to be carried out. It was not us who murdered him."

Considerable doubt has attended this allegation of innocence by the Shan leader, although his protests are understandable in the light of the brutal nature of the murder.

The story described Wolfgang's opulent home, and the many art treasures it contained—including their source. I had to read the sentence twice to absorb it.

The greatest find, however, was certainly some 126 works of art from the Hermann Goering Collection, believed until now to have been lost to the Russians during the Battle of Berlin (see box, p. 16).

I scattered the pages, ripping one, looking for 16. A browser next to me was staring at me. I barely noticed him. The box describing the cache of paintings in Wolfgang's office took up an entire page. Some of the finds were reproduced in color, including one of the Brueghels I had seen. Many more had been found, still in their original crates, the ones they'd been packed in at Goering's Carinhall residence.

I ripped back to the main article, crunching the *Time* up in my hands:

Further dramatic evidence that Wolfgang Krueger was the man behind the hoax came from no less than Abbot Tengid, present Head Lama of Tengboche Monastery. He was encouraged to speak by the Dalai Lama, who, until recently, has remained silent himself.

The abbot, a tall, intense man with an understandably harried look, has long been at the center of the controversy. As head monk under the late

Abbot Lobsang, he was present at Tengboche in
1959 during the Tibetan Crisis when a presumed
aide to the Dalai Lama arrived on a secret mission,
bearing what he said was a secret message from
the Tibetan god-king.

"I showed him into the monastery. He was a big
man and looked very tired and ill. Later Abbot
Lobsang called me into his inner chambers. The
man was there as well. There I was shown the
Buddha Head and the letter. I was told I was a
witness and that I was to memorize it. It was written in Tibetan. I have a very good memory but the
letter was long and it took me an hour. Afterwards
the man burned it in the candle. Then it was all
ashes" *(see box. p.17 for letter)*.

I snapped pages like whips. The letter was printed as
Abbot Tengid recalled it. The browser consciously moved
a step away from me. Tengid had to have a good memory.

To: Abbot Lobsang
Tengboche Monastery
Nepal

The recent tragic circumstances require the
transfer of This, the Most Precious Relic of Buddha—His Golden Head—to a temporary site until such time as it is safe for Its return to the
care of the Dalai Lama. Such a time can only
come with the Dalai Lama's eventual return to
Lhasa and the expulsion of the Chinese invaders.

Because of the great reverence and esteem
given to the most holy site of Tengboche, the
Dalai Lama deems this gravest of responsibili-
ties to fall upon you.

Secure It in the wall behind the main altar
personally.

Under no circumstances contact the Dalai
Lama, *even* if the Head is discovered by accident or should any tragedy befall It. The Dalai
Lama will *deny* knowing anything and all so as
not to endanger the creed of Buddhism.

Should tragedy befall, you are to take whatever steps are necessary to secure the Head.
Under no circumstances contact the European
gentleman who has delivered It. As an old
friend and confidant of the Dalai Lama, he *too*
will *deny* ever knowing It, or having brought It
to Tengboche Monastery.

Allow your head lama to read and memorize
these instructions in your presence. Always and
only the abbot and the head lama should know
about the Treasure.

Then destroy this Letter in the presence of
the carrier.

>My Eternal Blessings,
>Dalai Lama (And Seal)

I savaged the pages to find the main article again. The
person at the next rack gave me another sideways look,
shook his head in disgust, replaced his magazine, and
moved away.

Abbot Tengid had more to say:

"He was European, of course, but spoke Tibetan.
We weren't surprised but were honored. Everyone knew that the Dalai Lama had had two very
good friends for many years during and just after
World War II. They were two adventurous Aus-
trian mountaineers who had escaped a British
prison-of-war camp in India and made their way
to Lhasa, where the Dalai Lama gave them exile.
Their names were Heinrich Harrer and Peter
Aufschnaiter. We didn't know which of them it
was because he wore a balaclava, but we understood his need for this, and why he asked us not to
put specific questions about his identity."

But it certainly wasn't Harrer, who now lives in
Europe, or Aufschnaiter, who died in 1973. For
one thing, neither is or had been an amputee,
whereas the visitor bearing the Head had only one
arm.

Like most Tibetans, Abbot Tengid had never

seen a picture of Mr. Harrer or Mr. Aufschnaiter, but had only heard of them.

I slowly lifted my head. The eyes staring back at me in the window were huge.

"Wolf . . . gang . . . ?" I heard myself mutter in disbelief.

My eyes continued to gobble up the copy. It described how the visitor had only used one hand, and how that night Tengid, while checking his room to see if their guest was comfortable, had found him asleep—but had been shocked to see what he thought was his arm lying on the floor. Having never seen a manikin arm before, he didn't know what to make of it. But he had said nothing and the next day the visitor's strange limb was back in position, motionless under his coat.

I almost gasped when I plowed into the next section, headlined *Wolfgang Krueger—back of the head.*

> Krueger's background lends itself to this remarkable hoax attempt.
>
> Information about that past has been difficult to come by. Most has been derived from one remarkable source—a Mr. Kurt Klassen, of Bangkok, who has come forward with proof that he is the half-brother of Krueger. Klassen described his kin as a great patriot who didn't wish to remember the war, and who made him swear an oath of secrecy about his—Krueger's—past.
>
> Much of what Klassen has to say has been corroborated by family pictures, and documents that survived the Battle of Berlin. Klassen now runs a bar in the heart of Bangkok's notorious vice district, Patpong Road, one that he says his half-brother financed. He claims to be "flabbergasted" at this half-brother's lifestyle, about which he knew nothing until very recently

I was flabbergasted. *Kurt the Brussels Kraut?*

I scanned on at the speed of light. It described Wolfgang's short but brilliant flying career. Flying Messerschmitt 109s, he had shot down seven Mustangs during the Battle of Britain, becoming an ace by the age of twenty-two. But luck didn't stay with him—during a sortie over the English Channel, his fighter was shot up, forcing him to limp back to German-held France. In the subsequent crash landing, he lost his left arm.

After recovering, he began a new and equally brilliant career. Because of his flying record, no less than his family background—his father had been one of the leading art dealers in Berlin—he was taken under the ample wing of field marshal Hermann Goering, head of the German Luftwaffe, who appointed the young air hero one of his art collectors. Dressed in a Luftwaffe uniform with a lieutenant's stripes, and armed with the field marshal's personal letter of introduction, Krueger traveled freely all over the German occupied territories, inspecting and selecting works presented to him by the vast network of art agents coordinated by Goering's chief art administrator, Walter Andreas Hofer.

As well, he scoured museums and galleries, seeking out likely additions to the Hermann Goering Collection, which the field marshal often boasted, with some justification, was the largest in the world. Many of the works Wolfgang found were slated for the Hermann Goering Museum, which the Nazi leader planned to open on his sixtieth birthday in 1953.

But this was never to happen. By late April 1945, while the thousand-year reich, not yet a teenager, was going up in flames with Berlin, Hermann Goering was doing his best to safely transfer his enormous collection of plundered art treasures away from the fighting.

In with the long line of trucks laden with artworks, winding their way from Carinhall, Goering's 100,000-acre estate northeast of Berlin, were four carrying many of his most beloved treasures.

For years it was believed that these four trucks were lost in the confusion of the fiery Battle of Berlin. It has been widely presumed that at least one of them fell into the hands of the Russians and that many of the masterworks it was carrying now adorn the walls of Politburo members.

This speculation was fueled by the 1973 reappearance of Boucher's *Venus,* which turned up on the London auction market that year and is known to have been part of the famous lost shipment. Subsequent investigations traced the *Venus* back through Sweden, Finland and Poland to its ultimate point of origin—Russia.

Since the war's end it has been feared that the other three trucks had been whisked behind the Iron Curtain as spoils of war. But the recent discovery of the 126 masterworks hoarded by Krueger has put the lie to this almost universally accepted conclusion. The 126 works are mainly of the Dutch and Renaissance schools, of which Goering was especially fond and on which he was a recognized expert.

They were discovered in a study-gallery in Krueger's opulent home in Bangkok after his brutal murder. The whereabouts of the rest of the cache may never be known—the secret may have gone to the grave with this cunning German art expert. His half-brother, Kurt Klassen, denies all knowledge of the collection.

How Krueger managed to spirit such a collection out of war-torn Berlin and through Soviet lines is anyone's guess, but he appears to have done not only that, but to have transported it to Bangkok as well.

The story moved on to describe the Wolf's journalistic and collecting careers in the Far East following the war, and speculated on why he would cultivate the appearance of a man of modest means when, in fact, he was a multimillionaire. It also commented on what must be the diabolical character of any man who could pull this off for so long.

There was more. A few of the senior antiquities dealers on Madison Avenue in New York recalled doing business with Wolfgang as far back as the fifties and early sixties, when he was highly respected for his knowledge of Tantric Buddhism. Many also recalled that it was Wolfgang who used to talk the Rumor up, almost making a fetish of it. By the seventies, he had largely stopped doing business, and his old contacts rarely saw him again.

Certainly wealthy, no doubt from the private sale of an unknown number of the stolen works, he obviously had the money necessary to finance the making of such a piece as the Buddha Head. All of this is powerful evidence that this former German air ace was an alchemist trying to transform the base lead of a false head into the gold of a real one.

What he planned to do seems obvious now: having labored for a quarter of a century to create an atmosphere where the unbelievable was believable, he planned to cash in on what he fully expected would be a great surge of interest. Perhaps he never knew just how great.

In some ways, one must admire him for nearly succeeding.

I watched my head shake in disbelief in the darkened mirror that was the window. I quickly fumbled the page over. The next stories concerned François Giscard's role, and mine. My relief began to grow when I read a quote from Abbot Tengid in which he described having to turn to François as his only hope for recovering the Head. The abbot mentioned François had on several occasions tracked down and returned stolen property for monasteries in Nepal. François, in turn, was quoted as saying he had chosen me to act as his proxy because of my "unquestioned integrity and respect for Buddhism."

My risks and trials had finally been put in a favorable light. I let out an audible sigh of relief, hardly aware of the sideways stares of the other customers.

The story speculated on the whereabouts of three of the central figures, myself, Tysee San and Snake. There had been sightings of us everywhere, from Cairo to Rio to the Grand Caymans and even Timbuktu. It was suggested that we might be under the care and protection of the American government. The State Department was refusing to comment.

Ripping over another page, I found another boxed story that stated the Head would be on display for one month at the American Museum of Natural History in New York, after which it would be disposed of at the discretion of

Abbot Tengid of Tengboche. Fake Head or not, the monastery was still the de facto owner.

"Three days' time . . . ." I muttered as I crumpled the nearly destroyed magazine shut and stared at the cover picture. My eyes traced the contours of the familiar image, finally settling on the eyes. The photographer must have left on the light the gemologists had hooked up inside the Head, because the enormous gemmed peepers were shining brightly, so I would see into their vividly glowing interiors. I stared dumbly down at them.

Suddenly a spark seemed to go off behind *my* eyes. White-hot and ice-cold emotions flooded through me. My eyes burned down into the Buddha's. It must have been minutes before I looked up from the picture again. When I did I caught the reflection of my face in the window.

It was an expression of utter and absolute incredulity.

"Excuse me?"

"Huh . . . ?" I grunted, taken by surprise.

I turned to see a pretty, petite girl with her hands braided inside out, her chin pulled in and her twinkling eyes looking up at me.

"Excuse me, sir," she said politely, a trace of a smile on her lips. "But are you interested to *buy* the magazine, please?"

———— • ————

I caught the Lion just as he was coming out of the door of his bar. Or I should say, he caught me. There was a wide grin on his leathery face and his eyes sparkled as he grabbed my arm.

"Hey, Lee, good to fucken see ya! There's been some son of a bitch from New York trying to call you every day for the last coupla weeks. Got his fucken number writ down some goddamned place. Forget his name, but he's a frog, if that's any help."

"I can guess," I said numbly.

"I think he wants to get ahold of Brock Stambuck too, real bad. He says for you to keep an eye out for him."

"Will do. Thanks. I'm looking for him too."

"Well, be sure to check with fucken Lawson inside. He might have something on him. Maybe you can tell that New York frog to quit phonin' all the time. I hate the goddamned things anyway, though I suppose the things got their good points. Like I did jist get a good call on it for a change. I guess you obviously ain't heard the good fucken news yet?"

"No—what?" I asked, still distracted.

"Marrissa jist called from the doc's office. I sent her there because it was the second fucken month in a row she didn't get the ol' flag up. *I'm* gonna be a fucken pappy again! Sixty-nine fucken years old! Four months from our honeymoon and she still can't get enough of the ol' pipeline." The old iron worker did a sprightly jig before skipping over to the sidewalk to flag down a tuk-tuk.

I half-smiled but then my face just as quickly clouded over. He was so excited he didn't even mention the news about Wolfgang, but then it was probably old if *Time* had it.

I snapped the crumpled newsmagazine against my open palm and reached for the door handle. I needed a quiet drink. There ain't no such thing in the a-go-go bars of Patpong. The Crazy Horse was already forgotten.

"Texas Bitch" was on the jukebox. Hal was holding forth with a keen-eyed group of belt-stretchers, but immediately broke off when he spotted me and quickly made his way over. Taking me by the arm—a little too firmly—he pulled me into a corner.

"Lee, you son of a bitch," he said roughly between his teeth. "You got me in deep shit in Saigon."

"What are you talking about?" I said, pulling my arm loose. "Is this what I get for giving you the Wolfgang lead?"

I didn't need this crap. I was still trying to sort out the *Time* story.

"It has to do with that little transmitter you slipped into my baggage."

I looked him sharply in the eye.

"Go on."

"I was staying at the Caravelle Hotel, like the old days, eh? It was my last evening there and I was in my room when I heard a knock at my door. Before I could answer it I heard shouting, then this crash and some running. Next thing a firefight broke out. When it died down and I opened the door there was a bag full of beer smashed in front of it, and about four Charlies lying around quite dead, and these Vietnamese secret-service types running

all over the place, including some who'd been assigned to
look after me. Some were leaning over a big man
facedown on the floor at the end of the hall. It must have
been him who was coming to visit me, but before I could
recognize him, they pushed me back inside my room. But I
did see his hand—it was white. Whoever it was, I knew he
was dead by all the blood, eh? Then the Charlies turned
my room upside down till they found that little transmitter
in my baggage!"

He raised his voice sharply near the end.

The belt-stretchers rubbered their necks. His eyes were
flashing with accusation. I looked down and closed mine.

Brock Stambuck.

It had to be him. Why the hell would he have followed
the transmitter to Saigon? Why would he try to shoot it
out? Then I knew—he was a yank spook in a gook free-fire
zone. What other choice did he have?

"Charlie asked me a million questions but it was obvious
I had no idea what was the hell was going on, eh? They
tried to say it was just another Vietnamese but I pointed
out that he was too big so they dropped that ploy and
opened up a little more. But not much more." He stopped
to take a quick slurp of beer. His eyes were still on me.

"Well, come on. What's the rest?"

"They wouldn't tell me anything, didn't want it written
about, I'm sure. But one of them told a new arrival in
Vietnamese that the man had some kind of triangulation
unit on him, eh? They'd forgotten how after years in Nam I
spoke the language. I also learned that they spotted the
guy as a CIA agent at the airport, but they didn't collar him
then. Instead they followed him, looking to see who his
contact was and what he was up to, eh? To everyone's
surprise—particularly mine—he led them to *me!* It
seemed he wasn't about to be taken alive and when the
gooks moved in he opened up with a gun he'd managed to
smuggle in somehow, along with his electronic gear."

"Oh, Jesus."

Brock Stambuck was dead. Even if he was still alive, he
may as well be dead.

"Well, they were all very polite and all that, thank God,
eh? Because I was supposedly a VIP but they wouldn't tell
me a snip. Well, when I got back to Bangkok I checked the

airline lists for the week previous but I didn't recognize any names. I followed up on as many of them as I could, but no luck. I didn't know what the hell was going on, eh? Not till I told the Lion a bit about it all and *he* told me about that little transmitter the Brussels Kraut found in your gun." He fixed me firmly with his stare.

"You slipped it into my luggage didn't you?"

I nodded. There was no use denying it.

"I had *no* idea this would happen, believe me."

Hal grunted, totally unconvinced.

"Well, at least you can tell me where you got that Walther, eh? There's a big story here. I should get something out of it besides almost gettin' thrown in a gook slammer as a spy. Or worse."

"I can't tell you, Hal," I replied after a pause.

"You *can't* tell me! What *is* this bullshit, eh? Why?"

"Not until I check some sources."

I was thinking of the CIA. They should know first, before the story broke. It might give me a chance to find out why the hell that transmitter was placed there in the first place. If there was any hope for Brock, if he was still alive, it would be better that way.

"Listen—if anyone has a *right* to know, it's *me*, eh?"

I shook my head.

"Okay, one thing then, jerkoff, was it Brock Stambuck? This guy was big and wearing a jacket and tie and at a glance it looked like his back. He could have learned I was in town and dropped over for a beer."

"Hal," I said evasively. "I've already promised you an exclusive on me. Do you want it or not?"

The fire in his eyes danced down like a furnace with its gas cut.

"You're a bit of a cunt, you know that?"

"Well, you are what you eat. You can be a bit of a prick yourself, you know. If there's a story in that, I'll give it to you later. Now get out your bloody Nagra. Let's get the first bit over with."

Half an hour later, when we were through and I was at the door, I glanced behind me. Hal was on his stool checking the playback on his tape-recorder. He was also watching me like an eagle out of the corner of his eye. His hand was nowhere near his glass of beer.

———— • ————

"Nog! What the hell are you doing there?" I asked in English. "I didn't even expect the phone to ring!"

I heard a gasp of surprise on the other end of the line.

"Ah! Mr. River! It is much good to hear from you! How is you?"

"Fine. Keeping low. What are you doing there? I thought the home place was bombed out!"

"Oh no! Bomb went off nearby very bad and later one go off in courtyard behind van. It wrecked and birds and fish die. I sorry," he added apologetically, as if it were his own fault. "But house have little damage. There police guard since then so it okay. Po and I and kids we at another house where CIA men take us. We just come back few days ago. Only a few newspaper people around yet. Po okay. I just get out of bandage and able to work."

My heart leapt. For once I was glad the press got its facts wrong.

"Nog, I want you to bring me something. In the storage room you'll see a box marked 'For Insane Emergencies Only.' Remember the corner where we threw those two girls I had picked up at the Thermae Coffee Shop out of the car? The ones that were fighting?"

I'd been heading home after a night of mekhong flooding the Rivers and had a couple of bouncies in the back I had picked up at this Sukhumvit coffee shop where the hot cups you get have nothing to do with cream and sugar. I had planned on a late sandwich, though. Unfortunately, the two slices of bread didn't get along and started to tangle in the back of the car, and not the kind of tangle I like. We had stopped and sidewalked both of them.

"I remember." He laughed.

"Good. In an hour. And check to be sure you're not followed. The phone may be tapped."

"Oh, Mr. River," he asked worriedly. "One thing. I no can find my T-shirt with Foster's Beer on it and Four XXXX ball cap. You know where they go? I look everywhere!"

"Nog, don't you worry. I'm going to buy you a pet kangaroo once I get back."

SEVENTEEN

The American Museum of Natural History

BANSHEE WINDS THAT began somewhere in the horror of ice and snow above Labrador screamed down the great canyons of New York, slashing and slicing me to the quick as I slipped and slid down Central Park West from the Plaza to the American Museum of Natural History.

I swore to myself as I shifted uncomfortably under the huge, unfamiliar, mothball-reeking mound of clothes Nog had delivered to me. A light snow was falling, steeling on my shoulders and arms, and I tried to knock it off like it was an invasion of cockroaches.

I felt my forehead freezing through my toque, my ears cracking beneath the muffs, the frozen air searing my lungs, the hideous cold crystallizing the very film over my eyes. As I passed the Dakota I made out ahead of me through my blurring vision a long line of Ivan Denisovitch figures. That so many were there on opening day to view a fake Buddha Head surprised me. It disappointed me more: I would have to suffer in line.

I reached the end of the queue and looked ahead. As it wound forward and up the board steps into the museum, it resembled nothing less than the line up into Chilkoot Pass during the Klondike Gold Rush. I couldn't understand how some groups were able to talk and laugh together. Shuddering and shaking like an old Model T, I tucked in my chin, hunched my shoulders, and jumped up and down trying to keep warm. As the line inched forward we passed a building with a thermometer on the outside. It registered a murderous 42°F.

Just in time, my foot struck the first of the slippery gray-granite steps that led up to the American. Slowly the line inched forward. When I finally trudged through the revolving door and into the high-ceiling foyer with its brave and noble words by Teddy Roosevelt, my frostbitten senses immediately began to thaw. After paying five dollars at the turnstiles, I followed the snaking line into the echoing galleries.

After a quarter-hour more of shuffling we were there—in a large, rectangular gallery that had been given over for the exhibit itself. People strained on their tiptoes and peered around each other for their first glimpse of the Head, which was set up and spotlit inside a bulletproof glass pedestaled display case. In various corners of the room were stationed husky, sharp-eyed security guards with .38s and walkie-talkies.

From a distance it looked beautiful—the way the light gleamed off its golden curves, and the rubies radiated their Burmese crimson. I noted with relief that the gemologists' light had been left inside, to enhance those same ruby orbs.

Everyone had only a few seconds, ten at the most, for a close-up inspection as the line trickled by. I hoped it would be all the time I needed. It was my turn.

I glanced at the top of the Head. My eyes flashed over the features. Bending down, I peered into those glowing ruby eyes. The light enhanced the individual signatures of their huge interiors. It was like the cover picture in *Time* only clearer, much, much clearer: the large beautiful feather and rose-garden inclusions were visibly distinct even to the naked eye.

"Hey, buddy. Dere's other peoples here too, youse know."

"Sorry."

I pulled away and wandered in a daze toward the exit.

There was no doubt about it—it was brilliantly done. The goldsmithing was flawless, so much so that I wouldn't have noticed except for the illuminated eyes in that cover picture.

No two gems are alike. Each is as individual as a snowflake, or a pussy. These gems were beautiful, the inclusions enhancing that beauty.

The only trouble was that the stones in the Buddha Head Tysee and I spread out before us that day in the Chinatown teahouse had been absolutely *flawless,* unquestionably the finest rubies of that or any size I had ever seen.

Equally telling was the buck knife scar, which alerted me that not just the rocks had been switched. Whoever had tried to reproduce that scar in this head had missed. The wound wasn't behind the right eye—it was behind the left. And the broken portion of the blade was too large—it extended out an eighth of an inch. Previously it had been flush.

There had been a hoax, all right. But not the one the world was now hearing about.

The Head on display was not the same Buddha Head I had first seen in Kwan Mae, and which had been with us to the Philippines. It was an elaborate—and extraordinary—replica.

Not only that—I had seen those two gems before. You don't forget boulders like that. Not after you spend almost three months aboard the *QEII* studying and admiring them on the voyage from Pattaya to New York.

They had been part of Queen Supyalat's collection.

And I knew where they had gone. Directly across the frozen no-man's-land of Central Park.

———— • ————

"Mon Dieu! Monsieur Rivière! Thank God you're all right!" François Giscard exuded warmth as he drew me into his penthouse. "We have been so worried! Where have you been?"

"The American, François—to view the Head," I told

him, making no attempt to hide my suspicion. I made no move to remove my coat.

He searched my face for a moment.

"*Oui?* And did you see it?"

"I saw . . . what was there—"

"Really . . . !" he said, drawing back. He placed his elbow on the top of his wrist and scratched his chin thoughtfully. There was a tiny smile on his face.

"Very good. And what did you think of it?"

"Brilliant."

He nodded deeply, then smiled.

"What gave it away?" he asked, his eyes sparkling.

"The eyes, for one thing. The eyes . . . usually . . . give one away." I fixed his with mine.

"You recognized them, then?"

"Of course. Queen Supyalat's broaches."

"Ah! Good eyes! Yours too!" he exclaimed, then laughed. "And you're no doubt wondering how they got there, *oui?*"

"*Oui.*"

"*Alors,* your timing in some ways couldn't be better," he said, without explaining but reaching for my coat. "Come, come, don't be so stiff. I know you must be wondering what is going on. It's much too long a story for you not to be comfortable. Mainly, I'm just so relieved that you're okay!"

"Yeah, I'll bet."

Reluctantly I removed the bulky coat. I was still shaking from the deep freeze outside. He hung it on a hall horse, his nose twitching at the odor of mothballs rising from it. François was wearing a smoking jacket, though he was particularly well-groomed, as if in prelude to going out. Well, if that was the case, I thought, he could fucking well forget it. He'd explain it now if it took all night.

"I was hoping to just wait a little time before telling you," he was saying, "until the media vultures were finished with you . . . but perhaps the time has come. Please, come in. Come now. Don't look so puzzled, nor so suspicious."

He gestured me inside, and I followed.

"I insist you stay here," he said as he led me down the hallway of masks. "It isn't yet safe for you out there."

I paused at the door to his study but he continued on. Seeing me fall behind, he turned and gestured me ahead. "We are going to a different room. One you've never seen in my home before."

He led me through his bedroom into a large, walk-in wardrobe. At the back he pressed what appeared to be a nailhead, and a panel in the wall clicked open. We stepped inside. He clicked the door closed behind us. I instantly felt an overwhelming sense of déjà vu.

It was much like Wolfgang's study. The setting was luxurious and dignified. Thick leather furniture, an opulent desk, and rare art, including a great deal of pre-Columbian, was everywhere. Works of the same masters—Rembrandts, Vermeers, Brueghels, Avercamps, Raphaels and da Vincis—decorated the walls three and four paintings high, all of them from the schools that had been Goering's favorites. I noticed he had also brought in the two large oils of his father and grandfather, and given them a prominent, though off-center, position over the fireplace. A hammer lay on the mantelpiece; it appeared as if a nail had just been fixed in the wall to receive a third portrait. Huge windows overlooked Central Park. Snow was still falling outside. I tried not to look.

"*S'il vois plaît*, look around," he said, moving over to a thermostat on the wall. "I'll turn the heat up to what you like—ninety-five degrees, wasn't it? Good. Now I don't need to tell you that this is a most *private* study, and I ask you to please keep it that way."

I said nothing. I didn't know what to say. Some things were starting to fill in—connections that I didn't even know were connections. But far, far more questions were being generated here than answers.

The feeling of déjà vu grew when my eyes came to rest on a framed picture that looked familiar. I picked it up and studied the old, sepia-toned, five-by-seven black-and-white. A small, skinny boy with a prominent nose that the years couldn't change was standing warily beside a young lioness. Beside him stood what had to be his father. Behind him his heavy hand on the boy's shoulder, was a large man, grinning mischievously, in knee britches and a pompadour shirt. Field Marshal Hermann Goering.

"So you were a guest at Herr Goering's the same day as Wolfgang," I said blankly. My mind boggled.

"Comment?" he asked from where he was reaching into the liquor cabinet fridge.

I turned and stared at him as if he was a stranger. He clearly was. I held up the frame.

"I saw a similar picture at Wolfgang's."

"Ah, you *were* there," he said, a note of sadness entering his voice. "That makes explaining somewhat easier."

"Why don't you start," I rasped. "I'm waiting."

"First—Dom Pérignon!" he said, quickly forcing himself to recover. He began to uncork a bottle. "We have cases of it. Please tell me more about the Head across the park. Was it just the eyes that didn't fool you?"

I couldn't help but notice that he sounded a little like a craftsman asking an opinion of his handiwork. Just then the cork popped loudly and I started—it sounded like the Sikh's silenced .22 going off. Champagne ran over the bottle and down the sides. With his chin, he motioned me to a leather sofa chair before a coffee table.

"No. The knife scar gave it away too. It's on the wrong side."

"Really? I didn't know that." François neatly wiped the bottle dry before pouring out two glasses. "Well, our man had to do a hurried job and I guess he made a mistake!"

He passed me a glass of champagne and raised his.

"May I? This is for you. To a job well done!"

I didn't touch mine. He held his glass in midair for a moment before setting it back down in a display of disappointment. His face dropped noticeably.

"What do you mean, 'a job well done'? I didn't achieve what I set out to do. I didn't return the Head."

He looked me straight in the eye, nodded as if to himself, and leaned forward.

"This is not going to be easy to explain," he said, "and I'm not sure exactly where to start. But first of all, please understand that it could not have been done any other way. You couldn't be told what was going on. This was the only way for it to come off as if completely spontaneous, and to keep your name completely clear and clean, above suspicion, as it is now in the media. Though for a while it was a little rough. But I did my best to clear that up."

"What *are* you talking about?"

"Un moment, s'il vous plâit. Let me say also that you were always central to the plan, and that you did magnificently. Absolutely *magnifique!* Many times I thought it was all over! It's only your brilliance that pulled it off! But I expected that."

"Thank you for the compliment. Now exactly what in *hell* did I do?"

I looked at him like he was a loony. He saw it and laughed. The nervousness I had noticed during my previous visit was completely gone from him. In its place was euphoria.

"You, *mon ami,*" he said in a clear, soft voice, leaning toward me, "had a central role in one of the greatest antiquities hoaxes in history. It would be *the* greatest except for the one of my grandpapa. At the very least, it's the equal."

I felt my brow crinkling. He raised his glass again and bobbed his eyebrows at me.

"I salute you," he said, raising his glass and taking a sip. "And if Wolfgang were here, he would salute you as well."

I dropped my head and shook it in incomprehension.

"Wolfgang . . ." I muttered, then I looked up at the paintings. "You and Wolfgang obviously have known each other for some time."

"Oui, oui. Longtemps. As a matter of fact, the only other people in the world outside of you and myself who have been in this room are Breenda and Wolfgang"—he suddenly looked sad as that name passed his lips—"who with Papa, I should add, was instrumental in collecting these paintings in what we can call the Second Caper. Only the three of us ever knew. And now there is you. And in a few more years, Christopher."

His sadness while he thought of Wolfgang seemed to be genuine.

"Why do you risk showing it to *me?*" I asked him.

"You will never tell anyone. Because you are a part of the Third Caper. And you'll be rewarded suitably for your role in it."

"Third Caper. Second Caper? How many have there been?" I asked, exasperated.

"Just three, at least for now," he said, setting down his

glass. "One to a generation seems to be the present pacing."

A couple of things in the room caught my eye.

"My God," I said. "It's obvious you're in the game far more than I could have guessed." I rested my hand on a twelve-inch bronze of a Roman-era Jupiter that had been reported stolen a few years before. "Florence, right?"

"*Très observant! Oui!* Of course, I arrange antiquity deals that don't, ah, always meet the standards of the Rotary Club. In this business, don't we all?" He said that with a trace of pride.

"I see you haven't lost your interest in fine art either," I said cynically, nodding toward one of the paintings on the wall. It was Monet's *Impression soleil levant*, the painting that had given Impressionism its name. It had been stolen in '85, along with eight others, during a dramatic daytime robbery at the Marmottan Museum in Paris.

"Ah, that! I sold the others but I just couldn't part with this one. The same lads who handled that contract for me also managed to decorate my room with these pre-Columbians. They're from the National Museum of Archaeology in Mexico City. I've merely placed a number of these collections with people who really *appreciate* them, with those who are willing to make the sacrifice of a most precious commodity—money. Just like you were heard once to say," he added, smiling slightly.

"Wolfgang told you that?" I asked sharply.

"Everything."

"François, I've had a very hard time," I said, feeling exasperated. "I'm tired. I'm cold. I've still got a bit of a concussion. I haven't been laid in weeks. This is all very confusing. Please tell me what the hell has been happening?"

I also felt incredibly dumb. Used.

"It's a long and complex story, one that went so smoothly for a quarter of a century. Then overnight," he added, snapping his fingers, "the whole thing was almost lost! *Mon Dieu!*"

"Look, I don't know what you're talking about. Start with Wolfgang—first of all, what did he have to do with whatever this is?"

"Wolfgang . . ." he repeated, shaking his head as grief

seemed to flood back in. "He was my oldest and best friend. We had worked together on this project, as he had worked on a former one with Papa, since the beginning. His death made the whole thing almost not worth it, though we had always both understood that there would be certain dangers that had to be faced. But if we had had *any* idea! Or any idea how *big* it got! We never in any way expected *such* a response! It was even bigger than the project Wolfgang and my papa did. And certainly the equal of old Cecil's first!" He turned his head and gestured elegantly at the stiff portraits of the now-deceased founder of the family fortune, and his son.

My eyes hovered on the Egyptian ankh at the old man's fingertips. Then on the Iron Cross on his father's pedestal.

"Wolfgang would like to have been here to tell you all about it. You were like a son to him. But, sadly, it has become my duty—and pleasure. We always looked ahead to this moment as one of great celebration. So you and I will try to do our best despite the missing grand presence of that magnificent Teutonic knight. How far back do you wish me to go?"

"How about Genesis?"

He laughed.

"Très bon! For it is a story that goes back even more than a mere quarter century. Back, I suppose, almost *two* centuries."

"Is *that* where it *starts?*"

The champagne looked inviting but I ignored it.

"That's where it starts," he said quietly, sitting back for a moment to gather his thoughts. "I come from a long line of military careerists, but in the French Army, not the Swiss. Many of my ancestors served with distinction in a number of high-ranking positions when the Bourbons were reigning. One was in command of the musketeers when Louis XIV took Maastricht, where D'Artagnan was killed. Somehow they survived the purges in the military after the revolution and rose to positions in the Grand Army of Napoleon."

I clamped my arms around myself to slow my shivering.

"It was here that the story really began. My ancestor André Giscard was a colonel on Napoleon's staff during the 1799 Egyptian campaign. It was one of André's men who, upon finding the Rosetta Stone, brought it to my ancestor's attention. He, in turn, recognizing the stone's importance, brought it to the attention of Napoleon, who had it shipped back for study. It irks me to this day that it eventually ended up in the British Museum." François's voice grew slightly perturbed, then recovered. "But André's interest in Egyptology continued far past this. He took advantage of his position to collect a very great number of ancient pieces—large furniture and funeral trappings, including two mummies, one of a boy. Ancient objets d'art were considerably more numerous then than now, of course. By the time the campaign ended, André had compiled a thoroughly outstanding collection, no doubt the world's greatest single *private* collection of Egyptology—which it would still be today, I might add, if it hadn't been scattered."

"And what does Egypt have to do with the Buddha Head, François?" I asked. "I really wasn't serious when I said Genesis."

"It has directly to do with the First Caper," he said, holding up his hand. "The First Caper stimulated the Second, and the Second the present. What I'm telling you is the basis of what would later make his great-great-grandson a very wealthy man. That was, my grandpapa."

I settled in for the duration. The room was warming perceptibly anyway.

"As Napoleon's fortunes improved, so did André's. They rose together. My ancestor distinguished himself in many battles. Unfortunately in one of the later campaigns he was badly wounded, and so had to retire early. For his long service Napoleon rewarded him with a large land grant in Bordeaux, along with a healthy stipend. His forced early retirement was fortunate in some ways, for this was shortly before the fateful Russian campaign. In any case, André wasn't interested in growing grapes and almost immediately disposed of the property. He took his family and considerable profits, along with his enormous collection, to Geneva. He was hoping the drier climate there would alleviate his arthritis, which he attributed to his wound. There he purchased an estate and invested in a number of businesses, many of which were successful. Prospering, he moved onto a large estate by the lake. When André died, his son took no interest whatsoever in the collection, but stored it away in a room in one of the many towers, out of respect to his father. Through some workman's error the door was sealed and partitioned over. The room was effectively lost for almost a hundred years. It was only when my great-grandmama was planning some redecorating and the old wall was removed that the long-hidden room was rediscovered. And with it, the tremendous treasure. By this time the Western world's masses were reaping the benefits of mass public education, and were taking a bit of an interest in archaeology and Egyptology, and there were very few of the old pieces in Egypt that weren't in one museum or another already. But they said nothing about it. Old money is quiet money and they didn't want to advertise that they possessed such a treasure."

He stopped to hastily light a Gauloise, then quickly returned to the story. Recounting it was beginning to excite him.

"That's when my grandpapa Cecil first saw the collection," François said, motioning to the portrait. "He grew up with it. Fell in love with it. Became *obsessed* with it. Spent every waking moment away from school reading everything he could about Egyptology. At one point his papa had to take the boy on a summer vacation to the ruins at Memphis and Thebes to stop his incessant pestering.

"And to the disappointment of my great-grandpapa, Cecil took no interest in the family businesses, which were quite extensive by this time. He tried for two or three years to please his papa but in the end threw it in. He knew he had little talent for it. Instead he proved himself something of a gray sheep—he became adamant that he was going to study archaeology. There were the usual arguments but finally my great-grandpapa relented. It's a good thing, too, or you and I wouldn't be sitting here quite so comfortably right now."

Well, maybe *you're* comfortable, I thought. A few more degrees. . . . I should have asked him to turn the room up to ninety-eight.

"Grandpapa Cecil studied at the Sorbonne, then in London, which because of the British Empire had the most to offer in such study, which was then still a very young science. He finished his studies in Zurich and then his vocation was interrupted by the Great War. His papa died shortly thereafter. The family businesses, along with the estate, went to the next-eldest brother. Grandpapa wasn't given the short end of the breadstick entirely. He did inherit a comfortable sum of money, and as well was given a modest monthly allowance from the enterprises. It was natural that he would inherit the Egyptian collection."

François took a quick drag, then leaned forward, his eyes glowing. I glanced out at the snow swirling down from the rooftop, and shifted uneasily.

"Grandpapa Cecil began to spend most of his time in Egypt, digging at various sites. It was in 1921, during one of the digs in the Valley of the Kings, that he made an interesting discovery. He was in one of the long-ago looted tombs that had been dug deep into the hills there. He had noticed that a huge, solid granite sarcophagus had been shifted slightly on its base. With a complicated series of levers and pulleys he managed to move it to find out why. He found a broad passageway beneath that led to an adjoining tomb, and beneath that an even huger sarcophagus that had likewise been moved. Like the former, it had long since been looted—clearly by means of this same surreptitious entrance, for after probing around he found the main entrance still blocked completely by rubble. But it wasn't completely empty: the robbers had left a couple of enormous canopic shrines that were too big to have been removed, and some of the heavier furniture. By taking compass readings and measurements he was able to calculate the heights and angles to get a pretty good idea of where the outside entrance could be found."

"He wanted to dig out these few things?"

"Oh *non non non!* It would help you to know that he had discovered King Tutankhamen's tomb! Only it wasn't King Tut's yet! The hieroglyphics he found there described it as being connected with the former tomb."

"You're getting me a little confused here."

"Ah *pardon.* You see," François said, poking his cigarette with its lengthy ashes into the air, "King Tut hadn't been invented then. You see, he was a figment of my grandpapa Cecil's imagination."

"François—it's been a long flight," I said, heaving my chest, "and I'm a little tired for silly stories."

"Non! Why do you think there's no mention of Tut anywhere else? Why he was absolutely and totally unheard of until the so-called discovery? It's because Cecil *created* him!"

I stared at François. His eyes were on fire. He didn't look like he was lying. But then I knew that with him, I couldn't tell. Not anymore. I shook my head in disbelief.

"Oui, it's true! It was then that my grandpapa conceived what was, up until then, the greatest art and antiquities hoax in history—the First Caper. Why he did it I'll never know, for he died before I really knew him. But if he was anything like my papa, and I suspect he was, it was mainly for the sheer thrill of it—though he certainly needed money as well, his inheritance being, as I say, just modest, and him being used to a great deal more. But I like to think there was a more altruistic reason as well." He took another long drag.

"Yeah? Like what?"

"Such was his passion for Egyptology that I think he wanted everyone to hear about it. In this he certainly succeeded. He captured the imagination of the world! Today Egyptology is still at the pinnacle of archaeology! His passion is the *world's* passion. Perhaps if he had turned to a study of Turkey—which is so splendidly littered with the debris of some seven or eight civilizations—it would have been in ascendance over Egypt. But he chose Egypt."

I was having more than a little trouble believing this. Just the same, I took a tentative sip of the champagne. It tasted as dry as the Sahara.

"Being an expert in Egyptology, he was obviously a master at recognizing and even producing fakes—for you can't be absolutely sure of a piece without having a thorough knowledge of the antiquing processes. You know that yourself. His scheme was brilliant, really, though not without risks. He first of all spent a full year working in the hidden tomb, altering some of the hieroglyphics so they would have some continuity with the pharaoh he was creating, this King Tut. A good deal of this time was spent in applying a fully convincing patina some several thousands of years old. He also designed Tut's cartouche. It was quite incredible, really. In the collection back in Geneva were these two old, moth-eaten mummies that at one point he had almost thrown out. The one in slightly better condition was that of a boy. That's why he made Tut a boy-king. Want to know how he came up with the name?"

I cocked my chin slightly.

"Apparently when he broached the idea to his wife, my grandmama, she shook her head, as grandmamas will, and said, 'Tut-tut-tut Cecil, it's an *outlandish* idea.' Grandpapa took that as the name."

"Oh, *come on, François!* I can only take so *much!*"

"Non non! It's true! He had a bit of a sense of humor, if you will! That's a *very* inside family joke!" *"Ob* viously," I said, crossing my arms and shaking my head, my eyes rolling toward the ceiling. "And no one saw him mucking about all this time, of course?"

"Non. You must remember that this was before tourism. The Valley of the Kings then, as now, was completely dry, a place no one went to. He was able to take in supplies to last a long time. Grandmama then was still a young woman, only in her late twenties—Grandpapa was in his mid-thirties by this time—she took care of the tent and tutored my papa, who was then an adolescent. Here, look at this!"

He stood quickly and strode to a bureau. In a moment he was back with a framed picture. It was of a dusty old house tent, and the Valley of Kings stretched off in the background. Crates of supplies were piled here and there. In the foreground was standing a young woman in a flowing dress, a boy beside her. Behind them, his hands on their shoulders, was a man in breeches and hat.

"That little one is Papa. This was taken when Grandpapa was still preparing the tomb. That's where Papa developed *his* interest in antiquities, which would lay the groundwork for *his* amazing caper." François was speaking excitedly, his fifty-some years peeling away to reveal the boy inside. "Grandpapa had rigged up an alarm system, so that when the occasional inquisitive Arab did wander over Grandmama could signal him in the secret room and so he could quickly move back to the main chamber, cover the hole, and pretend to be translating hieroglyphics. Watching that bored even an Arab in less than a minute. Oh, they certainly had some close calls, no doubt, but overall they were left well enough alone."

François hastily butted his cigarette and fired up another.

"Once the chamber was ready, he smuggled in a carefully selected portion of his inherited collection. Such an act was considerably easier in those days, when customs was all but nonexistent. Of course, some of those pieces had been altered so they'd be identified with King Tut as well. The *pièce de résistance*— the gold lid from the mummy's smaller sarcophagus—was heartbreaking for him to give up, but it was necessary. He was risking everything. All of this he arranged in the room, which I'm sure you've seen in photographs. Then he dragged the sarcophagus back over the hole, and sealed it on his way out so it could never be moved. He also sealed up the old passageway so that there was only one way in, that is, through the actual rubble-filled entrance. The treasure was set. The next thing he did was assemble a team of archaeologists as accomplices, which took a bit of time. At this stage he made some mistakes, which caused him to have to take measures later on—quite drastic ones, I'm afraid—to protect the hoax."

François now looked troubled. He raised a finger to scratch an imaginary itch on a silvery brow.

"What do you mean?"

"I'll get to that. It's a bit of a blemish on the family, I'm afraid, but I feel I should tell you everything. Still, it's not the first fortune in this neighborhood that has a few skeletons rattling in the dark behind it. It's just there are so many in our family. Too many. Really, it is distressing."

He tapped his ashes methodically on the ashtray, then shook his head ruefully and took a thoughtful sip of champagne. Clouds of blue smoke hung in the still room like rain clouds.

"This team he sent out to the field—and mind you he was working behind the scenes completely now—made some initial 'discoveries' that 'led them to believe' that there might be more beneath. In this way they were able to garner some initial media attention. Grandpapa had studied how Schliemann had manipulated the press so well on his Troy dig, and made note of the lesson. As he hoped, the imagination of the world was soon caught up, and reporters from all over began to follow the dig. Each stage was carefully planned to exploit the newspapers to the maximum. Howard Carter had been a good choice to lead the actual dig—he was a good actor. Discovering that first step in the staircase that led into the ground was carefully timed for maximum exposure and effect. The dig was even slowed by various difficulties and obstructions they invented, so as to raise the suspense as they approached the so-called burial chamber. Grandpapa was brilliant in milking the problems! *Brilliant!* The Barnum of archaeology! By the time his men reached the wall and began chipping at it, they had all the world's press looking over their shoulders! The date they opened the tomb was February 16, 1923, and even this was planned! Cecil even took the seasons into consideration, making sure it was winter in Europe and North America, where everyone would be shut-ins, living from newspaper to newspaper, *National Geographic* to *National Geographic.*"

"Okay, this is an interesting story. But how did they make any money off it? Everything in there went to the National Museum in Cairo."

"They reaped the whirlwind! While the Tut treasure was being carted off triumphantly to Cairo, Grandpapa Cecil, pretending to act as a hush-hush agent for the archaeologists, began to sell off many of the remaining pieces in the collection André had collected on Napoleon's Egyptian campaign over a century before! These pieces were *said* to have been taken from a secret, fifth room adjoining, which was supposedly discovered when the media wasn't around. The diggers pretended to have formed a conspiracy around it. Of course it was never photographed, and was said to have been clandestinely sealed so that it supposedly lies un-rediscovered to this day. Of course the archaeologists themselves were always on hand to talk to prospective clients, which lent authenticity to the hoax. Grandpapa knew a great number of wealthy people who were only too pleased to be in possession of a piece from the famous King Tut treasure. Then, as now, there was an underground network of wealthy buyers. Believe me, I had no difficulty finding appreciative homes for my acquisitions from the Marmottan, and the National Archaeological Museum in Mexico City. Besides that, at the time of the First Caper the Industrial Revolution had begun to create

personal fortunes looking for places to exchange their
money. Secrecy was important, of course, as any owner
who has paid up to a half-million dollars for a piece will
testify. And because of that investment, even *their* heirs
are silent today. I know of a number of those pieces right
here in town. The grandsons and granddaughters of the
original owners think they share a very special secret with
me, but they don't know that there's a secret behind the
secret! Cecil sold virtually everything and made an absolute *fortune!* The only pieces left of the entire treasure are
what you see in my living room gallery, which we've kept
in the family as part of our private collection. The other old
mummy is out there. I know it's in terrible condition but
you must understand the sentimental value. Oh, and we
have this ankh, which he had framed."

I hadn't noticed it before. It was on the wall behind a
frame. Probably the same one used for the portrait I'd
seen.

"It was a great delight for me a few years ago," François
continued with a smile and a wink, "when the Tut treasure
was in town on tour, to go and have a look at Grandpapa's
work."

"Incredible," was all I could say. I didn't know if I could
believe him or not. But then recently I'd learned that
anything was believable.

"Yes, isn't it?" François agreed enthusiastically, enjoying
the telling of it. But then his face clouded up. "Then the
problems began. A great deal of money was made—millions. We moved to Zurich, which was at the heart then, as
now, of the antiquities business in Switzerland. The archaeologists began to demand more money or they would
'drop the vase,' so to speak. First one, then another tried to
blackmail him, and in fairness I suspect Grandpapa Cecil
didn't pay them enough, which was a mistake I tried to
avoid. In any case Grandpapa, being a stubborn man, refused. There were arguments, fights and threats. Then, I'm
afraid, Grandpapa took drastic action. If it came out that it
had all been a hoax, Grandpapa would, of course, have
been ruined, and the family name destroyed. He probably
felt he had no choice . . . ."

François took a long moment to light a fresh cigarette

and stare out the window at the light that was just starting to wane.

"Well? What did he do?"

"He began to have the troublemakers eliminated."

"*Kill* them?"

"*Oui*— I'm afraid so," he replied sadly, swirling the champagne around in his glass until it began to sizzle.

"Are you telling me that's the origin of the King Tut *Curse?*"

François nodded.

"*Oui*. Just about everyone connected with the dig died an unexpected and untimely death. I'm afraid that was because of Grandpapa. Like his men, he fell to greed. As much as he had, he wouldn't give up a little more. I suppose he felt that because the collection was his, and there was a great deal of expense and risk in the setup, he deserved the majority percentage. But he wasn't a good businessman, obviously—he said so himself. In any good business deal all parties have to be satisfied. Ironically enough, he himself was to die in the same sort of mysterious circumstances that he created for the others—a plane crash, while on a visit to the Roman ruins at Baalbek in Lebanon in '38. He was only fifty-four."

"It's a hell of a story, François. Utterly incredible. But when do we get to the Buddha Head?"

"Please be patient. It's a long story."

He took another drag of his cigarette and blew the smoke out thoughtfully into the air, where it hung like a mist among the other clouds. He set it down and went on.

"Papa naturally took over Grandpapa's antiquities business. By this time we were very well-established in Zurich, for Grandpapa had used the huge profits to invest heavily in all manner of objets. Papa was only in his mid-twenties then. I was only three years old or so. Papa showed a good deal of genius as well, and was the key figure in plotting out and executing the second great art hoax. The Second Caper."

He stopped for a sip and to light yet another cigarette. The first one still rested in the ashtray.

"Most people smoke one at a time," I said drolly, waving the clouds away.

He flushed and butted it, but quickly recovered. I looked

away and fixed my eyes on the Iron Cross beside his father's hand in the portrait. François cleared his throat, then continued.

"By this time our name was extremely prominent across Europe in the antiquities business, if I may be so immodest in saying so. But it is just a fact. One of Papa's and Grandpapa's regular customers before Cecil died was Hermann Goering, who had a great interest in art. He and my grandpapa got on extremely well, since they shared so many common interests. When Grandpapa was killed we received a handwritten letter of condolence and a wreath from the field marshal. His association with my papa continued to the end of the war, and on a number of occasions we were guests at his various estates in Germany. His favorite was Carinhall. It was built like a Scandinavian hunting lodge, and named in memory of his first wife, who was Swedish. I particularly liked going there. He used to dress so strangely—in togas and that sort of thing—quite outrageously, and he was very jovial. He also kept his own private zoo there and being a boy, of course I loved animals. It was on one of those visits there that that picture was taken." François motioned to the group photo with lion.

I took a long sip. This was getting interesting.

"Wolfgang had been an air ace, which you've probably read. Goering was an ace himself, of course—during the Great War he shot down twenty-two planes and commanded Baron Von Richthofen's Flying Circus after the Red Baron was killed. Among many of Goering's medals was the Iron Cross First Class."

I glanced again at the portrait of his father.

"That accounts for the medal in the second portrait?" François nodded.

"Yes. And that's the Wolfgang connection as well—he received it as well. And they both had an important part to play in the Second Caper."

"It obviously has something to do with all of this," I said, my hand sweeping over the masterworks on the walls.

"Obviously. Like the ones you saw at Wolfgang's, these are part of Goering's personal collection—his favorites that he kept in Carinhall. Many of these paintings you see here," François went on, in a low voice tinged with rever-

ence, "I saw as a child at Goering's. They're very close to
me. He loved art . . . But I was telling you about Wolfgang. His family were the leading dealers in art and antiquities in Berlin so, of course, my family had connections
with theirs, and Goering knew us all. When Wolfgang was
wounded, it was natural for Goering to give him a job as a
collector." François avoided my eyes as he hastily lit another cigarette. I snuck another sip of champagne.

"Naturally, Wolfgang had a good grounding in art and
antiquities because of his background, and in the next few
years helped build up the largest private collection of art
the world has ever seen!" François made a flourish with his
hand. "While on his travels, Wolfgang developed a special
interest in Far Eastern antiquities. This interest eventually
resulted in his moving to the Orient. Do you want another
glass of champagne? *S'il vous plaît*, help yourself. Drink all
you want. You deserve it."

François rose and set up an ice bucket with the champagne beside us. As inconspicuously as I could, I poured
another draught, topping his up at the same time.

"Goering had always been particularly fond of Wolfgang. When it was obvious the end was near, Goering
struck a deal with us to ensure us all a fortune—he of
course knew that everything he owned would be seized.
For some reason he had some incredible idea that the
Allies would let him go, and he wanted to salvage the best
of his collection for that eventuality. The plan was this:
because of our position in Switzerland, a neutral country,
we had access to the Soviets through their embassy.
Through these links, Papa made openings to the Russians,
negotiating a small deal. Stalin knew about Goering's art
treasures, of course. We offered him half the core of Goering's personal collection from Carinhall, provided he
would guarantee safe passage and transportation of the
other half along with Wolfgang to Switzerland. Half of this
was to be Goering's, with the rest split between Wolfgang
and Papa. Initially Stalin wasn't interested, for he thought
he could capture it all intact, but when he learned through
his intelligence service that Goering was going so far as to
requisition much-needed train cars and trucks to ship it to
the West, he quickly relented and arrangements were
made. Four trucks with the core of the collection, the

crème de la crème, were diverted from their original route between Carin and Berchtesgaden, to a prearranged point in Berlin, where they safely passed behind Russian lines. Wolfgang had to do this himself. You must remember that Berlin was going up in flames and was under constant artillery bombardment. Russian tanks were rolling through the suburbs. Fighting was from house to house. *Mon Dieu,* Wolfgang, with his one arm, was shuttling back and forth through the apocalypse to drive first one, then two, then all four trucks safely through to where he met my papa. Then the two of them drove to Switzerland, each with a truck."

"And Stalin actually kept his end of the deal?"

"Amazingly enough Juggling Joe did—that's what Papa used to call him around the house. It was partly because Papa kept him on the line with tentative promises of more treasures he would not otherwise have been able to grab. Over the next few years we were able to quietly sell off a good amount of the collection, to all the eager and extremely wealthy hands standing by to snatch them up. Many of the buyers were of the same families who still possessed pieces from the King Tut treasure. Wolfgang and my family made millions, and still were able to keep our favorites. Even Goering did his part, we learned later, by showing acute disappointment when the news came to him that the trucks had gotten lost—but that was just window dressing. He was a good actor, and always cunning. He even had the forethought to destroy all traces of Wolfgang's records, so the Allies would be unable to connect Wolfgang to him."

"I have to admit it's very interesting, François, and a little more believable than the King Tut stuff. But I'm surprised at how warmly you speak about the man—especially after what the Nazis did to the Jews."

"It's not surprising at all. He was a family friend. What he did at work didn't enter the parlor conversation. My father and he were friends sharing the same strong interest, a common bond—art. Papa disagreed strongly with Hitler's Jewish policies, as of course I did once I grew up and learned about them. *Mon dieu!* Many of my father's friends in the art and antiquities business were Jewish, particularly in Holland. Few of them survived. But Goering's attitude was rather pragmatic. He was quite indifferent to Jews except when it came to following official policy, though there he always did take care of business, so to speak. His wife, Emma, intervened a number of times to have Goering spring her old Jewish friends from her theater days from one jail or another. And privately, he told Wolfgang and his other collectors to ignore the background of the art dealers they worked with."

"Sounds like a real angel."

"There's good in the worst of us, bad in the best." François shrugged, reaching to replenish our glasses. "He kept his bargain to the end, literally—he said nothing. When he cheated the gallows by taking cyanide in '46, his share of the collection reverted to us. And that was the end of the Second Caper."

"So after the war, Wolfgang moved to the Far East."

"Correct. And *we* moved to New York. It was one thing to do business with Germans or have good friends among them, but another thing entirely to live with them—it was intolerable because of our background, and Zurich was German, so unlike Geneva, with its French atmosphere. Papa was only too glad to move when it became apparent that the new capital of the business was going to be here in 'La Grande Pomme,' as he called it. He had to be at the center of the action. Wolfgang as well had nothing left in Germany. All his family except for his half-brother Kurt were killed in the Battle of Berlin, and the family home and business were destroyed. Also he had been appalled when he learned of what happened in the concentration camps. Wolfgang stayed in seclusion with us for over a year. He didn't come out of hiding with us until after the Nuremberg trials. He managed to sneak in a couple of messages to Goering though his wife, Emmy, to let him know we had been successful. His old mentor responded with the advice to escape with his treasure to Buenos Aires, where Perón would certainly have accepted him in return for a painting or two. But Wolfgang couldn't stomach being anywhere near those war criminals—the revelations at the trial had appalled him. He was an intelligent, cultured man, and the so-called civilization that had borne him now disgusted him. In any case, he hadn't been named as a criminal, and besides that, no one was looking for him,

because of the cover up about his position with Goering.
All of which meant he had nothing to fear in the way of
prosecution. Partly out of his strong interest in Far Eastern
culture, and partly because he wanted to get away from
Germany completely, he came to the Orient. He looked
around and chose Bangkok as a base, because it's at the
center of the action, and because Thailand was the country
least touched by Western influence. As you well know, it's
the only country in the region that was never colonized."

"If he was so anti-Nazi, how could he put up with Kurt?"

"You have met him, *non?* Kurt is a half-wit, as dumb as
Wolfgang was smart. He didn't even have the brains to be
accepted by the army—during the war he worked as a
janitor. But he always idolized Wolfgang. Not only was
Wolfgang a genuine war hero, but he had such connections! Kurt apparently always had this fantasy about being
in the SS. Wolfgang brought him over to Bangkok from
Brussels in the fifties and later set him up in a bar. Wolfgang told me on numerous occasions that he had to feed
money into the place continually to keep it afloat, because
Kurt was such an awful businessman. But he didn't seem to
mind, as long as it made Kurt happy. Wolfgang had a special affection for Kurt, probably because he was his only
living kin."

"But why did Wolfgang bother doing the journalistic
career if he was so well-set? The rich don't usually write for
rags."

François took another sip before continuing. I joined
him.

"Many reasons, really. Remember he was still a young
man, in his mid-twenties. He was a man of action. He had
enjoyed the thrill of war, the dogfights. He also had a secret
passion for writing, which he expressed in journalism. The
Far East was an exciting place just after the war, with all
the European empires being dismembered. Bullets were
flying steadily, as they still do. Journalism gave him a cover
to go into restricted areas, often war zones, where many of
the old civilizations lay in jungle-covered ruins. He invariably came back out with incredible pieces for me—at the
time there was much, much less problem with Cultural
Properties restrictions that there is now. Despite this,
Wolfgang always kept his profile quite low in the antiqui-

ties business, as he did in most of his other ventures. Rarely would you learn the depth of his involvement in anything. He loved the antiquities business particularly, but thought he should keep it at elbow's length because of the Goering art caper. The pieces he did smuggle he marketed through Papa and then, after Papa was, ah, killed, through me, Although he did take a deeper interest in Tantric Buddhism, and spent much time collecting in the Himalaya. But in that case, the pieces he collected were more legitimate, and he sold them on the street. At least, he did until we started on the Third Caper."

His face took a downturn for a moment and he butted his long-ashed cigarette, which he had hardly taken a drag from.

"Before I tell you about the Head they're filing by at the American, if it isn't too late in the afternoon, let me tell you about the *real* Buddha Head—or whatever it is. Wolfgang had found it while covering the factional fighting in the north of Burma. The country had been devastated by the war with the Japanese—it was incredible the fighting that had gone on there. Chennault's Flying Tigers shot down as many as 1,400 Jap planes. Merrill's Marauders fought five major and around thirty smaller conflicts, with only 436 of the original 2,830 men surviving. Vinegar Joe Stilwell retreated 182 kilometers through the jungle without losing a man. Planes flying 'the hump' of the Himalaya to supply the Chinese lost a thousand men." François rattled the numbers off matter-of-factly. "After the war the country was torn apart, with no one really there to stitch it together. The British were licking their wounds and wanting to unload their Empire, and the result was a great deal of infighting between the various factions, Karen and Shan being the major two. Independence was declared in April 1947, when Aung San was elected Burma's leader, but only two months later he was assassinated and the new nation began to crumble. After Mao took China in 1949, some of the KMT generals under Chiang Kai-shek began to take refuge in northern Burma, and started getting involved in controlling the opium trade routes—and making the drug available in Rangoon, much to the shaky government's chagrin. The KMT were well-supplied with American guns through Taiwan, and began fighting the Burmese as well as the Reds. The country was in chaos, and the calm there even today is highly deceptive. There's still no real border to that country as you know."

I shifted uncomfortably in my chair. François was launching into another of his history lessons.

"You were saying something about Wolfgang and the Buddha Head . . . ?"

"Sorry," François said. "To the point: In 1955, Wolfgang was with the Shan in the jungle of northern Burma, doing a story on the factional fighting up there. That's when he first met Kun San, who was a rising young leader. While accompanying the Shan on one excursion against the Burmese, they were caught in an ambush. The Shan were shot to pieces, and Wolfgang was forced to take refuge in a small cave he stumbled on. To keep from being discovered he had to crawl far back into it, which he wasn't too eager to do, because of the snakes and other things that go chomp in the dark. But he had no choice—it was either that or be taken prisoner by the Burmese. Although he was merely a journalist, his chances of survival were questionable, since he was a guest of the wrong side."

François leaned forward conspiratorially. I set my glass down and got ready to pay acute attention. It was finally warming up in the room.

"It's a good thing he made that decision," François continued, "because way back in the cave he made an amazing discovery. It was in a small alcove he had squeezed into while a soldier was probing at the entrance. When he pressed his one hand into the corner, the cave wall suddenly crumbled—his hand went right through." François imitated the movement while he spoke. "It scared him more than anything at the time because the sound brought the soldier inside. But Wolfgang always had an imagination. He made a sound like a tiger and the soldier quickly retreated."

I nodded now with deep interest as François went on, his voice slowing, becoming deeper and more resonant. He let his most recent cigarette burn out.

"*Alors!* Upon investigating, Wolfgang discovered that behind this crumbling false wall was a smaller alcove, and in it a foot-square box covered in the mold, spider webs and slime of centuries. After dragging it out and wiping it

off, he saw that it was made of pure gold! It was well-sealed
and he didn't have the proper tools to open it, but he knew
that he had chanced on something amazing. None of the
patrol he'd come with had survived, so he was completely
alone. In what he later described as one of the two most
harrowing adventures of his life, he spent ten days making
his way back down jungle trails, slipping into the foliage
when he heard anyone approaching, until he made his way
back across the Thai border. You must remember that this
is a man with one arm, with only the food in his pack to
sustain him besides what he could scrounge off the land.
Once back in Thailand, he smuggled the box down to his
mansion in Bangkok, where he proceeded to open it. It
was, as I say, well-sealed. The craftsmanship of the box was
excellent, possibly of the same hand that did the incredible
work inside. For inside was—"

"The Buddha Head—"

"*Yes. If* that indeed is what it was! We've never been able to
know for sure! There was no inscription at all on the
box!"

"What happened to that box?" I interrupted, recalling
something of the kind in Wolfgang's study.

"The last time I saw it he was using it to grow a bonsai,"
François laughed. "Wolfgang immediately requested that
papa and I come to Bangkok, and we did—that was still in
the days when I flew. It was certainly intriguing. We *did*
run a carbon dating on some skull material."

I nodded in surprise, picturing the missing wedge from
inside the skull.

"To our delight it came out right on the money—2,500
years! And there was the protuberance of the cranium! It
was too much to be coincidental, *but . . . there . . . was
. . . no . . . proof!*" François jabbed a long finger in the
air with each word. "What, we asked ourselves, was it
doing walled up in a cave in the jungle? My papa, Wolfgang
and I sat up many a late night, pulling our hair, or I should
say Papa and I did—Wolfgang was already going prematurely bald. And we made some educated guesses, based
primarily on another carbon dating, that brought us to a
shared conclusion."

"My God. I don't believe what I'm hearing . . ."

"*Do.* Because it's true. We looked into Burmese history

for clues, and we found them. After a couple of initial minor cultures, the Mons and Pyu, the Burmese came in the second century A.D. They expanded rapidly, and built a great capital with enormous stone buildings at Pagan. The Burmese kingdom was already well-established by the time Kublai Khan sent his emissaries there. His own empire had begun its huge expansion by then, and the rulers in Pagan were perhaps getting a little too arrogant in their thousand-year-rule—or perhaps they simply didn't know just how powerful the Khan was. For when these emissaries refused to remove their shoes before the Burmese king, they were beheaded. That upset the Khan considerably, needless to say, and in 1287 he descended on the capital with his army. With one swat of his Mongolian hand he reduced the Burmese to a small enclave between two much larger factions, who quickly moved into the vacuum, as the Khan didn't stay any longer than was necessary to reap vengeance. The Mons took over the south, from their capital of Pegu near Rangoon; and the Shan, significantly enough, the center, from Ava near Mandalay. Pagan was abandoned. No one has lived there since, except for the few who take care of the modern-day tourist industry. Later the Burmese expanded again, of course; you can see that the country's factional warfare dates right back to the very roots of the nation. It was this situation that led to Wolfgang's amazing discovery. The significant date in our discussion is 1287—the date Kublai Khan bashed the Burmese. We are as sure as one can be from the circumstantial evidence that whoever placed that golden box in the cave was almost certainly fleeing the onslaught of the Khan's forces at Pagan! The cave was only fifty miles away!"

He paused to pour us more Dom and to light yet another Gauloise. He was taking his time now. I was now thoroughly intrigued.

"How did you tie in that date? By a coin in the box or something else?"

"No, not a coin. But there was well-preserved wood inside the box. It formed the frame that kept the Head still. We carboned *that!* Again, the date was right on the money."

"The Khan's year—1287?"

"About a century before, give or take fifty years. Close

enough. It seems whoever placed it there—it was probably a priest—did so with the intention of returning, but was probably killed or met with an accident before he—or they —could. It's happened before, the Dead Sea Scrolls being the obvious example. When we put our heads together over this, we came to some other circumstantial conclusions. Burma then, as now, is one of the most *firmly* Buddhist nations in the world, and it's also Hinayana, which is the more fundamentalist of the two branches of Buddhism. Was this just coincidence? Or was it because they had this special relic, even for a short period? Its existence was almost certainly *not* publicly known at the time, for the Pagan kings ruled in turbulent times, and despite the arrogance and over confidence that led to their destruction, they would have known that it was best to keep such a prize a secret. It probably was kept *very* quiet. None the less, its effect on the leaders of Buddhism was probably such that it inspired a great devotion in them. And these inspired leaders in turn would have inspired the followers. Buddhism grew so strong that later it almost strangled the economy of that nation, because so many men became monks, so few farmers. You just have to observe the thousands of little white *stupas* as you approach Mandalay to realize just how great an effect it had."

"But how would it have gotten to Pagan in the first place?"

"This was the time Buddhism was being pushed out of its prominent position in India, remember? Obviously someone secreted it from the Great Stupa at Sanchi, but instead of it going to the Himalaya, it must have come here! Otherwise, everything else about the probable route I described to you before remains the same! What do you think?"

I took a sip of champagne, my lips hovering at the glass's rim as I gropped with what he was saying.

"So it *could* be real . . ."

"*Oui.* I'm personally convinced, but there is . . . no . . . real . . . way . . . of knowing categorically."

"And I got all this bullshit from you about doing something good for mankind—"

"What *could* we do with it? With what we *suspected* but didn't really know? And that's *all* we really had, wasn't it? Tantalizing *suspicions,* and *circumstantial* proof. What would have happened had we brought it then to the attention of the world? What more could it have been than an immense curiosity? We would gain nothing and would most certainly have lost it. There's no doubt that had we told the world about Wolfgang finding it on Burmese soil, and our suspicions of it coming from Pagan, that the Burmese government would have surely demanded its return. If there had been written records—or *anything* about the possible existence of the Head beyond the hint about the Hedda Head that historically existed in Afghanistan—it would have been a different story. If it was unquestionably the Buddha Head we would have unquestionably presented it to the world. And why not? We would have gone down in the history books! That would have been reward enough! Certainly Wolfgang would have! But all there was was that nagging, persistent Rumor, which we chose to help along. There were many long discussions."

He removed his smoking jacket, undid his collar and top button, and leaned back.

"I can't say whose idea it was, Papa's or Wolfgang's, but the focus of the discussions just naturally began to shift; it was rather natural for them to begin thinking along the same lines as they'd developed during their excitement with the Goering collection. As you know, a extremely high percentage of antiquity dealing is black market at one stage or another. It's all part of the business and you, Lee Rivers, are extremely adept at it—the best there is, no doubt. So don't be too self-righteous." He smiled coyly as he said that. "We *all* think in these terms. And of course I might remind you you were willing to trade it yourself at one point."

"Well, at least I was considering to do a trade for love and not money," I said weakly, the thought of Tysee still nagging at me. "Though I sure the hell was promoted in the media in every other way."

"Ah! *Promotion!*" he exclaimed, seizing the word by the balls. "That is the *key* word. As you very well know again, promoting an item enhances its value greatly. Both of us have taken inexpensive pieces of some unusual item—take that wooden cobra head, that *naga* you bought in Sri Lanka that time." His eyes were shining now. "I know you paid about five dollars for it, to that Devil Dance cult of yours. I remember following you on that one, how you invested about 300 dollars to bring the colors up out of the patina, how you had it mounted, then wrote it up in a number of anthropological reviews, promoting its importance and rarity. That was very, very good. It took about two years, as I recall, but you created enough interest in that piece that when you eventually put it on the market, it was snapped up for—was it 2,500 dollars?"

"Your memory, as always, is infallible," I said, not without some pride in my success. *"But,* I might remind you—it was all *true.* It was a rare and little-known piece."

"No argument. But we're talking *promotion!* Like Grandpapa with his King Tut coup, Papa and Wolfgang knew it was just a matter of promotion. They knew that the only place where there's more politics involved than in art is Washington. Take Van Gogh's *Irises,* which sold for almost sixty million. What is so special about it, really? There's far, far more interesting paintings of equal and superior quality, even among his own works. In his own lifetime he only managed to sell one work for about seventy dollars. But a huge hype has grown around him. The same with diamonds—they're possibly the most boring of gems and not even the most valuable, but they've been promoted to the top of the heap. Look at Coca-Cola, certainly an acquired taste. *Promotion."*

"So, tell me about this promotion."

"Whenever they got together, and Papa and I used to travel to Bangkok a lot in those days because of the antiquities business, he and Wolfgang would talk, throw around ideas how they could do a caper to match the previous two. You must remember, of course, that both of them were wealthy and had no interest in playing the game, except for the sheer pleasure of it. They had time on their side, or so they thought. They decided that whatever they did would have to be a classic."

François cleared his throat, then continued.

"Their discussion always seemed to come back to the Cultural Properties problem. Whatever they did, they knew the country of 'origin'—in other words whatever country they planted it in—would certainly demand it back, and in this case would certainly get the piece back. Any western host government would see to that; after all, this was not merely the Elgin Marbles, which Greece has been nagging to get back for decades. That's when they decided that whatever they did, it would have to involve a switch."

I sat spellbound. Sweat was beginning to form on François's flushed forehead. It was still a little cool in the room but getting allowable.

"It was while they were still having a great deal of fun deciding what to do, that the Chinese invaded Tibet in 1959 to put down the revolt. They followed the events closely looking for a possible move, since it was one of the most staunchly Buddhist countries in the world. I remember being at Wolfgang's mansion listening to the six o'clock news on the shortwave radio when it was announced that the Dalai Lama had fled. *Mon Dieu!* I remember as if it were yesterday, how the two of them turned their heads and stared at each other. They didn't even have to say what they were going to do—they both *knew*. It was handed to them like a gift. They cheered and danced and broke into the champagne. It was the only time in my life I ever got a little tipsy, and saw Papa lose control." François's eyes sparkled as he recalled it.

He raised his glass of champagne, winked, and took a sip.

"And Wolfgang took it up there!"

"Right! They just had to work out the details. Wolfgang had studied the Tibetan language for some time—a result of his fascination with Tantric Buddhism. They spent the rest of the evening deciding exactly how they would take advantage of the situation. They knew about the Austrians Peter Aufschnaiter and Heinrich Harrer, particularly from the latter's book about the experience. Both were famous in Tibet. From the pictures, Wolfgang was about the same size as either of them. Perhaps a little larger. It was perfect. By the end of the evening they had decided what they were going to do." François gesticulated with all the flair of his European background. "Suddenly it was no longer parlor talk."

EIGHTEEN

Ahead of the Game

FRANÇOIS POPPED THE cork off another bottle of champagne.

"You talk like you weren't a part of it. You keep saying 'they.' "

"Oh, I *certainly* was part of it!" he began to explain. "But you must remember that I was a junior member. I was only in my mid-twenties in 1959, while Papa was in his mid-forties and Wolfgang in his late thirties. It was *my* idea to use Tengboche Monastery, which I had seen in pictures, as I too was developing an interest in Tantric Buddhism. I was integral, particularly since Papa knew that this was a long-term promotion. It was more for me than him—he had already had his fun with Goering. If only he had lived to see it to the end," he added, looking pained.

"How *did* your father die?" I asked, cushioning my curiosity with sympathy.

The air suddenly went out of François.

"Like his papa before him . . . a plane crash in 1967. His Beechcraft had developed engine trouble on a flight to the Yucatán and came down in the jungle. It seems like there very well *might* be a King Tut curse. Both my grand-papa and my papa died in planes and both at the same age —fifty-four. I haven't been in one since," he added, a little shakily, "and I'm fifty-three."

He methodically lit another cigarette, took a deep drag, and looked out at the snow. After a couple of minutes my embarrassed cough shook him back to the story.

"We forged various letters to meet all needs. The Dalai Lama's seal was in a book, and easy enough to duplicate. Wolfgang was a well-known figure in Kathmandu and had been bribing customs regularly since the early fifties, so the airport was a walk—not like today. Because the Dalai Lama escaped dressed as a soldier, Wolfgang purchased a soldier's outfit from a Tibetan deserter and had it modified to fit him. The trip almost did him in. Not only did he develop gastroenteritis on the nearly three-week trek to Tengboche, but he almost perished crossing the Tesi Lapcha La. Perhaps you know it—it's 18,885 feet high, it leads south to what was at the time the temporary refugee camp at Thami. He even lost his sleeping bag. He de-scribed the journey as his second most harrowing adven-ture, and swore the Head would someday kill him. Sadly, he was right." François's voice was growing lower. "The old Abbot Lobsang and his then head monk, Tengid, swal-lowed the story head, line and sinker. Wolfgang didn't even have to lie and say he was Aufschnaiter or Harrer— they took it for granted he was one or the other, they didn't even question his wearing a balaclava, they just assumed he wanted to be seen as little as possible. He never knew that his false arm had been spotted. I only learned about it from reading it in the papers. It's a good thing that it didn't come out any sooner—it would have aborted us from the beginning."

"That damned Wolfgang. All these years . . ." I stroked my new beard. Admiration for him seeped into my voice.

"Then we 'put the wine to age' as Papa called it—the end of Stage One. But at the same time we began to subtly enhance the tiny Rumor about the possible existence of the Head. Wolfgang was brilliant at this. Being a writer, he had a number of small articles published under assumed names discussing this possibility, some of them based on the so-called tablet finds of a field archaeologist. Well, you can guess who the archaeologist was! They watered the Rumor, and it grew. Papa was always a great party-giver and after his . . . demise . . . I continued the tradition, for I enjoyed them as much as he did. Whenever one of the articles was discovered at one it would just take a word or two to fan the flames, so to speak."

"What about the duplicate head?" I asked with growing disbelief.

"The physical anthropologists were right on the money when they said it was of Malay stock. Wolfgang had found it in one of the burial caves near Sagada in Luzon. The Filipinos are descended from the Malays. It was Benguet-Igorot, and similar to any of the hundreds you find stacked in those caves, except for an unusual protuberance in the top, which is what had attracted his attention to it years before."

"And sitting in a cave for 500 years, it's expected to be weathered and have a good bit of pollen embedded in it?"

"*Oui.* We hired an old master goldsmith in Hong Kong whom Wolfgang knew to do the goldwork. That was back when it was only 35 dollars an ounce, if you can imagine. The gems weren't set in the eyes until much later, of course. Gems that size aren't easy to come by. These turned up when Wolfgang was offered King Thibaw and Queen Supyalat's collection. His contacts in the field obviously were still good. He funneled the jewelry through you to me and I sold the entire collection—minus the heavy broaches, as you have so observantly noticed from the cover of *Time!* We had the same old gentleman in Hong Kong fly to Bangkok again to fit them, and had him specially prepare rather old-fashioned solders by traditional methods. We didn't want it to look like it came out of Tiffany's either. He was well-paid and loyal to Wolfgang and, best of all, old, which is one reason we chose him. He was eighty-seven when he passed on five years ago, which is longer than we expected him to live."

"Why did you get me involved in this a couple of months ago? Why didn't you handle it yourself?"

François glanced at me twice, both times quickly averting his eyes. I couldn't figure out why.

"Actually, for one thing you have been a part of the plan

considerably longer than two months," he said quietly, sneaking a third embarrassed glance at me as he nervously lit another cigarette. "It's hard to tell this to a friend, you see."

"What do you mean?" I asked suspiciously.

"Don't get angry. It *had* to be done this way and you'll agree when I finally finish this story. You see . . . you have been a part of it for over ten years."

"What!"

"It was partially because Grandpapa and Papa both had died in plane crashes. I had developed that phobia that no psychiatrist could rid me of. I kept thinking of that King Tut Curse. I'm not afraid of heights—not a bit—just airplanes. The mere mention makes me shiver like you are still doing now. They seem to give off . . . off horrible feelings, like they're living, evil things." He laughed nervously. "Perhaps I should have one of those Devil Dance exorcisms of yours."

He drained his glass and collected himself.

"It was obvious that whoever handled the final operation would have to be agile and very mobile. And it was true—when Abbot Tengid phoned me, as I expected he would after the robbery, I couldn't go personally to see him. That is, I *could* have, but it would have taken months by ship! You see, we were just about ready to put Stage Two into effect when Papa died. That threw the schedule *completely* out of whack."

"And obviously the Wolf couldn't go—"

"That's right. He had to play a supporting role after his initial active effort. So we began scouting around for someone suitable to, ah, take in. I mean take in as a partner, of course, even if he wasn't to know what was happening. It took a number of frustrating years but one day Wolfgang brought your name to my attention."

I was beginning to feel very uncomfortable.

"It was in the mid-seventies. You were starting to hang around The Lion's Den, and beginning to establish yourself in the business. Of course Wolfgang heard in the normal talk and flow of things about your Sri Lankan Devil Dance collection—that first big one you sold to London. Following on that your luck grew, and you picked up that contract from the Smithsonian. Well, I know both curators,

Dr. Marvin of the Museum of Man in London and Dr. Weenk of the Museum of Natural History in Washington. I gave them calls. They both were, I was happy to hear, even *more* than pleased with your acquisitions, particularly your documentation, which is always the Achilles' heel of all museums. You were young, bright, strong, in good health and adventurous. We had finally found our man! And none too late—we were worrying that it was a lost cause and were trying to think of alternative plans."

I stared at him speechlessly.

"Of course suitable candidates, if you will, weren't exactly abundant. This is a highly esoteric business. The only other person we gave any half-serious consideration to was Richard Haimes-Sandwich, who was starting out at about the same time as you. And we considered him only because of his growing knowledge and reputation in the field. He had a very talented, if myopic, eye. But we couldn't use a man with the eyesight and agility of a baby elephant, rest his soul. You, on the other hand, fit the bill perfectly. You even lived in Bangkok, where it was easy for Wolfgang to monitor your activities—and, to be frank, to manipulate your moves on occasion."

He said the last so softly it almost didn't bite.

"What *are* you talking about!"

"We began to cultivate you, to help your career along, to *promote* you. Now, make no mistake about it, we knew you would have developed an equal reputation on your own. There was no doubt about that, because you were and *are* very talented. You have a sharp eye and a good feel. The only thing we did was speed it up slightly with some rather spectacular finds."

In flooded the memories: of the trip to Kwan Mae with Wolfgang; of the marketing of the Burmese royal jewels; of the many lucrative smaller tips, for which I had paid Wolfgang his usual twenty percent commission; of the spontaneous meeting with François in New York, and our subsequent relationship; of my collecting trip to the Everest region, when he had given me a hello note to pass on to the abbot so I would meet him; and of the parties that always seemed to materialize whenever I was visiting him in New York. All so my reputation could grow. Anger mixed with my helpless frustration—a volatile mixture.

"I don't believe it," I said hollowly. Underneath I knew it could only be true.

"I'd say choosing you was the best thing we did. Now we were able to go back to enjoying the game. Time was suddenly no longer a threat. It took a dozen years to make you the best-known, most respected collector of primitive art and antiquities in the East—a star of sorts. We both enjoyed thoroughly the process of helping you along, and please believe me that we didn't laugh at you or anything. Both of us considered you a very good friend. I still do—indeed, my best friend now that Wolfgang . . . is gone. We have been through a great deal together, and you have my respect and admiration for pulling it all off so well when everything grew so out of control."

I took a sip of champagne, emptying the glass. The revelations flowing from François's elegant lips were stunning me into silence. He reached forward and poured me a refill.

"And of course, we promoted the package. I had spent considerable time cultivating Abbot Tengid's friendship, by frequent visits for Mani Rimdu—which was a problem getting to, of course. There I made a point of discussing the problem of antiquity thefts, and made sure he was thoroughly familiar with my position in the business. I was always adamant with him that I firmly believed that any and all stolen pieces should be returned and made a point of having a good number of those—including some that are quite priceless, I might add—returned to monasteries around Nepal. I didn't tell him about these Boy Scout deeds—I knew word of mouth would eventually spread, and that it's always far more effective to have others toot your trumpet. Like Ed Hillary and Aufschnaiter, the latter who took out citizenship, I became a friend of Nepal's, though I was careful to keep my profile rather low. There was no doubt in my mind at all that if there was a robbery or loss of any important kind, the abbot would contact me. I was convinced of this more than ever when he did just that three years ago. A trekker had made off with an ancient stone Buddha, and the old man called me. It took eight months to trace, after I put the word out to all the antiquity shops in the world to watch for the piece, that I wanted it. Luckily enough it found its way to a shop in

Rome. I bought it for no small expense and returned it. But then the cost was just all part of the investment. Abbot Tengid was ineffably grateful."

I looked at the fresh glass of champagne and decided not to drink anymore. Then promptly took another sip.

"At the same time, Wolfgang was working with Kun San, setting him up to do the robbery. That was your introduction to Kwan Mae."

And Tysee.

"Naturally, Kun San was in the sort of business that was amenable to this type of operation. Wolfgang had known for years that he was something of a lapsed Buddhist. Wolfgang offered him fifteen percent for what was, for him, quite a simple affair—the use of his plane and a couple of his men, a journey to Tengboche, followed by a drugging and a simple burglary. He wasn't told much—only what to steal and where to find it."

François sat back and took a thoughtful sip of his Dom Pérignon. After swirling the remaining bubbly around, he set down his glass and continued in a quiet, gentle voice, knowing that what I was hearing was hard on the ears.

"His men were to leave some clues for you, so you could track them down. Wolfgang said Kun San ordered one of his men to leave his gold talisman behind, to pretend to lose it. It would be easily identifiable as well as most convincing. Apparently this didn't make the man any too happy, but he agreed."

I reached into my pocket, juggled through some change, and tossed one of the gold amulets on the table. It tinkled around like a coin, then lay still. His eyes lit up brightly.

"*Ah, bien!* A wonderful souvenir!" he said animatedly, picking it up and examining it for a moment before handing it back. "As a backup clue there would be lots of rice, which could be traced . . . or made to look like it could be traced to Kwan Mae. Kun San cared not a nit that he and the Shan would be blamed. He was just interested in the money."

I needed that drink. I managed to raise it to my lips. The champagne sizzled going down. I felt myself relax a little.

"We also took two other people into our confidence. One was Peter Melville, my diplomat connection in Manila. As first secretary of the embassy there, he had considerable power, and the opportunity to move around. He'd also been posted all over the Far East and knew the various cities well, so he could find you easily. And of course, he had access to the diplomatic pouch, in which he could secretly move the Head. He was a little fainthearted but he still did his job in the end. We also decided to take one other person into our confidence, purely for your benefit."

"For *my* benefit . . . Seems to me everything has been done for *my* benefit." I was getting upset again.

"No, it's true. We knew this was going to be more dangerous than we had originally expected. The Islamic rebirth had taken place in the meantime. Sikhs were fighting Hindus in India, and Hindus were fighting Buddhists in Sri Lanka. We began to get a sense of how the world might react to the reemergence of the Buddha Head. We decided you needed a guardian angel. Someone to protect you."

The second Shan soldier who'd ran up to the plane as Tysee and I were escaping from Kwan Mae. The dead Hindu and Shan in Chinatown. The Walther. The transmitter.

"Don't say it . . . Brock Stambuck . . ."

François looked surprised.

"How did you know?" he asked, sounding astonished. "Or perhaps I should ask—how *long* have you known?"

"Just a couple of days. How? I found the transmitter."

I hadn't brought the Walther. Kennedy customs is bad enough even before they see all the Thailand stamps in my passport. If I wanted another gun I could pick up a Saturday Night Special at practically any candy store in New York.

"Aaaaaah! The one in the gun he sold you! That was his idea how to keep track of you."

"Jesus—I don't believe this," I mumbled while François refilled my glass again.

I had been afraid of this. Brock had been trying to protect me and I had inadvertently sent him to his death in Saigon. The Lion was going to choke me for being responsible for the death of some of his best customers.

"With his background he was ideal. Wolfgang knew, of course, that he wasn't with the DEA but with the CIA, which was a recommendation of sorts. Wolfgang approached him. Stambuck was amenable to the idea of moonlighting, on being like a double agent, when he learned of the sums we were talking about, and we offered him a percentage of the gross. What we proposed didn't jeopardize the security of his employer, which was his primary consideration. Indeed, once the wheels were turning he was even able to act in an official capacity, coordinating between you and the American government. And he knew you from The Lion's Den, so sliding into your confidence was an easy thing for him to do."

"So he was shadowing me from the time I met Wolfgang the day I returned from the Philippines?"

"He'd actually been shadowing you before that. Even *in* the Philippines."

"You're kidding—! But that might explain something. . . .Wolfgang told me he had phoned The Statue of Libertine in Angeles City, and I've always wondered about that —the bar owner said his phone wasn't working during that entire time so he couldn't have. I see that the Wolf got his information from Brock. . . ."

François wiped the sweat off his forehead, loosened his cuffs, and rolled his sleeves up. How could I tell him that Brock was done for? And as the result of a whim of mine? How could I have missed him in the Philippines? He wasn't exactly invisible. But then he was a spook.

"We had put the plan into operation, and knowing your exact movements was important," François continued. "With the Chinese opening up Tibet to the world so rapidly, and with there even being talk of the Dalai Lama returning, we had no time to waste. Stambuck kept us informed of your movements, though your day-by-day delays were a concern. Peter Melville, of course, was in Manila. He was standing by on the edge of his vacation so he would have time to move around freely for us. By the game plan, Kun San's men were to pull off the robbery and fly back to Kwan Mae, where Wolfgang would take possession of the Head. In the meantime, I would field the expected phone call from the abbot. By that plan we had some time to play with. I would have time to phone you, to tell you about the robbery and ask you to fly to Tengboche to investigate in my place. Even if the abbot hadn't phoned, I'd have sent you to him as my emissary, to tell him that I had heard a rumor to the effect the Head had been stolen and that perhaps you could help him. I knew he would take that bait. There was no doubt we had him wrapped up. Once you were there you were to find the Shan talisman and samples of rice. When you arrived back in Bangkok you were to be greeted by Wolfgang—who would admit no connection with me. He would be back from Kwan Mae by this time with the Head, though he wouldn't tell you this. Rather, he would tell you that he had just received an urgent message from Kwan Mae regarding a very rare Buddhist piece. He would ask you to be handy. Naturally, you would be drawn into confiding with him and would bring up the amulet, which he would verify. He would also pretend to have the rice analyzed, and of course it would come from the immediate vicinity of Kwan Mae. There would be no doubt: It would seen almost certain that Kun San had the stolen Buddha Head and wanted Wolfgang to market it. Wolfgang would pretend to go up to Kwan Mae and in a few days would 'return' with the Head. Then Wolfgang was to pass the Head to you, with the normal twenty percent terms you two have had, or—"

"Now, just a minute . . . who said that I'd necessarily be interested in selling it? We have to get this straight once and for all—"

"You didn't let me finish. I was also going to add, *or* bring it back to me as per the present agreement—that is, to return it to its supposed rightful owners. There seemed some question in your mind at the time. Both Wolfgang and I at separate times probed you on your feelings in this regard, so that we would know what psychological pose to take. He played the Devil's Advocate. I played the Saint. When Wolfgang phoned me to report on your conversation at The Lion's Den he said he found you rather ambivalent, and told me about you saying you'd sell it 'to the highest bidder.' But he also figured you were probably just talking through your hat, having been influenced to some degree by his stand. He advised me to play the moral role —to insist that returning it was the proper and honorable thing to do. We had known you long enough that we figured you would lean that way with such a piece and I agreed with the strategy. But if you had been *seriously*

interested in black marketing it in your conversation with
Wolfgang, I was ready to make it look like I was prepared
to betray the abbot. Either way, you would have deliver
the Head to me."

I couldn't even find my voice to comment.

"But it wouldn't have been *quite* that simple. It would
have taken you a while to smuggle the Head to me. You'd
probably have tried the luxury liner route again, and it
would have been some time before one pulled into Pattaya
where you could climb aboard. Once you had the Head we
were going to try to get you in as much trouble as we
could, while doing our utmost to keep you from getting
caught. Walking the red hot edge of the frying pan, as
Wolfgang so eloquently put it."

"Why . . . ?"

"Promotion, of course! To stir up maximum interest in
the Buddha Head through our various channels, to fan the
flames in the media and elsewhere. *Promotion.* And that's
what we did. First of all I leaked to the papers that it was
you and Tysee who crashed the plane into Wat Arun. I
learned this from Brock."

"You *what!*"

"*Oui,* of course. Then I followed this up by placing an
anonymous one-million-baht reward for your capture,
hinting that it had something to do with one of the relics of
the Buddha. *That* did a *lot* to raise interest," he said
smugly, holding a finger in the air.

"You did that?" I gasped, halfway out of my seat.

François smiled wickedly and waved his hand dismissively.

"We had to get the wolves to the scent somehow, didn't
we? But talking about wolves, it was right at this time that
he disappeared and I had to handle everything alone."

"You *insidious* son of a—"

"Now, now, now, sit down. Relax. The entire time you
were shadowed by your 'guardian angel,' Brock Stambuck,
who fended off the worst of the trouble."

"And how long was this to go on? Until I was caught? Or
shot?"

"Oh *non non non!* Once the heat got so high that it was
obvious your time in the field was very limited, we would
have the CIA in the person of Brock Stambuck sweep you

up. He would do the switch behind your back and Peter Melville would bring in the *real* Head to me. We would then sell it for a grand amount of money. Brock Stambuck deserved a great deal of credit for walking a razor-sharp tightrope."

"And at that point I would be left to the . . . sharks . . ."

It was beginning to sink in.

"*Non*, you would *not* have been! For one thing, you would have been under official American protection. The abbot and myself would testify that you had been working to return it. Your image would have emerged sparkling clean—just as it did! You would have been seen as a hero fighting overwhelming odds and danger for a great cause. And here it was absolutely imperative that there be no question of conspiracy on your part. You would have been heavily interrogated, no doubt subjected to a lie detector test. This, more than anything, is the reason you had to be kept in the dark. Do you understand now?"

"This duplicate I would have been left with. What would stop me from noticing it was a fake? Just like I did, in fact."

"Well, we honestly thought that duplicate was so good that you wouldn't have been able to, and there we *were* wrong. But if you had noticed, while the game was on, you would have been told to keep hush and we would have explained what was really going on—as I am doing now. We had a contingency for everything—or at least we *thought* we did. Things *did* turn out differently than expected."

"Why the fake in the first place? Why not just steal it like you do paintings?"

"This was too big. We needed a decoy. We expected it would be subjected to intensive investigation. It would be found to be obviously not the true Head. The Dalai Lama would, of course, deny any involvement at all, as 'His' letters said he would. That it was a fake would be accepted; there's enough pieces of the One True Cross around to build a fence from Jerusalem to Jericho with a loop through Harlem. And, having boarded it up for over twenty-five years, I'm sure Abbot Tengid wouldn't have been intimate with the visual details of it. That would have defused any adverse reaction from Buddhists or others and put out the flames of passion at their source."

"But how would you ever convince a buyer that the one you had was genuine . . . ?"

"We had ways planned, of course. For one thing, the carbon dating would go a *long* way. I would be able to provide a great deal of very convincing background, down to revealing to the potential buyer that I learned it had been placed in Tengboche in 1959 by one of the Dalai Lama's escaping entourage. I would be open with the buyer and tell him about all the arrangements—that the robbery had been planned by myself, and the fake manufactured to neutralize the heat. I could provide full details of the fake as well—the 500-year dating, details on the gems and settings, that the skull was of Malay stock and probably female, which the physical anthropologists would find and reveal. All this would have been quite overwhelming. You must remember that I have been dealing with my clientele for some time. It wouldn't have been the first time someone had knowingly purchased a purloined piece from me."

He sat back contentedly, a Cheshire cat's smile on his lips.

"Incredible," was all I could mumble.

François's face suddenly darkened and he leaned forward.

"Unfortunately, the best-laid plans of mice and men. . . ." His voice trailed off, leaving behind what could only be described as an elegant scowl.

"What do you mean?"

"The robbery went off more or less as planned. I sat on pins and needles until the abbot phoned. Fortunately, he had been well set up and call me was practically the first thing he did. But immediately after that, everything began to unravel! He told me that a monk had been injured. I didn't know until much later how badly—not until after you had come and gone. Then he died. *Mon Dieu*, it was very upsetting," he said sincerely. "It was like I was inheriting another less savory aspect of Grandpapa's legacy. And that was just the beginning! Wolfgang was in Kwan Mae, waiting for the Head, but he never got it! Once the Head was in Kun San's possession, the disgusting man changed completely! The cunning fox! Wolfgang had unwittingly told him at one point that the Head had been originally discovered in that cave which is on *traditional Shan territory!* Kun San now claimed that in the same way that gold or diamonds or ruins discovered on *Shan* land must be *Shan* property, so too the Head was obviously and rightfully theirs, and was now only being returned to its rightful owners! That snake! *Kun San claimed it as his!* As if Shan State had a Cultural Properties Act!"

François sat back with a fatigued look on his face, and shook his head slowly.

"I was skeptical about him from the beginning, and would have preferred hiring professionals here in New York to do the break-in. The team who handled the Marmottan Museum and Mexico City job for me could have done it—they could have disguised themselves as trekkers. But Wolfgang convinced me that because the Shan were remote and powerful, there was little chance of their being eventually arrested and broken. So, what we had for all our effort and over a million dollars invested, was the Head stolen from us right at the very start! I was stunned! Wolfgang had argued with him, of course, but all that happened was that he was badly beaten and thrown off Shan land. The only reason he wasn't killed was because of their long so-called friendship."

The pieces were popping into place.

"I was frantic. We knew we had to act quickly, before he disposed of it somehow, for surely that was his intention. He was greedy—he wanted one hundred percent rather than fifteen. And the fifteen he would have received through me would have made him *richer* than the full amount he or anyone he knew could have gotten. I have the best contacts by far! Kun San was a fool." He said it with disgust, throwing his hand dismissively in the air. "Then I began to receive information from my CIA friend here, that the abbot's phone call to me had been monitored! I liked the idea of the word getting around but hadn't figured on the *Russians* being one of my clients! Suddenly this created another immediate problem: I couldn't just *telephone* you, as I had originally planned, to ask you to go up to Tengboche. No, I had to *see* you personally—and urgently—to pass the information on! It was ob-

vious they had to have your name too. But how to get you
here? Right or wrong, we decided to risk dropping some of
the pretense of remoteness between Wolfgang and myself,
because he was the only one of us who could pass such a
message to you—Stambuck's invisibility was more important to the plan than Wolfgang's. We quickly thought up a
contingency whereby I had contacted Wolfgang because
of his reputation. Stambuck reported from the Philippines
when you had confirmed your flight back to Bangkok; I
ordered him back to Bangkok at once. He arrived back just
a day before you. It was Stambuck's idea to type out a note
telling you to meet Wolfgang as soon as possible at The
Lion's Den."

"But why couldn't Wolfgang just contact me and save all
the problem?"

"Wolfgang couldn't because of his beating. He was still in
the hospital in Chiang Mai, and had to check out and fly
down just in time to meet you. It took quite an effort on his
part to act more or less normal when he met you at The
Lion's Den."

I recalled that Brock had been in The Lion's Den at the
time as well. The bastard had even asked where I had been
when he knew all along. . . .

"Yes, and I remember you weren't quite yourself either
when I arrived here in New York," I said, trying to look
ahead.

"Goodness gracious no! I was worried sick about it all!"

"So then you briefed me. . . ."

"*Oui*. And you flew to Kathmandu, after a small stop-
over in Bangkok, where you met a pretty young lady—"

I flew to my feet.

"*You mean she was a plant?*"

"*Non non non, mon ami!* Not at all! Please sit down!
Quite to the contrary! She came along completely ser-
endipitously! A godsend! She proved to be the totally unexpected key to it all! Wolfgang saw years before that she had
a bit of a crush on you and helped nurture it, I suppose, on
his occasional visits to Kwan Mae by keeping her informed
about what you were doing. As she grew older she blos-
somed into a beautiful young lady. And apparently she
never lost that adolescent's fixated romantic dream of
you."

I sat back down, my heart back in my throat, as François continued.

"She had wrangled out of Wolfgang your hangouts, where she might meet you. She wanted to surprise you. He also knew she was very much at odds with her papa. Wolfgang was going to try to talk her into taking you in after the Head, but he wanted to give you two a chance to meet naturally first. As it turned out, relief upon relief, he didn't have to do any talking. You two worked it out on your own."

"Is *nothing* in my life private? I've been living in a goldfish bowl!"

François shrugged as if to say, what could we do? Then he continued.

"And into Kwan Mae you two went, and not a minute too late—they had brought in Richard Haimes-Sandwich to sell the Head for them. Another day and it would have been gone."

"And Brock was *there* as well?"

"Yes. Otherwise you never would have made good your escape. He's a very brave and capable man, no doubt. It was a tremendous risk for him, following you in there. But he'd had a lot of jungle experience in Vietnam. And working undercover with the DEA had already brought him up into the area a great deal."

"So he's the guy who took care of the other Shan I was sure I didn't hit?"

François nodded. "He said you almost picked him off at one point."

My eyebrows rose as I recalled whipping off a shot from the plane at a large shadow that took a dive. It had to have been Brock.

"Actually, there was more than one," François said. "He said he had to shoot four of them himself, altogether. In the confusion you were blamed and he was able to fade off into the jungle."

I nodded dumbly.

"He said it was a very dangerous operation. Apparently, at one point you found yourself staked out on some bamboo shoots or something. He was hiding nearby and was about to cut you loose when Tysee San appeared. She almost caught him in the act."

I took another sloppy drink of champagne. The snake in the grass—the bamboo grass.

"Luck continued to play an important hand after that. Your flight was rather eventful, particularly the landing. You have no idea how relieved I was at receiving your call from Bangkok. With things more or less back on track, I gave you some hope to hang on to by telling you about the diplomat who wasn't quite ready. I began to relax ever so slightly at that point."

He sat back, still visibly relieved as he relived the moment.

"Once you went into hiding it was an easy matter for Stambuck to find you with his directional equipment, and to pinpoint you at that, ah, brothel in Chinatown. And to secure you from a couple of Shan and a Hindu in the vicinity. He said you had no idea how many people recognized you. At one point he had to eliminate a couple of Palestinians and, God help his soul, a Jesuit who followed from a massage parlor in Patpong carrying a cross filed to a point—none of which made it to the papers. He had been quite badly wounded himself during the incident at your house just a day previously—he'd gone there in his official capacity to warn you about the Russian transmissions, and ended up shooting it out with a Bulgarian hit squad. He managed to go on but he said he was bleeding all over the place."

"It's too bad he didn't take care of Wolfgang as well." I said sadly. It was clear why Kun San had sent his killers down, why he had taken for granted I was working at Wolfgang's behest—I was. "I saw him. The Shan really made a mess of him."

François said nothing but slowly lit another Gauloise. He sat back for a very long time drawing on it, and turned his head to watch the falling snow out the window.

"He did take care of Wolfgang . . . but not in the way you imagine," he said finally, his words low and ominous. "He was there before you that night."

I was puzzled.

"I guess he must have just missed the visit by the Shan . . . ?"

"The Shan did *not* pay Wolfgang a visit. They didn't

know where to find him. They didn't know about the secret passage and the secret house."

"What are you talking about?"

"It took me a long, long time to realize it, after he had killed so many. He had done such a brilliant, cold-blooded job, absolutely heartless, but with such precision. I never suspected when Wolfgang's body was found. You see, the Shan didn't kill Wolfgang. Oh, it's not that they wouldn't have if they could have found him. . . ." His voice trailed off, his face showing the pain of losing his friend.

"What *are* you talking about?"

"I'm talking about why Brock Stambuck murdered Wolfgang Krueger."

"*What!*"

François looked even more pained.

"Brock Stambuck murdered Wolfgang and made it look like the Shan did it. It was a perfect cover-up. I had begun suspecting him of other things and this just added to the circumstantial evidence I was gathering. Consider—Kun San's successors *denied* that they had done it while *admitting* not only that they'd sent out men for *exactly* that reason, but also that they had killed the monk, Sonot, at Tengboche. That's why I became truly suspicious—why admit to one murder and not the other? Why would they not admit to doing away with Wolfgang when they could lay that murder at Kun San's feet as well? They had already passed off everything else on him, and besides, Chung Si Fu and Kayao had obviously been willing partners in the theft—in fact, they had been *eager!* It was *very* strange. It was particularly disconcerting because the news fell right on the heels of two peculiar deaths that followed the skyjacking—both of which had connections with Stambuck."

My brain was short-circuiting. François had to be trying to pull another one over me. He read my eyes at a glance.

"Let me explain," he said sincerely. "The first tiny crack in the armor came when I learned from the news that two Sikhs had been thrown from that train after having attacked you. The next time I spoke to him, when he called me from Raffles immediately after *you* did, I brought this up: why hadn't he been protecting you? I was furious. He apologized and said that although he was on the train, he had lost a lot of blood and that he had slept the entire way. I had to accept this at the time—Wolfgang hadn't been in contact with me for a few days but I wasn't terribly worried at that point. Stambuck told me that he thought Wolfgang had gone to some private hospital or another. In hindsight, I now know Stambuck was trying to get rid of you too."

"Why the hell would Brock have wanted to kill *me?*" I asked in disbelief. But that Brock had been on the train now seemed more than possible—the blood on the floor at our compartment door must have been his. And the trail of blood in the Chinatown alley surely was.

"I think that, as far as he was concerned, the promotion had gone far enough, and was getting too risky to carry on. You had completed your role. He had no further use for you. Wolfgang was already obsolete, which is why he murdered him when he did. It appears he wanted to let the Sikhs kill you—it was a hands-off way of eliminating you. Then he would nab the Head from them somehow. Unfortunately, it didn't work out that way. Or I should say— fortunately."

"I don't believe it," I said flatly. "What would *he* do with the Head? He doesn't know the markets!"

"Why, bring it to me, I'm sure! And I would sell it! You see, when I negotiated the original deal with him it was on a share basis. The original cut was twenty percent each to the principals: you, Wolfgang and myself. Then Kun San and Stambuck fifteen percent, and Peter Melville, merely for acting as a courier, ten percent. It had been agreed that, should any of the members succumb for whatever reason—for it was a risky venture—that their shares would be divided among the survivors. It was much like the deal my papa and Wolfgang had with Goering. We were probably talking about millions of dollars for each death. Is that not enough to kill for?"

Another thought came to my mind. "I recall him asking me for the Head after the shoot-out with the Bulgarians at my house."

"He *asked* for it then?"

"Yes. He tried to convince me that it was the safest thing for the Head. He almost succeeded."

François sat back and crossed his legs. He raised a palm in the air.

"Aah . . . I think I know. He was wounded, *oui?* He probably didn't know at that point if he could carry on protecting you, and thought he had better secure it while he could. But he soon found he could carry on and changed his mind."

"I'll still need a lot of convincing. Christ, he saved my life a number of times!"

"He only gave you temporary reprieves, *mon ami.* Temporary reprieves." François looked at me sadly before continuing. "He followed you to Penang, where he watched you board the *Riquer.* You were even tracked by surveillance satellites to the Changi Yacht Club."

I said nothing, just listened intently.

"It was at that point that I considered having the Head taken from you myself, because the publicity was already to a point where there was a good price built up on it, but Stambuck talked me out of it. He argued that you were now on board a boat and relatively safe. He recommended that I suggest you next go to the Philippines, 'if there was any possibility.' I readily agreed that it was a good idea, though we made it a little hot there too, by leaking to the press that you were on Cheever's boat and on your way."

"Why the hell did you do that? Christ, we were safer on the boat, if that's what you were worried about!"

"Oh, *oui,* certainly. But we wanted to make sure you'd get *off* the boat once you got to the Philippines. Can you think of a better way?"

"My God, you're diabolical. . . ."

François just smiled happily and continued.

"Peter Melville was in the Philippines as well, though he was having second thoughts because of all the publicity. That part was very true. Stambuck further suggested that you make contact at the Boeing 69 Club, which he told me was a CIA front. I could arrange to have Peter pick up the Head from you there, if his fears could be settled. You would be clean—the lie detector factor would be no problem. Though this purity is now compromised somewhat, to say the least, by all I'm telling you right now."

"Not necessarily. I already gave an exclusive interview

to Hal Lawson, a correspondent in Bangkok. This will all be yesterday's news tomorrow."

"Good," François said with visible relief. "Peter, of course, would take the Head from you, and bring it to me, while leaving the fake with the American government to be analyzed. The fake was already in Peter's care, he having picked it up from Wolfgang in Bangkok well ahead of time. Unfortunately, the story broke so big that Peter's feet really turned to ice. That's why Brock met you in Ermita alone, instead of with Melville."

My throat was dry. I downed the glass of champagne. François poured himself and me another, and popped the cork off a new bottle. I was trying not to be so convinced. There had obviously been a couple of other times I had been fooled. I recalled the pirate attack and brought that up. He listened with open eyes and ears.

"He made no mention about that one!" he exclaimed. "But I suspect that may have been legitimate. Stambuck was well out of range of your transmitter. And the weather was *terrible*— cloudy every day! The satellites lost you. At the same time the story was exploding all over the world! Additionally, I was growing more frantic about Wolfgang's disappearance. I had called all the hospitals in Bangkok, both public and private. There was no answer on his telephone. There was no one I could send over to his house except Brock, but he had to concentrate on tracking you, and that meant staying in the Philippines until you turned up. I didn't know what was happening. Above all, I was frantic for your safety."

"And the safety of the Head, of course."

"Of *course,*" he shot back with hardly a pause. "We had already decided that we had to gain control of the Head at the earliest possible opportunity, and wrap up the promotion end of the scheme before we 'blew it,' as you Americans say. I instructed Stambuck to tell you to hand it over to his safekeeping. I expected you to do just that. Then you called again. I had just arrived home from a late business dinner when Breenda said that you had, from the Boeing 69 Club. I immediately rushed out to a pay phone and called there but you had left by that time. To my shock, Stambuck informed me that you refused to hand over the Head because Tysee and Snake had been *kidnapped* by a

Russian submarine, and that you were actually discussing an exchange with the Russians! *Well! That* news was stunning, to say the least! I asked him, rather frantically, I recall, if he knew where you were. He said, he did, of course. That he knew as soon as you stepped into Ermita, because he had the area blanketed with directional finding devices that he could operate by remote control. He said that he knew it would take you at least a half-hour to return to your pension because you would have to shake off his men. He said the minute you boarded a jeepney after you left the Boeing 69, he had simply strolled a block over to your pension and flashed his Drug Enforcement Agency badge at the landlady."

I gulped the next glass. François dutifully filled it up. I didn't even try to say anything. I remember being surprised that Brock had let me go so easily.

"And then you made the switch," I said hoarsely. "But how did you handle arrangements to bring the real Head to you, if Melville was whinging?"

"Well, Brock handled that. He simply put considerable pressure on Peter, hinting at a few indiscretions in the CIA files that he could dust off. Peter reluctantly agreed to do his part. Brock presented the duplicate to the ambassador. You were above reproach. You would wonder about your guardian angel's work, but that would have been explained to you later, perhaps a year after, while I was presenting your share to you. That is what I originally planned. Unfortunately, Stambuck had less lengthy plans for you. He wasn't even prepared to wait until you had been sieved through the media."

François took another sip of his champagne, then leaned back, shaking his head.

"Just when we safely have the Head and Peter is more or less browbeaten into carrying it to me, this skyjacking comes out of the blue," François unconsciously punned, throwing his hands in the air with exasperation. *"Mon Dieu!* And then Ambassador Batten orders Stambuck to take the Head up to Clark just in case it can be used in some safe manner to free the hostages!"

He shook his head, finished his glass, then topped up both of ours again. Setting the Dom back in the bucket, he continued.

"Now, normally this really shouldn't have jeopardized anything. There was no way the U.S. government was going to let that Head be harmed. The worst thing would have been your finding out the Head had been nabbed from you by Stambuck before we actually told you about it, which we would have done later in any case. He didn't have to offer you an explanation of how he traced you to the pension, but he could have said that one of his men had already spotted you when you entered Ermita, that the area was surveillance-secured for you. He had, of course, told the ambassador about the submarine incident, and had been ordered, under the circumstances, to secure you at the base, since the skyjackers were asking for you. The same as with the Head, there might have been some role for you to play in freeing the hostages. Stambuck couldn't deny he didn't know where you were since he had been assigned to your case and had been successful in securing the Head from you."

"And that's when the MP s picked me up?"

"*Oui*, but I didn't learn of these details until later. At the time I didn't know *what* was going on. Most radio and TV stations were following the hijacking so closely that they were interrupting every time some new news came in. One of these announced that you had been located and that the Head was at the base. I knew it had to be the fake. Then after the hijacking was over, when it was announced that the Sikh and Richard Haimes-Sandwich had been called up to identify it, I almost collapsed. If either of them had announced to the world that the Head on the tarmac was a duplicate, the entire scam would have been jeopardized!"

I looked outside. The shadows were deepening in Central Park. The falling snow wasn't as visible.

"Well, when Peter finally did arrive here in New York after the hijacking—still shaking like an autumn leaf, by the way—he told me what had happened. Stambuck had frantically phoned him from Clark after he learned the Sikh was on board, demanding he bring the *real* Head up right away! Peter had it secured in his home not far from the embassy. Peter wasn't going to do it, but he gave in when Stambuck threatened to *kill* him! So Peter requisitioned a helicopter to fly himself to Clark with the Head. This they exchanged for the false head."

I recalled how Brock had left the control room immediately after it became known the Sikh was on the plane. And I vaguely recalled the controller saying something about a helicopter arriving from the embassy. And Melville *had* been acting beside himself when we had been introduced.

"Jesus . . . you know, I had a glimpse of the fake in General Casey's office before the jumbo arrived. . . ."

"And you didn't recognize it?"

"No! What you don't expect, you often don't see. I didn't look. Outside of the gems and the misplaced slash, it's an excellent copy."

"Peter also told me how Brock influenced General Casey to let you go out on the tarmac with it, and encouraged you to insist on it. That was another thing that added to the twinges of doubt I was having about Stambuck."

"Why?"

"Don't you see what he was doing? He was trying to have you killed! It would save him the problem later."

I nodded my head slowly. He was right. At least he was honorable enough to give me a fighting chance with the silencer.

"After the skyjacking was over, Brock Stambuck really went into high gear. He tried to imitate the Sikh's knife scar in the fake head, but he botched it. Then the bodies started dropping hard and fast. The day after the skyjacking ended and the day before Peter arrived, it was announced that Richard Haimes-Sandwich had had a heart attack and died. I was still in shock when Peter arrived in New York and left off the real Head with me. He was quite understandably exhausted, and didn't stay long after filing me in. He promised me a game of squash the next day, then headed straight for the Waldorf. It was the last time I saw him alive."

I perked up considerably.

"I heard from him once more, though, in a strange sort of way. The next morning, I was checking my calls on my telephone answering machine. One was strange—it was Peter's high-pitched voice but he sounded drunk or drugged. All he said was 'Brock Stambuck.' Then I think I heard the phone falling to the floor. I tried to call him back but there was no answer in his room. When the concierge sent someone up, they found a 'Do Not Disturb' sign on the door, so they didn't. Later, when he didn't appear for our game, I convinced the concierge that something was amiss. They found Peter sprawled in his clothes with the telephone receiver beside him on the floor. Well, *mon Dieu!* Not only did this come right on the heels of Richard's death, but it immediately reminded me of Brock's death threat to Peter! And now Peter's last words were Stambuck's name! A few days later the autopsy report came out, stating that he had died of a heart attack—no suspicion of foul play was put forward. And I found *that* unusual, because not only was he in top shape, but also the report added that the contents of his stomach indicated he had been drinking *beer!*"

François threw his hands up in astonishment.

"So . . . ?"

"Peter was an *absolute* teetotaler! A health nut. I was disturbed enough to phone my anonymous friend in the CIA. I told him that I was reading a spy thriller and just wanted to check the authenticity of something in it. He said *oui*, there was such a thing as a drug that could bring on a heart attack and yet be virtually undetectable. I changed the subject and we discussed the Head. We had been working closely together since they learned of my involvement, so they were keeping few secrets from me, and had told me Brock had been assigned to the case. I asked his whereabouts. What he said made me shudder. He told me that Brock had been *part* of the escort that flew 'the Head'—the false one—to Washington, on the very same day that Peter had brought the real one to me here in New York! My friend also told me that Stambuck's whereabouts weren't know, but that he had a ticket flying out of *New York* the next day to Bangkok! Brock was in *New York* and hadn't even phoned me! And at the same time Peter had had a 'heart attack'! Something was amiss. *Seriously* amiss."

"Interestingly enough, when I was in the hospital right after the skyjacking, he brought *me* a few beer. . . ."

François looked at me wide-eyed. I hadn't told him about Saigon yet. Uneasily, I recalled Hal Lawson telling me what had been left at his door the night the Vietnamese intercepted Brock. Or who I was sure was Brock.

"Obviously you didn't drink them!"

"No. When I woke up they were gone. Probably a nurse disposed of them. I didn't even think of them again."

"Whew!"

"Presuming Brock did away with Richard Haimes-Sandwich, the question is, why?"

"Because *he could identify the Head at the American Museum of Natural History as a fake, of course!* Stambuck was covering all bases. And it was a stupid, brutal way. Richard could have been bought off *easily*. But Stambuck was out for *everything* he could get!"

I could feel my breathing grow stronger. The connections were all too complex not to be believed. François shakily refilled our glasses.

"I tracked Stambuck down at his home in Bangkok," François said carefully, "and he went out to a pay phone and phoned me at the one here scheduled on the list. I made a pretext of wanting to know when he was coming to the States next so we could settle our business. He said that it would probably be fairly soon, since he hadn't 'been home in months.' Well! He was lying, of course! He asked if I had gotten 'the goods.' I said yes, and that I was working on a sale. He said he had heard of Peter's death, *then* he had the audacity to make casual mention that extra shares were now floating around, and that it was probably a good thing because he wasn't that pleased with his percentage, but that things were going to work out fine in the end. If I made a mistake, it was in giving him only fifteen percent rather than the twenty *we* had. I'm sure he was subtly threatening me. When I asked about you and Snake and Tysee, he told me that he had left you in the hospital, and that Snake and Tysee had gone off to Paris alone. Well, this made me feel very uneasy. I knew from Wolfgang how Tysee felt about you. It seemed unlikely they would run off together—though I don't know your relationships there, of course," François added sensitively.

My uneasiness turned into outright anxiety. Brock Stambuck had brought me that mote from Tysee. He had also brought me that fake note from Wolfgang. Could the Dear John have been a fake to throw me off? My heart started to beat wildly. He had also told *me* they had gone to *Hong Kong*— he couldn't even keep his lies straight. Paris —in winter—was an unlikely choice, and getting Snake to have a beer would be the easiest thing in the world to do. Tysee would love an orange juice. A mounting dread began to overwhelm me. They had to be dead. That's why there had been no word from them since Clark.

"Jesus. . . ." I muttered under my breath, the blood congealing in my heart.

"I phoned the hospital at Clark Air Base. They told me you had just checked out. No one knew where you had gone, but I suspected it would be back to Bangkok. That's why Brock was there—he would have been after you. It was no use phoning your house because I'd read it had been bombed, so I phoned that horrid Lion fellow with the shocking vocabulary. He promised he would tell you that I was looking for you. I couldn't count on this telephone not being clean so I was able only to give him a cryptic message to pass on to you. I told him to tell you 'to watch out for Brock Stambuck.' "

I'd tell him about my house being okay after all some other time.

"Yeah! I got it as 'keep an eye out for him.' I thought you *wanted* me to find him for some reason! It surprised me. I didn't see how you could know him."

"That was almost a fatal misunderstanding," he said, sitting back.

We both took another sip. François shakily lit another Gauloise, starting to show the effects of the bubbly. He was also sweating profusely. I was comfortable—physically.

"If my suspicions are correct he could just politely ask for his straight cut with the extra shares split. *Or* perhaps kidnap Breenda or Christopher, and press for more. I'm not taking any chances. He *knows* I can't go to the police. I swear I almost fainted when Security called up and said you were at the door! I had given you up for dead."

"I noticed the extra security you have here," I said. "Christ, they even searched *me!*"

"*Oui*, it's a bad situation. This Brock Stambuck is a definite worry. None of us has been out of here in almost a fortnight. I just can't understand what is taking him so long to act."

"Well, you don't have to worry about him anymore," I managed to say, my voice a hoarse whisper.

Thoughts of Tysee and Snake were overwhelming me. I knew I would never, ever see them again.

"Pardon?"

"I think Brock Stambuck is dead," I said in a voice that was scarcely audible.

"Comment! Ca' it be true?" His voice was beginning to slur.

I told him about slipping the transmitter into Hal Lawson's luggage, and what happened as a result. François listened with eyes the size of French rolls.

"Why don't you ring your mysterious friend in the Agency? Perhaps he can tell you if he's around."

François snapped fingers and reached for the phone. I didn't listen to the conversation, but when it was over François was beaming. He stood and staggered around the room, flicking on the lights that augmented the side lighting. We had almost been speaking in the dark the last while. With a flourish he slipped back down across from me and topped up our glasses.

"This is somethin' to drink to!" he exclaimed, taking up his glass. Champagne bubbled over the edges and onto the table. "An embassy of a foreign friend of ours in Saigon has reported that Brock Stambuck borrowed *directional-finding equipment* and a weapon two weeks ago! He has not been heard from since!"

I made no move. I hardly heard him. My dread had left, its place taken by sullen gloom. There was no doubt about it—they *had* been tricked. *I* had been tricked. They were dead. Their bodies would never be found. It would be presumed that they had been hunted down by terrorists.

He raised his glass. His eyes were sparkling more than the Dom, which was tying his tongue in knots now.

"To our tremendous success! To the Buddha Head Caper! The grea'est art and antiquities hoax in his'ory! Or at least since Grandpapa's!"

He was jolted a little from his champagne-driven reverie when he noticed that I didn't move.

"Alors! But of course! You don't know!"

"Don't know what . . . ?" I said, my voice devoid of emotion.

"The Head! You haven't asked wha' happened to the Head!"

I looked at him without expression. He sat down excitedly.

"Despite the uncertainties, I put the word out at certain levels an' at certain places, and contacted a certain high representative of a certain oil sheikhdom. He insisted upon complete and absolute secrecy, so please understand how I cannot even tell *you*, though I think you can guess. Of course I ha' a rather different story for him. I told him that Wolfgang and I were behind the robbery at Tengboche, and that you were an innocent brought in, but that you were working for us—all of which is very much the case. I didn't fib there. But then I told him that the so-called Tibetan in the Dalai Lama's entourage who told me that the Head had been placed at Tengboche also provided me with pictures and exact specifications, and that, using these, we had constructed the duplicate as part of the robbery plan—as a strategy to take off the heat. I explained how the robbery went wrong with Kun San, though I certainly didn't reveal exac'ly why. I said it was just an ordinary greed-induced double-cross. I described how you made your escape and how Stambuck, our man, had stolen it from you. I explained how it was used in the skyjacking. O' course he could easily see how the switch was done, and how Peter Melville was able to bring me the real Head."

"And it was all as simple as that," I said rather than asked, trying to suppress the leaden feeling in the pit of my stomach.

"Oh, there was more to it than that. He took a sample for carbon-dating. With his money, he had the clout to get it back the next day. It came back right on the money, of course—2,500 years."

"And tha' convinced them?"

I was speaking like an automaton, fighting down the building lump in my throat. I was also getting a little maudlin in my cups. I had reason to—besides Tysee and Snake being gone forever, there's nothing more depressing than America in winter.

"No, not completely. Through a stroke of very good luck, something that confirmed beyond a shadow of a doubt the absolute authenticity of the Head had fallen into my hands. It was the broken buck knife that the entire world knew had been stuck into it. The Arabs checked with the Libyans and sure 'nough their secret-service people had taken detailed pictures of the knife, as well as making exact measurements, while they were still planning the skyjacking; they knew how 'portant it was. But this time, I was dealing with a huddle of the highest members of the Royal Family, all of whom had flown in for a supposedly closed-door, emergency OPEC conference—at least that's wha' the world was told. I showed them the fit of the broken blade in the Head. The pictures an' specifications arrived by private jumbo jet from Libya via Jedda. There was no question: *that* was the buck knife, and *this* was the Buddha Head from Tengboche Monastery! The deal was finalized jus' a few days ago!"

He raised his glass again, this time without waiting. After throwing it back he merrily filled it up again. François was getting drunk for the second time in his life.

"That means the Head is gone," I said, barely caring. "That it's most likely been destroyed."

He nodded twice.

"The king said tha' it was a great pity to have to obliterate something so beau'iful and sacred but that it was necessary. He personally though' of the Buddha as a great prophet, but he had no illusions about the tremendous danger the existence of the Head created in upsetting the 'balance of religions,' as he called it. He spoke of grea' religious wars breaking out in the East. He recalled the recent massacre of Jews at their synagogue in Istanbul, and the bombing at the Mountain of Borobudur in Indonesia. He knew only too well the destructive cost of religious revivals, and of the particular volatility of his own creed. He was very much afraid Moslems would rise up, if threatened, and wipe Buddhism from the face of the earth. He said it was the grea'est irony of his life that he had to destroy the Buddha Head in order to save Buddhism. He was very eloquent. It was very difficult to disagree with him."

"So . . . what happened t' it in the end . . . ?" I asked, my own voice beginning to slur. I was fighting back tears.

"He confided to me tha' he had ordered all of it—including the gold and rubies—to be reduced to a fine powder.

This dust he had scattered from a plane over Mount Everest. He asked my 'pinion, if there was a more respectful way of bearing honor to th' remains. I could think of no other."

We were both silent for a long time while François fumbled a fresh cigarette to his lips and managed to light it.

"We ha' no proof it was the actual Buddha Head anyway, did we?" I said sadly.

It was karma. Somehow it was all karma.

"No. No, we didn'," he agreed quietly, then took a slightly inelegant sip.

But we both knew what the other thought—that maybe we'd been fooling ourselves.

"You mus' wanna know how much we made?" François finally asked, more than a hint of pride in his voice. "Wha' the price of th' priceless is?"

I looked up and shrugged. What is the cost of Tysee's life? Of Snake's? Of them all?

He sat back and settled himself in very comfortably, a small smile on his lips. He looked like a boy who's been in the cookie jar and gotten away with it. In a mischievous voice as clear as Czech crystal, he whispered:

"One billion dollars."

It was enough to shake me out of my morbid lethargy.

"One *billion* . . . dollars . . . ?"

It sounded too big to be believable. But then, the deal had been cut in the Orient, where the unbelievable is regularly believable.

"Your share will be equal to mine, af'er expenses—twenty percent!"

François fumbled into his jacket. He drew out a card and slid it across the glass table. I made no move toward it.

"On this is the name and address of a bank in Panama. The number is your account. I coul' have put it in one in Swi'zerland but, having a phobia of my own, I can understand yours to snow. Present it personally with your passport."

I looked at it blandly. It meant nothing.

"Incidentally, I'm opening a foundation for Wolfgang with his share. We'll use it to restore a good bit of Nepal. Do you agree?"

He took another sloppy, happy drink.

"Sure," I said quietly. "Sounds like a good idea. That's three shares . . . François, it jus' occurs to me tha' the champagne must be messing up your ability to add right."

"Why's tha' . . . ?"

"Well, if you and I get twenty percent each and we put another twenty into Wolfgang's foundation that adds up to only sixty percent. Or is Wolfgang's foundation taking a big share? I don't really care one way or another."

François held up his hands and stared at his fingers as he wiggled them around, then grinned wickedly.

"Gee, maybe I didn't plug in th' ol' Polish calculator," he laughed. His armpits were damp circles.

"I think I should go t' bed. . . ."

"Wait. Don' you wanna know where th' other two shares went?"

I shrugged.

"Why not?"

"Well, one went to Snake, of course."

"*What!*"

My head instantly cleared.

"You disagree?"

"*Snake!*"

"You *do* disagree—but I'm afrai' it's too late," he said with false gravity. "I wish I woulda been able t' discuss it with you earlier. Tsk-tsk-tsk. Missed oppor'—"

"*H . . . he's here!*"

François looked at me seriously, then dissolved into giggles.

"Come *on*, François! Is he *here?*"

He managed to get control of himself.

"No. Not exac'ly."

"What'd you mean, 'not exactly'?"

I couldn't be hearing right.

"You didn't even think to ask where I got th' buck knife from," he said, ignoring me and winking over his glass.

"I . . . I just presumed. . . ." I didn't know what.

"He managed to bring it here as a kind of souvenir. The story he had to tell was th' clincher, as far as what Brock Stambuck was up to. Excuse me, *mon ami?* You are all right?"

"N-no! Yes! You're saying that Snake . . . was *here* . . . ?"

"Oui. Of course! He an' Tysee came here a week after the skyjacking, just af'er I had begun negotiations with the sheikhs. Oh, with everything to tell, I didn't get aroun' to it," he added, that nefarious grin tracing his lips, which he dipped into the Dom a moment later.

I could barely hear him, my head was suddenly spinning so fast.

"Oui, Brock took them to wha' he described to them was a safe house in Manila and said tha' they were to stay there until everything died down. He gave them strict instructions not to contact anyone, or to leave th' place. Stambuck said he woul' be back in four days maximum or they would hear from him. On hin'sight it turned out this was a safe house only for Brock Stambuck—here he could safely dispose of them at his convenience. It's apparent tha' the reason he didn't righ' then was because he didn't have time. He had to do the switch, make arrangements for th' transfer of 'th' Head' to Washington—th' plane was leaving th' next day—then take care of Richard Haimes-San'wich and you."

"You say he *didn't* kill them?"

"How coul' he? You think of wha' the neighbors woul' say with a couple of bodies nex' door. You know how hot it is in Manila. Well, days came an' went. They heard about Richard's death on television. Then th' word of Peter Melville's demise was announced, though they didn' know who he was. Four days passed an' no Brock Stambuck. They waited two more days. They ran out of food. Snake was won'ering why if it was supposed to be a safe house, there were no bodyguards. On top of tha', he is not very good at taking advice, as I can testify. They thought it might be a good idea to contact the 'merican embassy—and 'bassador Batten was stunned to learn they were there," François finished. Then he burped.

I was starting to tingle all over with hope.

" 'scuse me. Stambuck had also told *him* that they had flown to Paris of their own accord. He knew of no such safe house, nor did any of the CIA staffers at th' embassy. Something was obviously amiss. The 'bassador arranged travel papers to fly them in a military aircraft here to New York, where they appeared on my doorstep. Well, not literally. I was contacted and asked to took, er, take them in. They never knew that Stambuck was part of the operation so they had no reason to suspect me. Snake knew that you were working through me, an' considered me th' obvious safe contact—and th' first person you would reach. They came here to wait for you in safety. They were still pretty shaken by their experience wi' the Russians an' th' terrorists. Th' last thing they wanted to do was speak to th' press."

François belched again. He batted his eyelids a couple of times in surprise before continuing.

" 'sccccccuse me again! Anyway, th' Russians had told them that no one would believe their story about being in an atomic submarine, an' they wouldn't remember much of it anyway. The Russians were smart an' had drugged them immediately upon taking them aboard, just for this reason. They may as well try to explain th' interior of a spacecraft. No one would believe them. But Tysee and Snake also know that as long as they don' make a big thing of it, their long-term chances of survival are enhanced when it comes to th' Russians, who don' want their involvement to come out. Righ' now everyone is holding back, keeping quiet. Th' State Department has quietly tol' th' Russians tha' they know about it, but for th' sake of settlin' the dust 'bout all of this, don' plan to make an incident out of it all." François merrily raised his glass up too fast. "Whooooops! I hope this doesn't stain. Hey, you all right? You're very white in th' face?"

"No—I'm not. . . ."

François laughed and reached for a fresh bottle of champagne. He began twirling off the wire.

"Well, have another drink. It'll cure wha' ails you. Boy. Does this champagne ever make one feel hot."

I drained the glass. The cork blew off, embedding itself in the middle of the *Impression soleil levant.*

"Oops," François said, putting his hand to his mouth. Then he shrugged and turned back to me and unsteadily refilled both glasses.

"So the note *was* false . . . ?"

"Whaddya mean?"

I managed to tell him about the letter that Brock Stambuck had given me at the Clark infirmary. François nodded raggedly.

"Did you ever see her handwriting?"

"Actually, never. The note was typewritten anyway."

"He was no dummy. He prob'ly suspected you would go off somewhere to lick your wounds. Being no fool he knew you would be psychologically down, easy prey, prob'ly alone. Have another glass of bubbles. Bu' you'll have to drink your presen' one first."

François laughed, then tried to light a cigarette. Blood was rushing to my ears and I felt like I was floating, maybe fainting. It didn't seem to be just the Dom. Then I saw François shake his head, which sent fresh tidal waves of hope crashing over me.

"Where are they . . . ? You say they were . . . here . . . !"

"Well, sor' of. Snake left for Europe. I couldn' keep him around. I tried to impress upon him how dangerous it was out there with Brock Stambuck cer'ainly looking for him but he would have none of it af'er a while. He insisted on leaving once he ha' his money, because he hadn't been 'laid' in weeks. Terrible language and sense of humor, that man. Lef' a dreadful mess in his room too. Beer cans an' bottles everywhere."

François shook his head, oblivious to the sweat pouring off his face.

"It's a goo' thing he's into th' money, because he was determined he was going to buy Errol Flynn's ol' *Sirocco* an' he's going to need every bi' of it. It's moored on the th' French Riviera an' tha's where he's headed! I've seen it— no masts, holes in th' sides. And hun'red an' some feet of bleached headache, but he's determined." François chuckled, then sloshed a little bubbly over the rim as he raised a finger to signal he'd remembered something. "Oh, he lef' something for you! I'm supposed t' give you this."

He weaved over to the wall and clicked open another wall-blended door. It was a closet of some not inconsiderable size. Stacked inside from top to bottom were cases of beer. All kinds of beer. He took a six-pack off the top and held it like it was a box of excrement. It had a picture of a goofy-looking moose on it.

"Unfortuna'ely, there's a lo' more in other closets in th' house tha' he requisitioned. There's . . . beer"—even the word was distasteful to François's lips—"from all over the

world! Andorra. Mali. You name it. I hope you'll manage to
get it out of here soon."

I was still in shock.

"But I almost never drink beer! What'd he do this for?"

"He said it was some kind of promise he made to you, I
don' know. He just told me tha' he's got to make sure
you're supplied with beer for th' rest of your life."
François's shoulders and arms were crunched up in an 'I
don't know either gesture. "Oh! An' he said t' save th'
empties fer somebody called Walter. He said somethin'
about you two sailin' to visit him again when he gets the
Sirocco shipshape an' it woul' be nice t' take 'im a gift."

I hardly heard him. My thoughts were elsewhere. Angel
wings were beating down, fanning my cheeks.

"Tysee . . . ?" I said, her name like porcelain in its delicacy.

"*Oui?* Wha' abou' her?" François said. I could see he was
trying to keep a straight face. And was losing.

"Don't . . . please . . . where is she?"

He made a Gallic gesture as if to say, what can I say?
Then he smiled.

"She stays up all night watching television. She says she's
ne'er seen so many channels. Mos' af'ernoons she practices
dance in the gym or plays wi' Christopher. Deligh'ful girl,
really. Tremendously interested in my collections and has
a million questions. She always has a late af'ernoon nap.
I'm sure tha's where she is now. Would you like to see
her?" He laughed. "Of course you do. Now follow me. An'
don' forget tha' card I gave you."

He picked up two glasses and the ice bucket, into which
he stuck a fresh bottle of Dom. He was about to lead me
out of the study when he thought of something. Setting
everything down, he reached into a drawer of his desk and
came up with the snuff case with the monogrammed N on
it, and the gilt-edged mirror. Gathering it all together sloppily in his arms, he bid me follow. He led me out of his
study, being careful to close and lock it behind us, then
weaved ever so slightly down one of the corridors.

As we passed the first gallery-sized room, he stopped to
address a man I hadn't seen before. There was an easel in
front of him and he was dabbing paint onto a partially
completed portrait. Beside him, on a small pedestal, sat a

small, golden Buddha. In the background were drapes. Christopher was romping nearby with his nanny. The toys he was playing with were full-size replicas of the English crown jewels.

"I'll be back sho'ly," he slurred into the room. "I'm sorry for the delay bu' some impor'ant business came up."

"No problem, Mr. Giscard. It gives me time to fill in some of the blocking."

I followed François down a white labyrinth of halls until we came to a door. He set the ice bucket, glasses, snuff box and mirror on the floor beside the door.

"Darn nice stuff, this champagne," he said, grinning gaily. "We'll have t' drink it a liddle more now an' again." Then he knocked quietly a few times.

He cleared his throat slightly and leaned forward to listen for an answer. The sleepy voice that replied sent rushes shivering up and down my spine.

"Chi?"

"We have a visitor, Mademoiselle San," François called. "It's somebody you've been waiting for. May I sen' him right in?"

His voice was light and cheerful, his eyes sparkling at me. He winked, then promptly turned, whistling merrily as he staggered back down the hall in the direction of the portrait artist.

I opened the door slowly. It was quiet in the room, the light subdued.

For a moment we just stared at each other, our eyes locked together, gleaming in the soft shadows. In another moment she had slipped out from under the quilt and was naked in my arms.

The card François had given me slipped to the floor.

EPILOGUE

The Bangkok Collection

CLEAR, CLEAN TROPICAL light spilled into the room as Tysee unlatched the shutters and swung them open. The cool, fragrant trades came in with it, softly caressing my cheek, along with the low murmur of waves gently washing against the white sand outside. It all blended into my dreams, brightening them. I felt a smile on my face as I drifted upward. For a moment I mildly wondered where I was. Then I saw the jungled volcanic slopes of Moorea rising from Oponoju bay on either side.

"Oh! You awake! I sorry!" she exclaimed, jumping back into bed with me.

Her mischievous smile told me she wasn't sorry one bit. She was stark naked and looked as beautiful and natural as a kitten.

I rolled around. Something cool touched my skin. It was an empty bottle of Dom. She laughed and took it away.

"Hey! What we do today? You teach me scuba dive?"

"Whatever you want, my little juiceburger," I replied, lazily reaching out for her.

She cuddled in close, and with one hand, held me just where she knew I liked being held most. She'd recovered well from the shock of learning what happened to her beloved Buddha Head, her practical nature seeing the necessity for it.

"I know! You first talk to me. I like that."

"What do you want to talk about? You name it, you got it."

I buried myself in her long hair. Our matching gold Shan talismans tinkled together musically.

She thought for a moment.

"You tell me about you collections. You big collector. You tell me about them and which you like best."

I did, while she lay beside me with that wonderful enthusiasm of hers and encouraged me with gentle strokes and caresses. I told her more about the start with the Devil Dancers of Sri Lanka. I told her about the treks into Mustang and Ladakh and to Everest for Tibetan pieces, and the jungle expeditions all over the Far East. I told her about the treasure diving. And the trips to European and American museums to sell it all. I told her that once I finished the Ifugao documentation for the Swiss museum I *might* take her to some of the places. She stroked me faster. I *promised* I would take her to *all* of those places, and to the moon and Andromeda.

"But you no tell me yet you favorite collection. What you like most?"

"Because I've been saving that for last," I said, kissing the tip of her little nose. "It's more precious and fascinating than all of them. It's from the Far East, of course, and is absolutely exquisite, unique, exceedingly rare—one of a kind in fact—and very, very beautiful."

"Is it old piece or new? From jungle or mountain?" she asked expectantly.

My breathing was coming in deeper and deeper draughts.

"Ummmm," I managed. "From the jungle. Definitely. I haven't done a thermoluminescence or had it carboned yet, but it's certainly not very old. But it'll develop a very nice patina with age, I'm sure."

"Is it big piece or little piece?"

"Little. Very, *very* little," I said, lightly stroking her slippery, little *him*.

"Will you ever part with it?"

"Part with it! No! Never! Whatever the price! It's the finest, uh, piece I've ever found. I'm absolutely mad about it! I love it!"

"What is it? I want know! I want see!" Tysee said excitedly, squeezing me hard.

"I call it The Bangkok Collection."

"Yes! But *what* is it?"

"You, my sweet," I said, nibbling her bottom lip and rolling her over onto her back. "You."

About the Author

JASON SCHOONOVER has been a field collector of primitive art and antiquities for over a decade. His collections, primarily ethnological, are found in museums around the world. His area of interest is the Far-East. Jason is a Fellow of the Explorers Club of New York, a member of the Foreign Correspondents Club of Thailand, single, lives comfortably out of a burgundy Samsonite and a khaki knapsack and can most often be found somewhere in Asia.

DON'T MISS
THESE CURRENT
Bantam Bestsellers

☐	27814	**THIS FAR FROM PARADISE** Philip Shelby	$4.95
☐	27811	**DOCTORS** Erich Segal	$5.95
☐	28179	**TREVAYNE** Robert Ludlum	$5.95
☐	27807	**PARTNERS** John Martel	$4.95
☐	28058	**EVA LUNA** Isabel Allende	$4.95
☐	27597	**THE BONFIRE OF THE VANITIES** Tom Wolfe	$5.95
☐	27456	**TIME AND TIDE** Thomas Fleming	$4.95
☐	27510	**THE BUTCHER'S THEATER** Jonathan Kellerman	$4.95
☐	27800	**THE ICARUS AGENDA** Robert Ludlum	$5.95
☐	27891	**PEOPLE LIKE US** Dominick Dunne	$4.95
☐	27953	**TO BE THE BEST** Barbara Taylor Bradford	$5.95
☐	26554	**HOLD THE DREAM** Barbara Taylor Bradford	$5.95
☐	26253	**VOICE OF THE HEART** Barbara Taylor Bradford	$5.95
☐	26888	**THE PRINCE OF TIDES** Pat Conroy	$4.95
☐	26892	**THE GREAT SANTINI** Pat Conroy	$4.95
☐	26574	**SACRED SINS** Nora Roberts	$3.95
☐	27018	**DESTINY** Sally Beauman	$4.95

Buy them at your local bookstore or use this page to order.

Bantam Books, Dept. FB, 414 East Golf Road, Des Plaines, IL 60016

Please send me the items I have checked above. I am enclosing $_____
(please add $2.00 to cover postage and handling). Send check or money
order, no cash or C.O.D.s please.

Mr/Ms _____

Address _____

City/State _____ Zip _____

Please allow four to six weeks for delivery.

FB–11/89

Prices and availability subject to change without notice.